EURIPIDES
ALCESTIS

EDITED WITH
INTRODUCTION AND COMMENTARY
BY

A. M. DALE

OXFORD
AT THE CLARENDON PRESS

Oxford University Press, Walton Street, Oxford OX2 6DP
Oxford New York Toronto
Delhi Bombay Calcutta Madras Karachi
Petaling Jaya Singapore Hong Kong Tokyo
Nairobi Dar es Salaam Cape Town
Melbourne Auckland
and associated companies in
Beirut Berlin Ibadan Nicosia

Oxford is a trade mark of Oxford University Press

Published in the United States
by Oxford University Press, New York

First published 1954
Reprinted from corrected sheets of the first edition
1961, 1966, 1971, 1974
First published in paperback 1978
Reprinted 1982, 1984, 1987

ISBN 0 19 872097 1

Printed in Great Britain
at the University Printing House, Oxford
by David Stanford
Printer to the University

PREFACE

THE imaginary audience to whom this commentary is addressed includes both pupils and professional colleagues. Younger school children were excluded, since there already exist simplified versions of this play designed for them, but I hope the Sixth Form may find things in it to interest them. Perhaps undergraduates were most often in my mind, but I have not felt able to discriminate for them in my notes between parts they need and need not read. The question *what* the poet wrote, even when we cannot hope to recover this with anything like certainty, is so intimately a part of the interpretation of his meaning that it seemed impossible to discuss it in isolation as so much 'textual' comment. The passages where in conclusion I have felt obliged to disagree with Professor Murray's text are so few that the plan followed in this series is amply justified.

The whole of my manuscript has been carefully scrutinized by Dr. Paul Maas. Many indeed are the scholars who, since he made his home in Oxford, have profited by his infinite patience and kindness and his superb scholarship, and none has exploited them more ruthlessly than I. For the imperfections and errors which stubbornly survive he is not responsible, but I owe him deep gratitude for the elimination of many more, and not least for delightful hours of friendly discussion. My thanks are also due to my husband, Professor T. B. L. Webster, for much valuable criticism, and to both him and the readers of the Clarendon Press for the removal of many blemishes from the proofs.

A. M. D.

LONDON
July 1954

CONTENTS

NOTE

The text reproduced here is that of Professor Gilbert Murray, O.M., which was published in 1902 in the series of Oxford Classical Texts.

INTRODUCTION

I. THE TETRALOGY

In the year 438 B.C. Euripides was placed second to Sophocles with the tetralogy *Cretan Women, Alcmaeon in Psophis, Telephus, Alcestis.* This is the earliest year for which the 'didascaliae', the festival records, have come down to us in a complete form for Euripides, and the *Alcestis*, played at the end of that programme, has survived to be our earliest play; but the poet was then, it seems, already in his late forties and had first appeared in the theatre seventeen years before, with the *Peliades*, like the *Alcestis* a play on a Thessalian legend. Of his youthful work, then, we know almost nothing,[1] nor does it seem to have impressed itself very forcibly on his contemporaries, or his admirers in the next generations. Perhaps there was not much of it, or at least not much that was 'granted a chorus'. The statement in the Hypothesis[2] to the *Alcestis*, *τὸ δρᾶμα ἐποιήθη ιζ'*, seems to mean 'was seventeenth in order of composition', and the most likely explanation of this number is that by the time of Aristophanes of Byzantium three at least of the earlier plays were already lost—probably satyr-plays, like the missing *Theristae* of 431.[3] This would give only three tetralogies for the years between 455 and 438. But this fifth tetralogy was memorable, and evidently left an impression for life upon the precocious child Aristophanes.

Of the *Cretan Women* little is known in detail, but the

[1] For a more optimistic view see W. Buchwald's dissertation *Studien zur Chronologie der attischen Tragödie 455–431*', Königsberg, 1939. If the *Rhesus* is genuine Eur., it was probably an early work, since the statement of Crates of Mallos (quoted *Σ Rhes.* 528) to this effect would seem to be taken from a didascalia.

[2] See below, p. xxxix and n. If the library edition was in alphabetical order, the chronological order would naturally be given by numbers in the Introductions.

[3] *Med.*, Hypoth. II, *οὐ σῴζεται.*

subject was the misdemeanours of the young Aerope (and perhaps also of her sister Clymene), whom an angry father gave to Nauplius to drown (cf. S. *Aj.* 1295 ff.), but he took them to Argos instead; whether the intrigue with Thyestes came into the story is uncertain. Evidently Aerope attempted to defend herself, to be told by her father that Hades should be judge of these things (Σ Ar. *Vesp.* 763). According to Σ Ar. *Ran.* 849 ὦ Κρητικὰς μὲν συλλέγων μονῳδίας, one ancient view was that this referred to Aerope, though it might also be an allusion to Pasiphae in the *Cretans*, or to Phaedra, or indeed to all these erring Cretan ladies.

The saga of Alcmaeon, as told in Apollodorus, is long and complicated (Euripides returned to another phase of it in one of his last plays, *Alcmaeon in Corinth*), and until a recently discovered papyrus fragment[1] cleared up the issue it was very doubtful which part of it was dramatized in the *Alcmaeon in Psophis*. Hounded by the furies of his murdered mother Eriphyle, Alcmaeon twice sought refuge, first with King Phegeus in Psophis, who purified him and gave him his daughter Alphesiboea in marriage, then, as the madness recurred, in the virgin land at the delta of the river Achelous, whose daughter Callirrhoe became his second wife. This play describes how he returns to Psophis, to recover by guile for Callirrhoe the fateful necklace of Eriphyle which he had given to Alphesiboea. He pretends that Apollo has commanded him to dedicate it in Delphi, but a servant betrays his real motive to Phegeus, who in anger gets his sons to ambush and kill Alcmaeon. It is uncertain how far Euripides takes the story, but probably Alphesiboea, still in love with him, laments his death and is punished by her father.

Telephus, the lame king disguised as beggar, was a favourite butt of Aristophanes, and his stratagems inspired not only whole scenes of *Acharnians* and *Thesmophoriazusae* but also the vase-painters of the next century. Aeschylus and Sophocles had already treated the legend of

[1] *Pap. greci e latini*, vol. xiii, 1, Florence, 1949, pap. 1302, pp. 54 ff., cf. Schadewaldt's reconstruction, *Hermes* lxxx. 46 ff.

the king of Mysia, Heracles' son, who, wounded by the spear of Achilles, came to the Greek camp because only 'the wounder could heal', and by some means persuaded them to make him whole again. Euripides made a new version full of intrigue, rhetoric, and excitement, with the disguised Telephus laying a secret plot with Clytaemnestra, pleading his own cause as if by proxy, and, when discovered, snatching up the baby Orestes with the threat to kill it if his request were not granted; with Agamemnon quarrelling with Menelaus and perhaps both with Achilles.

After all this, instead of a satyr-play,[1] came the *Alcestis*, the story of the wife who died in her husband's place, of the husband who found the life so dearly bought a worthless possession, of his noble hospitality and their marvellous deliverance by Heracles. Only excess of zeal has enabled scholars to discern in these four plays some common underlying theme, or specially significant correspondences and contrasts; any four plays of Euripides taken at random could with a little goodwill be made into as significant a group. What is noteworthy is how many of the characteristics of later Euripidean drama are present already, in one play or another, not in embryo but fully developed: the original approach, the liking for the by-ways of legend, the complex intrigues and deceptions, the 'strong' situations, the rhetorical subtleties and set debates, the interest in 'bad' women, the deliberate flouting of stage conventions. This earliest of our plays, the only one wholly outside the shadow of the Peloponnesian War, is the work of Euripides the mature artist.

II. THE LEGEND[2]

To trace a legend back and back to its dim sources in primitive consciousness is a task for the mythologist or

[1] As we learn from the Hypothesis, cf. infra, p. xxxix.

[2] A. Lesky's admirable article: 'Alkestis, der Mythus und das Drama', Wien, Sb. 203. 2 (1925), is fundamental for this question.

anthropologist, not for the commentator on Attic drama of the fifth century. If Admetus and Alcestis were originally chthonian deities, a sort of Hades and Persephone (cf. A. *Supp.* 149) to whom Apollo was made subject, that cannot have mattered to Euripides, nor does it add to our understanding of his play. Their legend as he knew it is firmly rooted in man's mortality, and the central core of it, the story of the young man (or woman; sometimes the sexes are reversed) who, though parents refuse, finds in a wife or lover a substitute willing to die in his place, is one of those wandering folk-tales which turn up among many different peoples. It is possible that the strong hero who wrestles with the black demon Death and wrests his prey from him is also a genuinely popular fancy, and had already been added as a happy ending to the other story in some of its folk-tale forms.[1] In Thessaly the whole tale attached itself to a local hero, King Admetus of Pherae, who in Hellenic mythology stood in a special relation to Apollo. The story is fullest in Apollodorus (*Bibl.* 1. 9. 15; 3. 10. 3–4). Asclepius, the god's son by the faithless Coronis, had used his healing powers to restore the dead to life, and for this had been blasted to death by the thunderbolt of Zeus, forged for him by the Cyclopes. Apollo in revenge killed the Cyclopes, and was sentenced by Zeus to a term of penance as serf to a mortal, Admetus. Admetus proved a kind and generous master, and was rewarded by Apollo's special favour; his flocks and herds twinned miraculously, and when against many rivals he wooed Alcestis, whom her father Pelias had promised to the man who should carry her off in a car yoked with wild beasts, Apollo harnessed a lion and a boar for him. So, naturally, in this version it is Apollo who, when Admetus is threatened with an untimely death, gains for him the privilege of offering a substitute, if he can find a willing one. In the folk-tale it is simply his destiny that claims the young

[1] The evidence is, however, not as clear as one could have wished that this part of the story is prior to and independent of the *Alcestis* version.

man, and so here it is from the Fates that Apollo wrings the concession, but the *Bibliotheca*, in its usual eclectic manner, adds another elaboration: that Admetus had offended the goddess Artemis by forgetting her in his wedding-sacrifices, so that when he opened the door of the wedding-chamber he found it full of coiled snakes (a symbol of death). This 'wrath of Artemis' motif, imported from other contexts, is clearly a later addition, designed to make the story more completely personal—if more commonplace. The source and date of it are unknown; there is no trace of it on the Attic stage. Of the happy ending Apollodorus frankly gives two alternative accounts: Kore (Persephone) sent Alcestis up to earth again, 'or, as some say', Heracles fought Hades and restored her to Admetus.

What version, or versions, of all this did Euripides know, and from what sources? The question, especially the second part of it, is not easy to answer. The subject had been dramatized before him by Phrynichus in the early days of drama, but that merely shifts the problem back a little farther: what sources were available to Phrynichus? We have no surviving fragments of epic or early lyric except on the fringes of the story, the myth of Apollo and Asclepius; one of the *Eoiai*, the 'Catalogue of Women' of Hesiod (Rzach, frs. 122–7), was devoted to Coronis and included the thraldom of Apollo, but this was an often told legend[1], and there is no evidence, or even likelihood, that as Wilamowitz imagines[2] it wandered on like an Arabian Nights' Tale to the further story of Alcestis. The Catalogue of Ships in *Iliad* 2 mentions Eumelus, son of Admetus and of Alcestis 'fairest of the daughters of Pelias', but any speculations about old Thessalian epics range through the empty air. One interesting hint of the existence of some kind of poetry celebrating the fame of Alcestis is contained in the play itself: the

[1] Of the list of authorities quoted in Σ *Alc.* 1 (cf. p. xxxii) Hesiod, Stesichorus, and Pherecydes the cosmogonist, the oldest Greek prose-writer, would have been available to Phrynichus.

[2] In the Introduction to his *Isyllos of Epidaurus*.

Chorus prophesies (445 ff.) that in days to come her deed will be sung by poets at the Carnean festival of Apollo in Sparta, and at Athens: 'much will the servants of the Muses have to sing of you, celebrating you both on the seven-stringed mountain tortoise-shell and in lyreless chants, in Sparta when the revolving season of the Carnean month comes round and the moon is aloft all night through, and in shining happy Athens.' Unfortunately this passage is the only evidence we have on the subject, and the words are allusive and ambiguous. (For text and sense see the Commentary.) Weber, in the Introduction to his edition, builds a massive superstructure on this slight foundation: Apollo is a late-comer to the Carnea, which at that time of year must have been an ancient harvest and vintage festival; Alcestis, hymned both with and without the lyre, i.e. in joyful music and unaccompanied dirge, was originally an Earth-goddess like Kore–Persephone, much older than this legend, and Admetus therefore a chthonian Hades; in Athens also there were similar cult-hymns, too well known to the audience to need further description. But it is very doubtful[1] whether *ἀλύροις ὕμνοις* here means unaccompanied songs of mourning—it might indicate either epic recitals (so Wilamowitz) or songs *to the flute*—and there is no indication that Alcestis was at the *centre* of the Carnean celebration; she could equally well figure in a minor episode of a great Apolline cult-festival. The reference to Athens *may* imply cult-hymns there too, but it is just as good a guess that Euripides' brevity covers a pretty allusion to his own drama.

It may be that we have here an example of those legends whose main currents of transmission were not literary but oral and popular, discernible to us only in some fleeting allusion in literature or art until a master gives them definition, or until they are codified by the professional mythographers. (The Scholiast on *Alc.* 1 speaks of *ἡ διὰ στόματος καὶ δημώδης ἱστορία περὶ τῆς Ἀπόλλωνος θητείας παρ' Ἀδμήτῳ . . . ᾗ κέχρηται νῦν Εὐριπίδης*, though making it clear

[1] See the Commentary.

that here this agrees with the version of Hesiod.) The songs at the Carnea were perhaps one early reflection of the Alcestis legend; another puzzling little echo may perhaps be heard in a popular *σκόλιον* partly quoted by Aristophanes (*Vesp.* 1238) and completed by Σ ad loc., who says it was attributed to Praxilla:

> Ἀδμήτου λόγον, ὦ 'ταῖρε, μαθὼν τοὺς ἀγαθοὺς φίλει,
> τῶν δειλῶν δ' ἀπέχου, γνοὺς ὅτι δειλῶν ὀλίγα χάρις.

This is often taken to mean that Admetus was 'traditionally a coward', regardless of the fact that no one could conceivably draw such a moral from the outcome of the story. It *might* be a comment on the goodness of Alcestis and Heracles and the cowardice of the parents, but there is some uncertainty whether in fact it refers to our part of the legend at all; the Scholiast mentions in the context a tradition that Admetus, exiled from Pherae with Alcestis and their youngest child Hippasus, was granted asylum in Athens by Theseus. It was evidently a favourite little drinking-catch at symposia (cf. Ar. *Pelargoi*, fr. 430K, Cratinus, *Cheirones*, fr. 236K), where a guest would be called on for the Ἀδμήτου λόγον or Ἀδμήτου μέλος (just as Ἐν μύρτου κλαδί was known briefly as the Ἁρμοδίου μέλος).

In Plato's *Symposium* (179b) we find a hint of another version of the legend: Phaedrus illustrates his discourse on the power of Love by a reference to Alcestis' story, and says the gods so admired her devotion that they sent her soul back from the dead; this is the version recorded by Apollodorus 1. 9. 15, that Kore let her go back to earth. Phaedrus goes on to draw the parallel of Orpheus and Eurydice, and conceivably it was the Orphics who sought to preserve the dignity of the nether powers by substituting this version for Heracles' wrestling-match. But Wilamowitz may be right in supposing the Mercy of Kore to be the original form of the story and the Rescue an invention of the satyric stage—in fact, probably, of Phrynichus. The connexion with the saga of Heracles, passing by on the way to his eighth labour, seems a little perfunctory, though of course if Lesky is right in seeing here an independent aspect of the folk-tale[1] this would be decisive for the priority of the Rescue version. However this may be, it seems that Euripides knew the other story. Heracles' assertion (850 ff.) that if he fails to snatch Alcestis from Thanatos he will go down to Hades and beg her back from the powers there looks like an attempt to reconcile the two versions; presumably Lucian is following up this hint when in the *Dialogues of the Dead* Protesilaus, adopting this more tactful form of the legend, reminds Pluto that τὴν ὁμογενῆ μοι Ἄλκηστιν παρεπέμψατε Ἡρακλεῖ χαριζόμενοι.

i. *The* Alcestis *of Phrynichus*

It is probable then that Euripides could assume an audience familiar with the general lines of the story but with no canonical version firmly fixed in their heads. Perhaps some of the older ones had actually seen the *Alcestis* of Phrynichus. Certainly in the scraps of our knowledge of that play there are indications that it had helped to define the story for the stage. In the first place, it is clear that Euripides owes to Phrynichus the action of Thanatos, like a priest officiating at a sacrifice, cutting off some hairs from the victim's head as a preliminary rite and so dedicating her to the nether powers. Servius, in his commentary on *Aeneid* 4. 694 (the death of Dido) says *alii dicunt Euripidem Orcum in scaenam inducere gladium ferentem quo crinem Alcesti abscidat* (cf. Macrobius, *Sat.* 5. 19. 4, in closely similar words, probably from the same source), *Euripidem hoc a †poenia* (F, *phenico* T) *antiquo tragico mutuatum.* Since we know from Hesychius (1. 61) that Phrynichus wrote an *Alcestis*, Jahn's emendation *Phrynicho* seems certain here. Euripides actually 'brought on' Thanatos with a drawn sword (74 ff.); it is of course not certain, though likely, that 'borrowed this from P.' means that Thanatos appeared on the stage in that play too. In any case the Death of Phrynichus was the popular

[1] Cf. supra, p. viii and n. 1.

demon-figure who comes to earth to fetch his victims, not Hades the throned king of the underworld of official mythology.

In Euripides' prologue *Μοίρας δολώσας* (12) is Apollo's discreetly brief account of the means by which he won a special concession for Admetus from the Fates. For further detail the Scholiast refers us to Aeschylus (*Eum.* 723 ff.), whose Eumenides reproach Apollo with his constant lack of respect for the elder gods: even so did he behave to the Fates on behalf of a favoured mortal when in the house of Pheres he made them drunk and tricked them into letting off Admetus. Evidently Aeschylus expected his audience to know the 'trick', and the natural assumption is that they knew it from the play of Phrynichus. Unfortunately we cannot deduce from this the answer to the important question: was it a tragedy or a satyr-play? In itself the incident suggests burlesque, but if it was merely reported—and it can hardly have been anything else—Phrynichus' play *need* not have been much nearer to burlesque than the *Eumenides* itself. It might also be argued (though inconclusively) that Aeschylus would not be likely to incorporate a feature of a satyr-play in his tragedy. In a later period one would imagine the appearance of Heracles in such a role to be decisive for a satyr-play (Euripides' *Alcestis* being the exception), but we know too little of what was possible in early tragedy to be confident on this point. The one surviving fragment of five words, one of them corrupt, adds puzzles of its own. Hesychius, s.v. *ἀθαμβές*, quotes *Φρύνιχος Ἀλκήστιδι* "*σῶμα δ' ἀθαμβὲς †γυοδόνιστον τείρει*". It is generally assumed, with some probability, that the reference is to the wrestling and the metre anapaestic, and *γυοδόνιστον* is emended to *γυιοδόνητον* ('limb-driven'?) or *γυιόδμητον* ('limb-mastered'). But this surely cannot be translated, as Weber does, 'fearlessly he thrashes his body, bruising him limb by limb'?[1]

1 Introd., p. 34, 'furchtlos walkt er seinen Leib, ihn Glied für Glied zerbläuend', cf. *Rh. Mus.* 79 (1930), 35 ff., where he rashly refers this to a 'messenger-speech'.

ἀθαμβές in such a position can only be another adjective, and, since 'fearless body' is likely to refer to Heracles, Death must be the subject of τείρει. It is a moment when the hero is hard-driven, and the obvious speaker of anapaests is the Chorus. How this fits into the structure of the play is not an easy guess. Perhaps while the hero is absent on his declared quest the Chorus is fearfully imagining the progress of the struggle—'perhaps even now . . .' or 'how can he hope to survive when . . . ?'

The possibilities of burlesque in the story of Admetus and Alcestis seem to have been occasionally exploited in comedy, by Phormis or Phormos the contemporary of Epicharmus, according to 'Suidas', and in Middle Comedy by Aristomenes in 388 (*Admetus*) and Antiphanes (*Alcestis*). For tragedy or satyr-play there is a slight discrepancy in the evidence. The Hypothesis[1] says that the subject has not been treated by Aeschylus or Sophocles, but Plutarch *de def. or.* 417f, claiming that the stories of exile and serfdom among the gods are untrue, complains of the ἁγνόν τ' Ἀπόλλω φυγάδ' ἀπ' οὐρανοῦ θεόν of Aeschylus (*Supp.* 214) and the οὑμὸς δ' ἀλέκτωρ αὐτὸν ἦγε πρὸς μύλην of 'Sophocles' *Admetus*' (fr. 851 P). 'My husband[2] brought him to the mill' should be spoken by Alcestis (Hera seems the only other possible candidate), but the only way of reconciling this with the Hypothesis is to assume that the plot concerned some other part of Admetus' career.[3] The words in any case sound remarkably un-tragic.

ii. *Euripides' Modification of the Legend*

We have seen that the essentials of the story were current before Phrynichus, being grafted on to the longer story of Admetus' association with Apollo; Phrynichus had dramatized the story complete with Thanatos and Heracles, or perhaps added this episode on his own account, ignoring, like Euripides after him, the inconsistency of this popular version with the underworld apparatus of official mythology,

[1] See infra, p. xxxix.

[2] Cf. Bacchyl. 4. 8.

[3] Cf. on the σκόλιον, p. xi.

and probably inventing also the detail of the trickery of the drunken Moirai. Just how much Euripides owes to Phrynichus is impossible to say, but we can safely assume that the general organization of the plot is his own, if only because so flexible and elaborate a dramatic technique would have been inconceivable before the middle of the century. The skilful alternation of hope and gloom, of despair and half-comic relief, is the mark of a sophisticated theatre; in particular the quarrel scene between Admetus and Pheres and the final dénouement must be new. Some of the improvisation in the last scene, indeed, will not bear too close a scrutiny—for instance, the grounds for Admetus' reluctance to take the strange woman into his house—but the whole episode of the Teasing of Admetus is carried through with a kind of light-hearted tension that is dramatically effective.

Like so many Greek tragedies, the *Alcestis* concentrates its action upon a limited part of the relevant story, leaving a great deal to be made known as *προγεγενημένα*. This puts a heavy burden of 'exposition' upon the opening scenes, and it is understandable that Euripides should often have chosen the short cut of an unashamedly explanatory prologue, an introductory monologue addressed direct to the audience. A god has great advantages here: his knowledge can if need be extend to the future and foreshadow coming events, he embodies the larger forces at work behind the human scene, and we accept the didactic tone more easily as his natural utterance. In this play, indeed, the explanatory monologue is kept short, and passes over (following Euripides' favourite pattern) quickly into vehement dialogue. Moreover, all is carefully motived: Apollo is at the palace because of his special link with Admetus, he leaves it to avoid the miasma of approaching death, and to his prophecy (64 ff.) he is goaded by the defiance of Thanatos. The gods came and went freely among men in these early legends; Apollo and Thanatos play important parts in the story, and their clash here epitomizes the struggle between light and dark in the succeeding scenes, but after the prologue they are seen no more as visible presences, though kept constantly in our minds by the words and songs, the struggles, fears, and prayers, of the human actors.

Once the poet has thus summarily expounded the initial situation, he may take up and amplify in the succeeding action any aspect of the προγεγενημένα which he wishes to dwell on. This, I think, is the explanation of a curious point of timing: between Alcestis' pledge of self-devotion and its fulfilment there has been an interval of time, and the play opens at the end of this, on the day when 'she is fated to die' (21). Euripides nowhere specifies the length of this interval; evidently it was pre-arranged, since not only Alcestis herself (158) and Apollo (27) but the Chorus (105) know that this is the 'appointed day'. Now clearly this was not the sense of the original legend, in which the threatened victim would be given time to make his threefold appeal, and his substitute would then be carried off.[1] In choosing to relegate the appeal, and Alcestis' response, to the antecedent incidents, Euripides has sacrificed the portrayal of her supreme moment of heroism. So he substitutes this undefined lapse of time, with an 'appointed day' on which the great issue again comes to a head, as it were, though in a different form. Not on a sudden brave impulse, but with quiet courage she makes her preparations 'for premeditated death'.

It is, I think, a mistake to see as one aspect of this interval a transformation of Alcestis from bride to wife and mother. Undoubtedly the play gains in depth and richness by placing the sacrifice of Alcestis at this later period in her life, and it

[1] Hence in the famous Alcsti krater (Beazley, *Etruscan Vase-Painting*, Pl. XXX. 1 and p. 133 f.) the Etruscan artist is sometimes believed to be representing some simpler pre-Euripidean version of the story, but 'this is more than can be said' (Beazley). I can myself see no reason to reject the older interpretation (Séchan, *E.T.G.*, p. 241) that this is a reminiscence of the death-scene of Eur.'s play. It is surprising that we have no Greek vase-painting inspired by it, though its influence can be seen on sculptured reliefs (Beazley, loc. cit.).

is very important for the plot that her last speech should be preoccupied with the thought of leaving the children rather than of leaving Admetus.[1] But there is no word in the play to suggest that the offer was made on her bridal night. Such a detail belongs if anywhere to the 'Wrath of Artemis' version (p. ix), and there is no suggestion—indeed quite the contrary—that the shadow has hung over the *whole* of their wedded life. Since the eldest child is of an age to sing a lament, it would mean that the Fates had demanded Admetus' death, or that of his substitute, within, say, five or six years—surely not the way these things are done. When Admetus claims (421) to 'have long been troubled by the knowledge', the word πάλαι is quite vague, and could as appropriately be used of months as of years. There is also the question of the length and the timing of Apollo's service. At first sight the natural sense of l. 9 τόνδ' ἔσῳζον οἶκον ἐς τόδ' ἡμέρας might seem to be that the term is just up and that (22) only the particular moment of his departure is determined by the approaching pollution of death, but the tense of ἔτλην (1) seems to put the whole episode in the past. The appropriate period in mythology for such penance seems to have been one year (so Pherecydes ap. *Σ Alc.* 1, Apoll. *Bibl.* 3. 10. 4, and cf. Apollo and Poseidon in *Il.* 21. 444 θητεύσαμεν εἰς ἐνιαυτόν and Theseus in *Hipp.* 37). But there is no indication at what stage Apollo made his bargain with the Fates over the life of Admetus (12), and in fact, of course, Euripides is deliberately vague about the whole timing of these προγεγενημένα; Wilamowitz is not justified in finding support in chronology for his view that we are to understand Alcestis the mother as repenting, though she will not repudiate, the sacrifice promised by Alcestis the bride. But the real answer to that famous pronouncement lies in our interpretation of the sense of the play as a whole. For here, and not in any modification of the story, lies the enormous originality, or in other words the characteristic quality, of Euripides' *Alcestis*.

[1] See infra, p. xxvi.

III. THE *ALCESTIS* AS A PRO-SATYRIC PLAY

Perhaps no other play of Euripides except the *Bacchae* has provoked so much controversy among scholars in search of its 'real meaning'. For many English readers it is their first introduction to Greek drama at school, and for this purpose it has some obvious advantages: it is short, the lyrics are simple and arise directly out of the action as it unfolds itself at each stage, and there is plenty of dramatic incident: strife between a god of light and a black-robed demon king, an affecting death-scene, an elaborate deception, a tremendous quarrel, a scene almost verging on drunken comedy, and a final Revelation—what Aristotle would have called ἀναγνώρισις with περιπέτεια. Yet this is not an easy play to begin on; in spite of its happy ending it has a curiously tart, almost bitter, flavour, and the young reader is apt to find himself puzzled by the figures of Admetus and Alcestis and uncertain about the whole tone of the play: how seriously is it meant to be taken? And not only the young reader; Browning wrote a part translation, part adaptation, *Balaustion's Adventure*, which he called a 'transcript', and it is most instructive to see where he has felt impelled to criticize, to paraphrase, to soften a harshness, to amplify in terms of motive. He admired the play, but he is all the time trying to pull it into the shape he feels it ought to have had. And since the stuff is strong and resists his pulling, at the end he appends a quite different version of his own, more edifying if less dramatic. (The same might be said of many other modern adaptations of this theme.)

The widely fluctuating judgements of scholars upon this play have followed in the main their disagreements on two fundamental matters, one, the 'pro-satyric' question, peculiar to the *Alcestis*, the other a problem posed here with unusual sharpness but affecting our general understanding of Greek drama: how Euripides conceived 'character in action' or in Aristotelian terms (much more applicable to Greek than to later drama) the relation of ἦθος and διάνοια to πρᾶξις. I shall start with the first; the second is a large subject and can be discussed only briefly in this Introduction.

Neither the Hypothesis[1] nor any other ancient source makes any comment on Euripides' departure from normal practice in producing the *Alcestis* instead of a satyr-play at the end of a tetralogy. One would expect this to mean that the phenomenon was by no means isolated, and indeed in the list of extant titles of Euripides the number of satyr-plays is for whatever reason far short of one-quarter of the whole, and a much smaller proportion than in Aeschylus and Sophocles. But since no other play, extant or not, is *known* to belong to this ambiguous category we can only inquire of the *Alcestis* itself what characteristics, if any, set it apart from the rest of Greek tragedy. In the first place it is short; the average length had increased since Aeschylus' day, and with 1163 lines the *Alcestis* is shorter than any other extant tragedy of Sophocles or Euripides (not counting the *Rhesus*), though even so the *Cyclops* is only about two-thirds as long. Should we add, secondly, that it only needs two actors? So does the *Medea*, for that matter, but that might mean only that a limitation normal for satyr-plays at this period could also extend to the occasional tragedy. The *Cyclops* has three actors,[2] but it is generally agreed to be of fairly late date; the *Ichneutae* evidently had only two. This point, then, is indecisive; all we know is that the play *could* be, and therefore probably was, run on two actors, one of them with a singing voice. The little boy's monody (393 ff.) is usually supposed to need an extra, a παραχορήγημα performing behind the scenes, or even to have been manageable by a (not too young) choir-boy in the part. Euripides alone of the dramatists gives voice parts to children, but (except

[1] Unless the adjective σατυρικώτερον (in place of κωμικώτερον) in § 2 is a surviving echo of some discussion of the point. See p. xl.

[2] Silenus, of course, must not be reckoned (as, for example, by Schmid–Stählin ii. 59, 2) as Chorus-leader of the satyrs; he acts on the stage and can hold an iambic dialogue with the coryphaeus. The fact that the Pronomos satyr-vase shows only eleven satyrs with Silenus and two other actors cannot affect the argument.

off stage) only singing, never speaking, parts: here a monody, in *Andromache* (504 ff.) a κομμός between mother and child, in *Supplices* (1123 ff.) apparently a supplementary chorus. The last *could* have been a choir of boys selected from the performers at the year's Dionysia, but Wilamowitz's view of these as a trained reserve, from which soloists could be drawn for such parts as Eumelus or Molossus, is very dubious. The training for choral singing was quite different from that of a soloist, which required much skill, and, in that great theatre, a powerful voice. *Andromache* is one of the few plays which require two adult singing actors, one for Andromache and Hermione, one for Peleus, and there can be little doubt that the latter sang the boy's part off stage. The case of *Alcestis* is more difficult. The heroine has the only other singing part, and the second actor is on the stage too. I have little doubt, strange as it may at first seem, that the child's song was sung by the protagonist himself. The head of the dead Alcestis would be propped comfortably high on a pillow on her couch[1] and hidden from the spectators by the child miming its part; thus the voice would proceed from very near the right spot.

But the main pro-satyric note in the *Alcestis* is struck by the scene after the departure of the Chorus for the funeral (747 ff.). Here we have the figure of Heracles presented in a manner discreetly reminiscent of the traditional burlesque Heracles, the coarse glutton and drunkard who rouses himself to perform prodigious feats of strength against the local monster or bully. This stock figure is perhaps most prominent in comedy, where we meet him as far back as the *Busiris* of Epicharmus and his existence is implied in half a dozen plays of Aristophanes and Cratinus; but he appears also in the satyr-plays *Heracles at Taenarum* of Sophocles, *Syleus* of Euripides, and *Omphale* of Ion, and is in fact a conspicuous example of the overlapping of comic and satyric themes. Perhaps too we might reckon the discomfiture

[1] Cf. πρόθεσις-scenes such as the one painted by Exekias, Technau, Pl. XVIII, *Ant. Denk.* Pl. XI. 2–4.

of Death as a potentially satyric feature, Death who is not the majestic king throned in the underworld but the ogreish creature of popular fancy, a monster like so many adversaries of the Hero; but the episode is passed over very lightly. As for the happy ending, that is of course the normal thing in satyr-play as in comedy, but the Greeks never recognized its exclusion from the concept of tragedy, and there is no lack of other instances.

It is clear, then, that while the *Alcestis* is recognizably pro-satyric, this does not constitute any very profound modification of its dramatic essence. Its relative shortness leaves room for an ample and fully developed action. The happy ending belongs to the type of story itself, as it does in the *Ion*, but the earlier scenes of tragedy are presented with as deep an earnestness as if there were to be no dispersal of the shadows. In the midst of these comes the scene of Heracles and the Manservant. The theme itself is satyric or comic, but not its treatment here; this is the *adaptation* of a satyric theme to tragedy (in the Greek sense). The description of Heracles gormandizing off stage is a stock piece, and so is the assertion of hedonistic materialism in his address to the Servant, but here these are subdued to the point where they can blend discreetly with the rest of the play. Even in this scene Heracles remains a man, not a caricature. It is not as a satyric or semi-satyric figure but as the forerunner of the great tragic personage of the *Hercules Furens* that his significance transcends the boundaries of this play.

In effect, the pro-satyric element gives the *Alcestis* a wider range of mood than any other extant Greek tragedy,[1] but this is a carefully calculated range, which does not destroy the unity of the whole. And Euripides has made the most of these contrasting moods by building the whole play on an alternation of dark and light; no tragedy of his is more flawlessly constructed. To seek to press the notion of a 'pro-satyric' play any further is I think mistaken. There is

[1] The nearest parallels would be perhaps some scenes of the *Helen*, and the episode of the Nurse in the *Choephori*.

nothing here of frolic, or inconsequence, or burlesque; the action moves to its conclusion by the strictest dramatic logic, and is meant, together with all the characters, to be taken seriously.

IV. THE CHARACTERS AND THE ACTION

The play is called *Alcestis* because the conspicuous glory is hers; she is ἀρίστη γυναικῶν—the adjective recurs time and again in dialogue and song. But the central theme of the tragedy—that in virtue of which it *is* a tragedy in the Greek sense of the word—is exemplified in the experience of Admetus. It might be summed up in his words ἄρτι μανθάνω (940): 'now—now when it is too late—I understand.' The same words are spoken in a flash of awful realization at the end of the *Bacchae*, and they might be made the burden of many tragedies, ancient and modern—a truly tragic ἀναγνώρισις in a sense not included in Aristotle's definitions. What Admetus realizes too late is that this life of which he has cheated Destiny is a useless possession; the loss of Alcestis and of his own fair fame has made it a desert for its owner κακῶς κλύοντι καὶ κακῶς πεπραγότι. The 'dark' scenes of the drama have been remorselessly leading to this climax, but in and out among them the beneficence of Apollo, working through Heracles, has been preparing a way towards the light, which dawns upon an incredulous Admetus and Chorus in the last scene.

The progress towards this insight into the real nature of 'what has been done'—τῶν πεπραγμένων—is a better clue to the understanding of each scene than the search for psychological complexities. To that school of thought which sees in ἠθοποιία, the creation of character, the chief and most original contribution of Euripides to the drama, scanning every turn of incident, every line of dialogue, for little touches to fill in some complex portrait, the chief interest of this play lies in an elaborately unflattering 'character-study' of Admetus, who is seen to be vain, shallow, egotistical, bad-tempered, lying, hysterical, and insincere; some would have him despicable, or at best ridiculous, to the very end, others reform him slightly in time for the happy ending. Now, some of this indictment has arisen from demonstrable misunderstandings of dramatic technique and of Greek usage (see, for example, the Commentary on 565, 1148), and in particular we ought to be suspicious of any such synthetic portrait as turns out to be at variance with considered, and unrepented, judgements expressed by one of the characters upon another in the course of the play. If Heracles declares privately at 857 his admiration for the noble and generous impulse (*not* the shallow vanity) which led Admetus to conceal the truth from him, we *cannot* interpret his μέμφομαι μέν, μέμφομαι at 1017, any more than his δίκαιος ὢν τὸ λοιπόν at 1147, as an indication of his (or the poet's) weighty moral disapproval of the same act. The explanation is simply that our portrait-painters have failed to understand the tone and level of these remarks. Heracles (1008) enters with the veiled woman, and begins: 'Admetus, to a friend one should speak candidly and not suppress one's grievances in the silence of the breast. Coming so close to your troubles I should expect to have been given the chance to prove my friendship; yet you did not reveal the presence of your wife's body laid out for burial, but entertained me as a guest in your house, . . . and I garlanded my head and poured libations to the gods under your afflicted roof. *I do protest* at being treated so; however, the last thing I want is to distress you in your grief.' μέμφομαι, in fact, is a gentle reproach near the level of our deprecating 'you shouldn't, you know, you really shouldn't have . . .'. Which of us, on discovering that a friend had put us under a heavy obligation of which he had intended us to remain ignorant, so that we appear to have acted unfittingly, would not react with just this mixture of feelings? Commentators are often finding touches of Thessalian 'local colour' in this play; what is much more remarkable is its echoes from the civilized courtesies of contemporary social life in Athens; in this respect the *Alcestis*, more perhaps than any other play, shows Euripides the forerunner of Menander.

But the real gravamen of the indictment built up against Admetus lies in the earlier scenes, in his attitude to Alcestis' sacrifice and death. In the first place, it is said, he ought never to have accepted it; in the second, his expression of grief at the death he has caused is too extravagant to be sincere (that image-business!), and shows the same lack of balance as his later outburst against Pheres. Most of the psychologists, however, relent towards the later Admetus; Pheres' home truths have punctured his self-esteem, and when he returns from the funeral his grief and contrition have somehow become genuine. Admetus in fact is seen as a clever, though unpleasant, 'character study'. Alcestis, considered from the same point of view, is a more awkward problem; the psychologists content themselves with labelling her an 'elusive' or 'complex' character, and it is usually left to young readers to voice a more open disappointment. She should not sing her own praises so loudly, they feel, and they remain unconvinced even when told that this was not considered such bad form in ancient Greece. And her severity towards Admetus, the lack of any word of love or affection for him in all her death-scene, are chilling to the romantic feelings. Hence Wilamowitz's belief[1] that if we read with the proper insight we shall see that Euripides is subtly conveying the disillusionment of her marriage which makes her now regret that impulsive promise given on her bridal night.

The root of the trouble is, I think, our inveterate modern habit of regarding a drama almost exclusively in terms of its characters. The modern conception of the actor's function, with each actor concentrating on the 'interpretation' of his single part, strongly reinforces this habit. It works quite well with modern drama, which is largely composed from the same point of view. It can be made to work with Shakespeare. But it will not work satisfactorily with Greek

[1] See p. xvii.

tragedy. Of course the Greek, like every serious drama, involves 'characters', whose part in the action, and therefore whose words, to some extent reflect their several natures. But in Greek tragedy their speeches, and the interplay of their dialogue, can rarely be interpreted as *primarily* or *consistently* expressive of their natures, and whenever we find ourselves trying to build up some elaborate or many-sided personality by *adding up* small touches gleaned from all parts of the play we can be pretty sure of being on the wrong lines. It usually means that we are not allowing enough for two considerations always very important to Greek dramatists, the trend of the action and the rhetoric of the situation.

Of the trend of the action in the *Alcestis* something has already been said. The bitter lesson Admetus learns in his ἄρτι μανθάνω is not 'I see now that I ought never to have accepted this sacrifice', but 'I see now that Alcestis in dying is better off than I in living, since I have lost my happiness and my reputation'. The gifts of the gods may by a kind of paradox prove ambiguous and self-defeating. So far as there is any 'ought to have' in the story it is Pheres or the mother who ought to have died instead; both Alcestis and the Chorus make that quite clear. But in a brilliant and shameless speech Pheres manages to stand that argument on its head and make it show Admetus to be a coward and a murderer. Paradox again. It is not Admetus' *conscience* that is eventually stricken by this; Pheres is hardly the mouthpiece of truth. What Admetus comes to realize is the handle he has given to malice—ἐρεῖ δέ μ' ὅστις ἐχθρὸς ὢν κυρεῖ τάδε: 'my enemies will say . . .', τοιάνδε πρὸς κακοῖσι κληδόνα ἕξω. That is Pheres' contribution towards the opening of his eyes. Alcestis did the rest, Alcestis who loved him and died for him. The strangest paradox of all. The whole play, or at least the whole dark side of it, is permeated by a sort of grave irony of plot, the irony of human intentions measured against their outcome. To safeguard her children's future, Alcestis exacts his promise never to marry again, and for the sake of the plot we must indeed be left quite certain that Admetus will know no more domestic felicity. If we do not realize the absolute sincerity of his response,[1] by which he pledges himself to turn his life into a desert, we miss half the point of the plot. We are not at liberty to argue that, because Alcestis makes no comment on his intentions except for what concerns the children, she is rebuking him for extravagance or expressing scepticism by her silent contempt. The *argumentum ex silentio* is never weaker than when it tries to make psychological deductions from what Euripidean speeches leave unsaid. The action requires that Admetus shall not be consoled and fortified in this scene by words of love and sympathy from Alcestis; and by making her concentrate upon leaving the children rather than leaving Admetus Euripides avoids the slightly ridiculous trap into which more than one of his successors has fallen, of showing Alcestis so devoted to her husband that she is only too happy and eager to die for his sake, thus deflecting our sympathies to the harder lot of the survivor.

Yet Euripides cares very much that we should know his conception of the character of Alcestis. The description by the Maidservant of her last hours in the house, the words of the Manservant about the mistress they are all heartbroken at losing, give us Alcestis as we know she must have been—brave, gentle, full of loving-kindness. And of course she loves Admetus—what else made her die for him? Our speech, songs, and literature are so saturated with the expression of this theme that we are apt to forget how unaccustomed Greek eyes and ears would be to the spectacle of a high-born young wife expatiating in public to her husband upon such a subject. *ἐγώ σε πρεσβεύουσα* is her prim little phrase: 'counting you more important than myself', 'putting you first'. But with beautiful reticence the strength of this feeling is conveyed in the Maidservant's description of her mistress's address to her marriage-bed, at sight of which her calm for the first time breaks down and she weeps and kisses

[1] See Commentary, l. 365.

it and suffers at the thought of a successor in her place. It is strange that so many commentators should deny that this means love and jealousy.

Of the characters in this play, Alcestis, Heracles, and Pheres stand out in much more definite outline than Admetus. Their part in the action is limited, and in itself goes a long way to characterize them, while for Alcestis we also have the benefit of description. Selfish father, unselfish wife, gluttonous and heroic son of Zeus: they have to be the sort of people they are or the action would not work. But for Admetus this applies only to his regal hospitality, which affects only a small area of his part in the action. For the rest, Admetus as a person is blown hither and thither by every wind of incident; he is a person to whom things happen, it is his experience that matters, his reactions to what people do or say to him, his *πάθος*, not his *ἦθος*. So far from considering the *Alcestis* a full-length study of *naïveté*, weakness, hysteria, egotism, character-development, and so forth, I do not believe that apart from the *ὁσιότης* (10) Euripides had any particular interest in the sort of person Admetus was. The situations in which the plot involves him are too diverse for much personality to appear, or to be intended. For in a well-constructed Euripidean tragedy what controls a succession of situations is not a firmly conceived unity of character but the shape of the whole action, and what determines the development and finesse of each situation is not a desire to paint in the details of a portrait-study but the rhetoric of the situation—what Aristotle calls *διάνοια*. Rhetoric is a concept which we tend to hold in some suspicion, as if in its nature there must be something slightly bogus; but we shall never properly understand Greek tragedy unless we realize how closely related were the rhetoric of Athenian life, in the assembly and law-courts and on other public occasions, and the rhetoric of the speeches in drama. Nourished on the psychological novel, we tend to assume that the poet had brooded on the story until the characters took shape in his mind, as if he had asked himself: What would X, being such a man, be likely to say in such a situation? whereas we might sometimes get nearer to the meaning by imagining the question: Suppose a man involved in such a situation, how should he best acquit himself? How gain his point? Move his hearers? Prove his thesis? Convey information lucidly and vividly? The aim of rhetoric is Persuasion, *Πειθώ*, and the poet is as it were a kind of *λογογράφος* who promises to do his best for each of his clients in turn as the situations change and succeed one another. This does not by any means exclude an interest in character; the skilful *λογογράφος* takes that into account in its proper place. But the dominating consideration is: What *points* could be made here? The points may be developed in a set speech, a *ῥῆσις*, or made and countered in stichomythia. Fertility in arguments, a delight in logical analysis—these are the essentials, though they may be skilfully made to produce an effect of spontaneity. Alcestis has to win her husband's promise never to marry again; her strongest arguments are the magnitude of her own sacrifice and the emotion aroused at the thought of the motherless children and her own death. So like a skilful pleader she makes the most of these things, and sometimes the skill of the pleading obscures the woman Alcestis, as when she emphasizes her own virtue in contrast to the conduct of the parents, or when at the end of the speech she says: 'And you, my husband, can boast that you had the noblest of women to wife, and you, my children, that you were born of the noblest of mothers.' It is a pleader's peroration, not the spontaneous cry of a noble heart. A modern actress, intent on 'being' Alcestis, might well find these lines embarrassing; not so the Greek actor, trained not in 'interpretation' but in rhetorical performance, before an audience that expected nothing less. And the dramatist as well as the actor has a technique to which we are unaccustomed. In an earlier scene he has conveyed to us, among other qualities, Alcestis' love for Admetus, which in any case is implicit in the story. But in this scene the action does not require it (it might indeed be a disturbing element), so he omits its expression and leaves only its effect, in her sacrifice; and all the emphasis goes into her anguish for the children. Our presuppositions about dramatic character lead us to expect that such a love will inform her whole utterance everywhere, and so we feel rebuffed. But if we start projecting these feelings into a Euripidean 'Portrait of Alcestis', we shall end up with the Alcestis of that delightful modern comedy 'The Thracian Horses' who was furious with Heracles for stealing her limelight and chiefly concerned lest she should become famous hereafter as the subject of his Labour number 8(a). It was great fun, but of course it was not Euripides.

V. THE TEXT[1]

i. *The Manuscripts*

The *Alcestis* was one of the ten plays of Euripides selected by some unknown authority, like the seven of Aeschylus and seven of Sophocles, for use in schools, perhaps towards the end of the second century A.D. The schools needed annotated editions, so the plays were accompanied by extracts from the old commentators with fresh accretions, especially paraphrases. Some of these notes have survived in the form of marginal scholia and interlinear glosses in a group of mediaeval MSS. dating from the twelfth and thirteenth centuries. Of this annotated group, cited in the Oxford text as MABV, neither M, the oldest and best, nor A contains the *Alcestis*. For this side of the tradition, therefore, we are dependent on two MSS., Parisinus 2713 (B) of the twelfth century and Vaticanus 909 (V) of the thirteenth, with their scholia (Σ). These two, though recognizably of the

[1] For a general account of the history of the text of Euripides see Méridier's introduction to vol. i of the Budé edition (1925), and D. L. Page's edition of the *Medea* (1938). The facsimiles of B, L, and P published by J. A. Spranger and available in some libraries have now added greatly to the ordinary scholar's opportunities of collation.

same family, contain many divergences; V has many more careless slips, though there are some fifteen places where it alone preserves the correct reading. Two Laurentian MSS. of the fourteenth century, O and D, though much inferior, are occasionally worth quoting in support of one reading or another, since in other plays they show a marked resemblance to the text of M.

The other group of MSS., LP, represents a different side of the tradition. In early Byzantine times a scholar apparently copied, without their scholia, a version of the select plays, with a unique addition—the text of nine other plays of Euripides, a segment of a complete edition arranged in alphabetical order of titles which had somehow come into his hands. From this copy are descended our two MSS., Laurentianus xxxii, 2 (L) of the early fourteenth, or perhaps late thirteenth, century, and P of the late fourteenth, now in two parts, of which the one containing *Alcestis* is Palatinus 287. The relation of P to L is obscure and somewhat puzzling. It is now generally accepted[1] that in the 'alphabetical' plays P is simply copied from L; many of its mistakes are only to be accounted for as misreadings of L's crabbed handwriting. Its only value here, therefore, is as a check on the original readings of L where these have been obscured by the hand of a later reviser (*l*). But in the select plays, though the relationship of the two is still close, P has some independent value. L does not contain *Troades* (it is doubtful whether it ever did) and has lost the second half of *Bacchae*; and in the plays common to both, divergences are no longer confined to the mistakes of P, nor do these seem to be related to L's handwriting. In *Alcestis* there are a score or so of places where P agrees with B or V or both[2] against L, and even one or two (e.g. *κατάρξωμαι* 74, *πάθῃ* 145) where P alone is right. It is true that in many of these, including the two quoted, only a slight correction of L's reading is needed, and

[1] See, however, Turyn, *The Byzantine MS. Tradition of Eur.*, 1957.

[2] There seems to be no adequate ground for Méridier's assertion that in this play V and P in particular show noticeable *rapports*.

in the alphabetical plays there are occasional signs[1] that P's copying, usually so careless and mechanical, was accompanied by a little independent thought; but it seems hardly credible that he should have had the adroitness and metrical observation required, for example, for the combination of ἐπάνωθε (ἐπάνω L) 463 and φιλίας (φίλας L) in the corresponding l. 473. It seems more probable that for the select plays P had another source closely akin to L, but expert opinion is far from united on this point.

Of the two classes of MSS., BV and LP, neither, in this play at least, is clearly superior to the other; in doubtful cases, therefore, there should be no bias towards one or the other as a 'better class' of MSS. Each case must be decided solely on its merits.

So far no papyrus find has contributed to the establishment of the text of *Alcestis*. The only relevant fragment is Hibeh I. 25 of the third century B.C., which contains (in a slightly inaccurate form) the anapaestic epilogue 1159–63, repeated at the end of *Andromache*, *Helena*, and *Bacchae*.

ii. *The Scholia*

The scholia available in the two annotated MSS. of *Alcestis* are relatively short, unlike, for instance, those of the three plays, *Hecuba*, *Orestes*, *Phoenissae*, which formed the shorter Select Edition of the Byzantines and are therefore much encumbered with useless paraphrases and nugatory displays of learning. Some scholia appear only in the one or the other MS., others are common to both. The majority consist of rather flat and painstaking prose renderings or explanations of any point where the poetic expression is keyed up a turn or two beyond the usage of ordinary speech; these are mostly aimed at the young and inexperienced reader, but occasionally, as in ποιμνίτας ὑμεναίους 577,[2] give a clear and unambiguous lead where modern commentators have

[1] v. P. Maas, *Textkritik*, § 27.

[2] Aelian also takes this in the right sense in his quotation: see *Testimonia*, p. xxxvi infra.

bungled, or, as at 447, 768, an apt and valuable citation of a parallel passage. Alternative explanations are sometimes added; thus 101 is said to mean either 'no one with hair cut short' or 'no shorn lock', and for the somewhat otiose διψίαν 560 (a Homeric reminiscence) we are offered, besides 'waterless', 'or *yearned after*, since thirst is a sort of desire'. Now and again there are echoes of literary criticism: at 779 the philosophy is said to be inappropriate (οὐκ εὐλόγως) for a drunken Heracles, and at 450 the turn of expression is commended (εὐφυῶς). At the first entry of the Chorus its composition, and division into two semi-choruses, is noted. There are no metrical scholia. As a commentary, the whole amalgam is of very varied quality, the sound core of Alexandrian learning, as quoted by the painstaking Didymus, having been reduced to small proportions and much overlaid. The scholion on l. 1 is quite exceptional, and appears to be an unabridged excerpt of Didymus. It gives a careful list of authorities, fourteen in all—poets, historians, and mythographers—for the conflicting reasons current in mythology for Apollo's service with Admetus and for the various versions of the crime of Asclepius. For the understanding of Euripides these pedantic details were of no importance, but we get an interesting sidelight on the wealth of mythological material available.

For us, however, the chief use of the scholia is textual. Besides the general protection they afford a text against later corruptions, they often record (with the formula γράφεται) ancient variants, and sometimes comment on a reading different from that of the MS. in which they appear. Occasionally this may be our only source for a correct reading; more often it coincides with that of some other source, and so throws light indirectly on the history of the transmission. At 58, where B reads πέφυκας and V λέληθας, each records the other in its Σ, and at 1153 B, reading πόδα, records both δόμον and ὁδόν as alternatives; evidently this was an old source of trouble. At 734 we owe the correct ἔρρων entirely to ΣV, and at 846 for the λοχήσας of all MSS.

the same source gives λοχίας as a variant, which would probably have put us on to the right λοχαίας even without the confirmation of one MS. of the *Etymologicum Magnum* where the line is quoted in this form. At 59, though V reads ὄνοιντ' and the first scholion explains μέμφοιντο κτλ., in the second the word ἀγοράσειαν clearly implies the correct ὠνοῖντ', while at 74, though the correct κατάρξωμαι appears only in P, the rest giving the future κατάρξομαι, the paraphrase in ΣVB ἀπαρχὴν τῶν τριχῶν λάβω indicates a text containing the subjunctive.[1] The comment on 843 εἰδωλοποιεῖται μελαίνας πτέρυγας ἔχων ὁ Θάνατος probably indicates an ancient variant μελάμπτερον for μελάμπεπλον. At 117–18 for ψυχάν (LP) VB had a genitive corrected into the accusative by the scribe of V and a later reviser in B; in the scholia of both the lemma is παραλῦσαι ψυχήν but the explanation assumes a genitive; similarly at 88 both V and B (like P) have the incorrect γόων, and the paraphrase of the scholiast in both assumes this, but while in V the lemma also gives γόων, in B, curiously enough, it is the correct γόον ὡς πεπραγμένων as in the text of L. Finally, at 820 ΣV has the valuable note that the three lines (818–20; see the Commentary) are omitted from some texts; since these lines are unsatisfactory in other ways it is interesting to find added grounds for regarding them as an interpolation.

iii. *The Testimonia*

One other possible source of evidence about a text is the citations of ancient authorities. Such a *testimonium* may on occasion be our oldest witness by some centuries, though not necessarily more reliable for that. There are four main classes of citation, in the works of (1) professional anthologists, (2) lexicographers, (3) scholiasts on other authors, (4) literary writers.

(1) The excerpting of quotable extracts from the poets in the form of anthologies was one of the symptoms of declining creative literary activity. The earliest workers in this field

[1] This is not noted in our apparatus critici.

must have read the originals in order to make their selection of moral and philosophical aphorisms arranged under appropriate heads, but their successors were content to excerpt the excerptors, whether to illustrate their own ethical essays or to provide handbooks of reference for lecturers and rhetoricians. Thus we constantly find the same pieces turning up in different anthologies. A considerable part of the Eklogai and Anthologion of 'Stobaeus' (John of Stoboi in Macedonia, probably of the fifth century A.D.) has survived, to be a prolific source of singularly uninformative fragments of the lost plays of the tragedians and of *testimonia* for the extant ones. Nine of these come from *Alcestis*;[1] one of them is the much quoted anapaestic tail-piece, three appear also in the similar anthology of the fifth-century grammarian Orion, and the same three again, or part of them, together with a fourth, in collections of trimeters called *Lines from Menander* (*Μενάνδρου γνῶμαι μονόστιχοι*) and *Couplets from Menander* (*Μενάνδρου Δίστιχα*), though Menander has certainly been credited with much that he never wrote. The MS. tradition of the anthologists has its own troubles, and in the course of repetition minor variants constantly appear (in 670, for instance, *Menandri Disticha* has πολὺν for μακρὸν), but now and again they are useful: at 880 Stobaeus supports LBP πιστῆς against V's φιλίας, and at 883 he alone has preserved the obviously correct τῆς (relative).

(2) The lexica and etymologies that have come down to us are mostly Byzantine overworkings or abridgements[2] based on various earlier works. The texts are often gravely corrupt, and peculiarly subject to interpolation, but used with proper caution they provide valuable evidence on tragic texts as well as diction, especially where their citations show a common word to have ousted (perhaps as a gloss) a rare one. For *Alcestis*, in fact, the only quotation of importance is in one MS. of the *Etymologicum Magnum*, which gives 846 in the garbled form κἄνπερ λοχαία σαυτὸν

[1] For references and details see under *Testimonia*, infra.

[2] Cf., under *Testimonia* infra, Stephanus on 577.

ἐξέδρας, and thus points to the correct reading.[1] A warning against indiscriminate use of such evidence is provided by Hesychius on 449 (see the Commentary).

(3) Parallel passages quoted in the scholia to other authors (e.g. *Σ* A. *Cho.* 151, for *Alc.* 424) or quotations to illustrate a parody in Aristophanes, usually go back to Alexandrian sources and are a useful and accurate check on the early state of the text. Thus on 181–2 *Σ* Ar. *Eq.* 1250 ff. gives the lines correctly, where the Byzantine lexicon 'Suidas' twice quotes them with *οὐχὶ μᾶλλον* for *οὐκ ἂν μᾶλλον*. The Latin author Macrobius, commenting on the death of Dido in *Aeneid* 4, quotes *Alcestis* 73–76 and gives welcome confirmation of P's *κατάρξωμαι*, though after that he either takes a bad text or misquotes. But the *Saturnalia* of Macrobius perhaps belongs rather to the next category than to the commentaries.

(4) On the whole, the citations in works of literature are the least useful of *testimonia*, since authors tend either to adapt the words quoted to the syntax of their own sentences or to quote from memory. (The adaptations of the parodist are of course a special case.) Often, naturally, the passages are the aphorisms already familiar from the anthologies or from other sources; 691, for instance, had evidently passed into a proverb by the time Aristophanes parodied it so allusively in the *Clouds*, and Arrian some centuries later is probably quoting from memory in his *θέλεις βλέπειν φῶς, πατέρα δ' οὐ θέλειν δοκεῖς*. A rather different class of quotation, however, was required by the Christian apologists, who —the earlier ones at least—had probably read the originals they pillaged. In the passages from the opening speech of Apollo quoted by Athenagoras, Clement, and Cyril, the only discrepancy is *δ' ἐς αἶαν* in 8, which is probably an old variant designed to avoid the simple accusative *γαῖαν*. The most useful quotations for us in this category come from the Stoic Chrysippus, quoted by Galen, which give (*a*) 1079 f. with *θέλοις* (*θέλεις* one MS.) and *τις ἐξάγει* (*b*) 1085 with

[1] See supra, p. xxxiii.

ἡβάσκει for the corrupt ἡβᾷ σοι of the MSS. For other implications of this context see the Commentary on 903 ff.

VI. TESTIMONIA

1–2. cit. Athenagoras, πρεσβεία περὶ Χριστιανῶν, p. 25 Schwartz.

2. Photius, *Lex.* s.v. θῆσσαν· μισθωτικὴν ἢ εὐτελῆ· [θῆσσαν τράπεζαν]· δουλικὴν τροφήν.

3–4. cit. Clem. Al. προτρεπτικὸς πρὸς Ἕλληνας 2. 30. 2, and Cyrillus Alex. *contra Julianum* 4. 201, Spanheim.

8–9. ἐλθὼν . . . οἶκον cit. Athenagoras ibid. 8. δ' ἐς αἶαν.

73–76. ἡ δ' . . . τρίχα cit. Macrobius, *Saturnalia* 5. 19. 4. 74. κατάρξωμαι. 75. τῷ . . . θεῷ. 76. ὅτῳ.

99. Hesych. 2. 953. πηγαῖον ὕδωρ· τὸ ὕδωρ τὸ περικαθαῖρον τὰ πρὸς [πρὸ] τῆς οἰκίας τῶν ἀποπεμπομένων, ὅτε ἐξεκόμιζον.

143. Hesych. 2. 1582. ψυχορραγεῖ· ἀποθνῄσκει.

181–2. cf. Ar. *Eq.* 1250 f. Σ παρῴδησε τὰ ἐξ Ἀλκήστιδος Εὐριπίδου. ἔχει δὲ οὕτως· σὲ δ' . . . ἴσως. Hence Suidas 3. 129, Adler, s.v. κλεπτής bis cit., each time with οὐχὶ μᾶλλον.

238–9. cit. (*a*) Stobaeus, *Flor.* 119. 10, (*b*) Orion, *Anthol.* 8. 23. 55, (*c*) *Menandri Monosticha* 552.

367–8. cf. Ar. *Ach.* 893.

417–18. Σ *Hipp.* 834 and 892 οὐ γάρ τι . . . ἤμπλακες.

424. cit. Σ A. *Cho.* 151.

449. Hesych. 2. 926. περι[ν]ίσσεται ὥρας· περιέρχεται τὰς ὥρας.

537. Hesych. 2. 1474. ὑπορράπτεις· συντίθης.

571. Hesych. 1. 1644. ἠξίωσε ναίειν· ἄξιον ἡγήσατο οἰκεῖν. *Etym. Gud.* 346 ἠ. ν.· ἄξιον ἡγήσατο τοῦ οἰκεῖν.

577. Aelian, *NA* 12. 44 (*On Horses*). λέγει δὲ Εὐρ. καὶ ποιμνίτας τινὰς ὑμεναίους κτλ. (with a correct account of the meaning). Cf. Steph. Byz. 531. ποίμνη ὡς αὐλή· ποιμνίτας ὑμεναίους. καὶ ποιμνιώτας. Meineke's note: *sine lacunis libri haec epitomatorum culpa obscurata sunt. St.*

dixerat, ut ab αὐλή *formatur* αὐλίτης, *ita* ποιμνίτης *formari a* ποίμνη. π. ὑ. Eur. *Alc.* 577.

669–72. cit. Stobaeus, *Flor.* 119. 1. 671. ἂν δ'. 669 f. *Menandri Disticha* (713 K). 670. πολὺν χρ.

675. cf. Ar. *Av.* 1244.

691. cit. Ar. *Thesm.* 194. cf. Ar. *Nub.* 1415, Arrian, *Epictetus* 2. 22. 11. θέλεις βλέπειν φῶς, πατέρα δ' οὐ θέλειν δοκεῖς;

732–3. *Etym. Mag.* xlv, s.v. Ἄκαστος· υἱὸς Πελίου, πατὴρ (*sic*) δὲ Ἀλκήστιδος. Εὐρ.· Ἡ τἄρ' Ἄκαστος οὐκέτ' ἔστ' ἐν ἀνδράσι· ἢ 'μῆς ἀδελφῆς αἷμα τιμωρήσεται.

780–9. cit. (*a*) 780–5. Plutarch, *Consol. ad Apoll.* 11. 781. δοκῶ μὲν. 783. ἔστιν αὐτῶν. (*b*) 782. *Men. Monost.* 69. ἅπασιν ἀποθανεῖν. (*c*) 782–4. Stobaeus, *Flor.* 118. 14. (*d*) 782–9. Orion, *Anthol.* 8. 4. 53. 785. ποῖ προβ. 786. οὐκ ἔστι διδ. 787. τοῦτ'.

846. cit. *Etym. Mag.* in cod. Flor. λοχαία σαυτὸν.

866–7. cf. Ar. *Vesp.* 751.

879–80. cit. Stobaeus, *Flor.* 69. 12. τί γὰρ . . . πιστῆς ἀλόχου.

882–4. cit. Stobaeus, *Flor.* 68. 13. 883. τῆς ὑπ.

889. Hesych. 1. 1049, δυσπάλαιστος· ἀκαταγώνιστος. Suidas 2. 152, Adler, δυσπάλαιστος· δυσκαταγώνιστος. οὕτως Εὐρ.

907. Hesych. 1. 234. ἅλις· ἱκανῶς, πλῆρες ἢ αὐταρκές. ἔστι καὶ μετρίως, ὡς Εὐρ. Ἀλκήστιδι.

960. Hesych. κύδιον· κρεῖττον, αἱρετώτερον.

962–6. cit. Stobaeus, *Ecl.* 1. 4. ἐγὼ . . . φάρμακον. 964. ἀρξάμενος.

966–9. *cit.* Σ *Hec.* 1267. οὐδέ τι . . . γῆρυς.

1078. cit. (*a*) Stobaeus, *Flor.* 114. 5. (*b*) Orion, *Anthol.* 8. 24. 55. cf. *Men. Monost.* 471, Cassius Dio 38. 18.

1079–80. cit. Chrysippus ap. Galen *de plac. Hipp. et Plat.* 5. 4. 1079. θέλοις στένειν ἀεί. 1080. τις ἐξάγει.

1085. cit. Chrysippus, ibid. διὸ καὶ τὸ τοῦ Ἀναξαγόρου παρείληφεν ἐνταῦθα, ὡς ἄρα τινὸς παραγγείλαντος αὐτῷ τεθνάναι τὸν υἱόν, εὖ μάλα καθεστηκότως εἶπεν, ᾔδειν θνητὸν γεννῆσαι, καὶ ὡς τοῦτο λαβὼν Εὐρ. τὸ νόημα τὸν Θησέα πεποίηκε λέγοντα "Ἐγὼ δὲ . . . δάκοι" [fr. 964N[2]]. οὕτω δὲ εἰρῆσθαί φησι καὶ τὰ τοιαῦτα, "Εἰ μὲν . . . κακῶν". [fr. 821N[2]].

ἔσθ' ὅτε τὰ τοιαῦτα μακρὸς "χρόνος μαλάξει, νῦν δ' ἔθ' ἡβάσκει κακόν".

1159–63. cit. (*a*) Cass. Dio 78. 8. (*b*) 1159–61. Lucian, *Symp.* 48, *Trag.* 325. (*c*) 1160–2. Stobaeus, *Flor.* 111. 6. (*d*) 1160. Plutarch, *de adul. et am.* 58, *de am. prol.* 497.

VII. THE HYPOTHESES

The word 'hypothesis' in this connexion seems at first to have been used in its natural sense of the story which the playwright found in the legends, or constructed out of them, as a 'presupposition' on which to base his drama. The first of these two Hypotheses to *Alcestis* is a skeleton story in this sense, and is attributed, by L alone, to Dicaearchus, the distinguished scholar who was a pupil of Aristotle and is known to have written a *Ὑποθέσεις τῶν Εὐριπίδου καὶ Σοφοκλέους μύθων*. It is the only extant Hypothesis so labelled, and when we find the *metrical* Hypothesis to S. *OT* accredited to Aristophanes of Byzantium we become cautious of accepting these attributions. That Dicaearchus did not merely compile such 'hypotheses' but also made some study of the tragedians' sources is clear from one of the Hypotheses to *Medea* referring to his view that Euripides borrowed the plot from Neophron. A certain Glaucus had already made the same kind of study for Aeschylus in his *περὶ Αἰσχύλου μύθων* (see the Hypothesis to the *Persae*). In any case such a summary of the story is found in our MSS. prefixed to almost all the plays, and there is nothing to distinguish Hypothesis I to *Alcestis* from any other of the kind except perhaps that it is shorter than the average.

The second Hypothesis is of a quite different type, showing the same characteristics as others which are attributed in our MSS. to Aristophanes of Byzantium, and there is little doubt that the first paragraph in substance goes back to that scholar. A 'hypothesis' in this sense is a kind of summary introduction, giving the kind of information that an ancient scholar would expect to find in a comprehensive library edition, for the complete identification of the play, together with its place in the poet's work and in relation to the other tragedians. Callimachus had earlier produced for the Alexandrian library a great Catalogue of all Greek literature, known as *Πίνακες*, and the tradition[1] which makes Aristophanes base on this work the idea of his Introductions to the dramas is probably reliable. Callimachus also produced, according to 'Suidas', a special didascalic πίναξ of all the dramas in chronological order (not by festivals), which Aristophanes doubtless used for some of his material. Our 'Aristophanean' Hypotheses have survived in a somewhat disjointed form, with omissions, interpolations, and variations in the order of items. The Hypothesis to *Alcestis* (preserved in V and partly in B) begins typically with a single sentence briefly indicating the plot, followed by the statement that 'neither of the [other] two has a play on this subject' (clearly Aristophanes' Hypotheses were limited to the three great tragedians). The next note, 'the drama was composed seventeenth', has no parallel except in the equally puzzling case of Sophocles' *Antigone*, which 'is reckoned thirty-second'—λέλεκται δὲ τὸ δρᾶμα τριακοστὸν δεύτερον. Since we are told below that *Alcestis* was the fourth of its trilogy, and since it is improbable that *Antigone* was a 'prosatyric' play, it seems simplest to assume that these are library numbers giving the chronological order and omitting plays that had been lost.[2] Next comes the didascalic information: the date (see app. crit.), the titles of the tetralogy, with its award in the competition (second to Sophocles; the third name is missing), and probably the name of the choregus, here displaced to l. 6 (so Dindorf) and corrupted beyond recognition. That at least is the most likely explanation

[1] Cf. Choeroboscus in *Etym. Mag.* 672. 27.

[2] Cf. above, p. v. It is just possible that in both cases the count is complicated by some earlier performances at the Lenaea, where only two tragedies were required, but the tragic agon was only established there in about 442 and was mostly patronized by minor poets; cf. Pickard-Cambridge, *Dramatic Festivals*, p. 38.

of V's rigmarole; the Hypothesis to the *Agamemnon* ends with the same items: date, award, choregus. Next is a short remark on the play's peculiarity, the happy ending[1] which in Aristotelian doctrine is normally the mark of comedy. Last comes a group of three identificatory items normally so associated in these Hypotheses: scene of the play, composition of the Chorus, *opening speaker*. Here the false equation of Apollo with Helios in V (B has Ἀπόλλων) cannot be laid at Aristophanes' door; it is the same kind of latter-day syncretism as the appearance of Charon for Thanatos in the list of dramatis personae. The technical sense of προλογίζει should be noticed; it does *not* mean, as it is usually translated, 'speaks the prologue', but 'speaks the opening words'. It would be absurd to call Antigone (S. *Ant.* Hyp. I) or Oedipus (*OC* Hyp. I) 'the speaker of the prologue'; moreover, according to the introductory scholion of V, which P has picked up from some source, Apollo προλογίζει ῥητορικῶς, a phrase which obviously refers (see Commentary, l. 1) to his opening words alone.

The second paragraph is a redundant addition from another source expanding κωμικωτέραν καταστροφήν above. The singularly inept grouping of the *Orestes* and the *Alcestis* is only intelligible if this was written after the Select Edition was made; of the ten plays, these are the only two which do not end 'tragically'.

[1] See supra, p. xxi.

ΑΛΚΗΣΤΙΣ

ΑΛΚΗΣΤΙΣ

ΥΠΟΘΕΣΙΣ ΑΛΚΗΣΤΙΔΟΣ [ΔΙΚΑΙΑΡΧΟΥ]

Ἀπόλλων ᾐτήσατο παρὰ τῶν Μοιρῶν ὅπως ὁ Ἄδμητος τελευτᾶν μέλλων παράσχῃ τὸν ὑπὲρ ἑαυτοῦ ἑκόντα τεθνηξόμενον, ἵνα ἴσον τῷ προτέρῳ χρόνον ζήσῃ. καὶ δὴ Ἄλκηστις, ἡ γυνὴ τοῦ Ἀδμήτου, ἐπέδωκεν ἑαυτήν, οὐδετέρου τῶν γονέων ἐθελήσαντος ὑπὲρ τοῦ παιδὸς ἀποθανεῖν. μετ' οὐ πολὺ δὲ ταύτης τῆς συμφορᾶς γενομένης Ἡρακλῆς παραγενόμενος καὶ μαθὼν παρά τινος θεράποντος τὰ περὶ τὴν Ἄλκηστιν ἐπορεύθη ἐπὶ τὸν τάφον καὶ Θάνατον ἀποστῆναι ποιήσας ἐσθῆτι καλύπτει τὴν γυναῖκα, τὸν δὲ Ἄδμητον ἠξίου λαβόντα αὐτὴν τηρεῖν. εἰληφέναι γὰρ αὐτὴν πάλης ἆθλον ἔλεγε. μὴ βουλομένου δὲ ἐκείνου ἔδειξεν ἣν ἐπένθει.

[ΑΛΛΩΣ]

Ἄλκηστις, ἡ Πελίου θυγάτηρ, ὑπομείνασα ὑπὲρ τοῦ ἰδίου ἀνδρὸς τελευτῆσαι, Ἡρακλέους ἐπιδημήσαντος ἐν τῇ Θετταλίᾳ διασῴζεται, βιασαμένου τοὺς χθονίους θεοὺς καὶ ἀφελομένου τὴν γυναῖκα. παρ' οὐδετέρῳ κεῖται ἡ μυθοποιία. τὸ δρᾶμα ἐποιήθη ιζʹ. ἐδιδάχθη ἐπὶ

1 Δικαιάρχου L: om. VBP Argumentum prius et alterius initium usque ad μυθοποιία extat in Scholiis Plat. Conviv. p. 179 b [usque ad ἀφελομένου τὴν γυναῖκα etiam in Pseudo Eudociae Violario p. 21.] Consentiunt Eudocia et Schol. Plat. cum V, uno loco excepto (vv. 6, 7) 3 τὸν ὑπὲρ ἑαυτοῦ ἑκόντα VB: τινὰ τὸν ὑπὲρ αὐτοῦ LP 4 τοῦ Ἀδμήτου om. LP 5 μηδετέρου LP 6, 7 Ἡρακλῆς παραγενόμενος LPB Schol. Plat. et Eudocia: om. V, qui mox post Ἄλκηστιν inserit ἐντυχὼν ὁ ἡρακλῆς 10 ἔδειξεν] ἀποκαλύψας ἔδειξεν LP

12 ἄλλως Schol. Plat.: om. codd. et Eudocia. Ἀριστοφάνους γραμματικοῦ ὑπόθεσις suprascripsit Wuestemann, collatis aliarum fabularum argumentis; e.g. Med. Or. Phoen. Secundum argumentum ex V descripsi: totum om. L; paucas nugas habet P: B habet Ἄλκηστις . . . γυναῖκα et ἡ μὲν σκηνὴ . . . προλογίζει ὁ Ἀπόλλων (sic); cetera omisit. Hauniensis totum habet nisi v. 16 τὸ δρᾶμα . . . καταστροφήν. τὸ δρᾶμα . . . ιζʹ non intellegitur

Γλαυκίνου ἄρχοντος †τὸ λ.† πρῶτος ἦν Σοφοκλῆς, δεύτερος Εὐριπίδης Κρήσσαις, Ἀλκμαίωνι τῷ διὰ Ψωφῖδος, Τηλέφῳ, Ἀλκήστιδι. . . . τὸ δὲ δρᾶμα κωμικωτέραν ἔχει τὴν καταστροφήν. ἡ σκηνὴ τοῦ δράματος ὑπόκειται ἐν Φεραῖς, μιᾷ πόλει τῆς Θετταλίας. συνέστηκε δὲ ὁ χορὸς ἔκ τινων πρεσβυτῶν ἐντοπίων, οἳ καὶ παραγίνονται συμπαθήσοντες ταῖς Ἀλκήστιδος συμφοραῖς. προλογίζει ὁ Ἥλιος. †εἰσὶ δὲ ε′ χορηγοί.†

Τὸ δὲ δρᾶμά ἐστι σατυρικώτερον, ὅτι εἰς χαρὰν καὶ ἡδονὴν καταστρέφει παρὰ τὸ τραγικόν. ἐκβάλλεται ὡς ἀνοίκεια τῆς τραγικῆς ποιήσεως ὅ τε Ὀρέστης καὶ ἡ Ἄλκηστις, ὡς ἐκ συμφορᾶς μὲν ἀρχόμενα, εἰς εὐδαιμονίαν δὲ καὶ χαρὰν λήξαντα, ⟨ἃ⟩ ἐστι μᾶλλον κωμῳδίας ἐχόμενα.

1 τὸ λ (= ὀ̄λ numero omisso)] ὀλυμπιάδος πε′ ἔτει δευτέρῳ Dindorf; tum enim Glaucinus Archon fuit πρῶτος . . . δεύτερος Dindorf: πρῶτον . . . δεύτερον V 2 ἀλκμαίονι τῶ διαψωφίλω V: correxit Dindorf Lacunam indicavit Kirchhoff: vide infra v. 6 3 καταστροφὴν suprascr. V[1]: κατασκευὴν V 5 ταῖς . . . συμφοραῖς B: τῆς . . . συμφορᾶς V: τῆς . . . συμφορᾷ Haun. 6 Ἥλιος V Haun.: ἀπόλλων B εἰσιδ' ἐχορηγοί V: εἰσὶ δὲ χορηγοί Haun. Et sane videntur quinque choreutarum prae ceteris eminere, cl. vv. 86 sqq., 213 sqq , 872 sqq., 888 sqq. Ἰσίδοτος ἐχορήγει Dindorf, his verbis post Ἀλκήστιδι collocatis, ubi lacunam reliquimus: sed ab Iside non appellabantur Athenienses saec. V: (Τεισίας ἐχορήγει Wilamowitz) 8 παρὰ τοῖς τραγικοῖς ἐκβ. codd.: corr. Leo. Cf. Schol. Orest. 1691 ἀνοικεία Haun.: ἀνοικείας V 10 ἃ add. Hermann

ΤΑ ΤΟΥ ΔΡΑΜΑΤΟΣ ΠΡΟΣΩΠΑ

Απολλων	Αδμητος
Θανατος	Παις Αλκηστιδος
Χορος	Ηρακλης
Θεραπαινα Αλκηστιδος	Φερης
Αλκηστις	Θεραπων

Ἐξιὼν ἐκ τοῦ οἴκου τοῦ Ἀδμήτου προλογίζει ὁ Ἀπόλλων ῥητορικῶς.

Personarum indicem eundem fere praebent L[2] (aut *l*) V B, longe alium P; vide infra *θεράπαινα ἀλκήστιδος* L : *θεράπων* hoc loco V B, omissa omni Famulae mentione *παῖς ἀλκήστιδος* scripsi : *εὔμηλος* L V B. Cf. P infra *Ἡρακλῆς. Φέρης* L V : *Φέρης. Ἡρακλῆς* B P sic : *ἀπόλλων. ἡρακλῆς. παῖς ἀλκήστιδος εὔμηλος. χάρων. φέρης. τρόφος. θεράπων. ἄλκηστις. χόρος. ἄδμητος.* Hic ordo quid sibi velit non video : prior ordo temporis est quo singulae personae in scenam progrediantur Verba *ἐξιὼν . . . ῥητορικῶς* habent V P (*τοῦ οἴκου ἀδμήτου* P) : om. L B

Alcestis fabula acta fuit anno A. C. 438. Codices B V L P : vv. 1159–1163 etiam Π : raro memorantur Haun. et O. Accedunt Σ brevia

ΑΛΚΗΣΤΙΣ

ΑΠΟΛΛΩΝ

Ὦ δώματ᾽ Ἀδμήτει᾽, ἐν οἷς ἔτλην ἐγὼ
θῆσσαν τράπεζαν αἰνέσαι θεός περ ὤν.
Ζεὺς γὰρ κατακτὰς παῖδα τὸν ἐμὸν αἴτιος
Ἀσκληπιόν, στέρνοισιν ἐμβαλὼν φλόγα·
οὗ δὴ χολωθεὶς τέκτονας Δίου πυρὸς
κτείνω Κύκλωπας· καί με θητεύειν πατὴρ
θνητῷ παρ᾽ ἀνδρὶ τῶνδ᾽ ἄποιν᾽ ἠνάγκασεν.
ἐλθὼν δὲ γαῖαν τήνδ᾽ ἐβουφόρβουν ξένῳ,
καὶ τόνδ᾽ ἔσῳζον οἶκον ἐς τόδ᾽ ἡμέρας.
ὁσίου γὰρ ἀνδρὸς ὅσιος ὢν ἐτύγχανον
παιδὸς Φέρητος, ὃν θανεῖν ἐρρυσάμην,
Μοίρας δολώσας· ᾔνεσαν δέ μοι θεαὶ
Ἄδμητον ᾅδην τὸν παραυτίκ᾽ ἐκφυγεῖν,
ἄλλον διαλλάξαντα τοῖς κάτω νεκρόν.
πάντας δ᾽ ἐλέγξας καὶ διεξελθὼν φίλους,
πατέρα γεραιάν θ᾽ ἥ σφ᾽ ἔτικτε μητέρα,
οὐχ ηὗρε πλὴν γυναικὸς ὅστις ἤθελε
θανὼν πρὸ κείνου μηκέτ᾽ εἰσορᾶν φάος·
ἣ νῦν κατ᾽ οἴκους ἐν χεροῖν βαστάζεται
ψυχορραγοῦσα· τῇδε γάρ σφ᾽ ἐν ἡμέρᾳ
θανεῖν πέπρωται καὶ μεταστῆναι βίου.
ἐγὼ δέ, μὴ μίασμά μ᾽ ἐν δόμοις κίχῃ,

8 δὲ γαῖαν] δ᾽ ἐς αἶαν citat Athenagoras suppl. pro Christ. p. 104
16 Versus suspectus; habuit Σ καὶ πατέρα γραῖάν θ᾽ Nauck
17 ὅστις Reiske : ἥτις codd. 18 θανὼν Reiske : θανεῖν codd.
(μηδ᾽ ἔτ᾽ Haun.)

λείπω μελάθρων τῶνδε φιλτάτην στέγην.
ἤδη δὲ τόνδε Θάνατον εἰσορῶ πέλας,
ἱερῆ θανόντων, ὅς νιν εἰς Ἅιδου δόμους
μέλλει κατάξειν· συμμέτρως δ' ἀφίκετο,
φρουρῶν τόδ' ἦμαρ ᾧ θανεῖν αὐτὴν χρεών.

ΘΑΝΑΤΟΣ

ἆ ἆ·
τί σὺ πρὸς μελάθροις; τί σὺ τῇδε πολεῖς,
Φοῖβ'; ἀδικεῖς αὖ τιμὰς ἐνέρων
ἀφοριζόμενος καὶ καταπαύων;
οὐκ ἤρκεσέ σοι μόρον Ἀδμήτου
διακωλῦσαι, Μοίρας δολίῳ
σφήλαντι τέχνῃ; νῦν δ' ἐπὶ τῇδ' αὖ
χέρα τοξήρη φρουρεῖς ὁπλίσας,
ἣ τόδ' ὑπέστη πόσιν ἐκλύσασ'
αὐτὴ προθανεῖν Πελίου παῖς.

Απ. θάρσει· δίκην τοι καὶ λόγους κεδνοὺς ἔχω.
Θα. τί δῆτα τόξων ἔργον, εἰ δίκην ἔχεις;
Απ. σύνηθες αἰεὶ ταῦτα βαστάζειν ἐμοί.
Θα. καὶ τοῖσδέ γ' οἴκοις ἐκδίκως προσωφελεῖν.
Απ. φίλου γὰρ ἀνδρὸς συμφοραῖς βαρύνομαι.
Θα. καὶ νοσφιεῖς με τοῦδε δευτέρου νεκροῦ;
Απ. ἀλλ' οὐδ' ἐκεῖνον πρὸς βίαν σ' ἀφειλόμην.
Θα. πῶς οὖν ὑπὲρ γῆς ἐστι κοὐ κάτω χθονός;
Απ. δάμαρτ' ἀμείψας, ἣν σὺ νῦν ἥκεις μέτα.
Θα. κἀπάξομαί γε νερτέρων ὑπὸ χθόνα.
Απ. λαβὼν ἴθ'· οὐ γὰρ οἶδ' ἂν εἰ πείσαιμί σε.
Θα. κτείνειν γ' ὃν ἂν χρῇ; τοῦτο γὰρ τετάγμεθα.

23 *τῶνδε φιλτάτην* Σ Hippol. 1437: *τήνδε φιλτάτην* L P: *τῶνδε φιλτάτων* V B 26 *συμμέτρως* L V B Σ: *σύμμετρος* P 28 ΘΑΝΑΤΟΣ] ΧΑΡΩΝ P hic, et plerumque (*θαν.* vv. 39, 72). Cf. Personarum indicem 29 *τί σοι* V 31 om. P: del. Nauck (*ἀποσπῶν ἀφορίζων* Σ) 34 *σφήλαντα* Earle 36 *τόδ'*] fortasse *τόθ'* 37 *αὐτὴ* B O D: *αὐτὴν* L P V 38 *τοι* V B: *τε* L P 40 *αἰεὶ* L: *ἀεὶ* V B P 41 *ἐνδίκως* V B 44 *βίαν* V B *l*: *βία* L P 47 *νερτέραν* P *l* 49 *γ' ὃν* V: *ὃν* L P B

Απ. οὔκ, ἀλλὰ τοῖς μέλλουσι θάνατον ἐμβαλεῖν.
Θα. ἔχω λόγον δὴ καὶ προθυμίαν σέθεν.
Απ. ἔστ' οὖν ὅπως Ἄλκηστις ἐς γῆρας μόλοι;
Θα. οὐκ ἔστι· τιμαῖς κἀμὲ τέρπεσθαι δόκει.
Απ. οὔτοι πλέον γ' ἂν ἢ μίαν ψυχὴν λάβοις.
Θα. νέων φθινόντων μεῖζον ἄρνυμαι γέρας.
Απ. κἂν γραῦς ὄληται, πλουσίως ταφήσεται.
Θα. πρὸς τῶν ἐχόντων, Φοῖβε, τὸν νόμον τίθης.
Απ. πῶς εἶπας; ἀλλ' ἦ καὶ σοφὸς λέληθας ὤν;
Θα. ὠνοῖντ' ἂν οἷς πάρεστι γηραιοὺς θανεῖν.
Απ. οὔκουν δοκεῖ σοι τήνδε μοι δοῦναι χάριν;
Θα. οὐ δῆτ'· ἐπίστασαι δὲ τοὺς ἐμοὺς τρόπους.
Απ. ἐχθρούς γε θνητοῖς καὶ θεοῖς στυγουμένους.
Θα. οὐκ ἂν δύναιο πάντ' ἔχειν ἃ μή σε δεῖ.
Απ. ἦ μὴν σὺ παύσῃ καίπερ ὠμὸς ὢν ἄγαν·
τοῖος Φέρητος εἶσι πρὸς δόμους ἀνήρ,
Εὐρυσθέως πέμψαντος ἵππειον μετα
ὄχημα Θρῄκης ἐκ τόπων δυσχειμέρων,
ὃς δὴ ξενωθεὶς τοῖσδ' ἐν Ἀδμήτου δόμοις
βίᾳ γυναῖκα τήνδε σ' ἐξαιρήσεται.
κοὔθ' ἡ παρ' ἡμῶν σοι γενήσεται χάρις
δράσεις θ' ὁμοίως ταῦτ', ἀπεχθήσῃ τ' ἐμοί.
Θα. πόλλ' ἂν σὺ λέξας οὐδὲν ἂν πλέον λάβοις·
ἡ δ' οὖν γυνὴ κάτεισιν εἰς Ἅιδου δόμους.
στείχω δ' ἐπ' αὐτήν, ὡς κατάρξωμαι ξίφει·
ἱερὸς γὰρ οὗτος τῶν κατὰ χθονὸς θεῶν
ὅτου τόδ' ἔγχος κρατὸς ἁγνίσῃ τρίχα.

50 ἐμβαλεῖν codd. et Σ: ἀμβαλεῖν Bursian 51 δὴ V B: γε L P 55 γέρας V B Σ: κλέος L P 58 λέληθας V L, γρ. B: πέφυκας B O D, γρ. V: ἐλήλυθας P 59 ὠνοῖντ' L et Σ duo: ὄνοιντ' V et Σ unus: ὤνοιντ' P B (ὄναιντ' l) οἷς L P Σ: οὓς V B γηραιοὺς codd. et Σ (sc. τοὺς φίλους): γηραιοὶ Hermann 64 παύσῃ] πείσῃ Schmidt 73–76 citat Macrobius v. 19. 4 74 κατάρξωμαι P et Macrob.: κατάρξομαι L V B 75 τῶν . . . θεῶν codd. et Σ: τῷ . . . θεῷ Macrob. 76 ὅτου τόδ' codd. et Σ (ὃ τοῦτο δ' V): ὅτῳ τόδ' Macrob.

ΧΟΡΟΣ

— τί ποθ' ἡσυχία πρόσθεν μελάθρων;
— τί σεσίγηται δόμος Ἀδμήτου;
— ἀλλ' οὐδὲ φίλων πέλας οὐδείς,
ὅστις ἂν εἴποι πότερον φθιμένην
βασίλεαν πενθεῖν χρή ⟨μ'⟩, ἢ ζῶσ' ἔτι
φῶς τόδε λεύσσει Πελίου παῖς
Ἄλκηστις, ἐμοὶ πᾶσί τ' ἀρίστη
δόξασα γυνὴ
πόσιν εἰς αὑτῆς γεγενῆσθαι.

— κλύει τις ἢ στεναγμὸν ἢ [στρ. α
χειρῶν κτύπον κατὰ στέγας
ἢ γόον ὡς πεπραγμένων;
— οὐ μὰν οὐδέ τις ἀμφιπόλων στατίζεται ἀμφὶ πύλας. εἰ
γὰρ μετακύμιος ἄτας,
ὦ Παιάν, φανείης.
— οὔ τἂν φθιμένης γ' ἐσιώπων.
— νέκυς ἤδη.
— οὐ δὴ φροῦδός γ' ἐξ οἴκων.
— πόθεν; οὐκ αὐχῶ. τί σε θαρσύνει;
— πῶς ἂν ἔρημον τάφον Ἄδμητος
. . . . . .
κεδνῆς ἂν ἔπραξε γυναικός;

77 ΧΟΡ. L P: ἡμιχ. V B. Totum hoc carmen inter ἡμιχόρια distribuunt codd. et Σ; quae nota cum fallacissima sit, malui cum Earlio paragraphos (—) praefigere, in ceteris plerumque Arnoldtium secutus 78 Nulla nota praef. in codd. 81 βασίλεαν scripsi cl. Pind. N. 1. 39: βασίλειαν codd. μ' add. Kirchhoff. Vulgo transponitur χρὴ ante βασίλειαν (Blomfield) et τόδε post Πελίου (Bothe): χρὴ ante πενθεῖν tr. *l* 88 γόον L et lemma Σ B: γόων V B P et lemma Σ V 90 ante εἰ ἡμιχ. praef. V B L: om. P 92 ὦ Matthiae: ἰὼ codd. 93 οὔ τἂν Matthiae: οὔτ' ἂν codd. φθιμένας codd. 94 Sic Kirchhoff Ἡμιχ. οὐ γὰρ δὴ φροῦδός γ' ἐξ οἴκων νέκυς ἤδη codd. (ἤδη νέκυς P: ἤδη del. *l*) 96 lacunam indicavit Hartung: cf. v. 110

— πυλῶν πάροιθε δ' οὐχ ὁρῶ [ἀντ. α
πηγαῖον ὡς νομίζεται
χέρνιβ' ἐπὶ φθιτῶν πύλαις.
— χαίτα τ' οὔτις ἐπὶ προθύροις το-
μαῖος, ἃ δὴ νεκύων πέν-
θει πίτνει· οὐ νεολαία
δουπεῖ χεὶρ γυναικῶν.
— καὶ μὴν τόδε κύριον ἦμαρ . . .
— τί τόδ' αὐδᾷς;
— ᾧ χρή σφε μολεῖν κατὰ γαίας.
— ἔθιγες ψυχᾶς, ἔθιγες δὲ φρενῶν.
— χρὴ τῶν ἀγαθῶν διακναιομένων
πενθεῖν ὅστις
χρηστὸς ἀπ' ἀρχῆς νενόμισται.

— ἀλλ' οὐδὲ ναυκληρίαν [στρ. β
ἔσθ' ὅποι τις αἴας
στείλας, ἢ Λυκίαν
εἴτ' ἐπὶ τὰς ἀνύδρους
'Αμμωνιάδας [ἕδρας],
δυστάνου παραλῦσαι
ψυχάν· μόρος γὰρ ἀπότομος
πλάθει· θεῶν δ' ἐπ' ἐσχάραις
οὐκ ἔχω ἐπὶ τίνα
μηλοθύταν πορευθῶ.

100 φθιτῶν L P : φθιμένων V B 101 Nulla nota praef. in codd. ἡμιχ. Hartung 103 πένθει V B Σ : πένθεσι L P οὐ Aldina : οὐδὲ codd. et Σ : (οὐδὲ νεαλὴς Dindorf) Ante οὐδὲ notam ἡμιχ. habent V B. Cf. v. 91 106, 107 Hoc ordine V B, inverso L P. Cf. v. 94 106 ἡμιχ. V B P : χορ. L 107 ἡμιχ. V *b* : om. B L P χρή] χρῆν P 108 ἡμιχ. V B : χορ. L P Tum ἡμιχ. ante ἔθιγες P 109 ἡμιχ. fortasse B : χορ. L P : notam om. V 112 χορ. V B : om. L P 114 Λυκίαν Monk : λυκίας codd. 115 seq. ἕδρας seclusi : εἴτ' ἐφ' ἕδρας ἀνύδρους 'Αμμωνιάδας Nauck. Cf. 125, 126 117 παραλῦσαι (vel -λῦσαι) codd. et Σ : παραλύσει Wakefield 118 ψυχάν L P (-ήν V[1] D) : ψυχῆς V : ψυχάς B (-ήν et -ᾶς *b*). Genitivum Σ ἀπότομος Blomfield : ἀπό**μος L : ἄπότμος V : ἄποτμος B P *l* 120 ἐπ' ἐσχάραν οὐκέτ' ἔχω τίνα Hartung, quo recepto μηλόθυτον pro μηλοθύταν Nauck. Cf. v. 130

— μόνος δ' ἄν, εἰ φῶς τόδ' ἦν [ἀντ. β
ὄμμασιν δεδορκὼς
Φοίβου παῖς, προλιποῦσ'
ἦλθεν ἕδρας σκοτίους
῞Αιδα τε πύλας·
δμαθέντας γὰρ ἀνίστη,
πρὶν αὐτὸν εἷλε διόβολον
πλῆκτρον πυρὸς κεραυνίου.
νῦν δὲ τίν' ἔτι βίου
ἐλπίδα προσδέχωμαι;

— πάντα γὰρ ἤδη τετέλεσται βασιλεῦσι,
πάντων δὲ θεῶν ἐπὶ βωμοῖς
αἱμόρραντοι θυσίαι πλήρεις·
οὐδ' ἔστι κακῶν ἄκος οὐδέν.

Χο. ἀλλ' ἥδ' ὀπαδῶν ἐκ δόμων τις ἔρχεται
δακρυρροοῦσα, τίνα τύχην ἀκούσομαι;
πενθεῖν μέν, εἴ τι δεσπόταισι τυγχάνει,
συγγνωστόν· εἰ δ' ἔτ' ἐστὶν ἔμψυχος γυνὴ
εἴτ' οὖν ὄλωλεν εἰδέναι βουλοίμεθ' ἄν.

ΘΕΡΑΠΑΙΝΑ

καὶ ζῶσαν εἰπεῖν καὶ θανοῦσαν ἔστι σοι.
Χο. καὶ πῶς ἂν αὑτὸς κατθάνοι τε καὶ βλέποι;
Θε. ἤδη προνωπής ἐστι καὶ ψυχορραγεῖ.
Χο. ὦ τλῆμον, οἵας οἷος ὢν ἁμαρτάνεις.
Θε. οὔπω τόδ' οἶδε δεσπότης, πρὶν ἂν πάθῃ.

122 μόνος] μούνως Wakefield 124 προλιπὼν O D 125 σκοτίας V 129 πλᾶκτρον *l* P 130 τίν' ἔτι βίου V : τιν' ἐπὶ βίου B O D : τίνα βίου L P : βίου τίν' ἔτ' Hartung 131 προσδέχομαι codd., corr. Musgrave 132 τετέλεσται βασιλεῦσι (vel -σιν) codd. et Σ : suspecta 135 οὐδ' L P : ἀλλ' οὐδ' V B. Cf. v. sequentem 136 ΧΟΡ. praef. V : ὅλος ὁ χόρος λέγει ταῦτα Σ B ; falso ὀπαδῶν] ὀπαδὸς L 140 ἂν L B : om. V P 142 αὐτὸς codd., corr. Aldina 145 πάθῃ P : πάθοι L V B

Χο. ἐλπὶς μὲν οὐκέτ' ἐστὶ σῴζεσθαι βίον;
Θε. πεπρωμένη γὰρ ἡμέρα βιάζεται.
Χο. οὔκουν ἐπ' αὐτῇ πράσσεται τὰ πρόσφορα;
Θε. κόσμος γ' ἕτοιμος, ᾧ σφε συνθάψει πόσις.
Χο. ἴστω νυν εὐκλεής γε κατθανουμένη
γυνή τ' ἀρίστη τῶν ὑφ' ἡλίῳ, μακρῷ.
Θε. πῶς δ' οὐκ ἀρίστη; τίς δ' ἐναντιώσεται;
τί χρὴ γενέσθαι τὴν ὑπερβεβλημένην
γυναῖκα; πῶς δ' ἂν μᾶλλον ἐνδείξαιτό τις
πόσιν προτιμῶσ' ἢ θέλουσ' ὑπερθανεῖν;
καὶ ταῦτα μὲν δὴ πᾶσ' ἐπίσταται πόλις·
ἃ δ' ἐν δόμοις ἔδρασε θαυμάσῃ κλύων.
ἐπεὶ γὰρ ᾔσθεθ' ἡμέραν τὴν κυρίαν
ἥκουσαν, ὕδασι ποταμίοις λευκὸν χρόα
ἐλούσατ', ἐκ δ' ἑλοῦσα κεδρίνων δόμων
ἐσθῆτα κόσμον τ' εὐπρεπῶς ἠσκήσατο,
καὶ στᾶσα πρόσθεν Ἑστίας κατηύξατο·
Δέσποιν', ἐγὼ γὰρ ἔρχομαι κατὰ χθονός,
πανύστατόν σε προσπίτνουσ' αἰτήσομαι,
τέκν' ὀρφανεῦσαι τἀμά· καὶ τῷ μὲν φίλην
σύζευξον ἄλοχον, τῇ δὲ γενναῖον πόσιν.
μηδ' ὥσπερ αὐτῶν ἡ τεκοῦσ' ἀπόλλυμαι
θανεῖν ἀώρους παῖδας, ἀλλ' εὐδαίμονας
ἐν γῇ πατρῴᾳ τερπνὸν ἐκπλῆσαι βίον.
πάντας δὲ βωμούς, οἳ κατ' Ἀδμήτου δόμους,
προσῆλθε κἀξέστεψε καὶ προσηύξατο,
πτόρθων ἀποσχίζουσα μυρσίνης φόβην,
ἄκλαυτος ἀστένακτος, οὐδὲ τοὐπιὸν
κακὸν μεθίστη χρωτὸς εὐειδῆ φύσιν.
κἄπειτα θάλαμον ἐσπεσοῦσα καὶ λέχος,

146 σώσασθαι L P 148 ἐπ' αὐτῇ V B et v. l. in Σ: ἐπ' αὐτοῖς L P Σ 151 et 152 paragraphum praef. L: 151 θερ., 152 τροφ. praef. P. Cf. Personarum indicem 151 μακρῶν V 167 ἀπόλλυται L P 172 μυρσίνης V B Σ: μυρσινῶν L P 173 ἄκλαυτος L: ἄκλαυστος V B P

ἐνταῦθα δὴ 'δάκρυσε καὶ λέγει τάδε·
Ὦ λέκτρον, ἔνθα παρθένει' ἔλυσ' ἐγὼ
κορεύματ' ἐκ τοῦδ' ἀνδρός, οὗ θνῄσκω πέρι,
χαῖρ'· οὐ γὰρ ἐχθαίρω σ'· ἀπώλεσας δ' ἐμὲ
μόνην· προδοῦναι γάρ σ' ὀκνοῦσα καὶ πόσιν
θνῄσκω. σὲ δ' ἄλλη τις γυνὴ κεκτήσεται,
σώφρων μὲν οὐκ ἂν μᾶλλον, εὐτυχὴς δ' ἴσως.
κυνεῖ δὲ προσπίτνουσα, πᾶν δὲ δέμνιον
ὀφθαλμοτέγκτῳ δεύεται πλημμυρίδι.
ἐπεὶ δὲ πολλῶν δακρύων εἶχεν κόρον,
στείχει προνωπὴς ἐκπεσοῦσα δεμνίων,
καὶ πολλὰ θαλάμων ἐξιοῦσ' ἐπεστράφη
κἄρριψεν αὑτὴν αὖθις ἐς κοίτην πάλιν.
παῖδες δὲ πέπλων μητρὸς ἐξηρτημένοι
ἔκλαιον· ἣ δὲ λαμβάνουσ' ἐς ἀγκάλας
ἠσπάζετ' ἄλλοτ' ἄλλον, ὡς θανουμένη.
πάντες δ' ἔκλαιον οἰκέται κατὰ στέγας
δέσποιναν οἰκτίροντες. ἣ δὲ δεξιὰν
προύτειν' ἑκάστῳ, κοὔτις ἦν οὕτω κακὸς
ὃν οὐ προσεῖπε καὶ προσερρήθη πάλιν.
τοιαῦτ' ἐν οἴκοις ἐστὶν Ἀδμήτου κακά.
καὶ κατθανών τἂν ὤλετ', ἐκφυγὼν δ' ἔχει
τοσοῦτον ἄλγος, οὗ ποτ'—οὐ λελήσεται.

Χο. ἦ που στενάζει τοισίδ' Ἄδμητος κακοῖς,
ἐσθλῆς γυναικὸς εἰ στερηθῆναί σφε χρή;

Θε. κλαίει γ' ἄκοιτιν ἐν χεροῖν φίλην ἔχων,
καὶ μὴ προδοῦναι λίσσεται, τἀμήχανα

178 damnat Nauck; habuit Σ   πέρι] πάρος Wilamowitz   179 δ' ἐμὲ] δέ με omnes, ut vid., codd.   180 μόνην] μόνον Blomfield: fortasse δέ με· μόνη πρ. γ. σ' κ.τ.λ.   182 οὐκ ἂν L P V B et Ar. Eq. 1252 cum Σ Ar. ad loc.: οὐχὶ Suidas s. v. κλέπτης   184 ὀφθαλμοτέγκτῳ P *b*: ὀφθαλμοτέκτῳ V B L   δεύετο L P, qui etiam κύνει paroxytone supra   187 θαλάμων Nauck: θάλαμον codd.   190 ἐν ἀγκάλαις L P   197 τ' ἂν codd.   δ' V B L: τ' P   198 *quod aliquando—non oblitus erit'*   οὗ ποτ' οὐ fere codd. (V L[1], οὔποτ' οὐ L B: οὗ ποτ' οὐ B[2]: οὔποτε P): οὔποθ' οὗ Nauck   199 τοῖσιν L P (τοῖσιδ' V B)   200 εἰ L P: ἦ B: ἧς V B[2]   σφε L P B: γε V

ζητῶν· φθίνει γὰρ καὶ μαραίνεται νόσῳ.
παρειμένη δέ, χειρὸς ἄθλιον βάρος
. . . .
ὅμως δὲ καίπερ σμικρὸν ἐμπνέουσ' ἔτι
βλέψαι πρὸς αὐγὰς βούλεται τὰς ἡλίου
ὡς οὔποτ' αὖθις, ἀλλὰ νῦν πανύστατον.
[ἀκτῖνα κύκλον θ' ἡλίου προσόψεται.]
ἀλλ' εἶμι καὶ σὴν ἀγγελῶ παρουσίαν·
οὐ γάρ τι πάντες εὖ φρονοῦσι κοιράνοις,
ὥστ' ἐν κακοῖσιν εὐμενεῖς παρεστάναι·
σὺ δ' εἶ παλαιὸς δεσπόταις ἐμοῖς φίλος.

Χο.
— ἰὼ Ζεῦ, τίς ἂν [πῶς] πᾷ πόρος κακῶν [στρ.
γένοιτο καὶ λύσις τύχας
ἃ πάρεστι κοιράνοις;
— αἰαῖ· εἶσί τις; ἢ τέμω τρίχα,
καὶ μέλανα στολμὸν πέπλων
ἀμφιβαλώμεθ' ἤδη;
— δῆλα μέν, φίλοι, δῆλά γ', ἀλλ' ὅμως
θεοῖσιν εὐχώμεσθα· θεῶν
γὰρ δύναμις μεγίστα.
— ὦναξ Παιάν,
ἔξευρε μηχανάν τιν' Ἀδμήτῳ κακῶν.
— πόριζε δὴ πόριζε· καὶ πάρος γὰρ
†τοῦδ' ἐφεῦρες†, καὶ νῦν

204 Post hunc v. lacunam Elmsley 208 (cum 207) delevit Valckenaer. Cf. Hec. 411, 412 213–243 Choro tribuunt V B P: 218-225 θεραπ. cetera choro L. Inter quinque choreutas distribui Hermannum secutus: inter quattuor ἡμιχόρια Pflugk, nulla nota ad vv. 222, 234 apposita 213 τίς ἂν πᾶ B D O: τίς ἂν πῶς πᾶ V: τίς ἂν πῶς ** L: τίς ἂν πῶς παι* P: τίς ἂν . . . ἢ πῶς ἢ ποῦ Σ. Antistrophicis non respondent 213, 214 215 αἰαῖ (h. e. ἒέ)· εἶσί τις Wilamowitz, cf. v. 228: ἔξεισί τις codd. 218 γ'] δ' V 219 εὐχώμεσθα B *l*: εὐχώμεθα L: εὐχόμεθα P: ἐχώμεθα V δύναμις V: ἁ δύναμις L P B μεγίστη L P V 221 μηχανήν τιν' B: μηχανὴν ἥντιν' V 223 τοῦδ' ἐφεῦρες codd. et Σ: del. Dindorf: σοῦ 'πηῦρε vel τοῦδ' ἐπηῦρε Headlam

λυτήριος ἐκ θανάτου γενοῦ,
φόνιον δ' ἀπόπαυσον Ἅιδαν.

— παπαῖ . . . . [ἀντ.
ὦ παῖ Φέρητος, οἷ' ἔπρα-
ξας δάμαρτος σᾶς στερείς.
— αἰαῖ· ἄξια καὶ σφαγᾶς τάδε,
καὶ πλέον ἢ βρόχῳ δέρην
οὐρανίῳ πελάσσαι;
– τὰν γὰρ οὐ φίλαν ἀλλὰ φιλτάταν
γυναῖκα κατθανοῦσαν ἐν
ἄματι τῷδ' ἐπόψῃ.
— ἰδοὺ ἰδού,
ἥδ' ἐκ δόμων δὴ καὶ πόσις πορεύεται.
— βόασον ὤ, στέναξον, ὦ Φεραία
χθών, τὰν ἀρίσταν
γυναῖκα μαραινομέναν νόσῳ
κατὰ γᾶς χθόνιον παρ' Ἅιδαν.

Χο. οὔποτε φήσω γάμον εὐφραίνειν
πλέον ἢ λυπεῖν, τοῖς τε πάροιθεν
τεκμαιρόμενος καὶ τάσδε τύχας
λεύσσων βασιλέως, ὅστις ἀρίστης
ἀπλακὼν ἀλόχου τῆσδ' ἀβίωτον
τὸν ἔπειτα χρόνον βιοτεύσει.

ΑΛΚΗΣΤΙΣ

Ἅλιε καὶ φάος ἁμέρας, [στρ.
οὐράνιαί τε δῖναι νεφέλας δρομαίου.

225 δ' V B : τ' L P 226, 227 παπαὶ ὦ V B : παῖ παῖ φεῦ φεῦ ἰὼ ἰώ L P. Lacunam Dindorf 227 σῆς P : τῆς σῆς L στερείς Monk : στερηθείς codd. Cf. 213, 214 228 αἶ αἶ αἶ αἶ V B : ἆρ' Hermann 229 καὶ om. B 230 οὐρανίῳ codd. et Σ : ἀγχονίῳ Wecklein πελάσαι codd. 231 φιλτάτην L P 232 ἔν γ' Musgrave εἰν Dindorf) ἄματι B : ἤματι L P V τῶδε γ' ὄψει L P 233 ἰδοὺ ἰδού om. L P 234 στέναξον ὦ βόασον L P 237 γᾶς V : γᾶν L P B 241 λεύσσων] λεύσων καὶ L P 242 ἀμπλακὼν (vel -ῶν) codd. : corr. Wakefield 244 ἡμέρας L P

ΑΔΜΗΤΟΣ

ὁρᾷ σὲ κἀμέ, δύο κακῶς πεπραγότας,
οὐδὲν θεοὺς δράσαντας ἀνθ' ὅτου θανῇ.

Αλ. γαῖά τε καὶ μελάθρων στέγαι [ἀντ.
νυμφίδιοί τε κοῖται πατρίας Ἰωλκοῦ.

Αδ. ἔπαιρε σαυτήν, ὦ τάλαινα, μὴ προδῷς·
λίσσου δὲ τοὺς κρατοῦντας οἰκτῖραι θεούς.

Αλ. ὁρῶ δίκωπον ὁρῶ σκάφος ἐν λίμνᾳ· [στρ.
νεκύων δὲ πορθμεὺς
ἔχων χέρ' ἐπὶ κοντῷ Χάρων
μ' ἤδη καλεῖ· Τί μέλλεις;
ἐπείγου· σὺ κατείργεις. τάδε τοί με
σπερχόμενος ταχύνει.

Αδ. οἴμοι, πικράν γε τήνδε μοι ναυκληρίαν
ἔλεξας. ὦ δύσδαιμον, οἷα πάσχομεν.

Αλ. ἄγει μ' ἄγει τις· ἄγει μέ τις—οὐχ ὁρᾷς;— [ἀντ.
νεκύων ἐς αὐλάν,
ὑπ' ὀφρύσι κυαναυγέσι
βλέπων πτερωτός—†αἴδας†.
[μέθες με·] τί ῥέξεις; ἄφες.—οἵαν ὁδόν ἁ δει-
λαιοτάτα προβαίνω.

Αδ. οἰκτρὰν φίλοισιν, ἐκ δὲ τῶν μάλιστ' ἐμοὶ
καὶ παισίν, οἷς δὴ πένθος ἐν κοινῷ τόδε.

Αλ. μέθετε μέθετέ μ' ἤδη.

247 θανῇ] θανεῖν L 249 νυμφίδιαι L P πατρίας Aldina : πατρώας codd. 252 ὁρῶ ante σκάφος erasum in L ἐν λίμνᾳ del. Aldina. Cf. v. 259 254 χέρ' Aldina : χεῖρ' codd. χάρων seclusit Matthiae 255 Fortasse ἐπείγου iterandum. Cf. v. 262 256 τάδε τοί με V B (τοι in τοῖα mut. *b*) : τάδ' ἕτοιμα L P. Fortasse ἑτοίμαν 259 Sic B D O ἄγει μ' ἄγει μέ τις *l* (et primitus L ipse ut videtur) : ἄγει ἄγει μέ τις L P : ἄγει μ' ἄγει τις V 261 αἴδας corruptum, cf. Robert *Thanatos* pp. 34 sqq. : fortasse ἆ δᾶ (sic larvam videns Io, A. Prom. 567; cf. Phoen. 1296) : αἴδαν Wilamowitz 262 Verba μέθες με om. L P, antistrophico v. 255 non respondentia ῥέξεις] πράξεις V 263 δειλαι** L : δειλαία *l* 266 μέθετε με μέθετε μ' V B

κλίνατ', οὐ σθένω ποσίν·
πλησίον Ἅιδας.
σκοτία δ' ἐπ' ὄσσοισι νὺξ ἐφέρπει.
τέκνα, τέκν', οὐκέτι δὴ
οὐκέτι μάτηρ σφῷν ἔστιν.
χαίροντες, ὦ τέκνα, τόδε φάος ὁρῷτον.
Αδ. οἴμοι· τόδ' ἔπος λυπρὸν ἀκούω
καὶ παντὸς ἐμοὶ θανάτου μεῖζον.
μὴ πρός ⟨σε⟩ θεῶν τλῇς με προδοῦναι,
μὴ πρὸς παίδων οὓς ὀρφανιεῖς,
ἀλλ' ἄνα, τόλμα·
σοῦ γὰρ φθιμένης οὐκέτ' ἂν εἴην·
ἐν σοὶ δ' ἐσμὲν καὶ ζῆν καὶ μή·
σὴν γὰρ φιλίαν σεβόμεσθα.

Αλ. Ἄδμηθ', ὁρᾷς γὰρ τἀμὰ πράγμαθ' ὡς ἔχει,
λέξαι θέλω σοι πρὶν θανεῖν ἃ βούλομαι.
ἐγώ σε πρεσβεύουσα κἀντὶ τῆς ἐμῆς
ψυχῆς καταστήσασα φῶς τόδ' εἰσορᾶν,
θνῄσκω, παρόν μοι μὴ θανεῖν, ὑπὲρ σέθεν,
ἀλλ' ἄνδρα τε σχεῖν Θεσσαλῶν ὃν ἤθελον,
καὶ δῶμα ναίειν ὄλβιον τυραννίδι.
οὐκ ἠθέλησα ζῆν ἀποσπασθεῖσά σου
σὺν παισὶν ὀρφανοῖσιν, οὐδ' ἐφεισάμην
ἥβης, ἔχουσ' ἐν οἷς ἐτερπόμην ἐγώ.
καίτοι σ' ὁ φύσας χἠ τεκοῦσα προὔδοσαν,
καλῶς μὲν αὐτοῖς κατθανεῖν ἧκον βίου,
καλῶς δὲ σῶσαι παῖδα κεὐκλεῶς θανεῖν.
μόνος γὰρ αὐτοῖς ἦσθα, κοὔτις ἐλπὶς ἦν
σοῦ κατθανόντος ἄλλα φιτύσειν τέκνα.

267 *κλίνατέ μ'* L P 269 *ὄσσοις* V B 271 *μάτηρ* V B : *δὴ μάτηρ* L P 272 *ὁρῴτην* Elmsley 273 *ὤμοι* P L[1] 275 *σε* add. Porson 276 *μὴ . . . ὀρφανιεῖς* om. L P 277 *ἄνα τόλμα* V *l* : *ἀνατόλμα* L P B 285 *Θεσσαλῶν* B et Σ B : *Θεσσαλὸν* L P V 289 *ἔχουσ' ἐν οἷς ἐτερπόμην ἐγώ* B O D : *ἔχουσα δῶρ' ἐν οἷς ἐτερπόμην ἐγώ* V : *ἔχουσα δῶρ'* (*δῶρον* L) *ἐν οἷς ἐτερπόμην* L P et *v* vel V[2] 294 *φιτύσειν* V γρ. B : *φυτεύσειν* L P B

καγώ τ' ἂν ἔζων καὶ σὺ τὸν λοιπὸν χρόνον,
κοὐκ ἂν μονωθεὶς σῆς δάμαρτος ἔστενες
καὶ παῖδας ὠρφάνευες. ἀλλὰ ταῦτα μὲν
θεῶν τις ἐξέπραξεν ὥσθ' οὕτως ἔχειν.
εἶεν· σὺ νῦν μοι τῶνδ' ἀπόμνησαι χάριν·
αἰτήσομαι γάρ σ'—ἀξίαν μὲν οὔποτε·
ψυχῆς γὰρ οὐδέν ἐστι τιμιώτερον—
δίκαια δ', ὡς φήσεις σύ· τούσδε γὰρ φιλεῖς
οὐχ ἧσσον ἢ 'γὼ παῖδας, εἴπερ εὖ φρονεῖς·
τούτους ἀνάσχου δεσπότας ἐμῶν δόμων,
καὶ μὴ 'πιγήμῃς τοῖσδε μητρυιὰν τέκνοις,
ἥτις κακίων οὖσ' ἐμοῦ γυνὴ φθόνῳ
τοῖς σοῖσι κἀμοῖς παισὶ χεῖρα προσβαλεῖ.
μὴ δῆτα δράσῃς ταῦτά γ', αἰτοῦμαί σ' ἐγώ.
ἐχθρὰ γὰρ ἡ 'πιοῦσα μητρυιὰ τέκνοις
τοῖς πρόσθ', ἐχίδνης οὐδὲν ἠπιωτέρα.
καὶ παῖς μὲν ἄρσην πατέρ' ἔχει πύργον μέγαν,
[ὃν καὶ προσεῖπε καὶ προσερρήθη πάλιν.]
σὺ δ', ὦ 'τέκνον μοι, πῶς κορευθήσῃ καλῶς;
ποίας τυχοῦσα συζύγου τῷ σῷ πατρί;
μή σοί τιν' αἰσχρὰν προσβαλοῦσα κληδόνα
ἥβης ἐν ἀκμῇ σοὺς διαφθείρῃ γάμους.
οὐ γάρ σε μήτηρ οὔτε νυμφεύσει ποτὲ
οὔτ' ἐν τόκοισι σοῖσι θαρσυνεῖ, τέκνον,
παροῦσ', ἵν' οὐδὲν μητρὸς εὐμενέστερον.
δεῖ γὰρ θανεῖν με· καὶ τόδ' οὐκ ἐς αὔριον
οὐδ' ἐς τρίτην μοι μηνὸς ἔρχεται κακόν,
ἀλλ' αὐτίκ' ἐν τοῖς οὐκέτ' οὖσι λέξομαι.

295 *ἔζων* V : *ἔζην* et *ἔζων* L : *ἔζην* B P et Etymol. M. p. 413, 9 298 *ἐξέπραξεν* L P suprascr. *υ* : *ἔπραξεν* V : *εἰσέπραξεν* B O D 299 *νῦν μοι* V : *μοι νῦν* B O D : *δή μοι* L : *δ' ἡμῖν* P 304 *τῶν ἐμῶν* L P 310 Post *ἐχίδνης δ'* suprascr. V[1] 312 del. Pierson : habuit Σ. Cf. 195 318 *σοῖσι θαρσυνεῖ τέκνον* L P : *τοῖσι σοῖσι θαρσυνεῖ* V B 321 *σμῆνος ἔρχεται κακῶν* Naber : nihil mutandum videtur : *μηνὸς* habuit Σ 321, 322 in textu om. in marg. infer. add. L[1] 322 *μηκέτ'* V B

χαίροντες εὐφραίνοισθε· καὶ σοὶ μέν, πόσι,
γυναῖκ' ἀρίστην ἔστι κομπάσαι λαβεῖν,
ὑμῖν δέ, παῖδες, μητρὸς ἐκπεφυκέναι.
Χο. θάρσει· πρὸ τούτου γὰρ λέγειν οὐχ ἅζομαι·
δράσει τάδ', εἴπερ μὴ φρενῶν ἁμαρτάνει.
Αδ. ἔσται τάδ' ἔσται, μὴ τρέσῃς· ἐπεὶ σ' ἐγὼ
καὶ ζῶσαν εἶχον καὶ θανοῦσ' ἐμὴ γυνὴ
μόνη κεκλήσῃ, κοὔτις ἀντὶ σοῦ ποτε
τόνδ' ἄνδρα νύμφη Θεσσαλὶς προσφθέγξεται.
οὐκ ἔστιν οὕτως οὔτε πατρὸς εὐγενοῦς
οὔτ' εἶδος ἄλλως ἐκπρεπεστάτη γυνή.
ἅλις δὲ παίδων· τῶνδ' ὄνησιν εὔχομαι
θεοῖς γενέσθαι· σοῦ γὰρ οὐκ ὠνήμεθα.
οἴσω δὲ πένθος οὐκ ἐτήσιον τὸ σόν,
ἀλλ' ἔστ' ἂν αἰὼν οὑμὸς ἀντέχῃ, γύναι,
στυγῶν μὲν ἥ μ' ἔτικτεν, ἐχθαίρων δ' ἐμὸν
πατέρα· λόγῳ γὰρ ἦσαν οὐκ ἔργῳ φίλοι.
σὺ δ' ἀντιδοῦσα τῆς ἐμῆς τὰ φίλτατα
ψυχῆς ἔσωσας. ἆρά μοι στένειν πάρα
τοιᾶσδ' ἁμαρτάνοντι συζύγου σέθεν;
παύσω δὲ κώμους συμποτῶν θ' ὁμιλίας
στεφάνους τε μοῦσάν θ' ἣ κατεῖχ' ἐμοὺς δόμους.
οὐ γάρ ποτ' οὔτ' ἂν βαρβίτου θίγοιμ' ἔτι
οὔτ' ἂν φρέν' ἐξαίροιμι πρὸς Λίβυν λακεῖν
αὐλόν· σὺ γάρ μου τέρψιν ἐξείλου βίου.
σοφῇ δὲ χειρὶ τεκτόνων δέμας τὸ σὸν
εἰκασθὲν ἐν λέκτροισιν ἐκταθήσεται,
ᾧ προσπεσοῦμαι καὶ περιπτύσσων χέρας
ὄνομα καλῶν σὸν τὴν φίλην ἐν ἀγκάλαις
δόξω γυναῖκα καίπερ οὐκ ἔχων ἔχειν·
ψυχρὰν μέν, οἶμαι, τέρψιν, ἀλλ' ὅμως βάρος

326 οὐχ ἅζομαι V B Σ: οὐ χάζομαι L P 327 ἥνπερ . . . ἁμαρτάνῃ L P 329 ἐμὴ] ἐμοῦ B O D 333 ἐκπρεπεστάτη L P (P ἐκ in ras. : εὐπρεπεστάτη V B 346 ἐξάροιμι L P : Aoristum Σ : ἐξάραιμι Wakefield

ψυχῆς ἀπαντλοίην ἄν. ἐν δ' ὀνείρασι
φοιτῶσά μ' εὐφραίνοις ἄν· ἡδὺ γὰρ φίλους
κἀν νυκτὶ λεύσσειν, ὅντιν' ἂν παρῇ χρόνον.
εἰ δ' Ὀρφέως μοι γλῶσσα καὶ μέλος παρῆν,
ὥστ' ἢ κόρην Δήμητρος ἢ κείνης πόσιν
ὕμνοισι κηλήσαντά σ' ἐξ Ἅιδου λαβεῖν,
κατῆλθον ἄν, καί μ' οὔθ' ὁ Πλούτωνος κύων
οὔθ' οὑπὶ κώπῃ ψυχοπομπὸς ἂν Χάρων
ἔσχον, πρὶν ἐς φῶς σὸν καταστῆσαι βίον.
ἀλλ' οὖν ἐκεῖσε προσδόκα μ', ὅταν θάνω,
καὶ δῶμ' ἑτοίμαζ', ὡς συνοικήσουσά μοι.
ἐν ταῖσιν αὐταῖς γάρ μ' ἐπισκήψω κέδροις
σοὶ τούσδε θεῖναι πλευρά τ' ἐκτεῖναι πέλας
πλευροῖσι τοῖς σοῖς· μηδὲ γὰρ θανών ποτε
σοῦ χωρὶς εἴην τῆς μόνης πιστῆς ἐμοί.
Χο. καὶ μὴν ἐγώ σοι πένθος ὡς φίλος φίλῳ
λυπρὸν συνοίσω τῆσδε· καὶ γὰρ ἀξία.
Αλ. ὦ παῖδες, αὐτοὶ δὴ τάδ' εἰσηκούσατε
πατρὸς λέγοντος μὴ γαμεῖν ἄλλην ποτὲ
γυναῖκ' ἐφ' ὑμῖν μηδ' ἀτιμάσειν ἐμέ.
Αδ. καὶ νῦν γέ φημι, καὶ τελευτήσω τάδε.
Αλ. ἐπὶ τοῖσδε παῖδας χειρὸς ἐξ ἐμῆς δέχου.
Αδ. δέχομαι, φίλον γε δῶρον ἐκ φίλης χερός.
Αλ. σὺ νῦν γενοῦ τοῖσδ' ἀντ' ἐμοῦ μήτηρ τέκνοις.
Αδ. πολλή μ' ἀνάγκη, σοῦ γ' ἀπεστερημένοις.
Αλ. ὦ τέκν', ὅτε ζῆν χρῆν μ', ἀπέρχομαι κάτω.
Αδ. οἴμοι, τί δράσω δῆτα σοῦ μονούμενος;
Αλ. χρόνος μαλάξει σ'· οὐδέν ἐσθ' ὁ κατθανών.

355 φίλους V : φίλοις L P B 356 χρόνον] τρόπον Prinz 358 ὥστ' ἢ Reiske : ὡς τὴν codd. (et Σ ?) 361 Χάρων] γέρων Cobet 362 ἔσχεν Earle 367, 368 Cf. Ar. Acharn. 893 372 ποτὲ L P : τινὰ V B et fortasse Σ ad v. 375 376 om. L P (in marg. add. *l*). Tum in L Alcestidi tribuuntur vv. 375, 377 378 πολλή μ' Monk : πολλή γ' codd. 379 χρῆν μ' O : χρή μ' V B : μ' ἐχρῆν L P (P in ras.)

Αδ. ἄγου με σὺν σοί, πρὸς θεῶν, ἄγου κάτω.
Αλ. ἀρκοῦμεν ἡμεῖς οἱ προθνῄσκοντες σέθεν.
Αδ. ὦ δαῖμον, οἵας συζύγου μ' ἀποστερεῖς.
Αλ. καὶ μὴν σκοτεινὸν ὄμμα μου βαρύνεται.
Αδ. ἀπωλόμην ἄρ', εἴ με δὴ λείψεις, γύναι.
Αλ. ὡς οὐκέτ' οὖσαν οὐδὲν ἂν λέγοις ἐμέ.
Αδ. ὄρθου πρόσωπον, μὴ λίπῃς παῖδας σέθεν.
Αλ. οὐ δῆθ' ἑκοῦσά γ', ἀλλὰ χαίρετ', ὦ τέκνα.
Αδ. βλέψον πρὸς αὐτοὺς βλέψον. Αλ. οὐδέν εἰμ' ἔτι.
Αδ. τί δρᾷς; προλείπεις; Αλ. χαῖρ'. Αδ. ἀπω-
λόμην τάλας.
Χο. βέβηκεν, οὐκέτ' ἔστιν Ἀδμήτου γυνή.

ΠΑΙΣ

ἰώ μοι τύχας. μαῖα δὴ κάτω [στρ.
βέβακεν, οὐκέτ' ἔστιν, ὦ
πάτερ, ὑφ' ἁλίῳ.
προλιποῦσα δ' ἁμὸν
βίον ὠρφάνισσε τλάμων.
ἴδε γὰρ ἴδε βλέφαρον καὶ παρατόνους χέρας.
ὑπάκουσον ἄκουσον, ὦ μᾶτερ, ἀντιάζω.
ἐγώ σ' ἐγώ, μᾶτερ,
καλοῦμαί σ' ὁ σὸς ποτὶ σοῖσι πίτ-
νων στόμασιν νεοσσός.
Αδ. τὴν οὐ κλύουσαν οὐδ' ὁρῶσαν· ὥστ' ἐγὼ
καὶ σφὼ βαρείᾳ συμφορᾷ πεπλήγμεθα.

Πα. νέος ἐγώ, πάτερ, λείπομαι φίλας [ἀντ.
μονόστολός τε ματρός· ὦ

386 ἄρ'] ἂν V 389 χαιρέτω L P 391 προλείπεις L: προλείπεις με V B P 393 et 406 Παῖς scripsi: εὔμηλος codd. 393 ἰώ μοι μοι L 397 ὠρφάνισσε Barnes: ὠρφάνισε codd. 399 χεῖρας L P 401 ἐγώ σ' ἐγὼ μᾶτερ P *l*: ἐγώ σε γάρ, μᾶτερ L: σ' ἐγὼ μᾶτερ ἐγὼ V B 402 σ' ὁ V B: ὁ L P: ⟨νῦν γε⟩ καλοῦμαι ὁ Aldina, cf. v. 414 404 τὴν γ' οὐ Hermann 406 πάτερ λείπομαι L P: λείπομαι πάτερ V B 407 τε L P Σ: om. rell.

σχέτλια δὴ παθὼν
ἐγὼ ἐργὰ . .,
σύ τέ μοι σύγκασι κούρα
συνέτλας· . . . . . ὦ πάτερ,
ἀνόνατ' ἀνόνατ' ἐνύμφευσας, οὐδὲ γήρως
ἔβας τέλος σὺν τᾷδ'·
ἔφθιτο γὰρ πάρος· οἰχομένας δὲ σοῦ,
μᾶτερ, ὄλωλεν οἶκος.

Χο. Ἄδμητ', ἀνάγκη τάσδε συμφορὰς φέρειν·
οὐ γάρ τι πρῶτος οὐδὲ λοίσθιος βροτῶν
γυναικὸς ἐσθλῆς ἤμπλακες· γίγνωσκε δὲ
ὡς πᾶσιν ἡμῖν κατθανεῖν ὀφείλεται.
Αδ. ἐπίσταμαί γε, κοὐκ ἄφνω κακὸν τόδε
προσέπτατ'· εἰδὼς δ' αὔτ' ἐτειρόμην πάλαι.
ἀλλ', ἐκφορὰν γὰρ τοῦδε θήσομαι νεκροῦ,
πάρεστε καὶ μένοντες ἀντηχήσατε
παιᾶνα τῷ κάτωθεν ἀσπόνδῳ θεῷ.
πᾶσιν δὲ Θεσσαλοῖσιν ὧν ἐγὼ κρατῶ
πένθους γυναικὸς τῆσδε κοινοῦσθαι λέγω
κουρᾷ ξυρήκει καὶ μελαμπέπλῳ στολῇ·
τέθριππά θ' οἳ ζεύγνυσθε καὶ μονάμπυκας
πώλους, σιδήρῳ τέμνετ' αὐχένων φόβην.
αὐλῶν δὲ μὴ κατ' ἄστυ, μὴ λύρας κτύπος
ἔστω σελήνας δώδεκ' ἐκπληρουμένας·
οὐ γάρ τιν' ἄλλον φίλτερον θάψω νεκρὸν
τοῦδ' οὐδ' ἀμείνον' εἰς ἔμ'· ἀξία δέ μοι
τιμῆς, ἐπεὶ τέθνηκεν ἀντ' ἐμοῦ μόνη.

409 ἐργὰ ⟨τλάμων⟩ coni. Hermann 410 σύγκασι μοί Hermann et ὠρφάνισεν v. 397 411 συνόμαιμε συνάδελφε τοσαῦτα ἔτλης ὅσα ἐγὼ Σ 412 ἀνόνητ' ἀνόνητ' L P 414 Verba ἔφθιτο γὰρ πάρος (cum καλοῦμαί σ' ὁ v. 402) delevit olim Wilamowitz: habuit Σ 420 γε L P: τε V B 426 πένθος L P λέγω] θέλω B D O 427 μελαμπέπλῳ στολῇ L P et *b*: μελαγχείμοις πέπλοις V et O: B et D post κουρᾶι ξυρ lacunam habent 428 θ' οἳ V B: τε L P 434 τιμῆς L P: τιμᾶν V B ἐπεί γ' ἔθνῃσκεν Usener μόνη L P: μόνην V D: λίαν B

Χο. ὦ Πελίου θύγατερ, [στρ.
χαίρουσά μοι εἰν Ἀίδαο δόμοις
τὸν ἀνάλιον οἶκον οἰκετεύοις.
ἴστω δ' Ἀίδας ὁ μελαγχαίτας θεὸς ὅς τ' ἐπὶ κώπᾳ
πηδαλίῳ τε γέρων
νεκροπομπὸς ἵζει,
πολὺ δὴ πολὺ δὴ γυναῖκ' ἀρίσταν
λίμναν Ἀχεροντίαν πορεύ-
σας ἐλάτᾳ δικώπῳ.

πολλά σε μουσοπόλοι [ἀντ.
μέλψουσι καθ' ἑπτάτονόν τ' ὀρείαν
χέλυν ἔν τ' ἀλύροις κλέοντες ὕμνοις,
Σπάρτᾳ κύκλος ἁνίκα Καρνείου περινίσσεται ὥρας
μηνός, ἀειρομένας
παννύχου σελάνας,
λιπαραῖσί τ' ἐν ὀλβίαις Ἀθάναις.
τοίαν ἔλιπες θανοῦσα μολ-
πὰν μελέων ἀοιδοῖς.

εἴθ' ἐπ' ἐμοὶ μὲν εἴη, [στρ.
δυναίμαν δέ σε πέμψαι
φάος ἐξ Ἀίδα τεράμνων
καὶ Κωκυτοῖο ῥεέθρων
ποταμίᾳ νερτέρᾳ τε κώπᾳ.

435 ὦ *l*: ἰὼ L P V B 436 εἰν V B: ἐν L P Ἀίδαο V B: ἀϊδ*, suprascripto α, L: ἅδα P δόμοις (non -οισι) omnes 437 οἰκετεύεις L: ἱκετεύοις V 438 ἀίδης L: ἅδης P 439 κώπη V B 443 ἀχεροντείαν L P: corr. *l* 446 ὀρείαν L P: οὐρείαν V B. Media syllaba corripitur ut Hip. 1127 447 κλέοντες Elmsley: κλείοντες codd. 449 κυκλο·s B περινίσσεται V L: περινίσεται B: περινείσεται P ὥρας Abresch ex Hesychio (περιίσσεται ὥρας· περι-έρχεται τὰς ὥρας): ὥρα B P *l*: ὥρ* L: ὥρᾳ V κυκλὰς . . . ὥρα Scaliger 451 παννύχου B *l*: παννύχους L P V σελήνας L P 452 Ἀθήναις L P 457 Ἀίδα V B: ἅδου L P 458 καὶ Κωκυτοῖο *l* vel, me iudice, L: καὶ κωκυτοῖς P: καὶ κωκυτοῦ τε V B κωκυτοῦ τε D O; ῥεέθρων V B P: ῥεείθρων L κωκυτοῦ τε ῥεέθρων deleto καὶ Matthiae. Versum damnat Bothe: habuit Σ B 459 κώπη L P

σὺ γὰρ ὤ, μόνα, ὦ φίλα γυναικῶν,
σὺ τὸν αὑτᾶς
ἔτλας πόσιν ἀντὶ σᾶς ἀμεῖψαι
ψυχᾶς ἐξ Ἅιδα. κούφα σοι
χθὼν ἐπάνωθε πέσοι, γύναι. εἰ δέ τι
καινὸν ἕλοιτο πόσις λέχος, ἦ μάλ' ἂν ἔμοιγ' ἂν εἴη
στυγηθεὶς τέκνοις τε τοῖς σοῖς.

ματέρος οὐ θελούσας [ἀντ.
πρὸ παιδὸς χθονὶ κρύψαι
δέμας, οὐδὲ πατρὸς γεραιοῦ,
. . . . .
ὃν ἔτεκον δ', οὐκ ἔτλαν ῥύεσθαι,
σχετλίω, πολιὰν ἔχοντε χαίταν.
σὺ δ' ἐν ἥβᾳ
νέᾳ προθανοῦσα φωτὸς οἴχῃ.
τοιαύτας εἴη μοι κῦρσαι
συνδυάδος φιλίας [ἀλόχου]· τοῦτο γὰρ
ἐν βιότῳ σπάνιον μέρος· ἦ γὰρ ἂν ἔμοιγ' ἄλυπος
δι' αἰῶνος ἂν ξυνείη.

ΗΡΑΚΛΗΣ

ξένοι, Φεραίας τῆσδε κωμῆται χθονός,
Ἄδμητον ἐν δόμοισιν ἆρα κιγχάνω;

Χο. ἔστ' ἐν δόμοισι παῖς Φέρητος, Ἡράκλεις.
ἀλλ' εἰπὲ χρεία τίς σε Θεσσαλῶν χθόνα
πέμπει, Φεραῖον ἄστυ προσβῆναι τόδε.

460 *μόνα, ὦ*] *σὺ μόνα* Wilamowitz 461 *αὑτᾶς* Erfurdt: *ἑαυτᾶς* L: *ἑαυτῆς* P: *σαυτᾶς* V B *ἀμεῖψαι* V B *l*: *ἀμείψασθαι* L P 462 *Ἅιδα* Lascaris: *ἀΐδα* V B: *ἅδαο* L P 463 *ἐπάνω* L 464 *πόσις λέχος* L P: *λέχος πόσις* V B *μάλ' ἂν* V B: *μάλ'* L P. Cf. v. 474 469 *δ' οὐκ* V B: *οὐκ* L: *κοὐκ* P *ῥύσασθαι* L P 470 *ἔχοντες* L P: corr. *l* 471 *νέᾳ* V B: *νέα νέου* L P, quo recepto legendum foret *ἔτλας ἔτλας* v. 462 472 *μοι*] *με* suprascr. L: om. P *κῦρσαι* Musgrave: *κυρῆσαι* codd. 473 *φίλας* L. Cf. v. 463 *ἀλόχου* del. Wilamowitz et *γύναι* v. 463: fortasse *μάλα τοῦτο* 474 *βιότῳ* V B: *βίῳ* L P *ἂν* erasum in L 477 *κιγχάνω* L B: *κιχάνω* V P 479 *χθόνα* V B: *πόλιν* L P Σ 480 *Φεραῖον* V B *l* Σ B: *φεραίων* L P

Ηρ. Τιρυνθίῳ πράσσω τιν᾽ Εὐρυσθεῖ πόνον.
Χο. καὶ ποῖ πορεύῃ; τῷ προσέζευξαι πλάνῳ;
Ηρ. Θρῃκὸς τέτρωρον ἅρμα Διομήδους μέτα.
Χο. πῶς οὖν δυνήσῃ; μῶν ἄπειρος εἶ ξένου;
Ηρ. ἄπειρος· οὔπω Βιστόνων ἦλθον χθόνα.
Χο. οὐκ ἔστιν ἵππων δεσπόσαι σ᾽ ἄνευ μάχης.
Ηρ. ἀλλ᾽ οὐδ᾽ ἀπειπεῖν μὴν πόνους οἷόν τ᾽ ἐμοί.
Χο. κτανὼν ἄρ᾽ ἥξεις ἢ θανὼν αὐτοῦ μενεῖς.
Ηρ. οὐ τόνδ᾽ ἀγῶνα πρῶτον ἂν δράμοιμ᾽ ἐγώ.
Χο. τί δ᾽ ἂν κρατήσας δεσπότην πλέον λάβοις;
Ηρ. πώλους ἀπάξω κοιράνῳ Τιρυνθίῳ.
Χο. οὐκ εὐμαρὲς χαλινὸν ἐμβαλεῖν γνάθοις.
Ηρ. εἰ μή γε πῦρ πνέουσι μυκτήρων ἄπο.
Χο. ἀλλ᾽ ἄνδρας ἀρταμοῦσι λαιψηραῖς γνάθοις.
Ηρ. θηρῶν ὀρείων χόρτον, οὐχ ἵππων, λέγεις.
Χο. φάτνας ἴδοις ἂν αἵμασιν πεφυρμένας.
Ηρ. τίνος δ᾽ ὁ θρέψας παῖς πατρὸς κομπάζεται;
Χο. Ἄρεος, ζαχρύσου Θρῃκίας πέλτης ἄναξ.
Ηρ. καὶ τόνδε τοὐμοῦ δαίμονος πόνον λέγεις·
σκληρὸς γὰρ αἰεὶ καὶ πρὸς αἶπος ἔρχεται·
εἰ χρή με παισὶν οἷς Ἄρης ἐγείνατο
μάχην συνάψαι, πρῶτα μὲν Λυκάονι,
αὖθις δὲ Κύκνῳ, τόνδε δ᾽ ἔρχομαι τρίτον
ἀγῶνα πώλοις δεσπότῃ τε συμβαλῶν.
ἀλλ᾽ οὔτις ἔστιν ὃς τὸν Ἀλκμήνης γόνον
τρέσαντα χεῖρα πολεμίαν ποτ᾽ ὄψεται.
Χο. καὶ μὴν ὅδ᾽ αὐτὸς τῆσδε κοίρανος χθονὸς

481 πόνον] πόνω V 482 προσέζευξαι V B : συνέζευξαι L P 487 μὴν πόνους scripsi : μ᾽ ἦν πόνους L : πόνους P : τοῖς πόνοις V B : τοὺς πόνους Monk τ᾽ ἐμοί] τέ μοι L : τέμει P 492 εὐμαρὲς V B *l* : εὐμαθὲς L P 497 δ᾽ ὁ L : θ᾽ ὁ P : δὲ V B 498 Ἄρεος V *b* L P : ἄρεως B *l* θρηκίας ζαχρύσου P : θρακώας ζαχρύσου L πέλλης V 500 αἰεὶ V L : ἀεὶ B P 501 οἷς L P : οὓς V B 504 συμβαλῶν L B : συμβαλὼν V P B 505 τόκον L 506 πολεμίων P et *l* in rasura

Ἄδμητος ἔξω δωμάτων πορεύεται.
Αδ. χαῖρ', ὦ Διὸς παῖ Περσέως τ' ἀφ' αἵματος.
Ηρ. Ἄδμητε, καὶ σὺ χαῖρε, Θεσσαλῶν ἄναξ.
Αδ. θέλοιμ' ἄν· εὔνουν δ' ὄντα σ' ἐξεπίσταμαι.
Ηρ. τί χρῆμα κουρᾷ τῇδε πενθίμῳ πρέπεις;
Αδ. θάπτειν τιν' ἐν τῇδ' ἡμέρᾳ μέλλω νεκρόν.
Ηρ. ἀπ' οὖν τέκνων σῶν πημονὴν εἴργοι θεός.
Αδ. ζῶσιν κατ' οἴκους παῖδες οὓς ἔφυσ' ἐγώ.
Ηρ. πατήρ γε μὴν ὡραῖος, εἴπερ οἴχεται.
Αδ. κἀκεῖνος ἔστι χἠ τεκοῦσά μ', Ἡράκλεις.
Ηρ. οὐ μὴν γυνή γ' ὄλωλεν Ἄλκηστις σέθεν;
Αδ. διπλοῦς ἐπ' αὐτῇ μῦθος ἔστι μοι λέγειν.
Ηρ. πότερα θανούσης εἶπας ἢ ζώσης ἔτι;
Αδ. ἔστιν τε κοὐκέτ' ἔστιν, ἀλγύνει δ' ἐμέ.
Ηρ. οὐδέν τι μᾶλλον οἶδ'· ἄσημα γὰρ λέγεις.
Αδ. οὐκ οἶσθα μοίρας ἧς τυχεῖν αὐτὴν χρεών;
Ηρ. οἶδ', ἀντὶ σοῦ γε κατθανεῖν ὑφειμένην.
Αδ. πῶς οὖν ἔτ' ἔστιν, εἴπερ ᾔνεσεν τάδε;
Ηρ. ἆ, μὴ πρόκλαι' ἄκοιτιν, ἐς τότ' ἀμβαλοῦ.
Αδ. τέθνηχ' ὁ μέλλων, κοὐκέτ' ἔσθ' ὁ κατθανών.
Ηρ. χωρὶς τό τ' εἶναι καὶ τὸ μὴ νομίζεται.
Αδ. σὺ τῇδε κρίνεις, Ἡράκλεις, κείνῃ δ' ἐγώ.
Ηρ. τί δῆτα κλαίεις; τίς φίλων ὁ κατθανών;
Αδ. γυνή· γυναικὸς ἀρτίως μεμνήμεθα.
Ηρ. ὀθνεῖος ἢ σοὶ συγγενὴς γεγῶσά τις;
Αδ. ὀθνεῖος, ἄλλως δ' ἦν ἀναγκαία δόμοις.
Ηρ. πῶς οὖν ἐν οἴκοις σοῖσιν ὤλεσεν βίον;

509 τ' om. L P 511 δ' om. L P 512 τρέπεις V 519 αὐτὴν L P 520 ἔτι V B : πέρι L P 521 δέ με V B : τέ με L : τ' ἐμέ P 526 ἆ μὴ L : ἆ ἆ μὴ V B : ἆ P (omisso μὴ) τότ' Wakefield : τόδ' codd. ἀμβαλοῦ Nauck : ἀναβαλοῦ codd. 527 Sic V B : χὼ θανὼν οὐκ ἔστ' ἔτι L : καὶ ὁ θανὼν οὐκέτ' ἐστιν P : καὶ θανὼν οὐκ ἔστ' ἔτι Schwartz 530 φίλων] οὖν P : ἦν L sed ipse correxit 531 γυναικὸς δ' B 533, 534 in textu om. L, add. ipse in margine : nunc abscisi sunt fines versuum post ἀναγ et σοῖσιν

Αδ. πατρὸς θανόντος ἐνθάδ' ὠρφανεύετο.
Ηρ. φεῦ.
εἴθ' ηὕρομέν σ', Ἄδμητε, μὴ λυπούμενον.
Αδ. ὡς δὴ τί δράσων τόνδ' ὑπορράπτεις λόγον;
Ηρ. ξένων πρὸς ἄλλων ἑστίαν πορεύσομαι.
Αδ. οὐκ ἔστιν, ὦναξ· μὴ τοσόνδ' ἔλθοι κακόν.
Ηρ. λυπουμένοις ὀχληρός, εἰ μόλοι, ξένος.
Αδ. τεθνᾶσιν οἱ θανόντες· ἀλλ' ἴθ' ἐς δόμους.
Ηρ. αἰσχρὸν παρὰ κλαίουσι θοινᾶσθαι ξένους.
Αδ. χωρὶς ξενῶνές εἰσιν οἷ σ' ἐσάξομεν.
Ηρ. μέθες με, καί σοι μυρίαν ἕξω χάριν.
Αδ. οὐκ ἔστιν ἄλλου σ' ἀνδρὸς ἑστίαν μολεῖν.
ἡγοῦ σὺ τῷδε δωμάτων ἐξωπίους
ξενῶνας οἴξας, τοῖς τ' ἐφεστῶσιν φράσον
σίτων παρεῖναι πλῆθος· εὖ δὲ κλῄσατε
θύρας μεσαύλους· οὐ πρέπει θοινωμένους
κλύειν στεναγμῶν οὐδὲ λυπεῖσθαι ξένους.
Χο. τί δρᾷς; τοιαύτης συμφορᾶς προκειμένης,
Ἄδμητε, τολμᾷς ξενοδοκεῖν; τί μῶρος εἶ;
Αδ. ἀλλ' εἰ δόμων σφε καὶ πόλεως ἀπήλασα
ξένον μολόντα, μᾶλλον ἄν μ' ἐπῄνεσας;
οὐ δῆτ', ἐπεί μοι συμφορὰ μὲν οὐδὲν ἂν
μείων ἐγίγνετ', ἀξενώτερος δ' ἐγώ.
καὶ πρὸς κακοῖσιν ἄλλο τοῦτ' ἂν ἦν κακόν,
δόμους καλεῖσθαι τοὺς ἐμοὺς ἐχθροξένους.
αὐτὸς δ' ἀρίστου τοῦδε τυγχάνω ξένου,

536 φεῦ om. L : add. *l* 538 ξένων B L[1] : ξείνων V : ξένον L P ἄλλων V B : ἄλλην L P 542 αἰσχρὸν δὲ Erfurdt : αἰ. φίλοις κλ. θ. πάρα Tate. Alii ἀσχάλλουσι vel πταίουσι ξένους L P : φίλοις V B 546 τῷδε B D : τῶνδε V L P 548 προθεῖναι Blaydes εὖ England : ἐν codd. 549 μεταύλους Ussing ex Moeride 551 τοιαύτης V B : τοσαύτης L P προσκειμένης Wakefield. Cf. 833. προκειμένης videtur habuisse Σ ad v. 747 552 ξενοδοχεῖν codd : vide Cobet. Var. Lect. p. 579 τί] ἦ Reiske 558 ἐχθροξένους L P : κακοξένους V B

ὅταν ποτ' Ἄργους διψίαν ἔλθω χθόνα.
Χο. πῶς οὖν ἔκρυπτες τὸν παρόντα δαίμονα,
φίλου μολόντος ἀνδρός, ὡς αὐτὸς λέγεις;
Αδ. οὐκ ἄν ποτ' ἠθέλησεν εἰσελθεῖν δόμους,
εἰ τῶν ἐμῶν τι πημάτων ἐγνώρισε.
καὶ τῷ μέν, οἶμαι, δρῶν τάδ' οὐ φρονεῖν δοκῶ,
οὐδ' αἰνέσει με· τἀμὰ δ' οὐκ ἐπίσταται
μέλαθρ' ἀπωθεῖν οὐδ' ἀτιμάζειν ξένους.

Χο. ὦ πολύξεινος καὶ ἐλεύθερος ἀνδρὸς ἀεί ποτ' οἶκος, [στρ.
σέ τοι καὶ ὁ Πύθιος εὐλύρας Ἀπόλλων
ἠξίωσε ναίειν,
ἔτλα δὲ σοῖσι μηλονόμας
ἐν δόμοις γενέσθαι,
δοχμιᾶν διὰ κλιτύων
βοσκήμασι σοῖσι συρίζων
ποιμνίτας ὑμεναίους.

σὺν δ' ἐποιμαίνοντο χαρᾷ μελέων βαλιαί τε λύγκες, [ἀντ.
ἔβα δὲ λιποῦσ' Ὄθρυος νάπαν λεόντων
ἁ δαφοινὸς ἴλα·
χόρευσε δ' ἀμφὶ σὰν κιθάραν,
Φοῖβε, ποικιλόθριξ
νεβρὸς ὑψικόμων πέραν
βαίνουσ' ἐλατᾶν σφυρῷ κούφῳ,
χαίρουσ' εὔφρονι μολπᾷ.

τοιγὰρ πολυμηλοτάταν [στρ.
ἑστίαν οἰκεῖς παρὰ καλλίναον
Βοιβίαν λίμναν. ἀρότοις δὲ γυᾶν

560 ὅταν ποτ' V B : ὅτανπερ L P 565 καί τῳ Heath 569 ὦ *l* : ἰώ codd. ἐλευθέρου post Purgoldium Wecklein 572 ἔτλα Matthiae : ἔτλη codd. 574 δόμοισι V 577 ποιμνήτας L P 582 χόρευσε Monk : ἐχόρευσε codd. 588 τοιγὰρ L P B Σ : τοι γάρ τοι V 589 οἰκεῖς codd. et Σ (sed τίθεται et κρατύνει infra) : οἰκεῖ Purgold

καὶ πεδίων δαπέδοις ὅρον ἀμφὶ μὲν
    ἀελίου κνεφαίαν
ἱππόστασιν αἰθέρα τὰν Μολοσσῶν . . τίθεται,
πόντιον δ' Αἰγαίων' ἐπ' ἀκτὰν
    ἀλίμενον Πηλίου κρατύνει.

καὶ νῦν δόμον ἀμπετάσας [ἀντ.
δέξατο ξεῖνον νοτερῷ βλεφάρῳ,
τᾶς φίλας κλαίων ἀλόχου νέκυν ἐν
δώμασιν ἀρτιθανῆ· τὸ γὰρ εὐγενὲς
    ἐκφέρεται πρὸς αἰδῶ.
ἐν τοῖς ἀγαθοῖσι δὲ πάντ' ἔνεστιν σοφίας. ἄγαμαι·
πρὸς δ' ἐμᾷ ψυχᾷ θάρσος ἧσται
    θεοσεβῆ φῶτα κεδνὰ πράξειν.

Αδ. ἀνδρῶν Φεραίων εὐμενὴς παρουσία,
νέκυν μὲν ἤδη πάντ' ἔχοντα πρόσπολοι
φέρουσιν ἄρδην πρὸς τάφον τε καὶ πυράν·
ὑμεῖς δὲ τὴν θανοῦσαν, ὡς νομίζεται,
προσείπατ' ἐξιοῦσαν ὑστάτην ὁδόν.
Χο. καὶ μὴν ὁρῶ σὸν πατέρα γηραιῷ ποδὶ
στείχοντ', ὀπαδούς τ' ἐν χεροῖν δάμαρτι σῇ
κόσμον φέροντας, νερτέρων ἀγάλματα.

ΦΕΡΗΣ

ἥκω κακοῖσι σοῖσι συγκάμνων, τέκνον·
ἐσθλῆς γάρ, οὐδεὶς ἀντερεῖ, καὶ σώφρονος
γυναικὸς ἡμάρτηκας. ἀλλὰ ταῦτα μὲν
φέρειν ἀνάγκη καίπερ ὄντα δύσφορα.
δέχου δὲ κόσμον τόνδε, καὶ κατὰ χθονὸς
ἴτω. τὸ ταύτης σῶμα τιμᾶσθαι χρεών,
ἥτις γε τῆς σῆς προύθανε ψυχῆς, τέκνον,

594 *ἱππόστασιν* L P B Σ : *ὑπόστασιν* V *Μολοσσῶν ⟨ὀρέων⟩* Bauer : cf. v. 603 595 *δ'* V B : *τ'* L P *Αἰγαίων'* Σ : *αἰγαῖον* codd. 598 *ξεῖνον* Aldina : *ξένον* codd. 599 *φίλας* Aldina : *φιλίας* codd. 603 *ἄγαμαι* delevit *l* 608 *πρὸς* L P : *εἰς* V B 617 *δύσφορα* L P *b* : *δυσμενῆ* V B et Σ B

καί μ' οὐκ ἄπαιδ' ἔθηκεν οὐδ' εἴασε σοῦ
στερέντα γήρᾳ πενθίμῳ καταφθίνειν,
πάσαις δ' ἔθηκεν εὐκλεέστερον βίον
γυναιξίν, ἔργον τλᾶσα γενναῖον τόδε.
ὦ τόνδε μὲν σώσασ', ἀναστήσασα δὲ
ἡμᾶς πίτνοντας, χαῖρε, κἀν Ἅιδου δόμοις
εὖ σοι γένοιτο. φημὶ τοιούτους γάμους
λύειν βροτοῖσιν, ἢ γαμεῖν οὐκ ἄξιον.
Αδ. οὔτ' ἦλθες ἐς τόνδ' ἐξ ἐμοῦ κληθεὶς τάφον,
οὔτ' ἐν φίλοισι σὴν παρουσίαν λέγω.
κόσμον δὲ τὸν σὸν οὔποθ' ἥδ' ἐνδύσεται.
οὐ γάρ τι τῶν σῶν ἐνδεὴς ταφήσεται.
τότε ξυναλγεῖν χρῆν σ' ὅτ' ὠλλύμην ἐγώ.
σὺ δ' ἐκποδὼν στὰς καὶ παρεὶς ἄλλῳ θανεῖν
νέῳ γέρων ὤν, τόνδ' ἀποιμώξῃ νεκρόν;
οὐκ ἦσθ' ἄρ' ὀρθῶς τοῦδε σώματος πατήρ;
οὐδ' ἡ τεκεῖν φάσκουσα καὶ κεκλημένη
μήτηρ μ' ἔτικτε; δουλίου δ' ἀφ' αἵματος
μαστῷ γυναικὸς σῆς ὑπεβλήθην λάθρᾳ;
ἔδειξας εἰς ἔλεγχον ἐξελθὼν ὃς εἶ,
καί μ' οὐ νομίζω παῖδα σὸν πεφυκέναι.
ἦ τἄρα πάντων διαπρέπεις ἀψυχίᾳ,
ὃς τηλικόσδ' ὢν κἀπὶ τέρμ' ἥκων βίου
οὐκ ἠθέλησας οὐδ' ἐτόλμησας θανεῖν
τοῦ σοῦ πρὸ παιδός, ἀλλὰ τήνδ' εἰάσατε
γυναῖκ' ὀθνείαν, ἣν ἐγὼ καὶ μητέρα
πατέρα τέ γ' ἐνδίκως ἂν ἡγοίμην μόνην.

623 εὐκλεέστερον V : εὐκλεέστατον L P B 625 τόνδε μὲν V B : τόνδ' ἐμὸν L P, fortasse recte 631 τὸν σὸν] τοῦτον Earle 632 Verba τῶν σῶν Prinzio suspecta, totus versus Nauckio 635 ἀποιμώξῃ Matthiae : ἀποιμώξεις L P : ἀποιμώζῃ B O D : ἀποιμώζεις V 636–641 proscripsit omnes Badhamus, unum 641 Wilamowitz : nos signa interrogationis posuimus 643 τηλίκος L : τ' ἡλίκος P 647 πατέρα τέ γ' L P : πατέρα τ' V B : καὶ πατέρ' ἂν Blaydes μόνην L P B : ἐμὸν V

καίτοι καλόν γ' ἂν τόνδ' ἀγῶν' ἠγωνίσω,
τοῦ σοῦ πρὸ παιδὸς κατθανών, βραχὺς δέ σοι
πάντως ὁ λοιπὸς ἦν βιώσιμος χρόνος.
[κἀγώ τ' ἂν ἔζων χἥδε τὸν λοιπὸν χρόνον,
κοὐκ ἂν μονωθεὶς ἔστενον κακοῖς ἐμοῖς.]
καὶ μὴν ὅσ' ἄνδρα χρὴ παθεῖν εὐδαίμονα
πέπονθας· ἥβησας μὲν ἐν τυραννίδι,
παῖς δ' ἦν ἐγώ σοι τῶνδε διάδοχος δόμων,
ὥστ' οὐκ ἄτεκνος κατθανὼν ἄλλοις δόμον
λείψειν ἔμελλες ὀρφανὸν διαρπάσαι.
οὐ μὴν ἐρεῖς γέ μ' ὡς ἀτιμάζοντα σὸν
γῆρας θανεῖν προύδωκας, ὅστις αἰδόφρων
πρὸς σ' ἦ μάλιστα· κἀντὶ τῶνδέ μοι χάριν
τοιάνδε καὶ σὺ χἠ τεκοῦσ' ἠλλαξάτην.
τοιγὰρ φυτεύων παῖδας οὐκέτ' ἂν φθάνοις,
οἳ γηροβοσκήσουσι καὶ θανόντα σε
περιστελοῦσι καὶ προθήσονται νεκρόν.
οὐ γάρ σ' ἔγωγε τῇδ' ἐμῇ θάψω χερί·
τέθνηκα γὰρ δὴ τοὐπὶ σέ· εἰ δ' ἄλλου τυχὼν
σωτῆρος αὐγὰς εἰσορῶ, κείνου λέγω
καὶ παῖδά μ' εἶναι καὶ φίλον γηροτρόφον.
μάτην ἄρ' οἱ γέροντες εὔχονται θανεῖν,
γῆρας ψέγοντες καὶ μακρὸν χρόνον βίου·
ἢν δ' ἐγγὺς ἔλθῃ θάνατος, οὐδεὶς βούλεται
θνῄσκειν, τὸ γῆρας δ' οὐκέτ' ἔστ' αὐτοῖς βαρύ.

Χο. παύσασθ'· ἅλις γὰρ ἡ παροῦσα συμφορά·
ὦ παῖ, πατρὸς δὲ μὴ παροξύνῃς φρένας.

651, 652 damnat Lenting. Cf. 295, 296 ἔζην B O D et Σ B 655 ἦν ἐγώ] ἦ γεγώς· Nauck 655, 656 θρόνων pro δόμων Schmidt: melius fortasse λάχος pro δόμον 657 διαρπάσαι L P: διαρπάσειν V B *l* 658, 659 ἀτιμάζοντα . . . προύδωκας L P Σ: ἀτιμάζων τὸ . . . προὔδωκά σ' V B 660 ἦ] ἦν codd. 665 τῇδε μὴ Weil θάλψω V 666–668 seclusit Badham 672 θνῄσκειν] θανεῖν B 674 ὦ παῖ ut e v. sequente huc retractum damnat Elmsley φρένας V B : φρένα L P

Φε. ὦ παῖ, τίν' αὐχεῖς, πότερα Λυδὸν ἢ Φρύγα
κακοῖς ἐλαύνειν ἀργυρώνητον σέθεν;
οὐκ οἶσθα Θεσσαλόν με κἀπὸ Θεσσαλοῦ
πατρὸς γεγῶτα γνησίως ἐλεύθερον;
ἄγαν ὑβρίζεις, καὶ νεανίας λόγους
ῥίπτων ἐς ἡμᾶς οὐ βαλὼν οὕτως ἄπει.
ἐγὼ δέ σ' οἴκων δεσπότην ἐγεινάμην
κἄθρεψ', ὀφείλω δ' οὐχ ὑπερθνῄσκειν σέθεν·
οὐ γὰρ πατρῷον τόνδ' ἐδεξάμην νόμον,
παίδων προθνῄσκειν πατέρας, οὐδ' Ἑλληνικόν.
σαυτῷ γὰρ εἴτε δυστυχὴς εἴτ' εὐτυχὴς
ἔφυς· ἃ δ' ἡμῶν χρῆν σε τυγχάνειν, ἔχεις.
πολλῶν μὲν ἄρχεις, πολυπλέθρους δέ σοι γύας
λείψω· πατρὸς γὰρ ταὔτ' ἐδεξάμην πάρα.
τί δῆτά σ' ἠδίκηκα; τοῦ σ' ἀποστερῶ;
μὴ θνῆσχ' ὑπὲρ τοῦδ' ἀνδρός, οὐδ' ἐγὼ πρὸ σοῦ.
χαίρεις ὁρῶν φῶς· πατέρα δ' οὐ χαίρειν δοκεῖς;
ἦ μὴν πολύν γε τὸν κάτω λογίζομαι
χρόνον, τὸ δὲ ζῆν μικρόν, ἀλλ' ὅμως γλυκύ.
σὺ γοῦν ἀναιδῶς διεμάχου τὸ μὴ θανεῖν,
καὶ ζῇς παρελθὼν τὴν πεπρωμένην τύχην,
ταύτην κατακτάς· εἶτ' ἐμὴν ἀψυχίαν
λέγεις, γυναικός, ὦ κάκισθ', ἡσσημένος,
ἣ τοῦ καλοῦ σοῦ προύθανεν νεανίου;
σοφῶς δ' ἐφηῦρες ὥστε μὴ θανεῖν ποτε,
εἰ τὴν παροῦσαν κατθανεῖν πείσεις ἀεὶ
γυναῖχ' ὑπὲρ σοῦ· κᾆτ' ὀνειδίζεις φίλοις
τοῖς μὴ θέλουσι δρᾶν τάδ', αὐτὸς ὢν κακός;

675 Cf. Ar. Av. 1244 679 ἄγαν μ' L 682 ὀφείλω δ' V B : ὀφείλων L P 688 ταὔτ' Purgold : ταῦτ' codd. 689 ἠδίκησα L P 691 Cf Ar Thesm 194, Nub. 1415 693 μικρόν V L : σμικρόν B P 697 λέγεις] ψέγεις Hervagiana altera 699 ἐφεῦρες V B : εὗρες L P (δέ γ' εὗρες L^2 vel *l*) 700 πείσεις ἀεὶ V B Σ : πείσειας ἂν L P

σίγα· νόμιζε δ', εἰ σὺ τὴν σαυτοῦ φιλεῖς
ψυχήν, φιλεῖν ἅπαντας· εἰ δ' ἡμᾶς κακῶς
ἐρεῖς, ἀκούσῃ πολλὰ κοὐ ψευδῆ κακά.
Χο. πλείω λέλεκται νῦν τε καὶ τὰ πρὶν κακά·
παῦσαι δέ, πρέσβυ, παῖδα σὸν κακορροθῶν.
Αδ. λέγ', ὡς ἐμοῦ λέξαντος· εἰ δ' ἀλγεῖς κλύων
τἀληθές, οὐ χρῆν σ' εἰς ἔμ' ἐξαμαρτάνειν.
Φε. σοῦ δ' ἂν προθνῄσκων μᾶλλον ἐξημάρτανον.
Αδ. ταὐτὸν γὰρ ἡβῶντ' ἄνδρα καὶ πρέσβυν θανεῖν;
Φε. ψυχῇ μιᾷ ζῆν, οὐ δυοῖν, ὀφείλομεν.
Αδ. καὶ μὴν Διός γε μείζονα ζῴης χρόνον.
Φε. ἀρᾷ γονεῦσιν οὐδὲν ἔκδικον παθών;
Αδ. μακροῦ βίου γὰρ ᾐσθόμην ἐρῶντά σε.
Φε. ἀλλ' οὐ σὺ νεκρὸν ἀντὶ σοῦ τόνδ' ἐκφέρεις;
Αδ. σημεῖα τῆς σῆς, ὦ κάκιστ', ἀψυχίας.
Φε. οὔτοι πρὸς ἡμῶν γ' ὤλετ'· οὐκ ἐρεῖς τόδε.
Αδ. φεῦ·
εἴθ' ἀνδρὸς ἔλθοις τοῦδέ γ' ἐς χρείαν ποτέ.
Φε. μνήστευε πολλάς, ὡς θάνωσι πλείονες.
Αδ. σοὶ τοῦτ' ὄνειδος· οὐ γὰρ ἤθελες θανεῖν.
Φε. φίλον τὸ φέγγος τοῦτο τοῦ θεοῦ, φίλον.
Αδ. κακὸν τὸ λῆμα κοὐκ ἐν ἀνδράσιν τὸ σόν.
Φε. οὐκ ἐγγελᾷς γέροντα βαστάζων νεκρόν.
Αδ. θανῇ γε μέντοι δυσκλεής, ὅταν θάνῃς.
Φε. κακῶς ἀκούειν οὐ μέλει θανόντι μοι.
Αδ. φεῦ φεῦ· τὸ γῆρας ὡς ἀναιδείας πλέων.
Φε. ἥδ' οὐκ ἀναιδής· τήνδ' ἐφηῦρες ἄφρονα.
Αδ. ἄπελθε κἀμὲ τόνδ' ἔα θάψαι νεκρόν.

706 τὰ] τὸ Wakefield 708 λέξαντος L P V Σ : λέγοντος B D O 713 μείζονα Schaefer et Σ primitus : μεῖζον ἂν codd. et Σ nunc ζῴης] ζώοις V B *p* 716 νεκρόν γ' V 717 σημεῖα γ' ὦ κάκιστε ταῦτ' ἀψυχίας L P τῆς σῆς ⟨γ'⟩ Herwerden 718 οὔτοι πρὸς ἡμῶν γ' V B : οὔτι πρὸς ἡμῶν L P 725 θάνῃς] θανῇ V : θάνηι B 726 μέλει L P : μέλλει V B 729 κἀμὲ V B : καί με L P

Φε. ἄπειμι· θάψεις δ' αὐτὸς ὢν αὐτῆς φονεύς,
δίκας δὲ δώσεις σοῖσι κηδεσταῖς ἔτι.
ἦ τἄρ' Ἄκαστος οὐκέτ' ἔστ' ἐν ἀνδράσιν,
εἰ μή σ' ἀδελφῆς αἷμα τιμωρήσεται.
Αδ. ἔρρων νυν, αὐτὸς χἠ ξυνοικήσασά σοι,
ἄπαιδε παιδὸς ὄντος, ὥσπερ ἄξιοι,
γηράσκετ'· οὐ γὰρ τῷδ' ἔτ' ἐς ταὐτὸν στέγος
νεῖσθ'· εἰ δ' ἀπειπεῖν χρῆν με κηρύκων ὕπο
τὴν σὴν πατρῴαν ἑστίαν, ἀπεῖπον ἄν.
ἡμεῖς δέ—τοὐν ποσὶν γὰρ οἰστέον κακόν—
στείχωμεν, ὡς ἂν ἐν πυρᾷ θῶμεν νεκρόν.
Χο. ἰὼ ἰώ. σχετλία τόλμης,
ὦ γενναία καὶ μέγ' ἀρίστη,
χαῖρε· πρόφρων σὲ χθόνιός θ' Ἑρμῆς
Ἅιδης τε δέχοιτ'. εἰ δέ τι κἀκεῖ
πλέον ἔστ' ἀγαθοῖς, τούτων μετέχουσ'
Ἅιδου νύμφῃ παρεδρεύοις.

ΘΕΡΑΠΩΝ

πολλοὺς μὲν ἤδη κἀπὸ παντοίας χθονὸς
ξένους μολόντας οἶδ' ἐς Ἀδμήτου δόμους,
οἷς δεῖπνα προύθηκ'· ἀλλὰ τοῦδ' οὔπω ξένου
κακίον' ἐς τήνδ' ἑστίαν ἐδεξάμην.
ὃς πρῶτα μὲν πενθοῦντα δεσπότην ὁρῶν
ἐσῆλθε κἀτόλμησ' ἀμείψασθαι πύλας.
ἔπειτα δ' οὔτι σωφρόνως ἐδέξατο
τὰ προστυχόντα ξένια, συμφορὰν μαθών,
ἀλλ', εἴ τι μὴ φέροιμεν, ὤτρυνεν φέρειν.

731 δὲ L P : τε V B σοῖσι L P B : τοῖσι σοῖσι V : σοῖσι del. V[1] 732 ἦ] ἢ codd. (ἣ V) ἄκλαυστος οὐκ ἔστ' ἐν ἀνδράσιν ἔτι V 734 ἔρρων γρ. Σ (τινὲς δὲ ἔρρων γράφουσι σὺν τῷ ν̄) : ἔρρου L *p* Σ : ἐρρο* P : ἔρροις V B lemma Σ 735 ὄντος L P : ὄντες V B *l* 736 τῷδ' ἔτ' Elmsley : τῶδ' ἴτ' L P : τῶδε γ' V B ταὐτὸν V B : ταὐτὸ L P 737 χρῆν V L[1] : χρὴ L P B 741 ἰὼ semel L P 742 ἀρίστα L P 743 seq. ἅδης ἑρμῆς τε δέχηθ' V 745 μετέχου V 746 νύμφῃ V : νύμφα L P B προσεδρεύοις L P 755 φέροιεν V

ποτῆρα δ' ἐν χείρεσσι κίσσινον λαβὼν
πίνει μελαίνης μητρὸς εὔζωρον μέθυ,
ἕως ἐθέρμην' αὐτὸν ἀμφιβᾶσα φλὸξ
οἴνου· στέφει δὲ κρᾶτα μυρσίνης κλάδοις
ἄμουσ' ὑλακτῶν· δισσὰ δ' ἦν μέλη κλύειν·
ὁ μὲν γὰρ ᾖδε, τῶν ἐν Ἀδμήτου κακῶν
οὐδὲν προτιμῶν, οἰκέται δ' ἐκλαίομεν
δέσποιναν· ὄμμα δ' οὐκ ἐδείκνυμεν ξένῳ
τέγγοντες· Ἄδμητος γὰρ ὧδ' ἐφίετο.
καὶ νῦν ἐγὼ μὲν ἐν δόμοισιν ἑστιῶ
ξένον, πανοῦργον κλῶπα καὶ λῃστήν τινα,
ἡ δ' ἐκ δόμων βέβηκεν, οὐδ' ἐφεσπόμην
οὐδ' ἐξέτεινα χεῖρ', ἀποιμώζων ἐμὴν
δέσποιναν, ἣ 'μοὶ πᾶσί τ' οἰκέταισιν ἦν
μήτηρ· κακῶν γὰρ μυρίων ἐρρύετο,
ὀργὰς μαλάσσουσ' ἀνδρός. ἆρα τὸν ξένον
στυγῶ δικαίως, ἐν κακοῖς ἀφιγμένον;

Ηρ. οὗτος, τί σεμνὸν καὶ πεφροντικὸς βλέπεις;
οὐ χρὴ σκυθρωπὸν τοῖς ξένοις τὸν πρόσπολον
εἶναι, δέχεσθαι δ' εὐπροσηγόρῳ φρενί.
σὺ δ' ἄνδρ' ἑταῖρον δεσπότου παρόνθ' ὁρῶν,
στυγνῷ προσώπῳ καὶ συνωφρυωμένῳ
δέχῃ, θυραίου πήματος σπουδὴν ἔχων.
δεῦρ' ἔλθ', ὅπως ἂν καὶ σοφώτερος γένῃ.
τὰ θνητὰ πράγματ' οἶδας ἣν ἔχει φύσιν;
οἶμαι μὲν οὔ· πόθεν γάρ; ἀλλ' ἄκουέ μου.
βροτοῖς ἅπασι κατθανεῖν ὀφείλεται,
κοὐκ ἔστι θνητῶν ὅστις ἐξεπίσταται
τὴν αὔριον μέλλουσαν εἰ βιώσεται·

756 χείρεσσι B : χείμεσι V L P. Nil mutandum. Vocem ποτῆρα habuit Σ 759 μυρσίνης Canter : μυρσίνοις codd. 760, 761 δισσὰ δ' . . . ᾖδε om. L P : add *l* 767 ἐφεπόμην V 769 ἡ 'μοὶ Wakefield : ἣ μοι codd. 780 οἶδας codd. (οἶσθ' L teste Wilamowitzio) et Σ et Plutarch. consol. ad Apoll. 11 781 οἶμαι] δοκῶ Plutarchus 783 ἔστιν αὐτῶν Plutarchus

τὸ τῆς τύχης γὰρ ἀφανὲς οἷ προβήσεται,
κἄστ' οὐ διδακτὸν οὐδ' ἁλίσκεται τέχνῃ.
ταῦτ' οὖν ἀκούσας καὶ μαθὼν ἐμοῦ πάρα,
εὔφραινε σαυτόν, πῖνε, τὸν καθ' ἡμέραν
βίον λογίζου σόν, τὰ δ' ἄλλα τῆς τύχης.
τίμα δὲ καὶ τὴν πλεῖστον ἡδίστην θεῶν
Κύπριν βροτοῖσιν· εὐμενὴς γὰρ ἡ θεός.
τὰ δ' ἄλλ' ἔασον ταῦτα καὶ πιθοῦ λόγοις
ἐμοῖσιν—εἴπερ ὀρθά σοι δοκῶ λέγειν;
οἶμαι μέν. οὔκουν τὴν ἄγαν λύπην ἀφεὶς
πίῃ μεθ' ἡμῶν τάσδ' ὑπερβαλὼν τύχας,
στεφάνοις πυκασθείς; καὶ σάφ' οἶδ' ὁθούνεκα
τοῦ νῦν σκυθρωποῦ καὶ ξυνεστῶτος φρενῶν
μεθορμιεῖ σε πίτυλος ἐμπεσὼν σκύφου.
ὄντας δὲ θνητοὺς θνητὰ καὶ φρονεῖν χρεών·
ὡς τοῖς γε σεμνοῖς καὶ συνωφρυωμένοις
ἅπασίν ἐστιν, ὥς γ' ἐμοὶ χρῆσθαι κριτῇ,
οὐ βίος ἀληθῶς ὁ βίος, ἀλλὰ συμφορά.

Θε. ἐπιστάμεσθα ταῦτα· νῦν δὲ πράσσομεν
οὐχ οἷα κώμου καὶ γέλωτος ἄξια.

Ηρ. γυνὴ θυραῖος ἡ θανοῦσα· μὴ λίαν
πένθει· δόμων γὰρ ζῶσι τῶνδε δεσπόται.

Θε. τί ζῶσιν; οὐ κάτοισθα τἀν δόμοις κακά;

Ηρ. εἰ μή τι σός με δεσπότης ἐψεύσατο.

Θε. ἄγαν ἐκεῖνός ἐστ' ἄγαν φιλόξενος.

Ηρ. οὐ χρῆν μ' ὀθνείου γ' οὕνεκ' εὖ πάσχειν νεκροῦ;

Θε. ἦ κάρτα μέντοι καὶ λίαν θυραῖος ἦν.

Ηρ. μῶν ξυμφοράν τιν' οὖσαν οὐκ ἔφραζέ μοι;

785 *τὸ* codd et Σ: *τὰ* Elmsley *οἷ* V B: *οὗ* L P: *ᾗ* Hauniensis 787 *τοῦτ'* Orion Anth. viii. 4 792 *ταῦτα*] *πάντα* Markland *πιθοῦ* Monk: *πείθου* L V B: *πίθου* P (voluit *πείθου*) 794 *Θε. οἶμαι μέν. Ηρ. οὔκουν κ.τ.λ.* B 795–796 *τάσδ' . . . πυκασθείς* del. Herwerden, cf. 829, 832 795 *τύχας*] *γρ. πύλας* Σ 797 *φρενῶν* L P: *κακοῦ* V B 809 *ἄγαν γ'* L P 810 *οὐ χρῆν μ'* V B et Σ: *οὔκουν* L P 811 *θυραῖος* B O D: *οἰκεῖος* V L P Σ. Cf. v. 814

Θε. χαίρων ἴθ᾽· ἡμῖν δεσποτῶν μέλει κακά.
Ηρ. ὅδ᾽ οὐ θυραίων πημάτων ἄρχει λόγος.
Θε. οὐ γάρ τι κωμάζοντ᾽ ἂν ἠχθόμην σ᾽ ὁρῶν.
Ηρ. ἀλλ᾽ ἦ πέπονθα δείν᾽ ὑπὸ ξένων ἐμῶν;
Θε. οὐκ ἦλθες ἐν δέοντι δέξασθαι δόμοις.
πένθος γὰρ ἡμῖν ἐστι· καὶ στολμοὺς βλέπεις
μελαμπέπλους κουράν τε. Ηρ. τίς δ᾽ ὁ κατθανων;
μῶν ἢ τέκνων τι φροῦδον ἢ γέρων πατήρ;
Θε. γυνὴ μὲν οὖν ὄλωλεν Ἀδμήτου, ξένε.
Ηρ. τί φῄς; ἔπειτα δῆτά μ᾽ ἐξενίζετε;
Θε. ᾐδεῖτο γάρ σε τῶνδ᾽ ἀπώσασθαι δόμων.
Ηρ. ὦ σχέτλι᾽, οἵας ἤμπλακες ξυναόρου.
Θε. ἀπωλόμεσθα πάντες, οὐ κείνη μόνη.
Ηρ. ἀλλ᾽ ᾐσθόμην μὲν ὄμμ᾽ ἰδὼν δακρυρροοῦν
κουράν τε καὶ πρόσωπον· ἀλλ᾽ ἔπειθέ με
λέγων θυραῖον κῆδος ἐς τάφον φέρειν.
βίᾳ δὲ θυμοῦ τάσδ᾽ ὑπερβαλὼν πύλας
ἔπινον ἀνδρὸς ἐν φιλοξένου δόμοις,
πράσσοντος οὕτω. κᾆτ᾽ ἐκώμαζον κάρα
στεφάνοις πυκασθείς; ἀλλὰ σοῦ τὸ μὴ φράσαι,
κακοῦ τοσούτου δώμασιν προκειμένου.
ποῦ καί σφε θάπτει; ποῦ νιν εὑρήσω μολών;
Θε. ὀρθὴν παρ᾽ οἶμον, ἣ ᾽πὶ Λάρισαν φέρει,
τύμβον κατόψῃ ξεστὸν ἐκ προαστίου.

815 τι κωμάζοντ᾽ ἂν ἠχθόμην σ᾽ V B : σε κωμάζοντ᾽ ἂν ἠχθόμην L P (ἠχθόμην* P) 817 δόμους L P 818–820 ταῦτα δὲ τὰ τρία ⟨ἰαμβεῖα⟩ ἔν τισιν οὐκ ἔγκειται Σ V ad v. 820: sed in V v. 819 tanquam duo versus scriptus est: τὰ τρία igitur 818–819 sunt 818 στολμοὺς . . . κουράν scripsi: κουρὰν . . . στολμούς codd. 820 τι φροῦδον ἢ B V[1] : τι φροῦδον γένος ἢ V ante corr. : τις φροῦδος ἢ L : τις ἢ φροῦδος ἢ P. Fortasse μῶν ἦν (ἆρα ἀφανὴς ἐγένετό τις τῶν παίδων Σ) 825 μόνον L 827 πρόσωπον] πεπλώματ᾽ Mekler ἀλλ᾽ ὅμως V, corr. V[1] 829 τύχας πύλας B: corr. b 831 κᾆτ᾽ ἐκώμαζον L : κἀπεκώμαζον P : κατακωμάζω V : κᾆτα κωμάζω B 832 σοῦ τὸ μὴ codd. et Σ 833 προσκειμένου Scaliger. Cf. ad v. 551 834 ποῦ νιν] ποῖ νιν Monk 835 Λάρισσαν codd. 836 προαστίου L B p : προαστείου V P

Ηρ. ὦ πολλὰ τλᾶσα καρδία καὶ χεὶρ ἐμή,
νῦν δεῖξον οἷον παῖδά σ' ἡ Τιρυνθία
Ἠλεκτρύωνος γείνατ' Ἀλκμήνη Διί.
δεῖ γάρ με σῶσαι τὴν θανοῦσαν ἀρτίως
γυναῖκα κὰς τόνδ' αὖθις ἱδρῦσαι δόμον
Ἄλκηστιν, Ἀδμήτῳ θ' ὑπουργῆσαι χάριν.
ἐλθὼν δ' ἄνακτα τὸν μελάμπεπλον νεκρῶν
Θάνατον φυλάξω, καί νιν εὑρήσειν δοκῶ
πίνοντα τύμβου πλησίον προσφαγμάτων.
κἄνπερ λοχαίας αὐτὸν ἐξ ἕδρας συθεὶς
μάρψω, κύκλον δὲ περιβάλω χεροῖν ἐμαῖν,
οὐκ ἔστιν ὅστις αὐτὸν ἐξαιρήσεται
μογοῦντα πλευρά, πρὶν γυναῖκ' ἐμοὶ μεθῇ.
ἢν δ' οὖν ἁμάρτω τῆσδ' ἄγρας, καὶ μὴ μόλῃ
πρὸς αἱματηρὸν πέλανον, εἶμι τῶν κάτω
Κόρης Ἄνακτός τ' εἰς ἀνηλίους δόμους
αἰτήσομαί τε· καὶ πέποιθ' ἄξειν ἄνω
Ἄλκηστιν, ὥστε χερσὶν ἐνθεῖναι ξένου,
ὅς μ' ἐς δόμους ἐδέξατ' οὐδ' ἀπήλασε,
καίπερ βαρείᾳ συμφορᾷ πεπληγμένος,
ἔκρυπτε δ' ὢν γενναῖος, αἰδεσθεὶς ἐμέ.
τίς τοῦδε μᾶλλον Θεσσαλῶν φιλόξενος,
τίς Ἑλλάδ' οἰκῶν; τοιγὰρ οὐκ ἐρεῖ κακὸν
εὐεργετῆσαι φῶτα γενναῖος γεγώς.

Αδ. ἰώ, στυγναὶ
πρόσοδοι, στυγναὶ δ' ὄψεις χήρων

837 καὶ χεὶρ] ψυχή τ' B. Cf. Or. 466 839 scribendum videtur Ἠλεκτρυώνη 'γείνατ' (sic Wilamowitz), cl. Hes. Scut. 86 et Inscr. Ialysiam Newtoni, *Trans. Roy. Soc.* xi, p. 442 843 μελάμπτερον Musgravius ex Σ (μέλανας πτέρυγας ἔχων) 845 πίνοντα codd. et Σ: πεινῶντα Schmidt 846 λοχαίας citatio in cod. Florentino Etymologici M. ap. Miller. Melanges p. 208. γρ. λοχίας (λοχαίας Schwartz) Σ: λοχήσας codd. 847 περιβαλῶ (sic) L P: περιβαλὼν V B *p* Σ 852 ἀνηλίου V

μελάθρων. ἰώ μοί μοι. αἶ αἶ.
ποῖ βῶ; ποῖ στῶ; τί λέγω; τί δὲ μή;
πῶς ἂν ὀλοίμαν;
ἦ βαρυδαίμονα μήτηρ μ' ἔτεκεν.
ζηλῶ φθιμένους, κείνων ἔραμαι,
κεῖν' ἐπιθυμῶ δώματα ναίειν.
οὔτε γὰρ αὐγὰς χαίρω προσορῶν
οὔτ' ἐπὶ γαίας πόδα πεζεύων·
τοῖον ὅμηρόν μ' ἀποσυλήσας
"Αιδῃ Θάνατος παρέδωκεν.

Χο.
— πρόβα, πρόβα· βᾶθι κεῦθος οἴκων. (Αδ. αἰαῖ.) [στρ.
— πέπονθας ἄξι' αἰαγμάτων. (Αδ. ἒ ἔ.)
— δι' ὀδύνας ἔβας, σάφ' οἶδα . . . (Αδ. φεῦ φεῦ.)
— τὰν νέρθε δ' οὐδὲν ὠφελεῖς. (Αδ. ἰώ μοί μοι.)
— τὸ μήποτ' εἰσιδεῖν φιλίας ἀλόχου
πρόσωπον ἄντα λυπρόν.

Αδ. ἔμνησας ὅ μου φρένας ἥλκωσεν·
τί γὰρ ἀνδρὶ κακὸν μεῖζον, ἁμαρτεῖν
πιστῆς ἀλόχου; μή ποτε γήμας
ὤφελον οἰκεῖν μετὰ τῆσδε δόμους.
ζηλῶ δ' ἀγάμους ἀτέκνους τε βροτῶν·
μία γὰρ ψυχή, τῆς ὑπεραλγεῖν
μέτριον ἄχθος·
παίδων δὲ νόσους καὶ νυμφιδίους

862 *μοί μοι. αἶ αἶ*] *μοι ἒ ἒ* V: *μοί μοι ἓ ἓ* B 863 *ποῖ στῶ* codd. et, ni fallor, Σ: *πῆ στῶ* *l*: *πᾷ στῶ* Porson 865 *μ' ἔτικτεν* VB 866 Cf. Ar. Vesp. 751 872–877 Chori sunt in L. 872–876 (usque ad *μοί μοι*) choro, reliqua usque ad 888 (*διὰ παντός*) Admeto tribuit P Paragraphos addidi 873 *αἰαῖ* om. P 877 v. antistrophico (894) non respondet: ⟨*σ' ἔν*⟩*αντα* Hartung 878 'Αδ. om. L: add. *l* *δμοῦ φρέν' ἥλκωσε* V 880 *πιστῆς* LPB et Stob. 69. 12: *φιλίας* V 883 *μία γὰρ ψυχή, τῆς* Stob. 68. 13 unus cod. *τῆς δ'*): *μία γὰρ ψυχὴ τῆσδ'* VB: *μιᾶ γὰρ ψυχῆ τῆσδ'* L: *ψυχῆ γὰρ μιᾶ τῆσδ'* P

εὐνὰς θανάτοις κεραϊζομένας
οὐ τλητὸν ὁρᾶν, ἐξὸν ἀτέκνους
ἀγάμους τ' εἶναι διὰ παντός.

Χο.
— τύχα τύχα δυσπάλαιστος ἥκει· (Αδ. αἰαῖ.) [ἀντ.
— πέρας δέ γ' οὐδὲν ἀλγέων τίθης. (Αδ. ἒ ἕ.)
— βαρέα μὲν φέρειν, ὅμως δὲ . . . (Αδ. φεῦ φεῦ.)
— τλᾶθ'· οὐ σὺ πρῶτος ὤλεσας . . . (Αδ. ἰώ μοί μοι.)
— γυναῖκα· συμφορὰ δ' ἑτέρους ἑτέρα
πιέζει φανεῖσα θνατῶν.

Αδ. ὦ μακρὰ πένθη λῦπαί τε φίλων
τῶν ὑπὸ γαῖαν.
τί μ' ἐκώλυσας ῥῖψαι τύμβου
τάφρον ἐς κοίλην καὶ μετ' ἐκείνης
τῆς μέγ' ἀρίστης κεῖσθαι φθίμενον;
δύο δ' ἀντὶ μιᾶς Ἅιδης ψυχὰς
τὰς πιστοτάτας σὺν ἂν ἔσχεν, ὁμοῦ
χθονίαν λίμνην διαβάντε.

Χο. ἐμοί τις ἦν [στρ.
ἐν γένει, ᾧ κόρος ἀξιόθρηνος
ὤλετ' ἐν δόμοισιν
μονόπαις· ἀλλ' ἔμπας
ἔφερε κακὸν ἅλις, ἄτεκνος ὤν,
πολιὰς ἐπὶ χαίτας
ἤδη προπετὴς ὢν
βιότου τε πόρσω.

887 seq. ἀτέκνους ἀγάμους τ' V B Σ: ἀτέκνοις ἀγάμοις τ' L P 889–894 Distributio versuum ut in B: omnia Choro dant L P: V sic, Χο. τύχα . . . αἶ αἶ. Αδ. πέρας . . . τιθεῖς. Χο. ἒ ἕ . . . ὅμως δέ Paragraphos addidi 890 δέ γ'] δ' L P 894 θνατῶν L: θνητῶν V B P 896 γαίαν V: γαίας Monk 898 καὶ μετ' V B *l*: κατ' P et sine dubio L κοίλην] κοινὴν Hoefer 901 σὺν ἂν ἔσχεν Lenting: συνανέσχεν V P et sine dubio L: γε συνέσχεν *l*: συνέχεν B, σ suprascr. B[1] 902 λίμναν L P 904 κόρος *l*: κοῦρος codd. 905 ὤλετ' V B: ᾤχετ' L P 907 ἅλις codd. et Σ et Hesych. s. v. 910 πρόσω codd.

Αδ. ὦ σχῆμα δόμων, πῶς εἰσέλθω;
πῶς δ' οἰκήσω μεταπίπτοντος
δαίμονος; οἴμοι. πολὺ γὰρ τὸ μέσον·
τότε μὲν πεύκαις σὺν Πηλιάσιν
σύν θ' ὑμεναίοις ἔστειχον ἔσω,
φιλίας ἀλόχου χέρα βαστάζων,
πολυάχητος δ' εἵπετο κῶμος,
τήν τε θανοῦσαν κἄμ' ὀλβίζων,
ὡς εὐπατρίδαι καὶ ἀπ' ἀμφοτέρων
ὄντες ἀρίστων σύζυγες εἶμεν·
νῦν δ' ὑμεναίων γόος ἀντίπαλος
λευκῶν τε πέπλων μέλανες στολμοὶ
πέμπουσί μ' ἔσω
λέκτρων κοίτας ἐς ἐρήμους.

Χο. παρ' εὐτυχῆ [ἀντ.
σοὶ πότμον ἦλθεν ἀπειροκάκῳ τόδ'
ἄλγος· ἀλλ' ἔσωσας
βίοτον καὶ ψυχάν.
ἔθανε δάμαρ, ἔλιπε φιλίαν·
τί νέον τόδε; πολλοῖς
ἤδη παρέλυσεν
θάνατος δάμαρτας.

Αδ. φίλοι, γυναικὸς δαίμον' εὐτυχέστερον
τοὐμοῦ νομίζω, καίπερ οὐ δοκοῦνθ' ὅμως·
τῆς μὲν γὰρ οὐδὲν ἄλγος ἅψεταί ποτε,
πολλῶν δὲ μόχθων εὐκλεὴς ἐπαύσατο.
ἐγὼ δ', ὃν οὐ χρῆν ζῆν, παρεὶς τὸ μόρσιμον
λυπρὸν διάξω βίοτον· ἄρτι μανθάνω.

913 πῶς δ' LP : πῶς VB 917 φιλίας] γρ. πιστῆς Σ. Cf. 880 921 ἀριστέων Dobree. Cf. Med. 5 εἶμεν Heath : εἰμὲν BP : ἦμεν VL 926 Χο. om. V 929 Post ψυχάν add. ἄδμητ. ἒ ἒ χορ. ὦ ἄδμητε V : ἒ ἒ B 934 δάμαρτας V et, ni fallor, Σ : δάμαρτος LPB πολλοὺς . . . δάμαρτος Canter 939 χρῆν Elmsley : χρὴ codd. 940 μανθάνων LP

πῶς γὰρ δόμων τῶνδ' εἰσόδους ἀνέξομαι;
τίν' ἂν προσειπών, τοῦ δὲ προσρηθεὶς ὕπο,
τερπνῆς τύχοιμ' ἂν ἐξόδου; ποῖ τρέψομαι;
ἡ μὲν γὰρ ἔνδον ἐξελᾷ μ' ἐρημία,
γυναικὸς εὐνὰς εὖτ' ἂν εἰσίδω κενὰς
θρόνους τ' ἐν οἷσιν ἷζε, καὶ κατὰ στέγας
αὐχμηρὸν οὖδας, τέκνα δ' ἀμφὶ γούνασι
πίπτοντα κλαίῃ μητέρ', οἱ δὲ δεσπότιν
στένωσιν οἵαν ἐκ δόμων ἀπώλεσαν.
τὰ μὲν κατ' οἴκους τοιάδ'· ἔξωθεν δέ με
γάμοι τ' ἐλῶσι Θεσσαλῶν καὶ ξύλλογοι
γυναικοπληθεῖς· οὐ γὰρ ἐξανέξομαι
λεύσσων δάμαρτος τῆς ἐμῆς ὁμήλικας.
ἐρεῖ δέ μ' ὅστις ἐχθρὸς ὢν κυρεῖ τάδε·
'Ιδοῦ τὸν αἰσχρῶς ζῶνθ', ὃς οὐκ ἔτλη θανεῖν,
ἀλλ' ἣν ἔγημεν ἀντιδοὺς ἀψυχίᾳ
πέφευγεν ῞Αιδην· εἶτ' ἀνὴρ εἶναι δοκεῖ;
στυγεῖ δὲ τοὺς τεκόντας, αὐτὸς οὐ θέλων
θανεῖν. τοιάνδε πρὸς κακοῖσι κληδόνα
ἕξω. τί μοι ζῆν δῆτα κέρδιον, φίλοι,
κακῶς κλύοντι καὶ κακῶς πεπραγότι;

Χο. ἐγὼ καὶ διὰ μούσας [στρ.
καὶ μετάρσιος ᾖξα, καὶ
πλείστων ἁψάμενος λόγων
κρεῖσσον οὐδὲν 'Ανάγκας
ηὗρον, οὐδέ τι φάρμακον
Θρῄσσαις ἐν σανίσιν, τὰς
'Ορφεία κατέγραψεν

943 ἐξόδου Lenting: εἰσόδου codd. et Σ 944 ἐξελᾷ V B *l*: ἐξελεῖ P et sine dubio L 948 πίτνοντα Wecklein 950 οἴκους L P: οἶκον V B 951 τ' Wakefield: γ' codd. 954 κυρῇ Monk 957 εἶτ' V B: κᾆτ' L P 960 κέρδιον Purgold: κύδιον codd. 964 ἁψάμενος] ἀρξάμενος Stob. i. 4. 3

γῆρυς, οὐδ' ὅσα Φοῖβος 'Ασκληπιάδαις ἔδωκε
φάρμακα πολυπόνοις ἀντιτεμὼν βροτοῖσιν.

  μόνας δ' οὔτ' ἐπὶ βωμοὺς [ἀντ.
ἔστιν οὔτε βρέτας θεᾶς
ἐλθεῖν, οὐ σφαγίων κλύει.
  μή μοι, πότνια, μείζων
ἔλθοις ἢ τὸ πρὶν ἐν βίῳ.
  καὶ γὰρ Ζεὺς ὅ τι νεύσῃ,
  σὺν σοὶ τοῦτο τελευτᾷ.
καὶ τὸν ἐν Χαλύβοις δαμάζεις σὺ βίᾳ σίδαρον,
οὐδέ τις ἀποτόμου λήματός ἐστιν αἰδώς.

καὶ σ' ἐν ἀφύκτοισι χερῶν εἷλε θεὰ δεσμοῖς. [στρ.
τόλμα δ'· οὐ γὰρ ἀνάξεις ποτ' ἔνερθεν
κλαίων τοὺς φθιμένους ἄνω.
καὶ θεῶν σκότιοι φθίνουσι
  παῖδες ἐν θανάτῳ.
φίλα μὲν ὅτ' ἦν μεθ' ἡμῶν,
φίλα δὲ †καὶ θανοῦσ' ἔσται,†
γενναιοτάταν δὲ πασᾶν ἐζεύξω κλισίαις ἄκοιτιν.

μηδὲ νεκρῶν ὡς φθιμένων χῶμα νομιζέσθω [ἀντ.
τύμβος σᾶς ἀλόχου, θεοῖσι δ' ὁμοίως
τιμάσθω, σέβας ἐμπόρων.
καί τις δοχμίαν κέλευθον
  ἐκβαίνων τόδ' ἐρεῖ·
Αὕτα ποτὲ προύθαν' ἀνδρός,

970 ἔδωκε Musgrave : παρέδωκε codd. 974 975 ἔστιν οὔτε . . . ἐλθεῖν G. A. Wagner : ἐλθεῖν οὔτε . . . ἔστιν codd. 981 οὐ βίᾳ P et γρ. *l* σίδηρον V P 984 σ' ἐν codd. et Σ: σέ γ' Nauck 985 τόλμα δ' L P : τόλμα τάδ' V : τόλμα τόδ' B 986 φθινομένους V 989 φθίνουσι L P : φθινύθουσι V B *l* 992 corruptus : cf. v. 1003 καὶ om. B O D et Haun. θανοῦσα sine elisione solus P ἔσται V B : ἐστίν L P δ' ἔτι καὶ θανοῦσα Barnes ex Aldina (δέ τι κ. θ.) : δὲ θανοῦσ' ἐς ἀεί Nauck 998 ὅμοιος V 1001 ἐκβαίνων L P : ἐμβαίνων V B 1002 προύθανεν codd.

νῦν δ' ἐστὶ μάκαιρα δαίμων·
χαῖρ', ὦ πότνι', εὖ δὲ δοίης. τοῖαί νιν προσεροῦσι
φῆμαι.

— καὶ μὴν ὅδ', ὡς ἔοικεν, Ἀλκμήνης γόνος,
Ἄδμητε, πρὸς σὴν ἑστίαν πορεύεται.

Ηρ. φίλον πρὸς ἄνδρα χρὴ λέγειν ἐλευθέρως,
Ἄδμητε, μομφὰς δ' οὐχ ὑπὸ σπλάγχνοις ἔχειν
σιγῶντ'. ἐγὼ δὲ σοῖς κακοῖσιν ἠξίουν
ἐγγὺς παρεστὼς ἐξετάζεσθαι φίλος·
σὺ δ' οὐκ ἔφραζες σῆς προκείμενον νέκυν
γυναικός, ἀλλά μ' ἐξένιζες ἐν δόμοις,
ὡς δὴ θυραίου πήματος σπουδὴν ἔχων.
κἄστεψα κρᾶτα καὶ θεοῖς ἐλειψάμην
σπονδὰς ἐν οἴκοις δυστυχοῦσι τοῖσι σοῖς.
καὶ μέμφομαι μέν, μέμφομαι, παθὼν τάδε,
οὐ μήν σε λυπεῖν ἐν κακοῖσι βούλομαι.
ὧν δ' οὕνεχ' ἥκω δεῦρ' ὑποστρέψας πάλιν
λέξω. γυναῖκα τήνδε μοι σῷσον λαβών,
ἕως ἂν ἵππους δεῦρο Θρῃκίας ἄγων
ἔλθω, τύραννον Βιστόνων κατακτανών.
πράξας δ' ὃ μὴ τύχοιμι—νοστήσαιμι γάρ—
δίδωμι τήνδε σοῖσι προσπολεῖν δόμοις.
πολλῷ δὲ μόχθῳ χεῖρας ἦλθεν εἰς ἐμάς·
ἀγῶνα γὰρ πάνδημον εὑρίσκω τινὰς
τιθέντας, ἀθληταῖσιν ἄξιον πόνον,
ὅθεν κομίζω τήνδε νικητήρια
λαβών· τὰ μὲν γὰρ κοῦφα τοῖς νικῶσιν ἦν
ἵππους ἄγεσθαι, τοῖσι δ' αὖ τὰ μείζονα

1005 φῆμαι omnes 1006 Χο. praef. L P B: om. V 1009 μομφὰς L B Σ: μορφὰς V P 1017 μέν V B: δή L: δέ P 1021 θρῄϊκας L P (-ίους suprascr. *l*) 1024 προσπολεῖν V B: πρόσπολον L P. De Σ non liquet 1025 πολλῶν δὲ μόχθων ἦλθε χεῖρας εἰς ἐμάς L P 1027 πόνον V: πόνων B O D: πόνου L P 1030 αὖ τὰ L P: αὐτὰ V B

νικῶσι, πυγμὴν καὶ πάλην, βουφόρβια·
γυνὴ δ' ἐπ' αὐτοῖς εἵπετ'· ἐντυχόντι δὲ
αἰσχρὸν παρεῖναι κέρδος ἦν τόδ' εὐκλεές.
ἀλλ', ὥσπερ εἶπον, σοὶ μέλειν γυναῖκα χρή·
οὐ γὰρ κλοπαίαν, ἀλλὰ σὺν πόνῳ λαβὼν
ἥκω· χρόνῳ δὲ καὶ σύ μ' αἰνέσεις ἴσως.
Αδ. οὔτοι σ' ἀτίζων οὐδ' ἐν αἰσχροῖσιν τιθεὶς
ἔκρυψ' ἐμῆς γυναικὸς ἀθλίου τύχας·
ἀλλ' ἄλγος ἄλγει τοῦτ' ἂν ἦν προσκείμενον,
εἴ του πρὸς ἄλλου δώμαθ' ὡρμήθης ξένου·
ἅλις δὲ κλαίειν τοὐμὸν ἦν ἐμοὶ κακόν.
γυναῖκα δ', εἴ πως ἔστιν, αἰτοῦμαί σ', ἄναξ,
ἄλλον τιν' ὅστις μὴ πέπονθεν οἷ' ἐγὼ
σῴζειν ἄνωχθι Θεσσαλῶν· πολλοὶ δέ σοι
ξένοι Φεραίων· μή μ' ἀναμνήσῃς κακῶν.
οὐκ ἂν δυναίμην τήνδ' ὁρῶν ἐν δώμασιν
ἄδακρυς εἶναι· μὴ νοσοῦντί μοι νόσον
προσθῇς· ἅλις γὰρ συμφορᾷ βαρύνομαι.
ποῦ καὶ τρέφοιτ' ἂν δωμάτων νέα γυνή;
νέα γάρ, ὡς ἐσθῆτι καὶ κόσμῳ πρέπει.
πότερα κατ' ἀνδρῶν δῆτ' ἐνοικήσει στέγην;
καὶ πῶς ἀκραιφνὴς ἐν νέοις στρωφωμένη
ἔσται; τὸν ἡβῶνθ', Ἡράκλεις, οὐ ῥᾴδιον
εἴργειν· ἐγὼ δὲ σοῦ προμηθίαν ἔχω.
ἢ τῆς θανούσης θάλαμον ἐσβήσας τρέφω;
καὶ πῶς ἐπεσφρῶ τήνδε τῷ κείνης λέχει;
διπλῆν φοβοῦμαι μέμψιν, ἔκ τε δημοτῶν,

1036 μ' V B: γ' L P   1037 ἀτίζων Scaliger (et Harleianus 5743): ἀτιμάζων codd. et lemma Σ   αἰσχροῖσιν L P (supple αὐτό): ἐχθροῖσιν V B, sed αἰχθροῖσιν primitus V   1038 ἀθλίους B O D   1039 προκείμενον V P   1040 εἴ του] εἴπερ L P   1045 μή μ' ἀναμνήσῃς L P: μή με μιμνήσῃς B D sed in B rasurae supra et post μι: μή με μιμνήσκεις V: unde μὴ 'μέ· μιμνήσκεις Kirchhoff   1051 κατ'] μετ' Hermann   δή τιν' οἰκήσει B   1055 θάλαμον εἰσβήσας B O D: εἰς θάλαμον βήσας V L P: θάλαμον ἐμβήσας Schmidt

μή τίς μ᾽ ἐλέγξῃ τὴν ἐμὴν εὐεργέτιν
προδόντ᾽ ἐν ἄλλης δεμνίοις πίτνειν νέας,
καὶ τῆς θανούσης· ἀξία δέ μοι σέβειν·
πολλὴν πρόνοιαν δεῖ μ᾽ ἔχειν. σὺ δ᾽, ὦ γύναι,
ἥτις ποτ᾽ εἶ σύ, ταὔτ᾽ ἔχουσ᾽ Ἀλκήστιδι
μορφῆς μέτρ᾽ ἴσθι· καὶ προσήιξαι δέμας.
οἴμοι. κόμιζε πρὸς θεῶν ἐξ ὀμμάτων
γυναῖκα τήνδε, μή μ᾽ ἕλῃς ᾑρημένον.
δοκῶ γὰρ αὐτὴν εἰσορῶν γυναῖχ᾽ ὁρᾶν
ἐμήν· θολοῖ δὲ καρδίαν, ἐκ δ᾽ ὀμμάτων
πηγαὶ κατερρώγασιν· ὦ τλήμων ἐγώ,
ὡς ἄρτι πένθους τοῦδε γεύομαι πικροῦ.
Χο. ἐγὼ μὲν οὐκ ἔχοιμ᾽ ἂν εὖ λέγειν τύχην·
χρὴ δ᾽, ὅστις εἶ σύ, καρτερεῖν θεοῦ δόσιν.
Ηρ. εἰ γὰρ τοσαύτην δύναμιν εἶχον ὥστε σὴν
ἐς φῶς πορεῦσαι νερτέρων ἐκ δωμάτων
γυναῖκα καί σοι τήνδε πορσῦναι χάριν.
Αδ. σάφ᾽ οἶδα βούλεσθαί σ᾽ ἄν. ἀλλὰ ποῦ τόδε;
οὐκ ἔστι τοὺς θανόντας ἐς φάος μολεῖν.
Ηρ. μή νυν ὑπέρβαλλ᾽, ἀλλ᾽ ἐναισίμως φέρε.
Αδ. ῥᾷον παραινεῖν ἢ παθόντα καρτερεῖν.
Ηρ. τί δ᾽ ἂν προκόπτοις, εἰ θέλοις ἀεὶ στένειν;
Αδ. ἔγνωκα καὐτός, ἀλλ᾽ ἔρως τις ἐξάγει.
Ηρ. τὸ γὰρ φιλῆσαι τὸν θανόντ᾽ ἄγει δάκρυ.
Αδ. ἀπώλεσέν με, κἄτι μᾶλλον ἢ λέγω.

1058 ἐλέγξῃ LPB: ἐλέγχῃ V 1059 ἄλλης LP: ἄλλοις VB 1062 τὰ αὐτά L[1] in marg.: ταῦτα codd. 1063 προσήοιξαι L: corr. *l*: δέμας προσεμφερές Nauck 1064 ἐξ VB: ἀπ᾽ LP 1066 δρᾶν] δρῶν V 1068 τλῆμον VP 1071 ὅστις εἶ σύ suspecta: cf. v. 1062: σὺ om. L: ἥτις εἴη Hayley: ὅστις εἶσι Hermann 1072 ὥστε σὴν om. LP: add. *l*: ἐκ θεοῦ add. alia manus in P: λειπ. in marg. scr. L[1] 1077 νυν ὑπέρβαλλ᾽ Monk: νῦν ὑπέρβαλ᾽ BOD: νῦν ὑπέρβαιν᾽ VLP (μὴ νῦν ὑπερβαλλόντως φέρε Σ) αἰνεσίμως VB 1079 θέλοις Haun.: θέλεις codd. et codex Galeni, p. 413 στένειν ἀεί Galen. 1080 τις Galen.: τίς μ᾽ codd.

Ηρ. γυναικὸς ἐσθλῆς ἤμπλακες· τίς ἀντερεῖ;
Αδ. ὥστ' ἄνδρα τόνδε μηκέθ' ἥδεσθαι βίῳ.
Ηρ. χρόνος μαλάξει, νῦν δ' ἔθ' ἡβάσκει κακόν.
Αδ. χρόνον λέγοις ἄν, εἰ χρόνος τὸ κατθανεῖν.
Ηρ. γυνή σε παύσει καὶ νέου γάμου πόθοι.
Αδ. σίγησον· οἷον εἶπας. οὐκ ἂν ᾠόμην.
Ηρ. τί δ'; οὐ γαμεῖς γάρ, ἀλλὰ χηρεύσῃ λέχος;
Αδ. οὐκ ἔστιν ἥτις τῷδε συγκλιθήσεται.
Ηρ. μῶν τὴν θανοῦσαν ὠφελεῖν τι προσδοκᾷς;
Αδ. κείνην ὅπουπερ ἔστι τιμᾶσθαι χρεών.
Ηρ. αἰνῶ μὲν αἰνῶ· μωρίαν δ' ὀφλισκάνεις.
Αδ. ὡς μήποτ' ἄνδρα τόνδε νυμφίον καλῶν.
Ηρ. ἐπῄνεσ' ἀλόχῳ πιστὸς οὕνεκ' εἶ φίλος.
Αδ. θάνοιμ' ἐκείνην καίπερ οὐκ οὖσαν προδούς.
Ηρ. δέχου νυν εἴσω τήνδε γενναίων δόμων.
Αδ. μή, πρός σε τοῦ σπείραντος ἄντομαι Διός.
Ηρ. καὶ μὴν ἁμαρτήσῃ γε μὴ δράσας τάδε.
Αδ. καὶ δρῶν γε λύπῃ καρδίαν δηχθήσομαι.
Ηρ. πιθοῦ· τάχ' ἂν γὰρ ἐς δέον πέσοι χάρις.
Αδ. φεῦ.
εἴθ' ἐξ ἀγῶνος τήνδε μὴ 'λαβές ποτε.
Ηρ. νικῶντι μέντοι καὶ σὺ συννικᾷς ἐμοί.
Αδ. καλῶς ἔλεξας· ἡ γυνὴ δ' ἀπελθέτω.
Ηρ. ἄπεισιν, εἰ χρή· πρῶτα δ' εἰ χρεὼν ἄθρει.
Αδ. χρή, σοῦ γε μὴ μέλλοντος ὀργαίνειν ἐμοί.
Ηρ. εἰδώς τι κἀγὼ τήνδ' ἔχω προθυμίαν.
Αδ. νίκα νυν. οὐ μὴν ἁνδάνοντά μοι ποιεῖς.

1085 νῦν L P : σε νῦν V : σ' νῦν B. Cf. v. 381 ἡβάσκει Galen. p. 419 : ἡβᾷ σοι codd. 1087 πόθος L : νέος γάμος πόθου Guttentag 1089 χηρεύσῃ λέχος] χηρεύεις μόνος L P 1090 τῷδε] τῷδ' ἀνδρὶ V 1093 μυρίαν V: corr. *v* 1094 1095 del. Wilamowitz 1094 supra ὡς scr. L[1] ἴσθι καλῶν L P B Σ : καλόν V 1097 γενναίαν L P 1098 ἄντομαι L P : αἰτοῦμαι V B 1101 πείθου V B τάχα γὰρ V 1102 μὴ λάβοις L, γρ. μ' ἤλαβεν *l* in marg. : μὴ λάβῃς P 1105 ἄθρει V B : ὅρα L P 1108 om. V (sed in marg. apposuit ipse), itaque 1109-1113 Herculis vv. Admeto, Admeti Herculi tributit

Ηρ. ἀλλ' ἔσθ' ὅθ' ἡμᾶς αἰνέσεις· πιθοῦ μόνον.
Αδ. κομίζετ', εἰ χρὴ τήνδε δέξασθαι δόμοις.
Ηρ. οὐκ ἂν μεθείην τὴν γυναῖκα προσπόλοις.
Αδ. σὺ δ' αὐτὸς αὐτὴν εἴσαγ', εἰ βούλῃ, δόμους.
Ηρ. ἐς σὰς μὲν οὖν ἔγωγε θήσομαι χέρας.
Αδ. οὐκ ἂν θίγοιμι· δῶμα δ' εἰσελθεῖν πάρα.
Ηρ. τῇ σῇ πέποιθα χειρὶ δεξιᾷ μόνῃ.
Αδ. ἄναξ, βιάζῃ μ' οὐ θέλοντα δρᾶν τάδε.
Ηρ. τόλμα προτεῖναι χεῖρα καὶ θιγεῖν ξένης.
Αδ. καὶ δὴ προτείνω, Γοργόν' ὡς καρατομῶν.
Ηρ. ἔχεις; Αδ. ἔχω; ναί. Ηρ. σῷζέ νυν, καὶ τὸν Διὸς
φήσεις ποτ' εἶναι παῖδα γενναῖον ξένον.
βλέψον πρὸς αὐτήν, εἴ τι σῇ δοκεῖ πρέπειν
γυναικί· λύπης δ' εὐτυχῶν μεθίστασο.
Αδ. ὦ θεοί, τί λέξω—θαῦμ' ἀνέλπιστον τόδε—
γυναῖκα λεύσσων τήνδ';—ἐμὴν ἐτητύμως;
ἢ κέρτομός με θεοῦ τις ἐκπλήσσει χαρά;
Ηρ. οὐκ ἔστιν, ἀλλὰ τήνδ' ὁρᾷς δάμαρτα σήν.
Αδ. ὅρα γε μή τι φάσμα νερτέρων τόδ' ᾖ.
Ηρ. οὐ ψυχαγωγὸν τόνδ' ἐποιήσω ξένον.
Αδ. ἀλλ' ἣν ἔθαπτον εἰσορῶ δάμαρτ' ἐμήν;
Ηρ. σάφ' ἴσθ'. ἀπιστεῖν δ' οὔ σε θαυμάζω τύχην.
Αδ. θίγω, προσείπω ζῶσαν ὡς δάμαρτ' ἐμήν;

1111 μεθείμην σοῖς γυναῖκα B 1112 εἰσάγαγ' V βούλει VB: δοκεῖ LP δόμους Monk (et apogr. Venetus codicis L): δόμοις LPVB 1114 δῶμα δ' LP: δώματ' VB 1115 μόνου Nauck 1117 προτεῖναι V: πρότεινε B: προτείνειν LP θίγε B 1118 καὶ δὴ VB: καὶ μὴν LP καρατομῶν Lobeck: καρατόμῳ codd. et Σ 1119 Vulgo post Monkium Αδ. ἔχω. Ηρ. ναί, κ.τ.λ. Nos signum interrogationis posuimus 1121 πρὸς V: δ' ἐς LPB σῇ Musgrave: σοι codd. 1122 δ' om. V 1123, 1124 Sic LP (λεύσων P): τί λεύσσω et γυναῖκα λεύσσω τὴν ἐμὴν VB λεύσω V) Interpuncta nos addidimus 1125 μ' ἐκ θεοῦ Buecheler ἐμπλήσσει P 1126 ἔστιν ἄλλη· Radermacher 1127 τόδ' ᾖ] τόδ' εἰσορῶ V γρ. τόδ' ᾖ V[1] 1130 τύχην] τύχῃ Reiske

Ηρ. πρόσειπ᾽. ἔχεις γὰρ πᾶν ὅσονπερ ἤθελες.
Αδ. ὦ φιλτάτης γυναικὸς ὄμμα καὶ δέμας,
ἔχω σ᾽ ἀέλπτως, οὔποτ᾽ ὄψεσθαι δοκῶν.
Ηρ. ἔχεις· φθόνος δὲ μὴ γένοιτό τις θεῶν.
Αδ. ὦ τοῦ μεγίστου Ζηνὸς εὐγενὲς τέκνον,
εὐδαιμονοίης, καί σ᾽ ὁ φιτύσας πατὴρ
σῴζοι· σὺ γὰρ δὴ τἄμ᾽ ἀνώρθωσας μόνος.
πῶς τήνδ᾽ ἔπεμψας νέρθεν ἐς φάος τόδε;
Ηρ. μάχην συνάψας δαιμόνων τῷ κυρίῳ.
Αδ. ποῦ τόνδε Θανάτῳ φῂς ἀγῶνα συμβαλεῖν;
Ηρ. τύμβον παρ᾽ αὐτὸν ἐκ λόχου μάρψας χεροῖν.
Αδ. τί γάρ ποθ᾽ ἥδ᾽ ἄναυδος ἕστηκεν γυνή;
Ηρ. οὔπω θέμις σοι τῆσδε προσφωνημάτων
κλύειν, πρὶν ἂν θεοῖσι τοῖσι νερτέροις
ἀφαγνίσηται καὶ τρίτον μόλῃ φάος.
ἀλλ᾽ εἴσαγ᾽ εἴσω τήνδε· καὶ δίκαιος ὢν
τὸ λοιπόν, Ἄδμητ᾽, εὐσέβει περὶ ξένους.
καὶ χαῖρ᾽· ἐγὼ δὲ τὸν προκείμενον πόνον
Σθενέλου τυράννῳ παιδὶ πορσυνῶ μολών.
Αδ. μεῖνον παρ᾽ ἡμῖν καὶ ξυνέστιος γενοῦ.
Ηρ. αὖθις τόδ᾽ ἔσται, νῦν δ᾽ ἐπείγεσθαί με δεῖ.
Αδ. ἀλλ᾽ εὐτυχοίης, νόστιμον δ᾽ ἔλθοις †δόμον.†
ἀστοῖς δὲ πάσῃ τ᾽ ἐννέπω τετραρχίᾳ,
χοροὺς ἐπ᾽ ἐσθλαῖς συμφοραῖσιν ἱστάναι
βωμούς τε κνισᾶν βουθύτοισι προστροπαῖς.
νῦν γὰρ μεθηρμόσμεσθα βελτίω βίον
τοῦ πρόσθεν· οὐ γὰρ εὐτυχῶν ἀρνήσομαι.

1132 *πάνθ᾽ ὅσαπερ* L P 1134 *οὔποθ᾽* V 1137 *φιτύσας* V : *φυτεύσας* L P B 1138 *σὺ γὰρ τἄμ᾽ ὤρθωσας* L P (*γὰρ δὴ τὰμά γ᾽ l*) 1140 *δαιμόνων* codd. et Σ *κυρίῳ* B O D et, ni fallor, Σ (sc. *ei qui proprius est*) : *κοιράνῳ* L P V 1141 *φῂς*] *ἔτλης* Prinz 1150 *τυράννῳ* V P L[1] : *τυράννου* L B 1153 *δόμον* L P *γρ.* B : *ὅδον* V *γρ.* B : *πόδα* B D : antiqua discrepantia codicum : *δρόμον* Wilamowitz : *πόρον* Headlam 1154 *πάσῃ τ᾽* B O D : *πᾶσι τ᾽* V L P 1155 *συμφοραῖς συνιστάναι* B O D 1156 *κνισᾶν* Haun. : *κνισσᾶν* codd. *προτροπαῖς* V P

Χο. πολλαὶ μορφαὶ τῶν δαιμονίων,
πολλὰ δ' ἀέλπτως κραίνουσι θεοί·
καὶ τὰ δοκηθέντ' οὐκ ἐτελέσθη,
τῶν δ' ἀδοκήτων πόρον ηὗρε θεός.
τοιόνδ' ἀπέβη τόδε πρᾶγμα.

1160 πολλά τ' Π 1161 δοκήσαντ Π 1163 τόδε] τόδε τὸ V
In fine τέλος εὐριπίδου ἀλκήστιδος V B P: εὐριπίδου ἄλκηστις L

COMMENTARY

1. Ἐξιὼν ἐκ τοῦ οἴκου τοῦ Ἀδμήτου προλογίζει ὁ Ἀπόλλων ῥητορικῶς, comments the Scholiast, making a fair deduction from the first speech: Apollo 'enters' (ἐξιέναι is, given the Greek stage-set, the normal word for the 'entry' of a player, cf. Ar. *Ran.* 946) and 'opens the play on a rhetorical note'—he begins, not with a bald ἥκω Διὸς παῖς, but with a (grammatically) floating apostrophe full of feeling, and it is not until 23 λείπω μελάθρων τῶνδε φιλτάτην στέγην that the implications of this address become clear: Dear house of Admetus, I must now depart from you. The intervening lines explain his affection for the house and his reason for leaving it, therewith furnishing the spectators with all the information they need at this stage. His name is not spoken till 30, but could be inferred without difficulty from the bow he carries (35) and from 'my father Zeus' and 'my son Asclepius'.

The same grammatical form of opening, a vocative of feeling deflected on to a relative, with no following 2nd pers. address (a sort of *vocativus pendens*) is found in *Andr.* Ἀσιάτιδος γῆς σχῆμα, Θηβαία πόλι, ὅθεν . . . , and *El.* ὦ γῆς παλαιὸν ἄργος, Ἰνάχου ῥοαί, ὅθεν . . . . Cf. *Bacch.* 521–2 and Dodds's n. The emotion gives as it were a natural start to the more frankly informative details that follow. **ἔτλην**: 'I brought myself to', cf. Monk's n. (at 275) on τολμᾶν, τλῆναι: 'est enim *sustinere* [Angl. *to endure*] non obstante vel periculo vel pudore vel superbia vel dolore animi vel misericordia.'

2. **θῆσσαν**, though in form apparently a substantive—θῆσσα from masc. θής like Κρῆσσα from Κρής—is used both here and *El.* 205 θῆσσαν ἑστίαν as an adjective; the substantival use is not attested earlier than Poseidippus (fr. 35K). **αἰνέσαι** is used of 'accepting' a situation, whether with approval or (as here and in 12, cf. *Hipp.* 37) with resignation.

3–4. Asclepius' offence was to have raised the dead to life, cf. Pind. *Pyth.* 3. 55 ff. Apollo not unnaturally suppresses the information here; the Chorus refer to it 123–9 with a sigh of regret for the dead Healer.

5. **οὗ**: Σ takes this 'gen. of cause' of an emotion as personal, like θυγατέρος θυμούμενος, *Or.* 751; it could equally well be neuter.

6. **κτείνω Κύκλωπας**: the oldest three earth-born Cyclopes, according to Hes. *Theog.* 139 ff. and fr. 112, Brontes, Steropes, and Arges, in later myth assistants of the master-smith Hephaestus. Σ, however, quotes Pherecydes as saying that it was their sons whom Apollo slew, a more exact requital.

7. ἄποιν': 'in requital for'. Eur. is rather fond of this use of an appositional substantive in either nom. or acc. case, cf. KG i. 284 f. The acc. *ἄποινα*, however, is by the fifth century well on the way to becoming a stereotyped substantive with dependent gen., having almost the force of a preposition, like *χάριν*, *δίκην*. Cf. *IT* 1459, A. *Pers.* 808, *Ag.* 1420, and *ἀμοιβάν*, *Or.* 843.

8. The simple acc. after a verb of motion, so common in Homer, occurs fairly often in the tragedians (cf. *Med.* 12, *ἀφίκετο χθόνα*); in quoting here δ' *ἐς αἶαν* Athenagoras (second century A.D.) may either have been misreading his copy or have found an old variant. **ἐβουφόρβουν**: *ἔνεμον* (i.e. pasture herds or flocks of any kind)· *ἀπὸ τοῦ διαφέροντος ζῴου, τοῦ βοός Σ*, who quotes *βουκολεῖν* used of horses *Il.* 20. 221, and Theocritus' *Βουκολικά* for a similar use of the particular term for the general.

9. ἐς τόδ' ἡμέρας: our earliest example of this curious idiom, which is found 3 or 4 more times in tragedy and reappears in late prose. It is clear from *Phoen.* 1085 and S. *OC* 1138 that the sense required is not 'to this day' but more narrowly, as it were 'to this hour'. LS quote it as an example of *ἡμέρα* used in the general sense of 'time', but S. *Aj.* 131 is not a parallel, and other instances are lacking. KG i. 279 explains it as 'to this hour of [this present] day', an unconvincing ellipse. Possibly 'day' should be regarded as a metaphor, like our colloquial 'at this time of day', 'so late in the day'.

For the timing of these antecedents to the story see Introd. p. xvii.

10. *ὁσιότης* is the piety of the man who fulfils the divine laws; it includes the observances of religion but also the protection of the weak and the suppliant, kindness, loyalty, hospitality, and a sense of obligation in matters where no legal code was applicable. It is hardly ever found as a divine attribute (see LS s.v. *ὅσιος*, II. 3), and in **ὅσιος ὢν** Apollo must be referring to his own human manifestation: the loyal hireling found a generous master.

11. θανεῖν: for the rarely used simple inf. after a verb of 'saving' cf. *Phoen.* 600 *αἵ σε σῴζουσιν θανεῖν.* Presumably the sense of 'save' is felt near enough to 'prevent' for it to exercise this right on occasion.

12–14. Eur. is not interested in the question why or when sentence of 'imminent death' was passed on Admetus; cf. Introd., pp. ix and xvii f. **δολώσας**: by making them drunk, as we learn from A. *Eum.* 723 ff., where the Furies reproach Apollo for his unedifying behaviour to the Elder Goddesses. **διαλλάξαντα**: 'if he gave in exchange.'

15. ἐλέγξας καὶ διεξελθὼν: 'having sounded all in turn'.

16–17. Nil mutandum. Suspicion has fallen upon 16 mainly because of *πάντας* in 15. It is claimed that either this must make *φίλους* = 'friends', so that we have the dubious (in Greek) form of copula A, B, and C in 'friends, father, and mother', or that if *φίλους* is in apposition to 'father and mother' it is absurd to say *πάντας* and then enumerate only two. Among various expedients the most commonly adopted are to read with Nauck ⟨*καὶ*⟩ *πατέρα γραῖάν θ' κτλ.* or with Dindorf to delete the line, though surely even in so short a summary Apollo must mention this vital point. In all forms of this widespread story the substitute has to come from the close circle of the family, and this is in fact the normal meaning of *φίλους*—certainly a sense of the word which *excluded* parents would be scarcely possible in Greek poetry. Those eligible in Admetus' case would in fact be three—father, mother, wife (the children, if they were already there, would not be asked). It is the magic number of the fairy story, and the third time works. All that has happened is that Eur. has phrased it in a characteristic Greek ellipse: having sounded all, A and B, he found only C who was willing. Of course *πάντας* at first *suggests* a larger number and makes Alcestis' sacrifice seem the more unique, but the three then enumerated, even if a minimum, do in fact make *πάντας* applicable.

17–18. The survival of **μηκέτ'** in the MSS. clearly shows Reiske's double emendation to be right. The sense 'no one who would' requires *ὅστις* (masc.); once the generalizing relative was misunderstood and *ἥτις* substituted, *θανών* would have to go too. The *μηδ' ἔτ'* of the Copenhagen MS. is a misleadingly simple attempt to get the syntax straight again. **κείνου** (not the reflexive) idiomatically from the point of view of the speaker or hearer; similar uses are common in prose.

19. ἐν χεροῖν. The omission of a possessive when the possessor does not occur in the sentence is so unusual that corruption or a lacuna has been suspected. Usener would read *ἣν νῦν . . . ψυχορραγοῦσαν,* and this may well be right, though a middle *βαστάζομαι* is not elsewhere attested. **βαστάζεται**: 'Suidas' says that *βαστάσαι οὐ τὸ ἆραι δηλοῖ παρὰ τοῖς Ἀττικοῖς ἀλλὰ τὸ ψηλαφῆσαι καὶ διασηκῶσαι καὶ διασκέψασθαι τῇ χειρὶ τὴν ὁλκήν* (cf. Fraenkel on A. *Ag.* 35, with whom I do not wholly agree). But as a matter of fact there does not appear to be any distinction between the uses of this word in Attic and in other poetry: it can mean 'lift', 'raise', as S. *Aj.* 827, S. *El.* 1470, and met. Pind. *Isth.* 3. 8; or 'hold', 'clasp', usually of something held off the ground, in mid-air as it were, like the hand of another infra 917, A. *Ag.* 35, the bow infra 40, S. *Phil.* 655, or the urn (the supposed ashes of Orestes) S. *El.* 1216, but here (*Alc.* 19) perhaps simply 'hold up' from falling, like A. *PV* 1019; or again, as 'Suidas' says, it can be 'hold to test the weight', hold a thing to see how it feels in the hand, as in *Od.* 21. 405, S. *Phil.* 657, or of the blind Oedipus *feeling* the body of his restored Antigone, *OC* 1105, and hence met. 'weigh' in the mind, 'consider', as *PV* 888, Ar. *Thesm.* 438.

20–21. See Introd., p. xvi ff. Pronouncements of life and of death are peculiarly apt to achieve solemnity by this kind of tautology, cf. 18, A. *Pers.* 299, *Il.* 1. 88.

22–23. So Artemis, Apollo's bright sister, abandons the dying Hippolytus: *καὶ χαῖρ'· ἐμοὶ γὰρ οὐ θέμις φθιτοὺς ὁρᾶν | οὐδ' ὄμμα χραίνειν θανασίμοισιν ἐκπνοαῖς Hipp.* 1437 f., where the Scholiast, quoting this passage, alone preserves the idiomatically right reading (which must have been in the archetype of our MSS.). The text of 538 shows a similar vacillation between gen. and acc.

24–26. Thanatos appears (*τόνδε*), a black-robed (843), winged (261) figure with a sword (74). There is no suggestion in the text of a supernatural manner of entrance. Since Heracles is to wrestle with and overthrow him, he is not represented as a majestic infernal Power but as an ogreish creature of popular mythology, like the Charon with whom he is later confused in the textual tradition (see the Dramatis Personae), snarling malignantly at Apollo, who treats him with a light disdain. 74 ff. even seems to suggest that his main function is to act as an officiating priest at the ceremony of death, *ἱερεὺς θανόντων*, dedicating the victim by the symbolic cutting of the lock of hair and haling him down to the underworld. But he is no mere subordinate demon; Apollo treats with him as with a sovereign, and Heracles' victory over him is a final decision. Elsewhere in the play, however, the more familiar underworld scene and figures are assumed, and once (see on 871) the two irreconcilable conceptions seem to hover in uncomfortable juxtaposition.

25. ἱερῆ. It is uncertain whether there is any difference, other than orthographical, between these occasional apparently Homeric accusatives in tragedy and the orthodox Attic *ἱερέ̮α*, &c., which were pronounced in verse with crasis.

26. συμμέτρως. The adverb is perhaps slightly preferable here to *σύμμετρος*. The nearest parallel in sense (= *εὐκαίρως*) is S. *Ant.* 387 *ποίᾳ σύμμετρος προὔβην τύχῃ*; where, however, the addition of the dat. makes a difference. P's divergence (which Méridier is mistaken in denying) may be due to deliberate conjecture, but is more probably a mere slip.

30–31. Nauck chose 31 for one of his many excisions, and the line is, as a matter of fact, omitted by P, probably by an oversight. *τιμὰς* as the object of *ἀδικεῖς* in the sense of 'trespass upon' is very dubious, whereas *ἀδικεῖς* used absolutely is idiomatic, cf. Ar. *Nub.* 25 (and S. *Ichn.* 178 *ἀδικεῖς ἀδικεῖς* suppl. Maas). The added part. gives the normal legal terminology, cf. Pl. *Ap.* 19b *Σωκράτης ἀδικεῖ . . . ζητῶν . . . καὶ . . . ποιῶν καὶ . . . διδάσκων.* Death is bringing a formal charge against Apollo: his guilt consists in 'limiting' for his own benefit and 'putting a stop to the prerogatives of the infernals'. *ἀφορίζομαι* is to 'stake a claim for oneself'; it is true that where this involves aggression against the territory of others one might expect the act. rather than the mid., cf. *Il.* 22. 489 ἄλλοι γάρ οἱ ἀπουρίσσουσιν ἀρούρας, but in the similar verb νοσφίζω the mid. can be used in act. sense, 'appropriate to oneself'.

30–34. Cf. on 12. G. Italie, 'De Euripide Aeschyli Imitatore' (*Mnem.* iv. 3. 3 (1950), 177 ff.), calls attention to the similarity of this scene, in general and in detail, to *Eum.* 179–234, where Apollo disputes with the Furies over the fate of Orestes.

34. Monk's σφήλαντα would avoid the double dat., but is not a necessary emendation. Possibly the question-mark should be postponed to the end of the sentence, making the whole of Death's remarks a series of nervous, angry questions.

36. The anticipatory **τόδ'** is perfectly in place (cf. *Hipp.* 466): this is *just what* she undertook to do.

The following dialogue, while leaving Death temporarily in possession of the field, enables Apollo to depart with honour and to give notice to the audience of the happy ending to be expected.

38. **θάρσει**: do not fear violence; my weapons are justice and reason. **δίκην** is a refutation of ἀδικεῖς.

41. **προσωφελεῖν**: sc. σύνηθες σοί (the bow was introduced to lead up to this). **καὶ . . . γε**: 'yes, and . . .', emphasizing the addition; so again 47. **ἐκδίκως**: Weber would read ἐνδίκως with V B, and it is true that such sarcasms are apt to be missed and the literal meaning substituted in our MSS. (cf. on 811). But the statement here would be so exactly in accord with Apollo's own claim that the irony would rather misfire. Earle may be right in suggesting that ἐνδίκως is due to a failure to realize that γὰρ ('yes, because . . .') in the next line is assenting to προσωφελεῖν alone, discarding ἐκδίκως.

47. νερτέρων or νερτέραν? The adjective is used *HF* 335 and fr. 450N², though even so the gen. would be preferable as *lectio difficilior*. It is highly probable that **νερτέραν**, in the source of P as in *l*, is due to conjecture. The preposition is 'pregnant': Death will carry her off 'beneath the earth' and 'into the land beneath the earth', the underworld, and **νερτέρων** 'of the nether beings' contributes this second meaning. Weber's 'gen. of aim' (which would require a verb of shooting) is inapplicable to **νερτέρων**, and in εἶμι τῶν κάτω 851 which he quotes as a parallel τῶν κάτω is simply possessive gen. with δόμους 852.

48. The same phrase recurs *Med.* 941 οὐκ οἶδ' ἂν εἰ πείσαιμι, πειρᾶσθαι δὲ χρή, and similar examples are found in prose (see KG i. 246). **οὐκ-οἶδα-εἰ** is treated simply as the equivalent of ἴσως οὐ rather than as a separate clause, so that if the following verb (as here the potential **πείσαιμι**) requires ἄν the particle is pushed forward as usual to an early place in the sentence **οὐκ οἶδ' ἂν εἰ** or **οὐκ ἂν οἶδ' εἰ**, regardless of the fact that it has thus strayed into a previous clause. It is something like the process by which δῆλον ὅτι becomes an inseparable combination δηλονότι instead of a separate clause.

49. V's emphatic **γε** is idiomatic: 'What, to kill my proper victim? Why, that's my office!'

50. 'No, to grant your intended victim (**τοῖς μέλλουσι** by a common idiom = *τῇ μελλούσῃ θανεῖν*) a respite from death'; cf. 527 *τέθνηχ' ὁ μέλλων*. Bursian's emendation *ἀμβαλεῖν* (for *ἀναβαλεῖν*, cf. on 526) is surely correct, and necessary. The metaphor *θάνατον ἐμβαλεῖν* would be curiously inappropriate; is death a sort of missile (cf. 4) or a halter (cf. 492)? But the chief difficulty with *ἐμβαλεῖν* is over *μέλλουσι*. This is usually explained in one of two ways: (1) 'the lingering'; so *Σ τοῖς γεγηρακόσι· βραδύνουσι γὰρ ἐν τῇ ζωῇ*, or (2) 'those ripe for death', i.e. the elderly, as being 'about to die' in any case. But in ordinary parlance Alcestis herself is *μέλλουσα θανεῖν* (cf. 527), and Death could justifiably reply that that is exactly what he *is* doing. If it be held that *μέλλουσι* could be spoken with some peculiar emphasis to convey unambiguously the meaning 'those who linger', the natural sense would be that Apollo is giving Death a positive hint to carry off Pheres or the mother instead. But this can hardly be brought in so allusively and then dropped altogether; 52, 54, and 56 make it clear that Apollo is in fact pleading that Alcestis be allowed to reach old age—i.e. what we want in 50 is a request for postponement. For the corruption cf. *Hec.* 1263 *ἐμβήσῃ* M A V O F for *ἀμβήσῃ*, and *Tro.* 1277.

51. **ἔχω** pregnantly: ah, *now* I understand.

52. **μόλοι**: the opt. is more tentative than the subj.

54. i.e. whether she dies old or young.

55–56. **γέρας**: the power and the glory; Apollo offers a rich funeral as an alternative bait.

57. **πρὸς τῶν ἐχόντων**: 'for the benefit of the rich', cf. *Supp.* 242, S. *Aj.* 157.

58. Jebb on S. *Phil.* 414 quotes this line as a parallel for the slightly redundant combination of *πῶς εἶπας* and *ἀλλ' ἦ* to introduce a surprised question, but here **πῶς εἶπας**; does not itself express surprise; it is a request for enlightenment: 'how so?', and is answered by Death in the next line.

59. There is confusion in the text here between three verbs: (1) *ὄνοιντ'* from *ὄνομαι* 'blame', which one scholiast does his best to defend; (2) *ὄναιντ'* from *ὀνίνημι* 'benefit', given by the corrector of L; (3) **ὠνοῖντ'** from *ὠνέομαι* 'buy', read by L and possibly intended by P B in *ὤνοιντ'*. Some edd. adopt (2), usually with the *οὗς* of V B, but surely (3) is the only version that answers Apollo's question: those with the means to do so would *purchase* length of days. This sense of course requires Hermann's *γηραιοί*. The scholiasts, who read *γηραιούς*, get bedevilled with the idea of 'buying old people' for somewhat obscure purposes; Murray gives the only possible interpretation with his 'sc. *τοὺς φίλους*'. Wealthy parents might of course want to buy it for their children, but it is doubtful whether the acc. is worth salving at the cost of this unnecessary complication. A similar corruption of nom. into acc. before inf. occurs in 37, where L P V all have *αὑτὴν*.

64 ff. Browning's stage-direction for this speech is 'more to himself than to Death'. Or more to the audience, perhaps. **παύσῃ** : it has been objected that forced cessation requires the passive, but the prophecy of the simple event is more menacing here. The verb is used absolutely, the sense being clear from the context. The conjecture *πείσῃ* is perhaps tempting, though not strictly compatible with *βίᾳ* in 69.

65–71. The anticipation of the plot in these lines has caused some offence, particularly because of the irrelevance of the details in 66–67. It seems to say either too much or too little; if it is intended for the audience's benefit, why not say 'Heracles' instead of this circumlocution which both names Eurystheus and anticipates unnecessarily what is made quite clear infra 476–506, while if Death is not to be put too much on his guard, why give details which must betray the hero's identity? Wheeler would delete 65–71; Hayley, perhaps rightly, suspects only 66–67. For other cases of interpolation in this play cf. on 818 ff., 1094 f.

66–67. The eighth labour of Heracles was to fetch away the man-eating mares of Diomedes king of Thrace. Though *ὄχημα* means literally 'vehicle', **ἵππειον ὄχημα** is the 'team', the four mares themselves (483 *τέτρωρον ἅρμα*); cf. *Rhes.* 621, where *ὄχημα πωλικόν* clearly refers to the horses alone. It is used on the analogy of *ἅρμα*, which can mean either chariot, chariot and horses, or horses alone; cf. *HF* 881 where *ἅρμασι* is distinct from *δίφροισι*, and *Andr.* 277 where *τρίπωλον ἅρμα δαιμόνων* refers to the three goddesses. *δίφρος* is never so used. This sort of 'metaphor' (in the Aristotelian sense) is characteristic of tragic style.

70. ἡ χάρις : the gratitude I should have owed you.

71. δράσεις θ' ὁμοίως ταῦτ' : i.e. you will give her up all the same. Strictly speaking, there is no *action* in the context for *δρᾶν* to pick up; it is really the passive 'you will have her taken from you by force'.

Exit Apollo; Death throws the next line after him as he goes. It would not do for his prophecy to make any impression on Death here.

72. ἂν repeated with both participle and verb: KG i. 246, nn. 7 and 8. The first *ἄν* is introduced as early as possible in order to show the contingency of the whole sentence; the second usually comes next the verb, but here the order gives rhetorical prominence to *πολλά* and *οὐδέν*.

73. δ' οὖν : dismissing irrelevancies—whatever you do or say.

74–76. Both Servius and Macrobius in their Virgiliana of the 4th century A.D. refer to this passage as an anticipation of *Aen.* 4. 698, where Virgil uses the theme for the death of Dido (cf. Introd., p. xii). The ritual as a preliminary part (κατάρχεσθαι) of the ordinary sacrificial ceremony is familiar enough from *Il.* 3. 271 onwards; the idea of applying it to the ceremony of death, with Thanatos as the officiating priest, cannot be traced farther back than Phrynichus' *Alcestis*, and may well have been invented by him for dramatic effect. Death's explanation 75–76 is circumstantial enough to suggest that the idea was not immediately familiar to his hearers.

Macrobius' citation[1] gives the correct subjunctive **κατάρξωμαι** found in P alone of the MSS. and implied in one of the scholiasts;[2] he misses the idiomatic possessive gen. with ἱερὸς, and in ὅτῳ (76) has probably misunderstood the construction. ἔγχος is used as 'weapon' in general (with reference to a ξίφος) several times in S. *Aj.* and *Ant.* **ἁγνίσῃ**: the omission of ἄν in this type of generalized relative clause is common in Homer and fairly frequent in the tragedians.

77–135. *Parodos.* Anxiety passes into hopelessness. Is Alcestis still alive? The house is silent, with none of the signs of recent death, and she cannot have been buried already, with so little stir. But no, there is no hope; this is the appointed day, and no oracle or altar can avail; it would need an Asclepius to restore her now, and Asclepius is dead.

The Chorus are so concerned for Alcestis that they approach on a series of anxious questions, without introducing themselves or explaining their presence further; even their age and sex only become clear later (212). Σ informs us that they are old men of Pherae, and (for this parodos) divided into two semi-choruses. The lines assigned to the one ἡμιχόριον or the other vary in the different MSS. (as often in such passages) and any arrangement of ours can only be tentative. The only places where the *sense* absolutely requires a division are in the anapaestic tail-pieces of strophe and antistrophe (v. infra); but it is probable that the hiatus between 78 and 79, instead of the synaphea to be expected in anapaests, is accounted for by change of speaker (as at S. *OC* 170), and if so, then 77–78 is likely to show a change also. 89 sounds rather like a rejoinder to the question before it, and the antistrophe could also split at the same place (101). The change registered in some MSS. after πύλας (90; the colon should probably end here, with εἰ transferred to the next line) raises the question of responsion; on the whole one would expect changes to correspond in *sung* lyric, and deviations in similar passages in other plays are nowhere quite certain. And since in 103 a change in the middle of a colon and in a correption (πίτνει οὐ[δὲ]) is inconceivable, both these are to be rejected. It is uncertain how far the incidence of *HM.* in our MSS. represents an original textual tradition and how far it is a deduction from other clear instances of question and answer. In 93, at

[1] See Introd., p. xxxvi. [2] Ibid., p. xxxiii.

least, the omission of *HM.* is probably due to the mistake by which OYTAN was interpreted as οὔτε ἄν instead of οὔτοι ἄν (v. app. crit.).

Hemichoric division is attested in only very few tragedies. (Cf. on this subject D. L. Page, *CQ* xxxi. 2. 94 (1937).) In S. *Aj.* 866–78 and in *Or.* 1258–60 = 1278–80 (trimeters) the Chorus has been assigned east and west areas of activity; in the final anapaests of A. *Sept.* it divides its allegiance. The anapaestic parodos of *Tro.* divides into two parts as first one (153) and then the other (176) semi-chorus emerges from the tent and engages in a κομμός with Hekabe. Probably something similar occurs *Rhes.* 531. All these except the last are spoken and recitative metres, and in some cases at least would be delivered by two coryphaei. *Sung* dialogue occurs, besides *Rhes.* 531, in Eur. *Supp.* 598 ff., and in the 'sight-seeing' parodos of *Ion*, and here it is natural to suppose two whole groups singing. *Alc.* 86–92 = 98–104 is of the same kind; for the anapaests it is impossible to say, and the same doubt occurs in the similar passages *Rhes.* 538–41, 557–61. In S. *Trach.* 863–70 and *HF* 815–21 (see Wilam. ad loc.) there appear to be not hemichoria but three single speakers, these counting as a quorum to represent alarm and indecision among a whole gathering.

This parodos contains introductory anapaests (77–85), strophe and antistrophe α′ (86–92 = 98–104), each followed by anapaestic dialogue (93–97, 105–11), strophe and antistrophe β′ (112–31), and (perhaps) a shorter anapaestic finale (132–5). Elsewhere when a parodos opens with anapaests these are regular dimeter 'systems', and there is little reason to doubt that 77–85, except for the hiatus in 78 referred to above, conformed to this regularity. 81–82 therefore, which appear in the MSS. as

βασίλειαν πεν - | θεῖν χρὴ ἢ ζῶσ'
ἔτι φῶς τόδε λεύσ - | σει Πελίου παῖς,

must be corrupt. Murray's βασίλεᾰν (cf. βασίλη, on the authority of Hesychius, in Soph. *Iphigeneia*, fr. 310P) brings the diaeresis to the right place in 81, but the form of the second metron – – – ⏑ ⏑ is very dubious. Perhaps the simplest of the emendations proposed is to transfer χρὴ (which in any case produces a hiatus where it is) to the beginning of 81, and with the Aldine to omit τόδε in 82, since the insertion of words to expand a paroemiac into a full dimeter is a common form of corruption.

79. ἀλλ': 'moreover'; what Denniston, *GP* 22, calls 'corrective or progressive ἀλλά, . . . sometimes reinforced by καί or οὐδέ'.

83–85. Alcestis' claim to ἀριστεία among wives is at the centre of the story, and is emphasized repeatedly, by the Chorus, by Admetus, by the household, and (to gain her end) by Alcestis herself.

86 ff. The signs from which a visitor could deduce death in the house are here given as the sound within of women's wailing and beating [of the breast?] with their hands, and, outside, the presence of a servant by the gate (presumably to give information), a bowl of water for the departing guests to besprinkle and purify themselves, and shorn locks (101) either lying on the threshold or affixed to the gatepost. Cutting the hair in token of mourning is a gesture familiar enough (cf. 215), but the next of kin usually did this over the corpse itself (or over the grave if the mourner had come too late for the funeral); this passage is our only evidence for the locks left at the outer gate, and it is not clear whether they were let fall there by the entering mourners or ceremonially affixed as a visible sign of death within. The **δὴ** (102) which indicates a *well-known* custom refers only to the actual cutting (**πίτνει**).

88. ὡς πεπραγμένων: absolute, 'as if all were over'. So *φθιμένης* in 93.

89. οὐ μὰν οὐδέ: 'why no, nor is there . . .'. The jingle **ἀμφιπόλων . . . ἀμφὶ πύλας**, since it has no echo in the sense, is perhaps simply accidental.

90. στατίζεται: passive like *ἵσταμαι*, in this form a *ἅπαξ λεγόμενον* in tragedy. *στατίζουσι* intrans. is used of *δμωαί El.* 316, and trans. *ποῦ δὲ χρὴ πόδα στατίζειν* in a new fragment of S. *Inachus*.

91. μετακύμιος ἄτας: an obscure phrase of which the general sense must be, as *Σ* says, *βοηθὸς παυστικός*. Hesychius and the scholiasts offer various explanations, which reduce themselves in the main to two: the lull *between* two waves, and the calm *after* a storm. Unfortunately, in the only other passage where the word occurs, in the neo-Pythagorean Numenius ap. Euseb. *PE* 11. 22. 1 *ναῦν ἁλιάδα . . . μετακυμίοις* (v. l. *-αις*) *ἐχομένην*, both the form and the meaning are uncertain. If such words as *μεταίχμιος, μεταμάζιος* can be taken as analogies, the sense *μεταξὺ δύο κυμάτων* might seem the more likely, and A. *Sept.* 758–63 would support this; but even so the form (from *κῦμα, -ατος*) is a strange one.

Thus far the Chorus, or semi-choruses, have sung in a series of iambics (with choriambic anaclasis 88) and prosodiac-enoplians:

⏑–⏑–⏑–⏑–   iamb. dim.
––⏑–⏑–⏑–   ,,
–⏑⏑–⏑–⏑–   aeolo-chor. octosyll. **dss**[1]
–––⏑⏑–⏑⏑–   **s̄̆ds**
⏑–⏑⏑–⏑⏑–   ⏑**dd**
––⏑⏑–⏑⏑––   –**dd**– (paroem.)
–––⏑––   **s̄s**–

They now turn to anapaestic dialogue, and the question at once arises:

[1] For this type of notation see my article 'The Metrical Units of Greek Lyric Verse', *CQ* xliv (1950) and N.S. i (1951), esp. Pt. II, p. 21.

should 93 ff. be accounted part of the strophe, and fitted into strict responsion with 105 ff.? As it stands (v. app. crit.) the text of 93–97 in V B L is unexceptionable in sense, and any addition between 96 and 97 would be quite otiose; metrically, the dubious points are the absence of metron-diaeresis in 94 *οὐ γὰρ δὴ φροῦ- | δός γ' ἐξ οἴκων* (but as these are not regular 'systems' this might be an early example of the heavy spondaic line in melic anapaests—cf. *IT* 140—which frequently ignored such diaeresis), and, more serious, a catalectic monometer, *νέκυς ἤδη* ⏑ ⏑ – – coming after a complete dimeter instead of (as 106) after a paroemiac, where it echoes the closing rhythm. Better than such a dubious anomaly would be the omission of these two words as a gloss; so Monk and older edd. In any case, I cannot feel any confidence in Kirchhoff's solution, although it appears to be now universally accepted. The Chorus divide into a more hopeful and a more pessimistic group, but they are all feeling puzzled and uncertain, and the sudden, unmotived assertion 'A corpse already!' seems to me quite impossibly abrupt, grammatically as well as emotionally. They are trying to account for the *silence*; if she were dead, there would be the sounds of mourning, since (the *γὰρ* is essential) it cannot be the silence of a deserted house, with the family absent at the funeral already; Admetus would never have buried his wife unattended (**ἔρημον τάφον**, 'a funeral without mourners').

A further difficulty is the sense of **πόθεν; οὐκ αὐχῶ.** *Σ* paraphrases *πόθεν οἶδας ὅτι οὐκ ἐξηνέχθη; οὐ γὰρ ἐγὼ αὐχῶ ἤτοι θαρρῶ* ('How do you know? *I* feel no such confidence'). All edd. accept this, and it may be right, but I can find no sort of parallel for this sense either of *πόθεν* or of *οὐκ αὐχῶ*. The normal idiomatic use of *πόθεν* after a negative statement, whether by the same speaker or another, is to underline the impossibility—'of course not; how could it?'—cf. 781. I have wondered whether this line could be continued to the same semichorus: 'She is not being buried already. How could she be? *I am sure she is not*' (cf. *Tro.* 770 *οὐ γάρ ποτ' αὐχῶ Ζῆνά γ' ἐκφῦσαί σ' ἐγώ*), while the other asks dubiously 'What makes you so confident?'

—οὔ τἂν φθιμένης γ' ἐσιώπων,
οὐ γὰρ δὴ φροῦδός γ' ἐξ οἴκων.
πόθεν; οὐκ αὐχῶ.
—τί σε θαρσύνει;
—πῶς ἂν ἔρημον τάφον Ἄδμητος
κεδνῆς ἂν ἔπραξε γυναικός;

For the lack of responsion with 105 ff. cf. the similar case of anapaests among lyric *Rhes.* 538–41, 557–61, where also changes of speaker cannot possibly be made to correspond.

100. πύλαις: unpleasantly redundant after *πυλῶν* 98. Maas suggests *ταφαῖς*.

101. ἐπὶ προθύροις: one of the rare instances in drama of the lengthening of a short final vowel before mute and liquid; Soph. and Eur. provide a special, though still small, class of instances in 'proclitic' words such as prepositions.

102. ἅ. Metrical considerations apart, one would certainly take this as = ᾗ, but since in the strophe the final syllable of *σταλάζεται* must suffer correption before the following vowel, ἃ must be neut. plur. This would be quite easy if it were possible to take **πίτνει** with *Σ* as = *συμβαίνει, εἴθισται,* 'befall', 'happen', but such a sense of *πίτνει* used absolutely, without some subject such as *ξυμφορά* or anything in the context to suggest the fall of the dice, would be extremely harsh; it must be used here of the literal falling of the cut hair. The collective idea in *χαίτα* may imply an antecedent like *τριχώματα* or *τομαῖα.*

103. νεολαία: normally a collective noun = *iuventus.* Did the feminine form suggest to Eur. its use as a poetic variant of *νέα*? There seems little point in emphasizing the 'youth' of the mourning women anyway (*Σ* suggests that their flesh would produce a more vigorous noise when slapped). Possibly the *ουδενεολαια* of the MSS. covers some deeper corruption than can be removed by the Aldine's deletion of **δε.**

108. Not, as Méridier, 'heart' and 'reason'; the two are simply cumulative.

109 ff. When the good are dying the loyal must mourn. *διακναίομαι* is a favourite word of the tragedians in anapaests. Lit. 'be grated to bits', it seems to be used simply of destruction of any kind, not necessarily a gradual 'wearing away', cf. *Med.* 164, *Hcld.* 296, A. *Ag.* 65.

112 ff. Neither oracles nor burnt offerings can avail now, not even the most distant oracles, only sought on grand occasions or in desperate need—those of Apollo in Patara or of Zeus Ammon (Amen-Ra) at the oasis of Siwa. *στέλλειν ναυκληρίαν,* 'make a voyage', is probably intrans. + internal acc. like *στέλλειν κέλευθον,* though in *Hel.* 1519 *ναυκ.* seems to be a mere variant of *ναῦς.*

114. The *Λυκίας* of all MSS. has been defended either (*a*) as fem. sing. of the noun by assimilation to the construction of *ὅποι αἴας,* or (*b*) as acc. plur. of the adjective with *ἕδρας* supplied out of the next phrase; either is just possible, but **Λυκίαν** is more natural, and very easily corrupted. For **ἢ . . . εἴτ'** cf. S. *Aj.* 176–8, and for **ἐπὶ** with only the second of the alternatives Monk quotes among other parallels *Phoen.* 284 [*πέμπειν με*] *μαντεῖα σεμνὰ Λοξίου τ' ἐπ' ἐσχάρας.*

115–16. Various expedients have been tried to bring this unmetrical line into responsion with 125–6, e.g. by reading *Ἀμμωνίδας ἕδρας* here (cf. *El.* 734 *ξηραί τ' Ἀμμωνίδες ἕδραι*—the forms of patronymic fem. *-ίδος* and *-ιάδος* are often confused in our MSS. cf. *HF* 785, S. *OT* 1108) and accommodating the antistrophe to either – – ⏑ ⏑ ⏑ – (dochmiac) or – – ⏑ ⏑ – – (reizianum). But since the antistrophe resists alteration and looks blameless, Nauck's *εἶτ' ἐφ' ἕδρας ἀνύδρους* | *Ἀμμωνιάδας* is the most satisfactory solution, *τὰς* being in any case unwanted. Strophe and antistrophe thus acquire an effective assonance.

118. μόρος ἀπότομος sounds at first like a variation on *αἰπὺς ὄλεθρος*, but with **πλάθει** the metaphor appears to have faded into something like 'grim', 'relentless', as in 981 (where see note) the *ἀπότομον λῆμα* of *Ἀνάγκη*. Contrast Soph.'s *ἀπότομον ὤρουσεν εἰς ἀνάγκαν* *OT* 877.

119–21. As it stands this would have to mean that the Chorus at the altars know of no priest to whom they could turn for help. The double *ἐπί* with two different cases is harsh, and though *μηλοθύτης* should mean literally 'sheep-sacrificer' is it likely to be so used in lyric diction? The only other instances of the word are both adjectival, dropping, as often with such words in *-της*, the notion of a personal agent: *IT* 1116 *βωμοὺς μηλοθύτας* and Bacchyl. 8. 17 Sn. *Πυθῶνά τε μηλοθύταν*. It is simplest to read *θεῶν δ' ἔτ'* (Bursian) *ἐσχάραν* (Reiske); *ἐπί* for *ἔτι* occurs again 130 in B O D, and *πορευθῶ ἐπί* is more natural with *μηλοθύταν ἐσχάραν* 'altar of sacrifice' than with 'priest'.

122. *Σ* indicates the slight anacoluthon by explaining *ἀντὶ τοῦ· εἶχεν αὐτὴν ἂν ζωοποιῆσαι*, 'only he could have brought her to life again'. **μόνος** is thrown forward for emphasis, the *ἂν* of the apodosis, as so often, hastens to assert itself as early as possible, and then the apodosis is after all given a different subject, leaving *μόνος* stranded outside the protasis to which it now has to belong.

125. ἦλθεν. The Chorus have so far despaired that they speak as if Alcestis were known to be already dead and in Hades.

127–9. 'For he used to raise the dead, *until* the Zeus-hurled bolt (lit. 'smiter') of thunder-fire slew him.'

The metre of this pair of stanzas contains, like the first pair, some ambiguous cola; it is impossible to say whether the opening of 114 = 124 and 117 = 127 conceals a contraction or not, e.g. *στείλας ἢ Λυκίαν* – – – ⏑ ⏑ – might be either a contracted form of the following line – ⏑ ⏑ – ⏑ ⏑ – or a choriambic 'dodrans' with opening 'drag' (i.e. a lengthened form of – ⏑ – ⏑ ⏑ –); there is the same uncertainty in *χαίτα* 101 and *δουπεῖ* 104. 116 *Ἀμμωνιάδας* is best explained as a choriambic pentasyllable, the reverse of an adonean – ⏑ ⏑ – –. 120 = 130 – ⏑ ⏑ ⏑ ⏑ ⏑ ⏑ *might* be a resolved hypodochmiac – ⏑ – ⏑ –, but would fit the context better if we could suppose that Eur. had invented a rare resolution of the above – – ⏑ ⏑ – (116) in the form – ⏑⏑ ⏑ ⏑ ⏑⏑.

⏒ – ⏑ – – ⏑ – }
– ⏑ – ⏑ – – } iamb.
– – – ⏑ ⏑ – } dodrans or contracted hemiepes
– ⏑ ⏑ – ⏑ ⏑ – } hemiepes.

– – ∪ ∪ – aeolo-chor. pentasyll.
– – – ∪ ∪ – – pherecratean or contracted hem. pendant.
⏓ – ∪ – ∪ ∪ ∪ ∪ – } iambic.
– – ∪ – ∪ – ∪ –
– ∪͡∪ ∪ ∪ ∪͡∪ } aeolo-chor. resolved dodecasyll.
– ∪ ∪ – ∪ – –

132–5. These anapaests have been suspected and indeed excised on grounds of diction, metre, and relevance to their context. Neither of the first two counts is decisive: *βασιλεῦσιν* = Admetus, cf. *δεσπόταισι* 138 and *Ion* 751, and for *πλήρεις* 'in full measure' cf. Eur. fr. 912N² *θυσίαν . . . πλήρη προχυταίαν.* Metrically it is possible to defend *βασιλεῦσιν* (in a line to itself) as a monom. cat. ∪ ∪ – – like *τί τόδ' αὐδᾷς* 106 between two paroemiacs, though admittedly this unusual colarion appears more easily as an interjection by a different speaker than in a continuous sentence. The most valid objection, however, is that this theme was dealt with in strophe *β'*, and its re-emergence here after the antistrophe is unwelcome. Wilamowitz believes these lines to have been inserted as a weak substitute for 112–31 when Asclepius became recognized as a god. I do not feel convinced that they are spurious.

136–7. This punctuation (comma rather than semicolon after *δακρ.*), making a single compound sentence with asyndeton, is probably right. *ἀλλά* has the effect of *ἀλλὰ . . γάρ.* 'But ([for] here comes a servant) I shall soon hear—what?' The inverse of this is found in A. *Ag.* 489–93 'We shall soon know . . . [for] I see a herald'.

138–9. μὲν . . . δὲ. Grief is excusable but we should like some information. **δεσπόταισι** plur. for *δέσποινα* as *Ion* 751. That 138–40 are spoken to (not merely apropos of) the entering *θεράπαινα* becomes clear only with her reply 141. The omission of any vocative in addressing a person newly arriving upon the scene is a singular breach of good stage manners—contrast, for instance, A. *Cho.* 730–2.

143. προνωπής. *Σ* takes this as a metaphor *προπεπτωκυῖα, προνενευκυῖα εἰς θάνατον*, but such a use is not possible without *εἰς* or *ἐπί*, cf. S. *Trach.* 976 *προπετής* with Jebb's note. It means 'drooping', of one who no longer has the strength to keep upright, as again 186.

144. A compliment to Admetus as well as Alcestis. The servant's allegiance is less divided; he will not fully appreciate her until he has lost her.

146. For **μὲν** in this sort of question cf. Denniston *GP* 366. (I suppose there really is no hope? I want to be quite clear about that first.) **σῴζεσθαι** V B: both pres. and aor. are common after the substantival *ἐλπίς ἐστι*, but the former is correct here because the meaning is 'keep her life in being'.

148. ἐπ' αὐτῇ: 'over her'. The *ἐπ' αὐτοῖς* of L P is unintelligible, but *Σ* ἐπὶ τοῖς εἱμαρμένοις τὰ προσήκοντα ὁ ἀνὴρ ποιεῖ. ἢ ἐπ' αὐτῇ τῇ Ἀλκηστίδι shows that both versions are old. The εἱμαρμένοις is evidently an attempt to find an allusion in αὐτοῖς to πεπρωμένη ἡμέρα.

153. An ambiguous and difficult line, variously interpreted or emended. Does τί χρὴ γενέσθαι; = ποία τις ἂν γένοιτο; 'What must she be like?' Is ὑπερβεβλημένην trans. 'surpassing her', or like ὑπερβάλλουσαν intrans. = *praestantissima* (cf. Pl. *Rep.* 558b εἰ μή τις ὑπερβεβλημένην φύσιν ἔχοι)? Neither 'What must the woman be who surpasses her?' nor 'How should there be any woman to surpass *her*?' (better with τήνδ' for τὴν) nor 'What [if not this] should the woman of rare excellence be?' seems really to translate τί χρὴ γενέσθαι; Lenting would read τίς δ' ἐναντιώσεται τὸ μὴ οὐ γενέσθαι τήνδ' ὑπ. γυν.; 'who will deny her to be a woman of surpassing excellence?', but the corruption would not be easy to account for. Perhaps we should simply obelize.

154. ἐνδείξαιτο: 'give proof of', with προτιμῶσα.

158. As Alcestis is forewarned of death (we are not told how) she administers to herself the necessary purifications and adornments.

159. λευκὸν: *not* proleptic, but simply the conventional epithet for women's flesh, the white-painted flesh on black-figure pots.

160. Cedar-wood protected clothes from damp and moth, cf. *Il.* 24. 191; in 365 coffins are made from it. **δόμων** is a somewhat unexpected word here. In *El.* 870 and S. *Trach.* 578 which Weber quotes as parallels the meaning is simply the ordinary one of 'house', not of the particular store-place in which the objects were kept. In Hes. *Op.* 96, also quoted by edd., Hope is left behind ἐν ἀρρήκτοισι δόμοισι, i.e. in the πίθος, Pandora's box or jar, but the word is used not as an appropriate synonym for πίθος but as a metaphor for the place inhabited by the living creature Hope. δοκῶν (from δοκή found in Hesych.) or δοχῶν (from δοχή, cf. *El.* 828 δοχαὶ χολῆς the gall-bladder) 'receptacle' have been conjectured. But Eur. probably has in mind Priam's 'high-roofed chamber of cedar-wood' (*Il.* 24. 191–2) from which he fetched the robes for Hector's ransom: αὐτὸς δ' ἐς θάλαμον κατεβήσετο κηώεντα | κέδρινον, ὑψόροφον, ὃς γλήνεα πολλὰ κεχάνδει. Alcestis fetches her garments from inner chambers or closets; she does not simply take them out of chests.

162. Ἑστίας or ἑστίας? In any case Hestia is the goddess addressed as δέσποινα in the next line, and not Hecate or Artemis as some would have it. No Greek prayer could be left as vague as that. But of course no statue is implied; there was just the altar of Hestia.

165. ὀρφανεύω = look after a fatherless or motherless child; so in the pass. 535, cf. κορευθήσῃ 313. The middle ὀρφανεύομαι *Hipp.* 847, *Supp.* 1133 is 'to be an orphan'.

167. αὐτῶν ἡ τεκοῦσ'. Participles expressing relationship, such as τεκών, προσήκων, occasionally assume enough substantival force to take a dependent gen.

172. ἀποσχίζουσα: she breaks off shoots for each altar. **μυρσίνης**: for the use of myrtle in ceremonial of the tomb cf. *El.* 324, 512. The mystae appear crowned with it Ar. *Ran.* 330 because it was sacred to Demeter (ap. *Σ* S. *OC* 681), and it was also favoured for festive celebration (cf. 759). In fact it was used chiefly for the decorative effect of its pretty, fragrant leaves.

173. ἄκλαυτος: L preserves the less familiar form. In most verbals where the alternative without -*σ* exists this is confined to poetry, like *κτιτός, καυτός, γνωτός*. When a verbal is formed from a trans. verb it can sometimes be used in the act. as well as the pass. sense—so here 'unweeping'.

175. Zeugma: *ἐς* = 'into' and 'on to'.

176. δὴ: then indeed she *did* fall to weeping.

178. παρθένεια κορεύματα (somewhat redundantly) = 'maidenhood'. Nauck deletes this line, but *παρθένεια* needs a substantive, and the unique *κορεύματα*, supported by *κορευθήσῃ* 313, is its own defence. For the whole phrase Méridier aptly compares *Tro.* 501, Pind. *Isth.* 8. 49. For **τοῦδ'** with very weak deictic force, in fact almost as the antecedent of *οὗ*, cf. KG i. 647–8. The one real stumbling-block is the use of *πέρι* for *ὕπερ*, which is absolutely unparalleled in tragedy; the other cases quoted by edd., such as the Homeric *ἀμύνεσθαι περὶ πάτρης*, are irrelevant, since they all contain expressions of fighting or competing, with the idea of a prize set in the midst. Wilamowitz is probably right in substituting *πάρος* for *πέρι*, quoting *Hcld.* 536 *ἀδελφῶν ἢ πάρος θέλει θανεῖν*.

179–80. οὐ γὰρ ἐχθαίρω σε explains the friendly *χαῖρε*. The next words are difficult. Some take them as 'you have lost me only' (not Admetus), but was it usual to lose both partners together? *ἀπώλεσας* is surely more naturally taken as 'you have brought me death', explained by the next clause. Blomfield's *μόνον* (with *δέ με* as codd.) would give a more obvious sense: 'you and you only . . .', but probably *μόνην* is all right; one might paraphrase more fully: *ἀπώλεσας δ' ἐμὲ μόνην· μόνη γὰρ προδοῦναί σ' ὀκνοῦσα κτλ.* Alcestis' fate is unique among women. *ἄλλη τις* is simply 'some other', not 'a different sort of', as Weber takes it.

182. This line, calculated indeed to linger in the memory, was parodied thirteen years later in one of the most devilish of Aristophanean parodies (*Eq.* 1252).

184. For the tendency of our MSS. to extend the (epic) licence of omitted augment beyond the limited number of places where it genuinely occurs cf. Page on *Med.* 1141, Bergson, 'The Omitted Augment in Gk. Trag.', *Eranos* li (1953). Since *δεύετο* here is prosodically impossible we can justifiably remove *δάκρυσε* 176 and *κύνει* 183.

186. στείχει προνωπὴς of her drooping, stumbling gait, cf. on 143. **ἐκπεσοῦσα**: 'tearing herself away from.'

187. θάλαμον codd., perhaps rightly, as acc. after ἐπεστράφη 'turned back into the room', cf. *Ion* 352.

195. Cf. (without the zeugma) 942.

197. τε . . . δέ are of course perfectly possible co-ordinates, though P emends δέ to τε. But τ' ἄν is a common mistake for τἄν (= τοι ἄν, cf. 93), and the latter should certainly stand here. The sense wanted is not 'there is evil either way' but 'mark my words: he is little better off for having escaped death'. The Servant ends with a bit of personal wisdom.

198. A surprising number of edd. accept Nauck's ugly οὔποθ' οὗ, mistakenly supposing that the sense meant is the banal 'such as he will never forget' (and rightly objecting to the inversion ποτ' οὐ for οὔποτε). ποτε, as Murray's note indicates, conveys 'the time will come when he remembers it all too well', οὐ λελήσεται being a litotes.

199. **ἦ που**: 'Admetus is grieved, no doubt?'

204. *Σ* τὴν ἰσχὺν τῆς χειρὸς (= *her* arms) παραλελυμένη, apparently taking βάρος as internal acc. after the pass. παρειμένη. But **χειρὸς ἄθλιον βάρος** would more naturally mean that she was a 'pathetic burden' in *his* arms, cf. ἄθλιον βάρος again *Bacch.* 1216. It is perhaps not necessary to assume a lacuna here if with Hayley we take καίπερ σμικρόν as parenthetic, construing ὅμως δὲ with ἐμπνέουσ' ἔτι instead of with βούλεται: 'But fainting, a pathetic burden in his arms, yet breathing still (though but faintly), she desires . . . .'

207–8. are the same as *Hec.* 411–12, only with ὄψεται for ὄψομαι. The construction here, ὡς with a finite verb after βούλεται with the same subject, is clumsy, and the repetition πρὸς αὐγὰς ἡλίου . . . ἀκτῖνα κύκλον θ' ἡλίου intolerable. Murray retains the first line, which would then have attracted the other. But the order becomes a little artifical with this addition, and the origin of these repetitions from play to play seems to have been the habit of writing parallel passages in the margin which then get incorporated in the text with a little perfunctory adjustment.

209–12. It is making too much of these lines to see in them an indication of Admetus' unpopularity with his disaffected subjects. Rather do they serve to characterize the Chorus.

213–37. A short ode, in matter and manner unlike a regular stasimon, in preparation for the entry of the king and queen. The singing of Alcestis then prolongs the lyric section. There are again some signs of division of parts; 215 and 218, though not exactly question and answer, belong most naturally to different speakers. The antistrophe could divide at the same place, though otherwise there is nothing in the words to suggest change of speaker. 220–1 and 232–3 might conceivably be spoken by the coryphaeus; the trimeter has a natural spoken rhythm. We are left making guesses; the whole might be sung by alternating semi-choruses, or the strophe might begin with three single voices to express general indecision, like S. *Trach.* 836 ff., *HF* 815 ff. (v. supra, p. 57), and pass at 220 into full chorus, while the antistrophe remained undivided except for 232–3 spoken by the coryphaeus. The strophe is a mixture of prayer and doubt (reading ἔξεισί τις 215); the antistrophe laments. Each contains five metrical 'major periods', clearly marked in conjunction with the rhetorical sense.

213–14. (1) O Zeus, is there no way out?

⏑ – – ⏑ – – ⏑ – ⏑ – doch. + hypodoch.
⏒ – ⏑ – ⏑ – ⏑ – } iamb. dim. + sync. dim.
– ⏑ – ⏒ – ⏑ –

The first line of the antistrophe is defective, though a series of exclamations culled from the varying MSS. *could* be made to yield a corresponding metre, e.g. παπαῖ ὤ· παπαῖ φεῦ· ἰὼ ἰώ. The text of 213 in V and *Σ*, possibly implied also in L P, gives a triple question τίς; πῶς; πᾷ; the last two of which are not necessarily tautologous, cf. Pl. *Legg.* 686b πῶς οὖν καὶ πῇ; In default of responsion certainty is unattainable, but metrically doch. + hypodoch. has a parallel in 393 and *Hipp.* 1380 and answers to 218 (double hypodoch.) below, whereas a double bacchiac + hypodoch. ⏑ – – ⏑ – – – ⏑ – ⏑ – is of more doubtful validity. **πόρος κακῶν**: 'way out of our troubles', like μηχανὰν κακῶν 221.

215–17. (2) Will someone be coming out to announce her death, or shall I take it for granted and assume mourning straightway (ἤδη)?

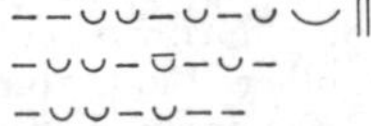

The metre is aeolo-choriambic, in recessive lengths: enneasyllabic, (cf. S. *Aj.* 399), octosyllabic, heptasyllabic (aristophanean). The Oxford text accommodates the strophe to the antistrophe by adopting Wilamowitz's suggestion of ἒ ἕ (i.e. αἰαῖ) corrupted to ἐξ-. The exclamation is then in both stanzas *extra metrum*, so that we are left with an octosyllabic colon like the following line, only with hiatus and pause. Metrically this is easy, but the strophe does not want lamentation at this point, and *does* want ἔξεισι rather than the simple verb. The alternative is to bring the antistrophe into line, and this is usually done by adopting Hermann's ἆρ' in place of αἰαῖ, making a rhetorical question of 228–30. But this rhetorical ἆρα (= *nonne*) is only used in iambic contexts, for pushing home a conclusion at the end of an argument: 'there! have I proved my point, that . . .?' cf. 341, 771, *et al. saep.*, and is out of place in lyric diction. Responsion might possibly be saved by reading ἒ ἕ for αἰαῖ in 228, and assuming that Eur. has treated the initial syllable as resolvable. ἒ ἕ is a prosodic chameleon, but can apparently be ⏑⏑; at least, that is the easiest assumption in *Supp.* 85, and in *Phoen.* 127 ἓ ἓ ὡς γαῦρος ὡς | φοβερὸς ὡς ἰδεῖν, where it would constitute the resolved initial syllable of the first dochmiac ⏑⏑––⏑–.

218–19. (3) There is really no doubt about the issue (**δῆλα** for δῆλον, cf. ἀδύνατά μοι *HF* 1058), but the gods are powerful; let us pray all the same.

–⏑–⏑– –⏑–⏑–   2 hypodoch.
⏑–⏑–⏒–⏑–   } iamb. dim. + aristophanean
–⏑⏑–⏑––   }

220–1. (4) Help him, Apollo. Iambic monom., trim. If 220 and 233 are not *extra metrum*, Παϊάν can be scanned with correption of the diphthong, as occasionally γέραϊος.

222–5. (5) Avert death as you did before.

⏑–⏑–⏑–⏑–⏑–– iamb. trim. cat.
––⏑––⏑–   } sync. iamb. dim. + enoplian[1] (blunt)
⏑⏑–⏑⏑–⏑–   }
⏑⏑–⏑⏑–⏑––   enoplian (pendant)

(The colometry of this section is uncertain.) The antistrophe appears to be sound, and 223 must be adapted to it. Headlam's σοῦ 'πηῦρε tries to account for the corruption palaeographically, but the obelized words (which *Σ* accepts) sound like part of an explanatory gloss, and if so they may be nothing like the original; so Dindorf, for instance, παρῆσθα, καὶ νῦν.

226–7. ἔπραξας intrans. 'you have fared', with **οἷα** internal acc.: 'what [ill-]fortune is yours'. Monk's στερεὶς for the unmetrical στερηθεὶς is inevitable.

229–30. πλέον ἢ . . . πελάσσαι (the question-mark should be deleted): 'more than hanging', i.e. more than enough to make him hang himself. Since one can say ἀγχόνη ταῦτα (cf. Ar. *Ach.* 125), what is yet worse becomes κρείσσον' ἀγχόνης (S. *OT* 1374) or πλέον ἢ and inf. in this circumlocution. βρόχος is any sort of running noose; οὐράνιος βρόχος makes it into a 'noose on high' in which one can hang oneself. The adjective is simply a conventional lyric exaggeration, as in οὐράνιον πήδημα *El.* 860.

232. The metrical problem here (in ἐν) is simple, though emendation is more difficult. A final *brevis in longo* (as here at the end of the iambic dimeter) is possible only if there is 'pause' (in the technical sense) before the following line. Pause does sometimes occur in trimeters between a preposition and its noun where an attribute precedes the preposition, and in Sophocles (*OT* 555, *Phil.* 626) even without such attribute (cf. Fraenkel, A. *Ag.* p. 587 and n.). But in

[1] I use 'enoplian' of cola in mixed double-short and single-short, in rising metre.

lyric this phenomenon is extremely rare; the only sort of parallel I can find is S. *Phil.* 184 *στικτῶν ἢ λασίων μέτᾰ | θηρῶν*, with a glyconic of the form – – – ⏑ ⏑ – ⏑ ⏑̆ ||, but here again the preceding attribute weakens the 'proclitic' force of the preposition (cf. Maas, *Gr. Met.* 135). In any case a pause in the antistrophe means a pause in the strophe, and at 218 there cannot possibly be one between *θεῶν* and *γάρ*. Schroeder ends the colon at *κατθανοῦσαν*, leaving the clausula ⏓ – ⏑ ⏑ – ⏑ – – (219 *θεῶ͜ν γὰρ δύναμις μεγίστα*). But this only produces another metrical anomaly in 218 *θεοῖσιν εὐχώμεσθα*, for I can find no parallel for a catalectic iambic dimeter with a long antepenultimate ⏑ – ⏑ – ⏒ – –. It seems, then, that 232 must end in a true long. Dindorf's *εἰν* would be simple but risky; the only parallels in tragedy are infra 436 (a direct reminiscence of *Il.* 23. 179, but see note ad loc.) and in the same phrase S. *Ant.* 1241, where, however, see Jebb's note. Musgrave's *ἔν* ⟨*γ'*⟩ is just possible, with the sense 'and on this very day too'. Maas, however, suggests *ἐν* ⟨*τ*⟩*ἄματι τῷδε*, on the analogy of *τῇδε θἠμέρᾳ, τοῦδε τἀνδρός*, &c.

235–6. μαραινομέναν παρ' Ἅιδαν: 'wasting away *to* Hades', the pregnant use of the preposition to convey the motion not expressed in the verb. *Ἅιδαν* echoes the close of the strophe.

238–43. The Chorus follows up the judgement of the *θεράπαινα* 198, but takes the case of Admetus, added to nameless others, as the basis of a generalization about marriage, which brings more grief than joy. The same rather negative attitude to experience is expressed by the Chorus in *Med.* 1090 ff., which (again in anapaests) concludes that it is a happier lot not to have children at all. The sentiment is not of great importance here; the anapaests allow time for the king and queen and their children to enter slowly and for attendants to bring on a couch for Alcestis, on which she sinks (cf. 250). After this *détente* the lyric tension is dramatically heightened again by the monody of Alcestis and her fevered vision of the summons of death. Engrossed in her own 'ecstasy' she does not heed or hear Admetus' despairing appeals, though he picks up and continues her words, his spoken iambics the foil to her lyric song (cf. *IT* 827–99, *Hel.* 625–97). She calls first upon the skies, then the familiar things of earth; then her vision darkens to the underworld which is claiming her. This is the only scene of 'natural' death on the Greek stage, and Eur. most powerfully brings home to the spectators the victim's sense of the terror and nearness of death.

244–5 = 248–9. – ⏑ ⏑ – ⏑ ⏑ – ⏑ – prosodiac (ibycean)
– ⏑ ⏑ – ⏑ – | – / ⏑ ⏑ – ⏑ – – prosodiac dicolon. (blunt + pendant)

244. 'Sun' is her first greeting; it was to look her last upon the sun that she had come outside (206)—the natural feeling of a dying mortal, especially one who associated any future existence with the darkness of the underworld.

245. Are the 'eddies of racing cloud in the heavens' a scientific concept, or simply a poetic description of moving cloud-drifts in a bright sky? (Cf. Schadewaldt, *Monolog u. Selbstgespräch*, pp. 112 f.) The second might seem more natural to us, but δίνη is too precise for 'drift', and **οὐράνιαι δῖναι** can hardly have failed to convey to the intelligent listener an allusion to the up-to-date cosmologies of Anaxagoras (cf. the περιχώρησις), Empedocles (οὐρανία φορά) and Leucippus (δῖνος), the views later expounded by the Socrates of the *Clouds* (*Nub.* 380 αἰθέριος δῖνος and Eur. fr. 593N² αἰθερίῳ ῥόμβῳ). The plural δῖναι are the patches of cloud carried round in the vortex of the upper air. Poetry, old myth, new learning, are already inextricably intertwined in Eur., though here with a light enough touch to avoid noticeable incongruity.

246–7. Admetus, with the matter-of-fact manner of the healthy, earth-bound individual, takes up 'Sun' and makes it the subject of ὁρᾷ, as if to indicate that Alcestis might have completed her apostrophe in this sense.

248–9. Should the close correspondence between strophe and antistrophe be further emphasized by adopting L P's νυμφίδιαι? (So Kakridis, *Ath.* 1929, 56.) Probably not, since with στέγαι just before the assonance might sound overdone. MSS. often tend to add the third termination, cf. 125 σκοτίας V. **πατρίας** (cf. νεφέλας 245) is a necessary correction here; see Page on *Med.* 431 (but γῆς ἀπὸ πατρῴτης which he cites as the only instance of this correption is a correption not of ῳ but of ω before ι adscript). Porson on *Hec.* 79 [82]: 'cum enim Attici πάτριος et πατρῷος promiscue usurpent, cur ad licentiam poeticam, nulla necessitate cogente, provocemus?'

Turning now to Earth, Alcestis calls upon the palace of Pherae before her and the bridal chamber in her childhood's home at Iolcus—this at least is the most natural way of taking the construction here, since these are the two focal points of her life's affections. *Σ* though informing us that Duris (fl. 300 B.C.) in his History records that Alcestis was married in Iolcus, has not preserved any comment on the inconsistency of this version with 177 and 911 ff. Probably it is simply due to an oversight; all that Eur. wants to convey here is that both scenes are present to her vision.

250–1. μὴ προδῷς: 'do not desert me', as in 202, 275. Admetus again urges the conventional prayer, which is far from her mind.

252 ff. Responsion with 259 ff. is variously achieved by edd. In the first line **ἐν λίμνᾳ** should on no account be deleted in order to accommodate 252 to the shorter version ἄγει μ' ἄγει μέ τις—οὐχ ὁρᾷς; of 259 in *l*. The words are essential to complete the vision and give it authenticity; she cannot see a boat in the void. The water is the λίμνα Ἀχεροντία of 443, with deep middle stream over which Charon rows with two oars, and stagnant marshy edges through which he poles the boat into the bank and holds it there. 259, unlike 252, obviously lends itself to muddle. The version of B D O corresponds exactly except for the first syllables of *ὁρᾷς* and *λίμνᾳ*. This might be explained as a 'final drag' in 252, but the whole stanza could be written as three dicola:

⏑–⏑–⏑⏑–⏑⏑– | ⏓–⏑⏑–⏑–– enop. and choriambic enop.
⏑–⏑⏑⏑⏓–⏑– | ⏓–⏑–⏑–– iamb. dim. and dim. cat.
⏑––⏑⏑––⏑⏑– | ––⏑⏑–⏑–– aeolo-chor. decasyll. + chor. enop.

The anceps then falls into place. The third dicolon is too long in the antistrophe in the text of all except L P, which omits *μέθες με*, but this is probably right; the words could be an explanatory gloss on *τί ῥέξεις; ἄφες*, and are in any case rather redundant. Wecklein keeps them by transferring them to the preceding line, substituting (with Weil) *ἆ· μέθες με* for *αἴδας* and (with Monk) *κυαναυγὲς* for *κυαναυγέσι*. The middle dicolon thus becomes

⏑ ⏓⏓⏑⏑⏑––⏑– | ⏓–⏑–⏑––

(The first syllable of *ὀφρύσι* can of course be either long, as above, or short, as in this version.) But is there anything wrong with *Ἅιδας*? The winged figure is clearly Thanatos, as already seen by the audience. It is true that Hades himself, the king of the underworld, is not usually represented with wings, but we have already seen why Eur. in this play gives Death his more popular, ogreish guise, and there is no reason why Alcestis should not here identify him by the more august name. (*ἄνακτα νεκρῶν* Heracles calls Thanatos 843, and uses the same word *τῶν κάτω κόρης ἄνακτός τε* 852 of Hades; the identification is purposely left shadowy and incomplete because the two conceptions are not easily reconciled.) At first she speaks only of a nameless figure, *τις*, who seeks to take her away to the hall of the dead, then she describes him: 'beneath dark-gleaming brows fixing me with his eyes, winged'—and then comes the final horror—*Ἅιδας*. Wilamowitz would read *ᾇδαν*, presumably internal acc. with *βλέπων*, like *φόβον βλέπων* A. *Sept*. 498. (To take *Ἅιδαν* with *ὁρᾷς*, as Weber does, seems to me impossible.) Monk's *κυαναυγὲς* (see supra) would bear the same construction. Possibly the epithet 'dark-gleaming' is more naturally used of the eyes than of the brows (though cf. *Phoen*. 308 *κυανόχρωτα πλόκαμον*), but even so this might be no more than a 'transferred epithet', not overbold in lyric diction; and this use of *βλέπων* without acc. to express the visible aspect occurs again *Phoen*. 397 *καλοῖς βλέπουσά γ' ὄμμασιν*. Wecklein's text gives three interjections of direct speech in each stanza, and among so much formal balance this might seem in its favour, cf. *ὁρῶ . . . ὁρῶ* = *ἄγει . . . ἄγει*, *νεκύων* = *νεκύων*; on the other hand *ὑπ' ὀφρύσι κυαναυγέσι* gives a more exact metrical correspondence.

256. τάδε κτλ: 'so, impetuous, he bids me hasten'. **τοι**: she is desperately trying to make Admetus see and hear what she does, cf. *οὐχ ὁρᾷς;* below. With the *ἕτοιμα* of L P nothing short of Hermann's alteration: *σὺ κατείργεις τάδ' ἕτοιμα σπερχομένοις· τάχυνε* gives satisfactory sense. (This is the text which Browning translates.) But the attempt to make a word *ἕτοιμα* out of the letters of *τάδε τοί με* is a far more likely corruption than the reverse process. A similar case occurs in *Ag.* 312 *τοιοίδε τοί μοι* dist. Schütz.

264. τῶν demonstrative, as in S. *OC* 741–2 *πᾶς σε Καδμεῖος λεὼς | καλεῖ δικαίως, ἐκ δὲ τῶν μάλιστ' ἐγώ.*

266 ff. Alcestis sinks exhausted on the couch, from which she must have risen (*ποσίν* 267) during the stress of her vision. Only L has the right accent on **ποσί⟨ν⟩**; the others read *πόσι*, 'O husband', and Σ explains *ὦ πόσι, οὐκέτι ἀντέχω,* but the plurals *μέθετε, κλίνατε* are decisively against this, and *οὐ σθένω* needs the completing dat. Nowhere in this lyric scene does she appeal to Admetus by name.

The colometry of this epode is quite uncertain, and probably the lines are best left in their rhetorical phrasing as in this text.

⏑⏑⏑⏑⏑⏑–– ithyph.
–⏑–⏑–⏑– lekythion
–⏑⏑–– chor. pentasyll. (adonean)
⏑⏑–⏑–|–⏑–⏑–– enop. colarion + ithyph.
⏑⏑⏑–⏑⏑–|| dodrans (chor.)
–⏑⏑––––– dragged chor. dim.
––⏑–⏑⏑⏑⏑⏑⏑⏑––iamb. trim. cat.

(The quantity of the first syllable of *τέκνα* is, however, ambiguous each time, and the third and sixth lines might possibly be anapaestic.) The dying fall of the dragged syllables of 271 is followed by the last 'vivite atque valete' to her children.

273. τόδ' ἔπος: not 'farewell' (especially as only the participle *χαίροντες* is available) but simply = *τάδε*, as often, cf. *Supp.* 1161–2, *Bacch.* 1269.

275 ff. With **θεῶν** as a monosyllable the line could be a paroemiac, but probably Porson is right in making these anapaests of Admetus into a single system. For **τλῆς** and **τόλμα** cf. Monk quoted on 1.

277. ἀλλ' ἄνα: 'up!', a rallying exhortation taken from Homer, here and probably *Tro.* 98 used absolutely, as in epic; in S. *Aj.* 193 *ἀλλ' ἄνα ἐξ ἑδράνων* it is more surprisingly construed as a verb.

278. In S. *OT* 314 the phrase *ἐν σοὶ γὰρ ἐσμέν* is used by itself; here *καὶ ζῆν καὶ μή* is an epexegetic addition, as in *IT* 1057 *καὶ τἄμ' ἐν ὑμῖν ἐστιν ἢ καλῶς ἔχειν | ἢ μηδὲν εἶναι,* and in prose Pl. *Prot.* 313a.

279. The exact sense of this line is not easy to grasp; translations such as Méridier's 'car nous vénérons ton amour' leave it unexplained. Browning has 'For in thee are we bound up, to exist Or cease to be—so we adore thy love'. Is this, then, the Greek way of saying 'We'—

or 'I' (for the plural might either mean Admetus himself or include the children)—'cannot live without you, your love means so much to me'? Whether **σεβόμεσθα** *without* 'so' can take all this weight is doubtful. Earle would put the emphasis on **σὴν**: '"For yours is the friendship (kinship, tie) that I reverence"; an anticipation of the renunciation of filial ties in the sequel'. But the audience could not take the point here, and *σὴν* simply picks up *σοὶ* in the line before. Wilamowitz paraphrases: 'zu deiner Liebe schauen, Gnade flehend, wir empor', implying, I take it, 'we address our prayers [not to desert us] to the affection we know you bear us'. *σεβόμεσθα* would then have to convey an act of worship implying supplication, which again is to ask a lot of the word. (Maas calls my attention to the interesting parallel in Aristotle's epigram Diehl² ii. 115, *εὐσεβέως σεμνῆς φιλίης ἱδρύσατε βωμὸν* | *ἀνδρὸς ὃν* . . ., where the altar makes the half-religious sentiment a natural one.) When applied to purely human relations *σέβομαι, σέβω*, or *σεβίζω* means not 'worship', but something more like 'regard', 'be true to', as in *Or.* 1079 *ἑταιρίαν σέβων* (between Orestes and Pylades) and *Med.* 156 *εἰ δὲ σὸς πόσις καινὰ λέχη σεβίζει* (whereas the normal husband *σεβίζει* his wife's *λέχος*). *σὴν φιλίαν* is I think less likely to mean 'your love for us' than (as Earle takes it) 'the tie between us'. Admetus says he is true to the love that is between them and therefore his life or death is bound up with hers.

280 ff. There are certain conventions in Greek drama to which we adjust ourselves with difficulty; such is the relation between stage-lyric and dialogue. The thread of action does not necessarily run continuously through both of these in a strict sequence of time. There are many scenes where a situation is realized first in its lyric, then in its iambic aspect—that is to say, first emotionally, then in its reasoned form. Where the latter appears as a development of the former, picking up and expounding for rhetorical conviction what passion had left only half-articulate (as, for instance, in the Cassandra scene *Tro.* 308–510, or where Phaedra, *Hipp.* 373–430, gives a clear analysis of her own emotional state) we accept the sequence as natural. But a death-scene treated under this dual aspect forces itself strangely on our notice. Alcestis' visions of death, the darkness closing over her eyes, the farewell to her children, all belong to her last minutes on earth; yet now we find her making a long speech, listening to Admetus' reply, and then at the end of the following stichomythia the darkness falls again and she renews her farewells. And there is no explanation offered as a concession to naturalism. On the modern stage we should have to play it with directions: 'recovering from her faint and by a superhuman effort summoning all her strength again . . .'. If Eur. had meant that, he could easily have made it clear in her opening words, but he has simply juxtaposed these two aspects of Alcestis' parting from life, rather than leave either incomplete. The anapaests of Admetus afford a perfunctory transition, so that the echoes of her lyric farewell can die out before her speech starts, but we cannot find in these anapaests, as Browning rather subtly attempts to do, a challenge to the truth, an empty protestation which galvanizes Alcestis to this renewed effort to make him understand. Her words show no such connexion of thought. (For some discussion of this subject see Schadewaldt, *M. und S.* 143.)

282. πρεσβεύουσα = *προτιμῶσα* 155: 'putting you first', counting him more important than herself. **ἀντὶ**: 'in place of', 'in exchange for'.

283. καταστήσασα with acc. and inf. as in Thuc. 2. 84. 3, aor. because the decision was taken once for all some time ago.

284–9. Is this one sentence or two? Most edd. give a full-stop after *τυραννίδι*, but the asyndeton in *οὐκ ἠθέλησα* comes as an unwelcome surprise each time we read it. 282 as the beginning of her exposition is in quite different case, and indeed an argument against another asyndeton here. It is usually explained as deliberately impressive ('eindrucksvoll' Weber) or emotional in effect. But she is building up her case in rhetorical periods, and the tone is not emotional; she is not saying, with feeling, 'I could not bear to live . . .', but 'I refused [virtuously] to live . . .'. Monk and oldcı edd. simply put a comma after *τυραννίδι*, but this still leaves one complex sentence with two main verbs, *θνήσκω* and *ἠθέλησα*, since *ἀλλ'* . . . *τυραννίδι* must continue subordinate to *παρόν μοι*. Weil's *παρὸν δὲ* for *παρόν μοι* 284 destroys the flow of the speech by parting *θνήσκω* from *μὴ θανεῖν*. Lenting's ⟨κ⟩*οὐκ* in 287 is the simplest solution.

288. οὐκ ἐφεισάμην: i.e. I did not grudge the sacrifice of . . ., cf. *ψυχῶν φειδόμενοι* Tyrt. 10. 14.

289. This line has two variants: *ἥβης ἔχουσα δῶρ' ἐν οἷς ἐτερπόμην*, out of which sc. *δώρων* with *ἐφεισάμην*, and the version in the text. Both are probably old. *δῶρα* is used like this elsewhere only with personal agents, as in the Homeric *δῶρ' Ἀφροδίτης*, *Hel.* 363 *δῶρα Κυπρίδος*. Conceivably we should write *Ἥβης* here, but it is not surprising that L has tried to convert to the objective gen. *ἥβης δῶρον*. Since *φείδεσθαι ἥβης* gives a better construction, and *ἐγώ* at the end of the line, standing in emphatic contrast to the following *ὁ φύσας χἠ τεκοῦσα*, is far from otiose, the text given here is preferable.

291–2. ἧκον αὐτοῖς = *καίπερ ἡκόντων αὐτῶν*, to be supplied with both *καλῶς μὲν* and *καλῶς δὲ*. The phrase appears to be an intricate mixture of *ἐς τοῦθ' ἥκειν τοῦ βίου ὥστε καλῶς κατθανεῖν* 'to have reached a good age for dying' and *καλῶς ἥκειν τοῦ βίου* 'to be well off as regards life', like *εὖ ἔχειν* + gen. But it must be admitted that the whole expression is strange, and *καλῶς ἥκειν τοῦ βίου* is a more natural phrase where *βίος* means 'livelihood', as it does in Hdt. 1. 30. 4 *τοῦ βίου εὖ ἥκοντι*. More serious is the weak repetition *κατθανεῖν*, which can only be explained as meaning (*a*) well placed for dying *anyway*, and (*b*) (by saving their son) well placed for dying *nobly*. If it is to be emended, Hayley's *καλῶς μὲν αὐτοῖς ἧκον ἐκστῆναι βίου*, assuming a suprascript gloss *κατθανεῖν*, has much to recommend it.

293–4. The reasoning recalls Antigone's (three years earlier) in her notorious speech 905 ff., but it is quite logical here, where the point of the argument is survival.

295. ἔζων: 'could have gone on living'. There is no reason to interpret this and the following verb-forms as the pathos of one who 'speaks as if she were already dead'; what other form could she have used? The reference is to **τὸν λοιπὸν χρόνον**; she is talking about the future as it might have been.

297 ὠρφάνευες: see on 165.

298. *ἐκπρᾶξαι ὥστε* or *ὡς* = to contrive that something shall happen, cf. S. *Ant.* 303, A. *Pers.* 723. **μὲν** is answered only by **εἶεν**, which dismisses one line of argument and turns to a new angle of the matter in question. It is in the rhetorical manner, not a sigh or 'a formula of resignation' (Jerram). The sentiment of Christian resignation is so familiar to us in such comments that it is only too easy to infuse some tone of it into this context, but what Alcestis says is not 'God's will be done', but 'Some god did this'. It is interesting to note the force of this association at work in translators (not Murray) and commentators. Wilamowitz: 'Doch das hat also ein Gott gefügt; *es musste wohl so sein*.' Meridier: 'Mais ces choses-là, *sans doute*, se sont accomplies par la volonté d'un dieu.' Weber: '. . . womit Alk. *resigniert* sich abgefunden hat.' Paley: 'The pious resignation in this sentiment is remarkable. Alc. is as religious as she is self-devoting.'

299. ἀπόμνησαι: the verb is only used of debts of gratitude, whether with *χάριν* as here, Hes. *Th.* 503, Thuc. 1. 137, or absolutely as *Il.* 24. 428.

300. ἀξίαν: sc. *χάριν*, as in Thuc. 1. 137.

302. δίκαια: not in terms of a requital but as something right in itself; natural affection, as the *γάρ*-clause shows, will support such a claim.

303. εἴπερ εὖ φρονεῖς: i.e. as a normal father. The words do not imply any doubt of his affection; they are merely a sort of safeguarding clause, against the presumption of making an assertion about the feelings of another. Cf. S. *Aj.* 547.

304. τούτους ἀνάσχου δεσπότας sc. *ὄντας* (or at least *δεσπότας* is predicative): 'suffer them to be masters in my house', i.e. to be brought up with that future before them, cf. 681. It will mean his remaining a widower, hence *ἀνάσχου* 'put up with'. **ἐμῶν** has been suspected, and the impossible *τῶν ἐμῶν* of L P has encouraged various unsatisfactory conjectures. But surely we need not boggle at the very natural *ἐμῶν*? 'Ce n'est pas une femme grecque qui peut s'exprimer ainsi'—

Méridier; but it need not denote exclusive, autocratic possession. Her thought seems to be: in what was once *my* home, and will be still through the presence of my children.

305. ἐπιγαμέω here can be taken in its ordinary sense, cf. *Or.* 589 ἐπεγάμει πόσει πόσιν and infra 372 γαμεῖν ἐφ' ὑμῖν, not marry and set a stepmother over the children, but take in second marriage on top of the one these children represent, cf. Hdt. 4. 154. 1 ἐπὶ ταύτῃ (his daughter) ἔγημε ἄλλην γυναῖκα.

311. This natural metaphor descends from *Od.* 11. 556 (Ajax, for the Greeks) to Alcaeus and the tragedians, see LS.

312. This intrusion from 195 is a peculiarly senseless example of the adscript (cf. on 207–8). The substitution of καὶ for οὐ is a miserable expedient to which a scholiast does his best to give some support: παρρησίαν γὰρ ἄγει πρὸς τὸν πατέρα.

313. **κορευθήσῃ**: see on 165.

314. In thus anticipating the evil she is seeking to avert Alcestis is 'talking at' Admetus, like a skilful pleader.

320–1. 'I have to face death *now*, not tomorrow or the day after' is an intelligible way of speaking, whether as spontaneous pathos or, more probably, as an echo of some phrase of familiar speech (still to be heard in the Levant), cf. Hes. *Op.* 410 μηδ' ἀναβάλλεσθαι ἔς τ' αὔριον ἔς τε ἔνηφιν. (Σ Ar. *Ach.* 172 explains εἰς ἔνην by εἰς τρίτην 'the day after tomorrow'.) The addition of **μηνὸς** is most unwelcome. On the assumption that τρίτην μηνὸς is a date, the 'third of the month', this has been explained as (1) a proverbial phrase arising from a habit of creditors, who might if kindly disposed postpone a repayment of debt, normally due on the first of the month, to the third (but this is an unfounded guess); (2) a somewhat oblique indication that the κύριον ἦμαρ of Alcestis' death was the first of the month, the νουμηνία sacred to Apollo. Weber also connects this reckoning with 1144 ff. where Heracles restoring her says she is to remain silent till the third dawn from that time, i.e. the fourth day of the month, which according to Hes. *Op.* 770 was also, like the first and seventh, a holy day. But by Greek reckoning the τρίτον φάος would be the third, not the fourth; and are we really to imagine Alcestis saying 'I have to die today the first of the month, not tomorrow or the third'? In any case it is doubtful whether τρίτην μηνός can express a date; normally the addition of ἱσταμένου, μεσοῦντος, or φθίνοντος is required, and the Scholiast, it may be noted, does not take it as a date: οὐκ εἰς τὴν αὔριον τοῦ μηνὸς τούτου οὐδὲ εἰς τὴν μεταύριον. Some scholars would delete the line, assuming that the somewhat elliptical phrasing of 320 was felt in need of a supplement (but that does not help to account for μηνὸς); others emend, e.g. Herwerden ἐς τρίτον μοι φέγγος.

322. **οὐκέτ'** codd. except V B μηκέτ'. Either the definite οὐ or the generic μή is possible, but οὐ is more likely to have been altered into μή than μή into οὐ, since in later Greek μή tends increasingly to be used with all participles.

324–5. That *ἀρίστης* is to be supplied out of **ἀρίστην** is perfectly clear, but I can find no other instance of this form of brachylogy in parallel clauses. No mention is made of it in KG or in Schwyzer.

326–7. As these two lines of Chorus belong to a formal pattern (cf. 369, 673, 706), we should beware of reading too much into the intervention, for which the Chorus itself half apologizes. We are not meant to see a hint that Admetus' goodwill was under suspicion, but to recognize that his consent can be taken for granted. Hence L P's *ἤνπερ . . . ἁμαρτάνῃ* is wrong; the Chorus is comforting Alcestis, not darkly criticizing Admetus. Cf. on 303.

329–33. These lines are built upon repeated use of zeugma: (1) = **καὶ. ζῶσαν εἶχόν** *σε μόνην γυναῖκα καὶ . . .* (2) **τόνδ' ἄνδρα** = *ἐμέ* (Hermann: 'nulla me Thessala ut sponsa alloquetur'), but the effect of the juxtaposition **ἄνδρα νύμφη** is to suggest an additional predicative sense for *ἄνδρα*: *Σ οὐδεμία ἄλλη γυνὴ ἐρεῖ μοι· ὦ πόσι.* (3) **οὕτως** belongs in grammar to **εὐγενοῦς**, in sense to **ἐκπρεπεστάτη**, which in effect picks up **πατρὸς εὐγενοῦς** as well as **εἶδος**. No other woman shall call me husband; *so* superlative, in birth or beauty, is no woman. **ἄλλως**: or so beautiful *either*.

334–5. Cf. *Med.* 558 *ἅλις γὰρ οἱ γεγῶτες οὐδὲ μέμφομαι. Σ* warns us to punctuate after *παίδων*, with following asyndeton. **γενέσθαι** sc. *μοι*, but the omission is harsh, especially with another dat. present to obscure the sense. One would expect an inf. of which 'I' could remain the subject; Maas suggests *ἑλέσθαι*, cf. A. *Ag.* 350.

338–41. Lasting hatred for his parents, flattering by contrast, is to be a part of his pious observance of grief for his wife. **ἦσαν, ἔσωσας**: he has projected himself into the future of his life of mourning, and looks back on these events. **ἆρα** = *nonne*: cf. on 215 ff., 771. **πάρα**: 'have I [not] cause?'

343–7. For these mourning observances cf. *Hipp.* 1131 ff. **βαρβίτου**: this instrument like the *λύρα* but with longer strings is put here for 'lyre' in general, not as a bit of local colour. The wood of the Libyan lotus-tree, according to Theophr. *HP* 4. 3. 4, was good for making flutes; but the original and simplest sort were of reed, and it is more probable that when Eur. uses *Λίβυς λωτός* (*Tro.* 544, *Hel.* 170, *IA* 1036) as a periphrasis for 'flute' he has in mind, rightly or wrongly, the *stalk* of a smaller sort of lotus-plant. This would be enough to account for **Λίβυν αὐλόν** here and in *HF* 684; whether Eur. knew of a tradition (as quoted by Athenaeus xiv, 618b from the historian Duris) that flute-playing was invented in Libya is doubtful. **λακεῖν**, in Homer an inanimate ringing or crackling sound, is extended by the tragedians to the voice of oracles, to the human voice raised in song, to loud human utterance, and finally (in Eur.) = 'utter' in general, a use which Aristophanes parodies *Ach.* 410, *Ran.* 97. Here it is simply 'sing'. Admetus plays the lyre himself but sings to (not plays) the flute, in accordance with the best amateur tradition of Athens. **ἐξαίροιμι** V B; the *ἐξάροιμι* of L P and Σ's paraphrase *οὐ πείσαιμ' ἂν τὴν ἐμὴν φρένα λακεῖν* might seem to point to the aor. here, but probably the pres. tense + aor. inf. **λακεῖν** is an intentional variant (for *οὐκ ἂν λάκοιμι*) on **οὔτ' ἂν θίγοιμι.** Strictly speaking, **οὐ γάρ ποτ'** 345 should carry on to *ἐξαίροιμι*, not to *λακεῖν*, and would again suggest the aor., but Eur. may quite well not have been speaking strictly.

348–54 σοφῇ: 'skilled'. Monk aptly quotes Perseus' first impression of Andromeda (fr. 125N²) as a figure carved on the rock, *σοφῆς ἄγαλμα χειρός.* **τεκτόνων**: probably 'sculptors', who are to make a painted statue. I do not think Eur. has in mind waxen images or any other form of representation of the absent for magic purposes. Wilamowitz's suggestion is very likely, that he is here borrowing from another Thessalian story, that of his own *Protesilaus*, in which (see Nauck, *TGF*² ad loc.) Laodameia in her transports of grief made an image in her husband's likeness and kept it in her bedchamber; whether or not there was some Thessalian magic ritual in the origins of this story, for Eur. in both plays the point was simply the assuagement of grief. H. J. Rose in *CR* xli (1927) recounts a real incident of a Hungarian mad with grief who had a waxen image of the beloved made and talked to it. The conclusion he draws is that Eur. here as elsewhere shows an understanding of morbid psychology, but I think Eur.'s meaning is that Admetus' grief was *extreme*, not that it was morbid. *ψυχρὰν μέν, οἶμαι, τέρψιν,* shows a disarming awareness of the touch of extravagance in his idea. The reminiscence of *Protesilaus* is made the more likely by the following appeal to Alcestis to return in dreams, which could well be a 'faded' version of the return of her husband's spirit by night to Laodameia.

353. τέρψιν: not the 'internal' acc. as in the superficially similar *Hel.* 35–36 *καὶ δοκεῖ μ' ἔχειν, κενὴν δόκησιν, οὐκ ἔχων,* but an acc. in apposition to the sentence, like *ἄποινα* 7. J. C. Kamerbeek calls attention to an interestingly similar expression in an epitaph: Kaibel, *Epigr.* 246. 5, *πενταέτους τε εἰκῶ τέκνου | κενὴν ὄνησιν ὀμμάτων χαράξατο.*

354. ἀπαντλοίην ἂν glossed by Hesychius *ἐπικουφίσαιμ' ἄν. ἄντλος,* properly 'bilge-water', is the starting-point of many metaphors in Greek tragedy. If it were pressed here, we might say that the soul is lightened of its burden of grief enough for it to survive, even as the ship whose hold is kept clear of flood-water (*Tro.* 691) can ride the storm. But it is unlikely that a metaphor so common was felt as fully as that. *ἀντλέω* and *ἐξαντλέω* in tragedy usually concentrate on the activity of 'drawing off', 'draining off' as a toilsome and disagreeable task, and so mean 'drain to the dregs', 'endure all the wretchedness of', without any prospect of relief; *ὑπεξαντλέω* in *Ion* 927 is a mixture of this sense and that of 'baling out' in order to survive; ἀπαντλέω is to 'draw off' an excess of something unpleasant (here βάρος ψυχῆς) and so obtain relief.

355–6. φίλοις L P B leaves λεύσσειν without any object; **φίλους** V supplies one, and is probably right, with φίλοις an easy corruption. **παρῇ** is usually taken impersonally, 'for such time as one may', but it would be quite idiomatic as a change from plur. (φίλους) to sing. (φίλος παρῇ) where the sing. has generalized collective force: 'however short their stay'. Cf. *Andr.* 421–2 οἰκτρὰ γὰρ τὰ δυστυχῆ | βροτοῖς ἅπασι, κἂν θυραῖος ὢν κυρῇ and the other examples in KG i. 87. Musgrave's φίλος is, however, a tempting conjecture, perhaps combined with ὅν τις ἂν (Blaydes). τρόπον (Prinz) 'in whatever guise', i.e. even as a dream, in place of χρόνον is meant to clarify ἐν νυκτί, but the sense is supplied clearly enough from ἐν ὀνείρασι φοιτῶσα just before. It is possible that an echo of *Protesilaus* again (he was released from Hades for three hours during the night) has led Eur. to phrase the sentence thus.

357–62. γλῶσσα καὶ μέλος: 'words and music', combined in **ὕμνοισι.** There may, or may not, have been an earlier version of the story, in which Orpheus *succeeded* in bringing back Eurydice, but there is nothing in this passage to indicate that Eur. is referring to such a version; still less can these lines be taken as evidence that a later tragic ending was not yet current in 438 B.C. Nor, when Σ explains τῇ μουσικῇ θέλξας τὸν Πλούτωνα καὶ τὴν Κόρην αὐτὴν ἀνήγαγεν ἐξ Ἅιδου, is there any reason why he should have added that at the last minute Orpheus failed; the scholiasts do not always pursue their comments beyond the point of relevance. The miraculous potency of Orpheus' music was a more arresting thought than the sad end of the story.

Cobet may well be right in reading γέρων for Χάρων 361. The parallel in 440 is no argument one way or the other, but **οὑπὶ κώπῃ ψυχοπομπὸς** does sound like the beginning of a periphrasis for the name, to match the three others in these lines. After Alcestis' visionary encounter with Charon, Admetus' hypothetical one; the irony is not to be missed. **ἔσχον**: Porson on *Hec.* 88 'Recte infertur verbum plurale, sive duo singularia nomina coniunguntur sive disiunguntur.' Just as in the former case the separate nature of the subjects' action may be emphasized by a singular verb, so with the disjunctives ἤ . . . ἤ, οὔτε . . . οὔτε a plural verb is occasionally used to emphasize cumulative action; so here he would have to surmount the opposition of *both* Cerberus and Charon. **σὸν βίον** = *te vivam*, cf. *Bacch.* 1339 μακάρων τ' ἐς αἶαν σὸν καθιδρύσει βίον.

363. ἀλλ' οὖν resigning himself to what *can* be done: 'but at least'. **ἐκεῖσε**, expect me *thither*, is a Greek pregnant construction of typical neatness, cf. Ar. *Ran.* 752 τοῖς θύραζε ταῦτα καταλαλῶν, and the opposite *IT* 1410 σοὶ τὰς ἐκεῖθεν σημανῶν τύχας.

364. Cf. Eur. *El.* 1143–5, there spoken in bitter scorn.

365–6. **κέδροις**: cedar-wood preserves corpses as well as clothes (160). **σοὶ** with **αὐταῖς**. Cf. *Or.* 1052 *πῶς ἂν ξίφος νὼ ταὐτόν, εἰ θέμις, κτάνοι, | καὶ μνῆμα δέξαιθ' ἕν, κέδρου τεχνάσματα;* But Electra and Orestes were to die together; Admetus' injunction to his children (**τούσδε**) hereafter is meant to have a touch of hyperbole. The closing sentence was doubtless spoken with tremendous feeling by the actor; thirteen years later Aristophanes (*Ach.* 893–4) was able to get a laugh with Dicaeopolis' culminating address to an eel: *μηδὲ γὰρ θανών ποτε | σοῦ χωρὶς εἴην ἐντετευτλανωμένης*—'embeetoned'.

Opinions have differed vastly as to the significance of this speech.[1] At one extreme it has been held that the formal pattern requires Admetus to speak at roughly the same length as Alcestis, but whereas she had a concrete request to make he has merely to dilate on his sense of grievous loss; consequently his speech has to be padded out with rather far-sought *motifs*. This is a reaction against the commoner 'psychological' interpretations, according to which Admetus, whether from lack of emotional balance or embarrassed by the first stirrings of a bad conscience, pours out this tasteless extravaganza, which is thus contrasted with his sincere grief later on in the play, after his spiritual reformation. W. Schmid (Sch.–Stählin, *Gesch.* i. 3. 342 ff.) finds this speech, and indeed the figure of Admetus in general, one of the deliberately comic aspects of this half-satyric play. Weber thinks Admetus indifferent to the children and egotistically preoccupied with his own sufferings; the emotion down to 361 is laid on a bit too thick to be genuine, but after that it settles down to a sincerely felt close—which is merely another way of saying that the sentiment and phraseology of 363 ff. are of the sort our ears are accustomed to, while the earlier part is not. It is a question of *our* taste, not of the taste of Admetus.

There can be no doubt, I think, that the whole speech is designed to express sincere, heart-rending grief. Alcestis, troubled by the thought of her deserted children, had asked him for their sake to pledge himself never to marry again; as this would be quite abnormal behaviour for a young, royal widower, she reminded him of the unparalleled magnitude of her sacrifice, for which this renunciation would be some return. Admetus, racked with grief, flings himself ardently into this idea of showing his gratitude by some corresponding sacrifice. Of course he will have no other wife and no more children; that is the least part of it and disposed of in few words; but he will do more, much more, to match the uniqueness of his wife's devotion with some unequalled tribute of mourning. Or almost unequalled—only Orpheus gave greater proof; but since, alas! he has

[1] Cf. on this subject Introd., pp. xxii ff.

not Orpheus' gift he will at least make his whole life one long dedication to her memory, until at last death reunites him to her. In fact Admetus is in all good faith proposing to lead a life which will make nonsense of her gift to him. Only one step more is needed for completeness: that his despair should lead him to wish to die and even seek to make an end of himself; this, apart from a momentary impulse 382 (but this is Alcestis' death-scene and we must not be distracted from it), is left for later realization, after the funeral.

369. καὶ μὴν ἐγώ: 'And be sure that I . . .'.

371–3. Alcestis concentrates on the practical object she had sought to gain; the rest is lightly alluded to in *μηδ' ἀτιμάσειν ἐμέ* as if it were a mere corollary of his promise about the children. (See Introd., p. xxvi.)

373. ἐφ' ὑμῖν: see on 305.

374. Either 'I both say it now and will do it hereafter', or 'I say it again now, and what is more I will do it.' Only the emphasis given in speaking could determine which.

375–6. The taking over of the children is a symbolic pledge of his acceptance of the conditions (**ἐπὶ τοῖσδε**). Cf. the phrase *δέχομαι τὸν ὅρκον*. The initial anapaests in successive lines are the result of adopting part of a regular formula from everyday life.

377. MSS. usually make no distinction between *νῦν* and *νυν* enclitic, even when the metre obviously requires the second, so we are at liberty to restore *νυν* wherever it makes better sense. Often, as here, the choice is difficult. The enclitic is common in entreaties, and perhaps we should follow Monk in writing *σύ νυν* here, which makes it easier to throw the emphasis on *σύ*.

378. Denniston, *GP* 144: 'Emphatic and limitative *γε* are sometimes found in close proximity', with examples *Phoen.* 554, S. *OC* 387. This is an even clearer instance, and the first *γ'* should not be emended.

379. *Σ νέα οὖσα δηλονότι.* Possibly also with a feeling that this was not strictly her own fate she was meeting but her husband's. **χρῆν**: the tendency of later Greek to recognize only *χρή* and *ἐχρῆν* leads to many faults of transmission.

380–1. τί δράσω δῆτα: 'then what shall I do?' Denniston, *GP* 269–71. Wilamowitz, followed by Weber, rejects these two lines as an interpolation on the grounds that (1) they are a doublet of 382–3, and of the two couplets *ἄγου με σὺν σοί* is clearly the genuine response to *ἀπέρχομαι κάτω*. But the repetition of *κάτω* at the end of adjacent lines is hardly tolerable, not so much for the jingle as that the word itself becomes superfluous. Nor is the sense of these two couplets obviously alternative; (2) the lines are a patchwork, since *χρόνος μαλάξει* has been inserted here as a repetition from 1085, where *κακόν* is to be supplied as the object, whereas the personal object *σε* is unsuitable for *μαλάσσειν*. It is true that *μαλάσσειν* usually has some object such as *ὀργάς* (771) or *θυμόν* or *σπλάγχνον*, but the passive in S. *Phil.* 1334 *πρὶν ἂν . . . νόσου μαλαχθῇς τῆσδε*, 'until you are relieved of this malady', is a near enough parallel. It is difficult to know just where to draw the line in accepting repetition of phrase, but this might be considered to fall within the limit; (3) the sensitive reader must at once reject such a sentiment from Alcestis, especially after the appeal to honour her memory. But the sentiment is not so different from that of 387, and in any case in stichomythia we are meant to look not so much (in Aristotelian terms) for the *ἦθος* of the speaker as for the *διάνοια* of the repartee.

383. i.e. *ἀρκεῖ τὸ σοῦ προθνῄσκειν ἐμέ*, the personal construction being preferred in Greek, cf. S. *Ant.* 547 *ἀρκέσω θνῄσκουσ' ἐγώ*, *OT* 1061 *ἅλις νοσοῦσ' ἐγώ*. The use of the article in *οἱ προθνῄσκοντες* here is noteworthy (*Rhes.* 329 *ἀρκοῦμεν οἱ σῴζοντες Ἴλιον πάλαι*, sometimes quoted as a parallel, is a quite different sense of *ἀρκεῖν*); the participle is made to do duty twice over: *ἡμεῖς οἱ προθνῄσκοντες σέθεν ἀρκοῦμεν θνῄσκοντες*.

384. ὦ δαῖμον: for this sense of the word cf. S. *OT* 1311 *ἰὼ δαῖμον ἵν' ἐξήλλου*. This is Admetus' individual fortune indeed!

385. καὶ μὴν heralds the coming of darkness.

393. Murray is undoubtedly right in printing *ΠΑΙΣ* rather than *ΕΥΜΗΛΟΣ*. Children are usually kept anonymous in Greek tragedy (except where, as with Eurysaces in S. *Aj.* or Astyanax in *Tro.*, the name has a special significance), but their names were the kind of detail that the commentators loved to supply, cf. *Andr.*, where the form *Μολοττός* betrays itself. So too in the *δράματος πρόσωπα* of A. *Ag.* the Herald appears as *Ταλθύβιος κῆρυξ*.

393–415. Monody.

393 *ἰώ μοι τύχας. μαῖα δὴ κάτω* 406 *νέος ἐγώ, πάτερ, λείπομαι φίλας*	⏑ ⏖ – ⏑ – – ⏑ – ⏑ –
βέβακεν, οὐκέτ' ἔστιν, *μονόστολός τε ματρός·*	⏑ – ⏑ – ⏑ – ⏝
ὦ πάτερ, ὑφ' ἀλίῳ. *ὦ σχέτλια δὴ παθὼν*	– ⏑ ⏑ ⏑ – ⏑ –
προλιποῦσα δ' ἀμὸν *ἐγὼ ἔργ'· ⟨ἰώ μοι·⟩*	⏑ ⏑ – ⏑ – –
βίον ὠρφάνισεν τλάμων. *σύ τε σύγκασί μοι κούρα*	⏑ ⏑ – ⏑ ⏑ – – –
ἴδε γὰρ ἴδε βλέφαρον *. . . . . συνέτλας·*	⏑ ⏑ ⏑ ⏑ ⏑ ⏑ ⏑ –
καὶ παρατόνους χέρας. *. . . . . ὦ πάτερ,*	– ⏑ ⏑ ⏑ – ⏑ ⏝ ‖

400 ὑπάκουσον ἄκουσον, ὦ ⏑⏑–⏑⏑–⏑–
412 ἀνόνατ' ἀνόνατ' ἐνύμ-

μᾶτερ, ἀντιάζω. –⏑–⏑––‖
φευσας, οὐδὲ γήρως

ἐγώ σ' ἐγώ, μᾶτερ, ⏑–⏑–––
ἔβας τέλος σὺν τᾷδ'·

. . . . –⏑⏑–⏑–
ἔφθιτο γὰρ πάρος·

σὸς ποτὶ σοῖσι πίτνων στόμασιν νεοσσός. –⏑⏑–⏑–|–⏑⏑–⏑––
οἰχομένας δὲ σοῦ, μᾶτερ, ὄλωλεν οἶκος.

The restoration of the text is very difficult; the end of the strophe and the middle of the antistrophe can only be left as a problem in which we have not the data to arrive at a solution. The main trouble is that the antistrophe is shorter than the strophe, and since the sense is complete it is not clear where the lacuna falls (or is to be distributed). The metre is by no means self-developing, there are several ambiguous quantities, and the responsion may, within limits, be inexact. The first three cola are straightforward; they can of course go into perfectly orthodox iambo-dochmiac, with ὦ in each stanza at the end of the second line, but I have substituted the 'long dochmiac' (see my *Lyric Metres*, 113–14) to keep the rhetorical phrasing and to anticipate the same colon in *καὶ παρατόνους χέρας* below. The next clear responsion is 400 = 412. The only way to reduce the intervening lacuna in the antistrophe to a single patch is, with Wilamowitz, to delete *ἐγὼ ἔργα* and change *ἀμὸν* 396 to *ἐμὸν* (Weber retains *ἀμὸν* in his text, but the first syllable is never short). But these changes, the latter especially, are difficult to account for palaeographically; moreover, the metre thus produced is an anapaestic trimeter with some freedom of responsion as in recitative anapaests: *προλιποῦσα δ' ἐμὸν βίον ὠρφάνισεν τλάμων· ἴδε γὰρ* = *σύ τε σύγκασί μοι κούρα συνέτλας* ⟨––⏑⏑–⟩. Any statement about what is probable or improbable in the metrical sequence of a polymetric stanza is apt to sound arbitrary; I can only say for what it is worth that such a trimeter here, especially with the separation of *ἴδε γὰρ* | *ἴδε* by pause and final *brevis in longo*, would even with a unanimous textual tradition have aroused my deepest suspicion. It is better to let the lacuna be split, filling in 409 with something like *ἰώ μοι*, or Hermann's *τλάμων*. The responsion of 397 to 410 is puzzling. The Oxford text adopts Barnes's *ὠρφάνισσε*, thus making an anacreontic ⏑⏑–⏑–⏑–– in free responsion to an ordinary ionic dimeter ⏑⏑––⏑⏑––. This would be in order in a clear ionic context, but an isolated ionic colon here is in any case rather unwelcome. Hermann's *σύ τε σύγκασί μοι κούρα* (with *ὠρφάνισεν* 397) slightly alters the effect of *μοι* but is the easiest line of escape, giving an enoplian ⏑⏑–⏑⏑–––, a variant with dragged close (*κούρα, τλάμων*) of 400 = 412 ⏑⏑–⏑⏑–⏑–. In 399 = 411 the question turns on the quantity of the syllable before *βλέφαρον*. If it *must* be long, one solution would be to emend (with Wilam.) to *βλέφαρα* and move the lacuna in the antistrophe:

ἴδε γὰρ ἴδε βλέφαρα· ⏑⏑⏑⏑–⏓⏑⏑
. . *συνέτλας· ὦ πάτερ* (followed by lacuna)

with free responsion in the close of a long dochmiac. But I suspect the less obvious *βλέφαρον* of being right, and in that case we must either admit a strange intruder in the shape of a choriambic colon ⏑⏑⏑⏑–⏑⏑– or assume that the occasional ambiguity which affects *βλ* and *γλ* has produced a short quantity here.

Finally, since neither *καλοῦμαί σ' ὁ* nor *καλοῦμαι ὁ* can respond to *ἔφθιτο γὰρ πάρος*, the strophe, which in these lines betrays a muddled tradition, must be accounted at fault. The Aldine's *νῦν γε* is a feeble stopgap. Wilam. transfers *σ' ἐγώ* 401 (and *ἔβας* 413) to the end of the line before, and then continues

ἐγώ, μᾶτερ, καλοῦμαί σ' ὁ σὸς
⟨σὸς⟩ ποτὶ σοῖσι πίτ-νων στόμασιν νεοσσός.

The short dochmiac *ἐγὼ μᾶτερ* ⏑––– is perhaps possible, and also the free responsion of dochmiacs ⏑––⏑– = –⏑⏑–⏑– in *καλοῦμαί σ' ὁ σὸς* = *ἔφθιτο γὰρ πάρος*. The last line echoes the metre of 245, and the antistrophe seems sound, but the repetition of *σὸς* is a clumsy expedient, and I am doubtful about the long first syllable of *πίτνων*, since this form is nearly always used by the tragedians where *πίπτω* would be impossible metrically. The metre appears to be throughout dochmiac, iambo-dochmiac, and prosodiac-enoplian.

Childishness on the stage, in anything approaching a realistic sense, would be unthinkable within the Greek tragic convention. Here as in *Andr.* 505 ff. the child sings the sentiments its elders feel for it. Macduff cries 'all my pretty chickens', but Alcestis' child calls himself 'I, your chick', and Andromache's says to her *ἐγὼ δὲ σᾷ πτέρυγι συγκαταβαίνω*. **μαῖα** 393 is in the Odyssey a familiar and affectionate form of address to old women-servants (nurse or housekeeper), cf. also *Hymn to Demeter* 147, Ar. *Eccl.* 915. Its presence here without an article suggests that it could be used by children either to their nurse or to the mother who nursed and fed them, like the negro Mammy. In this sense it probably belongs to nursery language, even though elsewhere (A. *Cho.* 44, S. fr. 959P) it can be used in tragic diction, by a metaphor, of Earth or the land of one's birth.

404. τὴν picks up *σε*. Without *γε* this is certainly abrupt, but abruptness may have been intended.

407. μονόστολος: *Σ ἀπὸ μεταφορᾶς τῶν μόνων στελλομένων πλοίων. μονόστ. οὖν ἀντὶ τοῦ ἔρημος.* Cf. *Phoen.* 742 *μονοστόλου δορός*, where the metaphor has faded to nothing, S. *Phil.* 496 *αὐτόστολος*, *OT* 212 *ὁμόστολος*, *OC* 1055 *διστόλους*.

410. σύγκασι: a *ἁπ. λεγ.* used adjectivally with *κούρα*. *IT* 800 *συγκασιγνήτη*.

416–9. The usual *Non tibi hoc soli.*

420–1. The choice between the easily confused *γε* and *τε* is not easy. There appears to be no other well-attested instance of 'emphatic' *γε* —'Oh I *do*'—answering a previous command (v. Denniston, *GP* 131 and Fraenkel, A. *Ag.* 539), but the difference in sense between *γίγνωσκε* 418 and *γιγνώσκεις* is so slight here that not much need be made of this objection. *τε καί* is of course quite normal in such an answer; Fraenkel compares S. *Trach.* 626 and *OC* 113. Perhaps a preference might be given to the slightly less obvious and familiar *γε*. **προσέπτατ'**: the metaphor can be used of the approach of something intangible—sound or smell—through the air, as in A. *PV* 115, 555, or of the hostile swoop of some evil, as of a bird of prey: so here and *PV* 644, S. *Aj.* 282. *αὔτ'* is of course *αὐτό*. Weber takes it as *δ' αὖτε* (*sic*) 'underlining the sharp contrast'. There is a similar ambiguity S. *Ant.* 462, where Bruhn would read *αὖτ'* with L, but see Jebb ad loc. *αὖτε* would there make grammatical sense; *δ' αὖτε*, which is found only with preceding *μέν*, would here make none.

422–4. πάρεστε: 'attend' the funeral procession (not 'stand by to help', a meaning which requires a context of danger or struggle); **μένοντες ἀντ.**: sing while you are waiting for it to appear. *παιάν* in connexion with suffering and the powers of death has probably always the force of oxymoron. It is sometimes expressly distinguished from *θρῆνος* (A. *Cho.* 342 f.) and rejected from the worship of the infernal powers (A. *Niobe* fr. 161N² *μόνος θεῶν γὰρ Θάνατος οὐ δώρων ἐρᾷ, | οὐδ' ἄν τι θύων οὐδ' ἐπισπένδων ἄνοις, | οὐδ' ἔστι βωμὸς οὐδὲ παιωνίζεται*, and *IT* 182–3 *τὰν ἐν θρήνοις μοῦσαν νέκυσι μελομέναν, τὰν ἐν μολπαῖς Ἅιδας ὑμνεῖ δίχα παιάνων*). In *Tro.* 578 Hec. *οἴμοι*. Andr. *τί παιᾶν' ἐμὸν στενάζεις;* it is used in bitter irony. Aesch. uses it with deliberately unexpected genitives: *τοῦ θανόντος Cho.* 151, *Ἅιδα Sept.* 869, *Ἐρινύων Ag.* 645; in the present context the anomaly is heightened by the epithet in *ἀσπόνδῳ θεῷ*, the paean being especially associated with *σπονδαί* (A. *Ag.* 246–7, Xen. *Symp.* 2. 1). This raises the question of the force of the dat. *θεῷ* with the verb *ἀντηχήσατε*. Is this 'sing to the god a responsive paean', or 'sing a paean in response to the god'? If the former, it might mean 'make the echoes ring', i.e. sing it very loud and clear, or (more probably) sing an antiphonal, antistrophic song. But in all other cases where the verb is used with the dat. this takes up the *ἀντί*, and in the only other instance in tragedy, *Med.* 427 *ἀντάχησ' ἂν ὕμνον ἀρσένων γέννᾳ*, the meaning is quite definitely 'in answer to the male breed'. I am inclined to think that Admetus means in effect sing a paean of Alcestis which will be a kind of *challenge, echoing upon* the ears of the god who is so deaf to this form of human approach.

426. *πένθος* L P is doubtless an ancient variant, and equally good grammar.

427. V O appear to have conflated this line with *κάρα ξυρῆκες καὶ πέπλους μελαγχίμους Phoen.* 372, doubtless written here as a marginal gloss because of its similarity (and therefore probably genuine in *Phoen.*). So too *κουρᾷ ξυρήκει* intruded into the text of *Tro.* 141. 'Razor-sharp cropping' is a more natural use of the adjective than *κάρα ξυρῆκες*, but this appears again *El.* 335.

428–9. All horses, whether in chariot-teams or ridden singly, are to display cropped manes. This mourning usage appears to be common to all northern Greece (Plut. *Pelop.* 33, *Alex.* 72) and to the Persians (Hdt. 9. 24). **μονάμπυκας**: cf. Pind. *Ol.* 5. 7 *ἵπποις ἡμιόνοις τε μοναμπυκίᾳ τε*, an abstract which implies the existence of the concrete already. They are single horses ready bridled (and thus with a frontlet), **ζεύγνυσθε** containing a slight zeugma. The compound attribute is of the type where each component refers separately to the substantive; the first, the numerical one, conveys the immediate point, while the second adds a detail (of varying importance) to the background. 'Single-frontleted' does not imply that a horse might sometimes have more than one frontlet. Cf. S. *OT* 846 *οἰόζωνος* a solitary traveller, girt up, *Hel.* 1129 *μονόκωπος ἀνήρ*, a single man in a rowing-boat. See also infra 906 *μονόπαις* and note.

434. **τιμῆς**: Porson on *Hec.* 309 *ἡμῖν δ' Ἀχιλλεὺς ἄξιος τιμῆς, γύναι* compares this passage. The old variant *τιμᾶν* is equally possible, cf. for the act. voice infra 1060 *ἀξία δέ μοι σέβειν*.

Alcestis is carried within, and Admetus and the children go to put on mourning. The Chorus has no opportunity to change for the funeral.

435 ff. The Chorus sings a most moving Praise of Alcestis, addressed throughout to her in the second person: Let Hades recognize your uniqueness among women; on earth your fame shall be widely celebrated in song. Would that I could redeem you from death as you, with devotion unequalled, redeemed your husband.

ὦ Πελίου θύγατερ, –⏑⏑–⏑⏑–
πολλά σε μουσοπόλοι hemiep.
χαίρουσά μοι εἰν Ἀίδαο δόμοις ––⏑⏑–⏑⏑–⏑⏑–
μέλψουσι καθ' ἑπτάτονόν τ' ὀρείαν enop.
τὸν ἀνάλιον οἶκον οἰκετεύοις. ⏑⏑–⏑⏑–⏑–⏑––
χέλυν ἔν τ' ἀλύροις κλέοντες ὕμνοις. enop.

ἴστω δ' Ἀίδας ὁ μελαγχαί- – – ⏑⏑ – ⏑⏑ – –
Σπάρτᾳ κυκλὰς ἀνίκα Καρνεί- enop. +

τας θεὸς ὅς τ' ἐπὶ κώπᾳ – ⏑⏑ – ⏑⏑ – – prosodiac
ου περινίσσεται ὥρα (hemiep. pendant)

πηδαλίῳ τε γέρων – ⏑⏑ – ⏑⏑ –
μηνὸς, ἀειρομένας hemiep.

νεκροπομπὸς ἵζει, – ⏑ – ⏑ – –
παννύχου σελάνας, ithyph.

πολὺ δὴ πολὺ δὴ γυναῖκ' ἀρίσταν ⏑⏑ – ⏑⏑ – ⏑ – ⏑ – – ||
λιπαραῖσί τ' ἐν ὀλβίαις Ἀθάναις. enop.

λίμναν Ἀχεροντίαν πορεύ- – – ⏑⏑ – ⏑ – ⏑ –
τοίαν ἔλιπες θανοῦσα μολ- enop. +

σας ἐλάτᾳ δικώπῳ. – ⏑⏑ – ⏑ – – prosodiac
πὰν μελέων ἀοιδοῖς. (aristophanean)

The general metrical type is clear; the stanza is a study in prosodiac-enoplian, the cola having either double-short[1] (**dd, dd–, –dd–, –ddd**) or double-short changing to single-short (**‸ddss–, –dss–, ds–**). The form of the second line is doubtful; as given in this text it requires the scansion *ὀρεῐαν* 446. (Wilamowitz, *GV* 537, accepts this correption, though he adopts a quite different and to my mind inferior colometry). Murray compares *Hipp.* 1127 *ὦ δρυμὸς ὄρειος, ὅθι κυνῶν*, where the iambic dimeter is most easily saved by making *ὄρειος* a tribrach. The text more usually adopted in 436 is the *εἰν Ἀίδα δόμοισ⟨ιν⟩* of *l* giving the enoplian – – ⏑⏑ – ⏑⏑ – ⏑ – – (= A. *PV* 135). There are, however, some grounds for suspicion of the text of the strophe here anyway. The line is a remarkably close echo of *Il.* 23. 179 *χαῖρέ μοι, ὦ Πάτροκλε, καὶ εἰν Ἀίδαο δόμοισι*, and this is held to account for the epic form of the preposition (see on 232) and of *Ἀίδαο* if that is read here. It must also account for the rather singular redundancy of expression in 436–7. The phrase *χαίρουσά μοι τὸν ἀνάλιον οἶκον οἰκετεύοις* (cf. 852) would by itself be a discreet tragic reminiscence of Homer, and the reference (438) to *Ἀίδας ὁ μελαγχαίτας θεὸς* sounds more like a first reference than a second within the stanza. (S. *Trach.* 689 *κατ' οἶκον ἐν δόμοις* is different, see Jebb ad loc.) If, however, *εἰν Ἀίδαο δόμοις* is due to a parallel quotation in the margin it has displaced the original words beyond hope of restoration, and we can only leave the text as it stands.

437. οἰκετεύοις: 'may you dwell in'; the verb is a *ἅπ. λεγ.* except for Hesych. *οἰκετεύεται· συνοικεῖ.* Though *οἰκέτης, οἰκέτις* have usually the special sense of 'household servant', this does not make the verb mean 'be an attendant in the house' [of Persephone], hinting at some

[1] See note, p. 60.

special status of Alcestis in the royal household in anticipation of 744–6. The basic meaning of *οἰκέτης, οἰκέτις* is simply 'inhabitant of an *οἶκος* (so in S. fr. 866P *οἰκέτιν τ' ἐφέστιον περιστεράν*, cf. Theocr. 18. 38 and Suid. s.v. *οἰκέται*), and this would naturally prevail in a derivative, if indeed the form was not simply coined *ad hoc* as a lyric variant on *οἰκέω*.

438 ff. Cf. on *ἀντηχήσατε* 423. The Chorus addresses itself to Hades–Thanatos (cf. on 262) and Charon, the two figures of Alcestis' vision. The construction is clear in spite of its compression: *ἴστω* includes both Hades and Charon, though *ἴστω πορεύσας* is grammatically appropriate only to Charon. The emphatic word is of course *ἀρίσταν*: they are to know that this woman whom Charon has ferried over Acheron is the noblest of her kind. Jebb on S. *Trach.* 559 *ποταμὸν . . . βροτοὺς . . . 'πόρευε* quotes this passage as a parallel instance of double acc. of a rare kind, object + space traversed.

442. It is most improbable that Ar. *Av.* 539, twenty-three years later, meant *πολὺ δὴ πολὺ δὴ χαλεπωτάτους λόγους* as a reminiscence of this; the repetition is neither otiose nor operatic but a natural way of achieving emphasis, cf. the precisely similar *θανάτῳ θανάτῳ πάρος δαμείην* *Med.* 648.

445. *μουσοπόλος* is one who 'busies himself about the muses' (cf. *θαλαμηπόλος*), an 'attendant on the muses', hence a poet; the word is usually adjectival, though cf. Sappho inc. lib. 35 Lobel.

446. From 'seven-stringed lyre' to 'seven-toned tortoise' is easy; 'the seven-toned mountain-tortoise' because there were also water-tortoises—*Σ*. In making the first lyre Hermes took the life of a *χέλυς ὄρεσι ζώουσα* (*H. Herm.* 33). The Hymn naturally credits Hermes with the full 7 strings of the sixth-century lyre, and this remains the traditional number, though by 438 it may have had 8 or even more.

447. ἀλύροις: the negative word is unfortunately ambiguous. Elsewhere in tragedy—cf. *IT* 146, *Hel.* 185, *Phoen.* 1028, S. *OC* 1222 (combined with *ἄχορος*), and *ἀφόρμικτος* A. *Eum.* 332—*ἄλυρος* negatives the idea of joy, dance, festivity, usually associated with music, and the context always brings this out clearly. 'Lyreless' thus commonly means 'unfit for music', 'anything but festive'. But here 'celebrating you with hymns both to the lyre and lyreless' is clearly quite different. *Σ* compares *καὶ πεζὰ καὶ φορμικτά* in Soph.'s *Locrian Ajax* (fr. 16P), adding as a note on *πεζά* that hetairai who came to banquets without a musical instrument were [jestingly] known as *πεζαί*. *πεζός*, then, which *Σ* takes as the equivalent of *ἄλυρος*, means 'without music', cf. Com. adesp. 601K *παῦσαι μελῳδοῦσ', ἀλλὰ πεζῇ μοι φράσον*, though it can also be limited more precisely to 'prose', as in Pl. *Soph.* 237a *πεζῇ τε . . . καὶ μετὰ μέτρων* and in general in later Greek. *ἄλυρος* is also used in this general sense of 'without music' in Pl. *Legg.* 810b *πρὸς δὲ δὴ μαθήματα ἄλυρα ποιητῶν κείμενα ἐν γράμμασι,* where, however, as the context is about lyre-playing this was the natural word to use. In Arist. *Rhet.* 3. 6. 7, on the other hand, the poets are said to speak of the music of, for example, the trumpet as ἄχορδον μέλος or ἄλυρον μέλος. Eur. might here then mean either 'sung and spoken poetry' (e.g. rhapsodic performances, or tragic iambics) or 'songs sung to strings and to stringless instruments', and of these two μέλψουσι, like μολπὰν μελέων ἀοιδοῖς below, would be more appropriate to the second. We are far too ignorant about the Carnean festival at Sparta to get help there. As it was a festival of Apollo the story of Admetus and Alcestis would be among the appropriate subjects for celebration, but this passage is the limit of our evidence. The reference to Athens is vaguer; it has been suggested that Eur. is delicately alluding to his own play but it is perhaps more likely that he is thinking of the two instruments for accompanying melic poetry in his time, the lyre and the flute, calling the latter type of song ἄλυρον μέλος as in Arist. *Rhet.* quoted above. In any case 'Sparta and Athens' conveys that her fame will spread beyond Thessaly over the Greek world.

448–51. Undoubtedly the simplest grammatical construction of this much vexed passage is given by retaining the ὥρα of the majority of MSS. and with Scaliger reading κυκλὰς for κύκλος (for the form cf. φθινὰς ἁμέρα *Hcld.* 779): 'when at Sparta the revolving season of the Carnean month comes round and the moon is aloft all night through.' ἀειρ. παν. σελ. is gen. abs. and may either be intended merely as an indication of the time of the Carnean festival (during the full moon of the month called at Sparta after Apollo Κάρνειος) or, more probably, may imply that the songs were actually sung by moonlight. The month is fixed on the ἐνιαύσιος κύκλος, the cycle of the year, so that on this its own κυκλὰς ὥρα 'comes round'. The difficulty (by no means decisive) is that κυκλάς in this sense is attested for nothing earlier than the Orphic Hymns and Nonnus, and there only in simpler phrases—ἐνὶ κυκλάσιν ὥραις, κυκλάδος ὥρης. If κύκλος is retained as the subject we must either (1) with V read ὥρᾳ, which then carries the gen. Καρνείου μηνός, and we have then to decide what to make of κύκλος. (*a*) Monk, citing *IA* 717, takes κύκλος σελάνας together as the orb of the full moon, but the wide separation and the use of the verb περινίσσεται are unnatural; (*b*) Weber: 'when the cycle comes round to its beginning again', this being the New Year's month in Sparta. But κύκλος without an explanatory 'of the year' is unparalleled in this sense, and the meaning of περινίσσεται is also forced: (*c*) LS cites this passage with Ar. *Ran.* 445, Simon. 148, 9B (Antigenes in Diehl) for κύκλος as 'a round dance', cf. κύκλιος χορός. But κύκλος is there not a technical term, but simply the 'circle' or 'ring' of the dance, and for this meaning needs a clear lead from its context, which περινίσσεται certainly does not give; and Σ is surely right in connecting this phrase somehow with Homer's περιτελλο-

μένους ἐνιαύτους. Or (2) we can trust Hesychius: *περι⟨ν⟩ίσσεται ὥρας* which can be pretty safely assumed to refer to this passage. But his explanation *περιέρχεται τὰς ὥρας* does not help us much with the construing of it. Neither *περιέρχομαι* nor the rare *περινίσσομαι* (or -*νῑσομαι*) is ever used in the trans. sense '*bring* round', and 'goes round the seasons' does not make sense. If *ὥρας* is right there must be a rather clumsy double gen.: 'when the cycle of the season of the Carnean month comes round'—a different gen. from the normal *ἐνιαυτοῦ κύκλος*, though perhaps not impossible. To add to the confusion Hesych. also has *ἀειρομένας· περιερχομένας*, which looks as if it might refer to this passage, and if so shows him to have mistaken the case, the construction, and the meaning of *ἀειρομένας*.

450. ἀειρομένας παννύχου σελάνας: *μετεωριζομένης πλησιφαοῦς τῆς σελήνης* Σ. There is no exact parallel, but Hipp. *Aer.* 6 has *ἄνω ἀρθῆναι* of the sun in mid-sky, and S. *Phil.* 1331 uses *αἴρειν* intrans. of the sun's rising.

455 ff.

1	εἴθ' ἐπ' ἐμοὶ μὲν εἴη	–⏑⏑–⏑––	arist.
	ματέρος οὐ θελούσας		
2	δυναίμαν δέ σε πέμψαι	⏑––⏑⏑––	pher.
	πρὸ παιδὸς χθονὶ κρύψαι		
3	φάος ἐξ Ἀίδα τεράμνων	⏑⏑–⏑⏑–⏑––	enop.
	δέμας οὐδὲ πατρὸς γεραιοῦ—		
4	ποταμίᾳ νερτέρᾳ τε κώπᾳ.	⏑⏑⏑––⏑–⏑––	
	ὃν ἔτεκον δ', οὐκ ἔτλαν ῥύεσθαι,		sync. iamb. trim.
5	σὺ γάρ, ὦ μόνα, ὦ φίλα γυναικῶν,	⏑⏑–⏑⏑–⏑–⏑––	enop.
	σχετλίω, πολιὰν ἔχοντε χαίταν—		
6	σὺ τὸν αὑτᾶς	⏑⏑––	anap. monom. cat.
	σὺ δ' ἐν ἥβᾳ		
7	ἔτλας πόσιν ἀντὶ σᾶς ἀμεῖψαι	⏓–⏑⏑–⏑–⏑––	enop.
	νέα νέου προθανοῦσα φωτὸς οἴχῃ.		
8	ψυχᾶς ἐξ Ἅιδα. κοῦφα σοι	–––– ––––	anap. dim.
	τοιαύτας εἴη μοι κῦρσαι		
9	χθὼν ἐπάνωθε πέσοι, γύναι. εἰ δέ τι	–⏑⏑–⏑⏑–⏑⏑–⏑⏑	
	συνδυάδος φιλίας ἀλόχου· τὸ γὰρ		dact. tetram.
	καινὸν ἕλοιτο πόσις λέχος, ἦ μάλ' ἂν	–⏑⏑–⏑⏑–⏑⏑–⏑⏑	
	ἐν βιότῳ σπάνιον μέρος· ἦ γὰρ ἂν		dact. tetram.
10	ἔμοιγ' ἂν εἴη στυγη-	⏑–⏑––⏑–	
	ἔμοιγ' ἄλυπος δι' αἰ-		sync. iamb. dim.
	θεὶς τέκνοις τε τοῖς σοῖς.	–⏑–⏑––	+ ithyph.
	ῶνος ἂν ξυνείη.		

Echoes from strophe to antistrophe (in 2, 6, 9, 10) are again noteworthy. The transition from 9 to 10, with the initial anceps of an iambic following on the uncontracted tail of a dactylic tetrameter, so characteristic of Soph., is not found elsewhere in Eur.

455–6. There is no contrast between **ἐπ' ἐμοὶ εἴη** and **δυναίμαν,** in spite of the *μέν* . . . *δέ*: 'would that it lay in my power and I could.'

457. For the acc. **φάος** without a preposition after *πέμπειν*, 'bring to the light', cf. 479, *Tro.* 883.

458. There is no corresponding line in the antistrophe, and we have to decide between a lacuna there or a deletion here. This line, in its various forms, might have originated, as Wilamowitz, *GV* 537, suggests, from an *ἐκ Κωκυτοῖο ῥεέθρων* substituted for the previous line because *κώπᾳ* 459 was felt to need a river to row on. It adds nothing to the sense or the picture. In the antistrophe the first sentence appears to lack a main verb, which might at first suggest a lacuna—except that it is all but impossible to think of anything to put in it. Weil's punctuation, with a dash after *γεραιοῦ* and another after *χαίταν*, thus putting 469–70 into parenthesis, makes it possible to take *σὺ δ' ἐν ἥβᾳ* as the main sentence, the *δέ* after a participial clause being akin to 'apodotic *δέ*'. Cf. Pl. *Symp.* 220b; I am unable to find any precise parallels in Attic poetry.

459. A highly affected use of co-ordinate epithets to convey a participial phrase 'plied on the underground river'.

460. The traditional text here is perfectly intelligible, even though hard to pin down grammatically. **φίλα γυναικῶν** as *Hipp.* 848, cf. *Hcld.* 567, *Hec.* 716; but instead of *σὺ γὰρ μόνα γυναικῶν, ὦ φίλα γυναικῶν, ἔτλας*, we find *μόνα* attracted into the voc. also, as if it were going to be *ὦ μόνα γυναικῶν τλᾶσα.* It is probably not necessary to write exclamatory *ὢ* (as in *ὤμοι*) so as to leave *μόνα* nom. 'For you, O alone, O dear among women, have dared . . .' seems a possible licence in lyric poetry.

462. **ἀμεῖψαι** pregnantly with **ἐξ Ἅιδα,** as it were 'redeem out of Hades' in exchange for her own life.

463. The earliest extant expression of this prayer, so common in later epitaph, Greek, Latin, and English. For a rhetorical development of the theme cf. *Hel.* 851–4.

471. If L P's *νέα νέου* be adopted (for *ἐν ἥβῃ* by itself cf. *Cyc.* 2), both must be pronounced monosyllabically, cf. A. *Sept.* 327 *νέας*, A. *Supp.* 64 *νέον*, and *νεανίδων Eum.* 959, *νεανικὴν* Ar. *Vesp.* 1067, *νεανιῶν* 1069. This may very well be right, since *φώς* is not used elsewhere absolutely, without the support of an adjective, except in its most general sense of 'man' = 'human being', cf. A. *PV* 549, E. *Rhes.* 773, never as 'husband'. The irrelevance of Admetus' youth here need be no objection in such an antithesis.

472. κῦρσαι: restored for the unmetrical *κυρῆσαι*. Eur. hardly uses *κύρω* except in the aor., but then very commonly.

473. The simplest way of restoring responsion here is with Erfurdt to read *τὸ γὰρ* for **τοῦτο γὰρ** (with the same meaning). Wilam. later (*GV* 537) accepted this solution. But **συνδυάδος φιλίας** is enough by itself to convey 'dear wedded wife' (*φιλίας* simply = *φίλης*, as often in Eur.), and the pleonasm with **ἀλόχου** spoils the effect of the word. (A similar question arises in A. *Ag.* 1108 *τὸν ὁμοδέμνιον πόσιν*, where see Fraenkel's note.) Since it is a *ἅπ. λεγ.* we cannot appeal to usage. If *ἀλόχου* be deleted as a gloss, Murray's *μάλα τοῦτο γὰρ* would be a possible way of filling the lacuna; for the position of *γάρ* cf. Fraenkel on *Ag.* 222.

474. ἄλυπος could mean (1) act. 'without causing me pain', (2) pass. 'without pain', 'untroubled'. The latter is commoner in tragedy, but the former is almost certainly right here. The Chorus does not mean to imply 'I (*ἔμοιγ'* emphatic, in contrast to Admetus) should know how to value her'; no such comparison can be intended, since *ξυνεῖναι δι' αἰῶνος* was the one thing that Fate did not allow to Admetus and Alcestis. The sentiment is simply one of the conventional endings to a choral stasimon: the personal wish, often only loosely connected with the actual situation, cf. *Hcld.* 926, *Phoen.* 1060. Nor is there any reason to suppose that these words, inappropriate to an elderly Chorus, are a sigh from the poet's own heart. 472–5 are an echo of a locus communis about the (rare) good wife, and therefore naturally give the effect from the husband's point of view. Cf. *IA* 1162–3 and Sem. Amorg. 7. 83 ff. D. *τήν τις εὐτυχεῖ λαβών· . . . θάλλει δ' ὑπ' αὐτῆς κἀπαέξεται βίος· φίλη δὲ σὺν φιλεῦντι γηράσκει πόσι.*

476. As the sad song dies away the heroic voice breaks in with invigorating contrast. The abrupt, unheralded entry is deliberate. 'Good citizens of this land of Pherae.' I do not think that **κωμῆται** is a special bit of Thessalian local colour (= members of a rural community grouped round the ruling prince's house), still less that *ἄστυ* 480 is intended as the mild rebuke of hurt local pride. In Athenian political life a *κώμη* was an urban ward, as distinct from a rural *δῆμος*, so that *κωμῆται* in Ar. *Nub.* 965 (cf. *Lys.* 5) is 'fellow-parishioners'. Arist. *Poet.* 1448a 36 notes that in the Peloponnese the *κώμη* was a *rural* community, and in Pl. *Legg.* 762a with its Peloponnesian colour *κωμῆται* is clearly used to mean 'members of a rural community'. But here (476) the word is no different from *δημόται* 1057; both can mean members, or fellow-members, of any kind of local community. There is certainly no need to emend, with Nauck and Wecklein, *χθονός* to *πόλεως*.

480. προσβῆναι: an unusual inf., generally explained as 'inf. of result without the normal *ὥστε*', but perhaps one should say rather that *τίς* *χρεία πέμπει σε* [*Θ. χθόνα*] is followed by an inf. as if it were the equivalent of *τί χρή σε; τί σ' ἀναγκάζει;*

482. The MSS. are divided between *προσέζ.* and *συνέζ.* as again *Hipp.* 1389 (*συμφορᾷ*, v. l. *συμφοραῖς*). *συζ.* is found in *Andr.* 98 (with *δαίμων*), *Hel.* 255 (with *πότμος*), cf. S. *Aj.* 123 *ἄτῃ συγκατέζευκται κακῇ.* In these last three the metaphor could be pressed to make *δαίμων, πότμος, ἄτη* an uneasy yoke-*fellow*; in *Hipp.* 1389 *συμφορᾷ* might give the same meaning, but *συμφοραῖς* would require *προσ-*, the calamities being as it were the heavy plough, or task to which one is harnessed. With **πλάνῳ** the metaphor is in any case getting rather moribund, but *προσ-* is perhaps more appropriate than *συν-*.

483. ἅρμα: see on 66.

484. ἄπειρος εἶ ξένου: probably not simply 'connais-tu l'étranger?' (Méridier), but 'have you no experience of his hospitality?'

486. ἵππων: mares, like all chariot-teams. **μάχης**: with their master, of course.

487. οὐδ': the Chorus has just said 'you cannot . . .' and Her. replies 'but neither can I . . .' (strengthened by **μὴν**, cf. Denniston, *GP* 338, 340). Whether the compulsion is of his sentence or his character, he cannot 'refuse to face labours' because they are difficult. There can be no doubt that **πόνους** acc. (as in *HF* 1354), not *πόνοις* dat. is required here. **ἀπειπεῖν** can be used with a dat. of person, e.g. 'to fail one's friends' as *Med.* 459, but 'labours' can hardly be personified ('say no to') here, since *ἀπειπεῖν πόνοις* would naturally mean 'to give up exhausted under toil', cf. *Hec.* 942, *Or.* 91, and was probably so taken by V B. *μὴν* (Dobree, Weil, Murray) is the only satisfactory way of accounting for *μ' ἦν* in L, which could not possibly have been inserted 'to fill up' (Weber) when *τοὺς* or *τοῖς* dropped out. That the article was inserted when the unintelligible *μ' ἦν* was dropped (cf. P) would on the contrary be quite easy to suppose.

488. Perhaps an echo of some proverbial phrase, cf. *Ion* 1038.

489. τόνδ' ἀγῶνα: i.e. the *ἀγών* of life and death, cf. *Or.* 878 *ἀγῶνα θανάσιμον δραμούμενον.* 'It would not be the first time I had faced that issue.'

493. εἰ μή γε: see Denniston, *GP* 132. *γε* does double duty, affirming, or rather contradicting a denial, and limiting, cf. *Hcld.* 272.

494. ἀλλ': 'no, but . . . .' **ἀρταμοῦσι**: according to the lexicographers used of cooks 'jointing' carcases; so, appropriately, in the *Peliades*, fr. 612N², cf. *El.* 816. **λαιψηραῖς**: lit. 'nimble'.

495. χόρτον: as it were 'lion-fodder'.

498. *Σ* describes the *πέλτη* as a rimless shield, and asserts *ἀπὸ τῶν ὅπλων τοὺς ὁπλίτας φησίν*, i.e. **πέλτης** = *πελταστῶν*, wherein he is followed by some edd., but the picture here is of a single barbarian warrior-king, not a company-commander. **ἄναξ** thus used is a regular tragic metaphor; a man is 'lord' of his weapon or tool. A. *Pers.*

378–9 πᾶς ἀνὴρ κώπης ἄναξ and πᾶς ὅπλων ἐπιστάτης means every rower and every marine, not just the officers; so too *IA* 1260 ὅπλων ἄνακτες, *Cyc.* 86 κώπης ἄνακτας, and Wakefield aptly quotes Ovid, *Met.* 13. 2 'clipei dominus septemplicis Ajax'. Diomedes' crescent-shield is 'much gilded' like that of Rhesus (*Rhes.* 370, cf. ibid. 305) because he is a king; even in golden Thrace the ordinary peltast has no such costly armour.

499. τοὐμοῦ δαίμονος: characteristic of, in accordance with, my destiny.

500. πρὸς αἶπος ἔρχεται = προσάντης ἐστί, i.e. arduous. It is hardly necessary to see in 'for it is ever hard and uphill' an allusion to the Choice of Heracles and the Hesiodic paths of Virtue and Vice (*Op.* 287–92, Xen. *Mem.* 2. 1. 21 ff.).

502. The obscure Lycaon seems to have been (ap. Etym. Flor. s.v. Pyrene, E. Miller, *Mélanges* 258, cited by Weber) a son of Ares and the nymph Pyrene, who challenged Heracles to single combat. It seems likely that this is the same character as the Cycnus of Apollodorus 2. 5. 11, to be distinguished from the more famous Cycnus of 503, son of Ares and Pelopia (Apoll. 2. 7. 7, *HF* 391, Hes. *Sc.* 327 ff.).

507. Admetus must have been summoned by an attendant leaving the stage for that purpose, with news of Heracles' arrival. He retires again at 567, since at 606 the natural assumption is that he comes out of the house once more with the information that all is ready. He is in mourning, with hair cut short (512). Otto Hense, *Die Modificirung der Maske in der gr. Trag.*, p. 24, n. 5, argues that this clearly meant a fresh mask, but in our comprehensive ignorance of the detail of fifth-century stage conventions this must be regarded as uncertain.

509. Perseus was grandfather of Alcmene; farther back Admetus does not go, since Perseus was himself son of Zeus.

511. For the play with χαῖρε Monk compares *Hec.* 427 and *Phoen.* 618.

514. A formula for avoiding an ill-omened question.

519–21. Cf., of Castor and Pollux, *Hel.* 138 τεθνᾶσι κοὐ τεθνᾶσι· δύο δ' ἐστὸν λόγω: they had killed themselves but they had been transformed into immortal stars. Admetus prevaricates—only her unburied body still 'is', so far as his own knowledge goes, and the feeble explanation he presently gives is rightly rejected by Heracles (528). But to the audience, of course, the real savour of this interchange is the unintentional truth of ἔστιν τε κοὐκέτ' ἔστιν—Alcestis, they knew, was not *irretrievably* dead; the μῦθος about her was really ambiguous at this point.

520. For the 'gen. of reference' without a prep. cf. S. *El.* 317 τοῦ κασιγνήτου τί φῄς; and Jebb's note. The idiom is rare enough to account for the substitution of πέρι for ἔτι in L P.

523. μοίρας: an acc. attracted into the oblique case of a following rel. occurs again S. *Trach.* 152 *τότ' ἂν τις εἰσίδοιτο . . . κακοῖσιν οἷς βαρύνομαι*, and is occasionally found in prose.

524. κατθανεῖν ὑφειμένην: 'that she submits to die.'

526. Perhaps *τόδ'* is just possible: 'this point of time of which you speak', picking up *τάδε* of the previous line. **ἀμβαλοῦ**: Nauck's contraction is certain, since Eur. has no resolutions in the third metron of the trimeter in any play written before 420 (*Andr.* 444, a parallel case to this one, should read *ἀμμένει*). The familiar uncontracted forms tend constantly to replace the contracted in MSS., cf. *Andr.* 1137, *El.* 868, *Phoen.* 297.

527. ὁ μέλλων: sc. *θανεῖν*. There is not much to choose between the version of the text (V B) and L's *χὠ θανὼν οὐκ ἔστ' ἔτι*, but the order in L is slightly more logical, with the conclusion (cf. 525) left to the end. V B's version might perhaps have been contaminated from 530. Schwartz's *καὶ θανὼν* would keep *ὁ μέλλων* as the subject all through, but there is no reason to suppose that P's unmetrical version conceals a different tradition.

528. χωρὶς . . . νομίζεται: 'are considered two different things', as S. *OC* 808 *χωρὶς τό τ' εἰπεῖν πολλὰ καὶ τὰ καίρια*, and cf. *δίχα* in A. *PV* 927.

529. A formula of unaltered conviction, cf. *Supp.* 466, *S. Aj.* 1039. There was a proverbial expression (*λόγος παλαιός*) according to Evenus ap. Stob. 80: *Σοὶ μὲν ταῦτα δοκοῦντ' ἐστίν, ἐμοὶ δὲ τάδε.*

531. The doublé sense of **γυνή** is of course untranslatable in English. **ἀρτίως**: Heracles takes 'just now' as the words of 513—the corpse I have been speaking of just now is a woman; Admetus inwardly refers it to 519–27.

533. ἄλλως δ' again with two possible meanings: (1) = *ὅμως δέ*, 'and yet' (2) 'but in another sense' with close ties to the family.

537. i.e. what [ill] design lies at the back of those words?

538. Either **ἄλλων** or *ἄλλην* gives the same sense.

542. ξένους and *φίλοις* are doubtless old variants. *ξένους* is a little repetitive after 540, and if the phrase is proverbial (see below) *φίλοις* is perhaps more likely.

Is **παρᾱ κλαίουσι** possible? This lengthening of a final short vowel before mute + liquid is occasionally found in 'proclitic' words (prepositions, articles, &c.) in the lyrics of Soph. and Eur., though never in Aesch. (see Fraenkel, A. *Ag.*, Appendix E). Cf. supra 101 *ἐπῑ προθύροις*. But in trimeters there is no instance other than the present passage, whether in a proclitic or any other word, in any extant play of the three tragedians; in any apparent instances (cf. Denniston on *El.* 1058) there are strong objections to the text on other grounds. Three are quoted from the fragments of Eur. by Tucker on *Cho.* 854, of which curiously enough one (fr. 642) also concerns παρά, while in fr. 620 παρά is so scanned in anapaests; but rather than admit the conclusion that παραί should be admitted as a tragic form we should perhaps prefer to regard this as a coincidence. Thus ὁ δράσας in the *Gyges* fragment (ed. Lobel, 1950) finds little support in fifth-century tragedy, where even after an augment mute + liquid very rarely 'make position', though there are two instances in S. *Ichneutae* (39, 224). Yet this line in *Alc.* as it stands is exactly right, and any suggested emendation makes it less effective; even ⟨δὲ⟩ (cf. *Cyc.* 425) spoils the proverbial sound of it. It may conceivably be an echo from some earlier setting, such as the work of an iambographer, where the lengthening was in place.

544. '. . . infinitely grateful': all through this interchange we catch echoes of the polite courtesies of everyday Athenian social life.

546 ff. **σύ**: such κωφὰ πρόσωπα would always attend the entrances and exits of a king. For the convention by which a speaker breaks off to address one of these as σύ cf. J. Jackson on *Phoen.* 1279, *CQ* 1941, p. 181. **τῷδε** is better than τῶνδε, cf. *Hel.* 865 ἡγοῦ σύ μοι, and is more likely to have been assimilated to the case of δωμάτων than v.v. 'Take him along and open up the guest-chambers away from the [main] palace . . . and make sure they close (κλῄσατε plur.) the doors between the courts.' These lines are usually taken as evidence (v. Pickard-Cambridge, *Theatre*, p. 52) for three stage doors, but no extant tragedy needs more than one. The directions are designed to make the interior scene clear to spectators who could *not* see it (cf. the escape of the Phrygian *Or.* 1366 ff., where Σ, misunderstanding a similar passage, has led to the rejection of sound lines and a ludicrous misconception of the actual scene). It is not very clear whether the θύραι μέσαυλοι are the doors between the ξενῶνες and the main court or the doors leading to the γυναικωνῖτις at the back, where the wailing would be in progress. **ἐξωπίους**: (lit. 'out of sight of') = 'away from', a Euripidean word, cf. *Med.* 624, *Supp.* 1038, each time with δόμων or δωμάτων, and parodied by Ar. *Thesm.* 881 αὐτὸς δὲ Πρωτεὺς ἔνδον ἔστ' ἢ 'ξώπιος; **εὖ**: the objection to ἐν δὲ κλῄ. is not the tmesis, since this does occur, though rarely, in tragic dialogue, cf. *Hec.* 1172, *HF* 53, S. *Ant.* 420, but the meaning of ἐγκλείω, 'shut in', or 'shut up', 'confine'. It is hardly possible to take ἐν here adverbially ('close it within' Weber, or 'close it withal' Hadley); wherever (after Homer) at the beginning of a sentence the order is preposition –particle–verb the explanation is always tmesis; in adverbial uses more words intervene. And for the meaning 'withal', 'also', there must be traceable in the context the notion 'and among these'.

551. Many edd. adopt Wakefield's προσκειμένης here, and Scaliger's προσκειμένου in 833, and it is true that in 1039 the MSS. are confused between the two words. But προσκ. is used in such contexts—of κακά and the like—either of an *accumulation* (one thing coming 'on top of' another, as in 1039) or of an *inherent* evil, as in S. *Ant.* 1243 *τὴν ἀβουλίαν ὅσῳ μέγιστον ἀνδρὶ προσκεῖται κακόν.* To *be involved in* a misfortune is, conversely, *προσκεῖσθαι κακῷ*, as S. *El.* 1040. *προκ.*, apart from its special sense of the *πρόθεσις* of a corpse, as in 1012, is used of something which *lies before* you, either in the future, temporally considered, as 1149 *τὸν προκείμενον πόνον*, or (by a metaphor), spatially, as S. *Ant.* 1334 (contrasted with *μέλλοντα*), of something present before you, waiting to be dealt with: so here and 833. The Scholiast also uses the verb in the same sense (v. app. crit.) in paraphrasing 747: the Servant speaks *δυσφορῶν ἐφ' οἷς ὁ Ἡρ. πένθους προκειμένου οὐκ ᾐσχύνετο κτλ.*

552. This use of *τί* is unexpected. Monk quotes 'Galle, quid insanis?' but one would suppose the Greek for 'What is this folly?' to be *τί μωραίνεις;* Reiske would emend to *ἦ*—'are you a fool?' not 'why are you a fool?' But exactly the same phrase is found in Men. *Epit.* 766, and attempts there to split it up into *τί; μῶρος εἶ*, or the like, are misguided. The phrase must be accepted.

558. ἐχθροξένους: probably an Aeschylean coinage (*Sept.* 606, 621, *PV* 727) from the familiar *φιλόξενος.*

560. διψίαν: Homer's *πολυδίψιον Ἄργος* (*Il.* 4. 171).

565. τῷ μέν: not, as some edd. surprisingly take it, 'to Heracles', but (whether written *τῷ* or *τῳ*) 'to one man or another'. This is quite clear from the use of the pres. *δοκῶ*, since Heracles was not yet in a position to appraise his conduct; and the whole sentiment is a variation on the type of concluding formula in which a speaker expresses a settled attitude of mind that may seem exaggerated or foolish to the uninstructed, cf. S. *Aj.* 1038, *Ant.* 469, *OC* 1665 *εἰ δὲ μὴ δοκῶ φρονῶν λέγειν, οὐκ ἂν παρείμην οἷσι μὴ δοκῶ φρονεῖν.* One may guess it to be a rhetorical cliché in the speeches of public life.

This scene is of course not designed to illustrate either the sophistic nature of Admetus or the stupidity (or honest simplicity) of Heracles. The plot requires a Deception of the Guest, and Eur. has chosen to use stichomythia as the most entertaining way of effecting this; amid thrust and parry Admetus defends his secret and wins his point against Heracles. A round lie would have been both shocking and inartistic; the ingenious deception does indeed raise a moral issue, but not the issue of candour or untruthfulness. The question, which the Chorus next proceeds to raise, is whether hospitality carried to these lengths is foolish and excessive (551–2) and whether a friend is not entitled to know one's griefs (561–2). Admetus defends his decision on the grounds that the duty of hospitality, at least for his house with its princely tradition, is paramount. The heroic scale of this sentiment in him is a pivot of the whole story, and to suggest that Eur. is trying to convey that it was just folly and vanity is to misunderstand the technique of emphasis. To a Greek dramatist the natural way to make such a point tell is by rhetorical argument—to raise an objection (the Chorus shows at first the shocked disapproval which is the ordinary man's reaction to such conduct) and then to overrule the objection, stating the moral grounds for such a *προαίρεσις*. The Chorus is convinced, and sings its praise and admiration, and as the story develops we see the decision of Admetus win him back Alcestis. By any human moral calculus the reward is out of all proportion to the issue at stake, but the gods in visiting reward or punishment show a comprehensive indifference to any such standard.

α′ 569–87.	1 –⏑–––⏑⏑–⏑⏑–⏑⏑–⏑–⏓ ‖	**s– ddds–**
	2 ⏑–⏑⏑–⏑⏑–⏑–⏑––	⏑ **dd** ⏑ **s–**
	3 –⏑–⏑–– ‖	ithyph. (**ss–**)
	4 ⏑–⏑–⏑–⏑⏑–	⏑ **s** ⏑ **d**
	5 –⏑–⏑––	ithyph. (**ss–**)
	6 –⏑–⏑⏑–⏑–	glyc. (**sds**)
	7 ––⏑⏑–⏑–––	**–dss̄**
	8 –––⏑⏑––	pher. (**s̄d–**)
β′ 588–605.	1 ––⏑⏑–⏑⏑–	**–dd**
	2 –⏑–––⏑⏑–⏑⏑–	**s– dd**
	3 –⏑–––⏑⏑–⏑⏑–	**s– dd**
	4 –⏑⏑–⏑⏑–⏑⏑–⏑⏑–⏑⏑–⏑–– ‖	**ddddds–**
	5 ––⏑⏑–⏑⏑–⏑– –⏑⏑–⏑⏑–	**–dds | dd**
	6 –⏑–––⏑⏑––	**s– d–**
	7 ⏑⏑⏑– –⏑– ⏑––	iamb. trim. cat. (^{r}**s | ss–**)

(In *β*′ 6 I have taken *Αἰγαῖον* 595 with *θράσος* 604, v. infra.) Perhaps *β*′ 3 and 4 should be run together in one long period, in view of *ἐν* 599, but the length seems excessive for tragedy. A pause after *δαπέδοις* 591 = *ἀρτιθανῆ* 600 would be possible, but there is no support in the context for the opening on double-short which would have to follow. There are objections to each alternative.

The metre is akin to dactylo-epitrite, but is based on a greater variety of units, some of them nameless in the traditional nomenclature. The regular dactylo-epitrite units, –⏑– (**s** in my terminology) and –⏑⏑–⏑⏑– (**dd**), with anceps interspersed, appear in *α*′ 2 and *β*′ 1, 2, 3. The type of phrase which changes from double- to single-short at the end is found in *β*′ 5 (**dds**), the *ἅλιε καὶ φάος ἁμέρας* of 244; a longer form **ddds** in *α*′ 1, and a still longer one (with this colometry) in *β*′ 4. The admixture of such common cola as the ithyphallic, glyconic, and pherecratean is found elsewhere in the dactylo-epitrite of drama. There are 'drags' in *α*′ 7 and 8.

Stanza 1 is addressed to the *οἶκος*, the 'house' or 'household' (possibly with a change at 573, v. infra); stanza 2 to Apollo. In 3 and

4 the subject, unexpressed but unmistakable, of the verbs *τίθεται, κρατύνει, δέξατο* is Admetus, and *οἰκεῖ* must surely be accepted for *οἰκεῖς* 589 to avoid unnecessary harshness and confusion.

569 ff. With the MS. text **ἀνδρὸς** must = *Ἀδμήτου*, which is perhaps just possible, but awkward. Purgold's *πολυξείνου καὶ ἐλευθέρου* is much easier, and probably right. The **οἶκος** is so far identified with its master that from the more literal **σέ . . . ναίειν** the angle can change to the personal **σοῖσι . . . ἐν δόμοις**—this, at least, seems better than to take *δόμοις* as the actual building, since as *μηλονόμας* Apollo's life would be passed mainly out of doors. **ἐλεύθερος**: 'liberal', in prose *ἐλευθέριος*.

573. ἔτλα: cf. on 1; Apollo was 'not too proud' to become a herdsman. The question where to write *ᾱ* for *η* against the MS. tradition is a thorny one; on the whole subject see G. Björck, *Das Alpha Impurum und die tragische Kunstsprache* (Uppsala, 1950), who thinks that *ἔτλη* here and *ἔτλης Hel.* 218 are perhaps better left.

575. *δόχμιος* is used of something which 'runs athwart' the main axis, whether 'slanting' on the flat plane as in 1000, or 'sloping' on the upright, as here. *Σ τῶν πλαγίων καὶ ἀνακεκλιμένων ὀρῶν*, since *πλάγιος* is also used in this double sense. 'Over the tilted hill-slopes piping to your flocks.'

577. ποιμνίτας: adjectival. The 'pastoral wedding-chants' Apollo pipes to the flocks are not premonitions of Theocritus; it is the herds, not the herdsmen, who are to wed. *Σ ποιμενικὰς ᾠδὰς δι' ὧν ἦγεν τὰ βοσκήματα εἰς τὸ ἀλλήλοις μίγνυσθαι* is a sound if prosaic paraphrase of Eur.'s charming conceit.

579 ff. Apollo's music, of pipe (576) or lyre (583), lays its spell not only on the flocks and herds but on wild creatures also, swift, fierce, and shy alike. Spotted lynxes come to graze placidly among the flocks, a tawny troop of lions stalks down from the mountain-clefts, the dappled fawn steps dainty-footed out from the shelter of the high-crowned firs and dances in the open.

579. χαρᾷ μελέων: Maas points out that the phrase recalls *φθογγῆς χαρᾷ* (of Orpheus) in a closely related context A. *Ag.* 1630, and strengthens the case there for D. A. Rees's conjecture *πάντα πο⟨υ⟩*, *CR* lxi, (1947), 74. This miracle was already a familiar part of the Orpheus myth in poetry and art, cf. Fraenkel on A. *Ag.* 1629. **τε . . . δὲ** is sometimes found as a form of antithesis, or where the emphasis is on the second, cf. S. *Trach.* 143 with Jebb's note. In such cases, in effect, *τε* is substituted for *μέν*. But here there is simply an enumeration *τε . . . δὲ . . . δ'*, which can only be explained as a slight anacoluthon.

583. ἀμφὶ σὰν κιθάραν: 'to your lyre', a rare use of this preposition instead of *ὑπό* or *πρός*, for which J. Tate compares *Phoen.* 1028 *ἄλυρον ἀμφὶ μοῦσαν.*

588 ff. The grace of Apollo has brought unexampled prosperity to Admetus, both in the numbers of his flocks and in the extent of his dominion. The modest domain of a Thessalian princeling round Boebeis, which we find in the possession of his son Eumelus, *Il.* 2. 711–15, is magnified by the Chorus in vague language to suggest the whole of the Thessalian plain with its ring of mountains, Othrys on the south (580), Molossia in Epirus to the west (a claim possibly suggested by the name of the historical Admetus king of the Molossians with whom Themistocles took refuge), and eastward the steep, harbourless coast of the peninsula formed by Pelion round the gulf of Pagasae. The flocks graze on the foothills, and the flat acres are cornland. In spite of this vast imaginative sweep, the actual location of the play is simply Pherae with its immediate country-surroundings, extended at most to the later tetrarchy of Pelasgiotis (1154).

588. πολυμηλοτάταν: cf. the traditional names of his children, *Εὔμηλος* and *Πολυμήλη*.

589. καλλίναον: a conventional epithet hardly applicable to a stagnant piece of water. **Βοιβίαν** appears to be unique; the usual form is *Βοιβηίς*, as in *Il.* 2. 711, Hdt. 7. 129, &c., from the town *Βοίβη*.

590 ff. The *general* sense is clear; **μὲν . . . δ'** (or possibly *τ'*, as lectio difficilior) give the western and eastern limits respectively, in the direction of the sunset and on the Aegean side. But the *precise* meaning is very uncertain and the text doubtful. 603 in the antistrophe is longer by ⏑ ⏑ –, and though **ἄγαμαι** is perhaps detachable (but see below) its emphatic affirmation is admirably placed and its interpolation would be extremely difficult to account for. Since the opening of 595 looks sound, it seems that the lacuna must fall before *τίθεται*, and it might be easier to fill if we knew the meaning or construction of the peculiar phrase **αἰθέρα τὰν Μολοσσῶν**. 'The sky of the M.' is perhaps somewhere on the verge of possible Greek; 'the sky of the M. mountains', reading with many edd. ⟨*ὀρέων*⟩ seems to me slightly beyond it. To take *αἰθήρ* as 'quarter of the sky', hence 'clime', 'region', is entirely without parallel. An adjective such as *δροσερὰν* or *ζοφερὰν* might make the expression a little easier. The usual practice is to make *αἰθέρα* the object of *τίθεται* and *ὅρον* predicative: 'makes the sky his boundary', but the normal phrase is *ὅρον τιθέναι* or *τιθέσθαι*, 'sets the boundary of his cornlands where the sun stables his horses in the west', and in that case *αἰθ. τ. Μ.* must be in apposition to *ἱππόστασιν*, 'the western stables of the sun, the sky of the M.'. But it is unlikely that the stables were imagined *in the sky*; certainly in the *Phaethon* (773. 5) the eastern stables of Helios are on solid earth, though as these rival stables must belong to separate fantasies we should not perhaps make too much of this. In any case it seems desirable to obelize *αἰθέρα τὰν*. Pohlenz suggests *εἰς τὸ πέραν*, with which of course Bauer's ⟨*ὀρέων*⟩ would be unobjectionable.

Eastward also the prospect is somewhat hazy. The MSS. all have *Αἰγαῖον*, to which there is no metrical objection; responsion can be saved by reading *θράσος* for *θάρσος* 604 (for their interchangeability see Wilam. on *HF* 624). In that case *πόντιον*, *Αἰγαῖον*, and *ἀλίμενον* would all be attributes of *ἀκτὰν Πηλίου*, and *κρατύνει* would be used absolutely. *Σ* construes in this way with *both* versions, *Αἰγαῖον* and *Αἰγαίωνα*, which he gives without comment or explanation. Edd. generally accept the latter, with the construction implied in LS. '*πόντιον Αἰγαίωνα* = the Aegean Sea', i.e. the phrase is the object of the verb *κρατύνει*, and 'Aegaeon of the sea' is an eponymous being. In *Il.* 1. 404 he is a giant, identified with Briareos, and we can no longer trace the process which led to his identification—if indeed it is the same Aegaeon—with Poseidon in Lycophron 135 and Callim. fr. 59. 6 Pf. But we do not want Admetus ruling 'over the Aegean as far as the headland of Pelion'; his was no thalassocracy, and the context requires simply the sea as his eastern boundary. It seems then that we must construe as *Σ* does, and in that case, unless *ἐπί* is to be taken *ἀπὸ κοινοῦ*, an adjective rather than a noun is wanted. *Αἰγαῖον* is certainly an adjective; whether *Αἰγαίωνα* can be one is doubtful. No argument is possible on metrical probabilities here.

600 ff. *ἐκφέρεσθαι* is more often used of undesirable impulses. cf. S. *El.* 628 *πρὸς ὀργὴν ἐκφέρῃ*, the metaphor suggesting a chariot plunging off the course. Nobility tends to carry its chivalry almost too far, but in the noble (*οἱ ἀγαθοί* practically = *οἱ εὐγενεῖς*) are to be found all qualities, wisdom included: the Chorus are confident that this apparent excess is really good sense; Admetus has an instinct for the right which is denied to them, and they can but admire—and hope that virtue will again be rewarded.

603. πάντα σοφίας is a curious phrase, and possibly we should punctuate after **ἔνεστιν.** *σοφίας ἄγαμαι* would then be a close parallel to *Rhes.* 244 *ἄγαμαι λήματος* in the same grammatical detachment. The implication of *πάντ' ἔνεστιν* would still be felt as including *σοφία*.

605. θεοσεβῆ φῶτα may be a generalization, but more probably = Admetus, *this* god-fearing man, cf. 830 *ἀνδρὸς φιλοξένου*. For **κεδνὰ πράξειν** = *εὖ πράξειν* Monk compares *Tro.* 683 *οὐδὲ κλέπτομαι φρένας πράξειν τι κεδνόν*.

606 ff. Enter Admetus, and servants carrying Alcestis on the bier. The procession halts for the Chorus to pay their last greetings (610), but the entry of Pheres to pay *his* postpones this ceremony till 741 ff. The 'customary' sentiments are heard in *χαῖρε* 626 and 743, *εὖ σοὶ γένοιτο* 627, &c., and the words of praise. The stasimon 435 ff. is really an anticipation of the farewell greeting, of which 741 ff. is merely a summary repetition.

606. 'Gracious attendance of Pheraeans': cf. a similar abstract with gen. *Hcld.* 581 *ὑμεῖς τ', ἀδελφῶν ἡ παροῦσ' ὁμιλία*, S. *Trach.* 964 *ξένων γὰρ ἐξόμιλος ἥδε τις βάσις*.

608. τάφον τε καὶ πυράν: since Alcestis' story requires simple burial (and cf. 365 ff.) it is probable that *πυρά* is used here in the sense of tumulus = *τύμβος, κολώνη*, as in Pind. *Isth.* 8. 57 *πυρὰν τάφον θ'*, S. *El.* 901, *Hec.* 386, *IT* 26, irrespective of whether the body had been, or was to be, burned upon it.

614 ff. Pheres' sentiments, especially 621–2, have in the circumstances a smooth *ἀναίδεια* which makes Admetus' outburst hardly surprising.

617. The v.l. *δυσμενῆ* of B V, glossed by *Σ* B with *δύσκολα*, 'troublesome', is hardly tolerable; elsewhere when it is used of things, as *Andr.* 468, S. *El.* 440, there is unmistakably a personal hostile agent in the background.

619. ταύτης σῶμα, rather than *τόνδε νεκρόν*, in deliberate contrast to **σῆς ψυχῆς**: this poor return is all I can make.

623. V's comparative gives much better point than the superlative.

625. *τόνδ' ἐμὸν* L P *tout court* would be an unnatural expression for Pheres to use of his son, and can only be a corruption of **τόνδε μὲν**. The shape of this line gives it a particular solemnity.

627–8. 'Such a marriage profits a man, or he had better not marry' is not a logically expressed alternative, though the meaning is clear. Musgrave quotes from Aristides, *or.* 50, 65, p. 442 Keil *τὸ τῆς παροιμίας, ἔφη, ἐρεῖς, ἢ τοιαύτην χρὴ γαμεῖν, ἢ μὴ γαμεῖν*, an obvious trimeter, quoted by Kock, *CAF* iii as fr. adesp. 235, p. 452, with Cobet's *ἤ⟨τοι⟩ κτλ.* Possibly the line is descended from this passage.

630. φίλοισι: prob. masc. *κατὰ σύνεσιν*: 'nor do I count your presence as that of a friend.'

631–2. The echo in these two lines is probably for rhetorical effect rather than a sign of corruption.

633. τότε: the abrupt asyndeton of rising passion.

635. ἀποιμώξῃ: ζ and ξ are easily confused, but the majority of MSS. seem to be trying to give a future. In fifth-century Attic this must be middle, so that *ἀποιμώξῃ* is probably right, and that commits us to an indignant question here. From this it is easier to pass on to a rising temperature of questions in the next lines.

636 ff. These lines are a locus conclamatus, in which the main problems are two: (1) Could Admetus, however carried away by fury, have attributed a servile origin to himself by way of accusation against his father? (2) Should any of them be excised as superfluous, having belonged perhaps to another play or to an alternative version which at the time of collation was added instead of rejected?

It is true that in an *ἀγών* when passions are sufficiently roused no holds are barred, but so much more mud is left sticking to Admetus than to Pheres by this accusation in its positive form that it seems surprising Pheres did not point it out in his reply. And it is rather early in the indictment for so drastic a conclusion to be drawn. It may be objected that the whole point is that Admetus does not see the absurdity of the figure he cuts here, that his blind rages were of just this quality. I do not believe Eur. did wish to exhibit Admetus in so ridiculous a light, nor is it in general part of his technique to use a rhetorical *ἀγών* to bring out subtle details of the psychology of the disputants; the general tone is in keeping with the whole character of the speaker, but the arguments used are as good and as hard-hitting as his case allows. The contradiction between the sentiment here and 644–6 just below makes nonsense of both points. Earle suggests that 636–9 may be an interpolation from the Euripidean *Oedipus*, part of a speech of Oedipus to Polybus; Wilamowitz deletes 641 as intolerably flat after 636–9 (but 641 cannot be separated from 640, and 642–7 amplify and explain 640–1). But Murray's expedient of adding question-marks at 636–8–9 gives an entirely different tone to the whole passage, which becomes a highly effective *reductio ad absurdum.* You could hardly have shown less concern over my fate if I had been some miserable slave-child passed off as your own by the fraudulent connivance of your wife. In 640 Admetus answers his own angry questions: Pheres may be *ὀρθῶς τοῦδε σώματος πατήρ*, but spiritually he has disqualified himself by his *ἀψυχία*, and Admetus now formally rejects him: **οὐ νομίζω** 'I no longer count myself your son'; henceforth Alcestis shall take the place of father and mother in his regard. Perhaps the plur. **εἰάσατε** 645 might be taken as a slight additional reason for retaining the mention of the mother in 637–8.

646–7. For the thought in a very different context edd. compare *Il.* 6. 429 (the orphaned Andromache). *τέ γε* is rare, and usually meets with some resistance in the MS. tradition (see the examples in Denniston, *GP* 161). If we accept L P here **καὶ . . . τε** must not be taken as corresponsive; *τε* is substituted for a second *καί* in order to show that the meaning is *not* 'both . . . and', but 'yes, and father too'—in spite of the awkwardness of the sex.

648 ff. As Murray says, Admetus could almost have composed Pheres' speech of renunciation for him. . . .

651–2. An intolerable repetition from 295–6, here interrupting the connexion of thought.

655. **ἦν**: if correct, the earliest appearance of this form of the 1st pers. sing. It is not found in Aesch. or Soph. (v. Jebb on *OT* 1123), and it should probably be removed from our texts wherever the metre does not require it, e.g. infra 660, *Hec.* 284. As *Hipp.* 1012, in a relatively early play, appears to be genuine, there is no compulsion to reject it here, but it must be admitted that Nauck's *ἦ γεγώς* makes excellent sense.

658. A neat illustration of a corrupt reading in the making. L P are of course right; it is strange that several edd. have chosen the other alternative. There is no question, even in Admetus' heated imagination, of Pheres' accusing him of giving his father up to death. What he is saying is, in effect, 'You cannot allege as an excuse for giving me up to die that I had failed in respect for your age'. *Σ* read *προύδωκας* correctly but had *ἀτιμάζων τὸ σὸν*, which he construes through a brick wall by saying that *ἀτιμάζων* is here put for *ἀτιμάζοντα*.

666. τοὐπὶ σέ here not 'quod ad te attinet', but 'quantum in tua potestate fuit', cf. Porson on *Or.* 1345.

668. Admetus speaks in legalistic terms, regardless of the inapplicability of these words to his actual saviour. 666–8 are not detachable; they are needed to complete 665.

669–72. These lines recall the subject of the Aesopic fable (90 Halm) of the old man and the bundle of faggots. 669–70 (with *πολὺν* for *μακρὸν*) appear, presumably by error, in a collection of distichs from Menander (713K), and the passage has quite unnecessarily been suspected here, especially in view of the violation of 'Porson's Canon' in 671. (There seems, however, to be almost a case for a special licence for *οὐδείς, οὐδέν* in this position; see *Phoen.* 747, *Cyc.* 120, 672, *Mel. Desm.* fr. 6, 27, S. *OC* 1022, and cf. Maas, *Metrik* 135.) It is certainly common form for Eur. to end a long agonistic speech with a bit of trenchant popular morality.

673–4. The close formal parallel with 706–7 protects these lines. Mekler rewrites them *Ἄδμηθ', ἅλις γὰρ . . . παῦσαι, πατρὸς δὲ κτλ.*, but the repetition of *ὦ παῖ* in 675 need not worry us. Where a speaker turns in the middle of a speech to a new addressee, with a voc. and a postponed *δέ*, it is usual to insert some case of *σύ* before the *δέ*, cf. S. *Ant.* 1087 *ὦ παῖ, σὺ δ' ἡμᾶς ἄπαγε*, but here *πατρὸς* takes that place for the sake of the juxtaposition *παῖ πατρός*—a juxtaposition which is itself the main reason for this unusual form of address from the Chorus.

675. Anachronisms did not worry Eur. Ar.'s parody *Av.* 1244–5 so many years later (cf. infra 691, *Thesm.* 194, *Nub.* 1415) suggests that this was a famous passage.

679–80. ἄγαν, like *λίαν*, in later Greek shortened its final syllable, and is apt to appear in MSS. with these additions (*μ'* L), cf. 809, S. *OT* 439, intended to lengthen it. **νεανίας** in the sense of *νεανικός*. *οὐχ οὕτως* = 'non impune' Elmsley. **ῥίπτων** and **βαλὼν** could be merely synonyms—as it were 'you shall not merely finish your hurling and go'—but *βαλών* with some verb of going off appears to have been a proverbial phrase. 'Suidas' s.v. *βαλὼν φεύξεσθαι οἴει· πρὸς τοὺς κακόν τι δράσαντας καὶ οἰομένους ἐκφεύγειν*, cf. Pl. *Symp.* 189b, *Rep.* 344d, Plut. *de s. n. v.* 548b.

683–4. i.e. neither the law of the land nor the Rights of Man contain such a provision.

685–6. Your life is your own responsibility, not mine, even if you have the misfortune to be fated to die young.

687–8. **πολλῶν**: probably neut., though the meaning 'much *land*' is to be supplied out of **γύας**. Like his father before him (cf. 654 ἥβησας) Pheres had handed over the kingdom to Admetus but retained some private domains of his own. Purgold's **ταῦτ'** is an improvement on ταῦτ'.

697. ψέγεις in the second Hervagian reprint of the Aldine is clearly a conjecture prompted by the unusual sense of **λέγεις**, 'talk of'.

In the theatrical ἀγών, as in the law-courts, it is usual for the plaintiff to speak first; but there is also a tendency to put the stronger case, if there is one, second—stronger either in justice or in debating-points—and occasionally, as with Helen v. Hecuba in *Tro.*, this is allowed to invert the normal order. Here Pheres is the defendant and so naturally speaks second, but there can be no doubt that he also wins on points with this superb speech, in its mordant wit hardly surpassed in Greek tragedy. Not that Eur. approves of the old rascal; the judgements of Alcestis and the Chorus have united with Admetus in condemning him, but the plot requires that Admetus shall be defeated here, so that when his temper has cooled he shall realize what the ill-disposed can make of his situation. Sorrow and ill fame are what he has gained by living on, the first he has begun to feel already, the second only the malice of Pheres could bring home to him. It is not just, or fair, or objective, or the general judgement on Admetus; it is the counterblast of selfishness driven to self-defence, but Admetus has provoked it by putting himself in the wrong with the unfilial violence and exaggeration of his attack.

706. The slight anacoluthon in **τὰ πρὶν** does not require emendation; it also picks up more pointedly the last words of Pheres—*those* κακά.

708. **λέξαντος**: i.e. I made my accusation and it stands, whatever insults you heap on me. Σ gives λέγε ὡς καὶ ἐμοῦ κακῶς ἐλέγξαντος (v.l. ἐλέγξοντος) δι' ὧν οὐκ ἠθέλησας ὑπὲρ ἐμοῦ ἀποθανεῖν, on the strength of which Weber reads ἐμοῦ 'λέγξοντος in this line. But what would κακῶς ἐλέγχειν in Σ mean? (Hermann, who first proposed 'λέγξοντος, would emend Σ κακῶς to καλῶς.) Schwartz in his edition of the scholia reads κακῶς λέξαντος, but surely Dindorf's κακῶς σὲ λέξαντος is palaeographically more satisfactory.

712. Pheres does not answer the question directly, since he has made his point already 691 ff., but goes on from ἐξημάρτανον 710; it would have been a worse wrong because no one has any right to dispose of an extra life.

713. It appears from ἀρᾷ in the next line that this must be taken as a wish, and therefore ἂν is an intrusion due to a misunderstanding. In its extravagance the wish has the force of a malediction (cf. the story of Tithonus). The supposed etymological connexion of *Ζεύς* with *ζῆν* comes out more clearly in *Or.* 1635 with the Ionic gen. *Ζηνός*, but the idea was clearly a proverbial one, cf. *Tro.* 770–1: Helen cannot be sprung from Zeus since she brings death, not life.

716. σὺ: a *tu quoque*.

718. The **οὔτοι . . . γ'** gives support to Hermann's version of *Med.* 1365 *οὔτοι νιν ἡμὴ δεξιά γ' ἀπώλεσεν.*

719. *Σ*'s misinterpretation *εἴθε χρειάν μου ἔσχες ἵνα σοι ὑπηρετήσω* seems to have misled both Wilamowitz and Weber. The sense, of course, is menacing: 'just wait till you need my help one day . . .'. Cf. Xanthias in Ar. *Ran.* 532–3.

722. For **φίλον . . . φίλον** cf. *Bacch.* 963, where Dodds cites, besides this passage, *Hipp.* 327, *Rhes.* 579.

723. οὐκ ἐν ἀνδράσιν = *ἄνανδρον*, but the phrase is a curious one; elsewhere (infra 732, *Or.* 1528, *IA* 945) it is, as one would expect, only used of *persons*.

724. The phrase is highly elliptical; apparently it means 'you are baulked of the pleasure of carrying your old father out to burial as a substitute for yourself'.

725. You will come to die one day, and you will die infamous.

726. The disclaimer is just as deliberately cynical and shocking to common sentiment as Admetus indicates; a clear comment on the moral level at which Pheres has won.

728. Not old and shameless, but young and foolish.

730 ff. A well-barbed final thrust; his acceptance of Alcestis' sacrifice might entitle him to rank as a murderer who could be pursued by blood-feud. The allusion to Acastus, son of Pelias, a far from famous mythological figure, is of a highly unusual type in drama or indeed in any form of narrative, apart from lyric. Maas suggests that the family may have become familiar to the Athenians through Micon's paintings in the Anakeion, cf. Lippold in *RE* s.v. 'Mikon', 1932, p. 1559, 10 ff. Acastus may conceivably have been a character in the *Peliades*, but that was already seventeen years ago.

731. *τε* V B is quite probably right; the external sanction will be *added* to the religious offence.

734. ἔρρων which *Σ* found in some texts is undoubtedly right; *ἔρροις* makes an awkward asyndeton in the following words.

735. ὄντος was bound to be corrupted to *ὄντες*, not v.v. As Paley pointed out, *γὰρ* in 736 requires *παιδὸς ὄντος*, of which it gives the explanation.

736–7. τῷδ' ἔτ' Elmsley is a very probable origin for the divergent corruptions of L P and V B. **νεῖσθ'**, as usual in its finite forms, with fut. sense.

737–8. Fathers could publicly disinherit their sons; he would have liked to disown his parents in the same formal way.

741. σχετλία: *καρτερική Σ*, probably rightly, not 'pauvre victime d'un fier courage' (Méridier). As with *τλήμων*, the earlier meaning of *σχέτλιος* was 'enduring', 'steadfast', and this occasionally survives in tragedy, though the sense 'miserable' became much the commoner. The gen. is possible with either meaning, cf. *Ion* 960 *τλήμων σὺ τόλμης*.

743. The welcome of Hermes Psychopompos and Hades is a modest wish; the thought of a seat as *πάρεδρος* by the side of Persephone is a measure of how far Alcestis is the noblest of women. The concept of a *πάρεδρος* varies with the context; sometimes it is technical: 'assessor', as of Aeacus in Isoc. 9. 15; here it is perhaps hardly more than a specially honoured Lady-in-Waiting, as the Loves 'attend upon' Wisdom *Med.* 843. Helen may be destined for some less subordinate position by the side of Hera and Hebe *Or.* 1687, but to be Zeus-born was a higher claim than mere moral virtue—'if even there virtue has its reward'; the gentle piety of the Chorus is less than optimistic.

The Chorus, or the Coryphaeus, speaks these anapaests to music as it turns and follows Admetus and the funeral procession. The scene is left empty, as the action requires, since Heracles must make his resolve without witnesses. So again *Hel.* 385, *Rhes.* 565, and in the *Phaethon*, but also (with a change of scene) A. *Eum.* 231, S. *Aj.* 814. It does not commonly happen, but any dramatist could adopt this expedient when his plot required it.

747. The monologue of the Servant on an empty stage is in effect spoken directly at the audience, as again the monologue of Heracles 837–60. The same technique is employed for Menelaus in *Hel.* 386–434 and 483–514; elsewhere in extant Greek tragedy it is found only in the prologues. It became common, of course, in any part of the chorusless New Comedy, and presumably Epicharmus used it freely. But even in the middle of a tragedy such a speech makes no very unusual impression, since often enough the address to the Chorus is little more than a perfunctory form.

748. ξένους μολόντας οἶδ': 'I have known strangers to come.'

750. κακίον'. This is the earliest extant appearance of what was to become so common a gambit in the dramatic monologues of comedy—the assertion of a superlative by the denial of a comparative (or by *οὐχ οὕτω* with the positive), in describing the behaviour of someone within the house; the speaker enters bursting, as it were, with irrepressible feelings about it, as Socrates (*Nub.* 627) about the stupidity of Strepsiades. E. Fraenkel, *Plaut. im Plautus*, pp. 165 ff. gives many examples from Greek and Latin comedy.

754–5. συμφορὰν μαθών: the Servant naturally assumes that Heracles knows of Alcestis' death, since he had met Admetus at the gate. A tactful guest (**σωφρόνως**), assuming he had come in at all, would have 'taken it as he found it' (**τὰ προστυχόντα ξένια**); evidently the fare was a scratch meal, and Heracles, knowing the standards of hospitality Admetus would wish his household to observe, would feel justified in calling for more. So each motif of the traditional burlesque can be modified to suit this context.

756. ποτῆρα: the word occurs again *Cyc.* 151 of a drinking vessel, but not elsewhere; presumably it is meant to convey a large size of *ποτήριον*. **κίσσινον**: cf. *Cyc.* 390, fr. 146N² for the association of ivy with *large* vessels or pails; I have tried to show in *CR* n.s. ii (1952) 3 that this is simply because Eur. is rendering in iambic form the Homeric *κισσύβιον* (*Od.* 9. 346). **χείρεσσι**: an epic form not found elsewhere in dialogue, though it appears in a lyric trimeter S. *Ant.* 1297.

757. μελαίνης μητρὸς: the black grape, cf. A. *Pers.* 614–15 *ἀκήρατον δὲ μητρὸς ἀγρίας ἄπο | πότον*. In the mouth of a slave the mannered periphrasis sounds incongruous; Eur. least of the tragedians varies the tone and style of his dialogue to the person speaking.

760. Cf. frag. inc. 907N² (probably from the *Syleus*) *κρέασι βοείοις χλωρὰ σῦκ' ἐπήσθιεν | ἄμουσ' ὑλακτῶν*. This 'discordant braying' is the climax of Heracles' revelry here. The Cyclops (*Cyc.* 425 *ᾄδει . . . ἄμουσα*) was affected by drink in the same way.

766. τινα. The Servant does not know who the guest is, hence the candour of these remarks, unawed by the great name.

768. *Σ* aptly compares A. *Cho.* 8–9, lines for which he is our only source.

773. οὗτος. This form of address by the demonstrative pronoun is not, except where the further context makes it so, rough or insulting. It demands the hearer's attention with a touch of peremptoriness or impatience, as when the divine voice called Oedipus and asked why he delayed (*OC* 1627). It is usually amplified by *σε καλῶ* or the like (as S. *Aj.* 71, 89, *Trach.* 402) or, most commonly, introduces a protesting question, as here, cf. *Med.* 922, *Hec.* 1127, 1280, A. *Supp.* 911, S. *OT* 532. **πεφροντικὸς**: 'worried', the state of mind which arises from overmuch *φροντίζειν*. For the combination of adjective and perf. part. in an internal acc. cf. Theocr. 20. 14–15 *σεσαρὸς | καὶ σοβαρόν μ' ἐγέλαξεν*.

778. *Σ σπουδάζων εἰς ἀλλότριον πένθος· ἐνόμιζε γὰρ ὅτι ξένη ἦν ἡ ἀποθανοῦσα.*

780. The regular Ionic forms *οἶδας, οἴδαμεν, οἴδατε, οἴδασι*, common in the later *κοινή*, are occasionally found in archaic and Attic Greek, though it is of course often difficult to decide whether they should be emended (for instance *Od.* 1. 337, E. *Supp.* 1044) when they are not protected by metre. **οἶδας** appears here only in tragedy, and there are two or three instances in New Comedy, but the form *οἶσθας* is commoner in Mid. and New Comedy.

781. πόθεν γάρ; cf. on 95.

784. τὴν αὔριον μέλλουσαν: 'the day which will be on the morrow' cf. the slightly different phrase S. *OC* 567 τῆς εἰς αὔριον ἡμέρας.

785. οἶ προβήσεται V B: a dat. form of adverb, οἶ or ποῖ, is normal with this verb, cf. *Med.* 1117, *Hipp.* 342, 936, *Or.* 511.

785–6. *τύχη . . . τέχνη*: the antithesis beloved of stage philosophers. **διδακτὸν**: neither by theory (διδαχή) nor practice (τέχνη) can we acquire knowledge of the processes of *τύχη*.

790. Such a double superlative is a not uncommon form of emphasis; cf. Page on *Med.* 1323.

792. ταῦτα: these things that are troubling you.

795–6. Herwerden's deletion (v. app. crit.) is to be commended; the double repetition so soon afterwards (829, 832) is highly suspicious, especially as *Σ* notes a variant *πύλας* (from 829) here too. **τύχας** looks like a perfunctory attempt to give better sense here but 'surmounting these chances' is wholly superfluous after *τὴν ἄγαν λύπην ἀφείς*.

797–8. The general sense of this rather involved metaphor is clearer than the exact significance of each detail. *τὸ ξυνεστὸς φρενῶν*: his state of mind, 'clotted' as it were with sullenness (cf. *Hipp.* 983), will be loosened into gaiety with drink. *μεθορμίζω*: the change of heart becomes a transference to a better anchorage. **πίτυλος ἐμπεσὼν σκύφου**: it is difficult to twist this into the 'plash' of the wine 'falling into' the tankard; rather *πίτ. σκ.* is the rhythmical elbow-lifting and gurgling of the carouse, and with *ἐμπεσὼν* sc. *σοι* out of *σε*—it will 'get hold of' you (like a passion or a disease, cf. S. *Ant.* 782) and 'transport' you to a better place.

802. συμφορά: just one long misery. He supposes the Servant to be no more than sulky and ungracious.

803. πράσσομεν: our present fortunes.

807. τί with a word repeated in surprise or indignation—'how do you mean, *live*?'—has clearly a colloquial flavour. See P. T. Stevens 'Colloquial Expressions in Euripides', *CQ* xxxi (1937), 184, for parallel instances in Greek and Latin comedy.

809. *γ'* L P: see on 679.

810. 'Was I to lack hospitable treatment just because of a stranger's death?' *οὐκοῦν* L P must have been combined with *εὖ πάσχει*, the *-ν* having dropped out before *νεκροῦ*. The subject of course would be *ἐκεῖνος*, and the sense none.

811. The stronger MS. tradition, with *Σ*, gives *οἰκεῖος*, which would be a simple, emphatic declaration from the Servant, giving the show away prematurely and forcing Heracles to the direct question (in fact not reached till 820). Nevertheless nearly all edd. adopt *οἰκεῖος*, to the detriment of the sense; Weber gives two reasons: (1) the accumulation of particles to express painful emotion—but much more necessary with **θυραῖος** to express irony; besides, **ἦ . . . μέντοι** (Denniston, *GP* 399 ff., 410) is emphatic affirmative, not the equivalent of *μὲν οὖν*; (2) the Servant is not up to irony—but this is the common confusion between what Aristotle would call *ἦθος* and *διάνοια*. Eur. is not concerned with the minor characteristics of the Servant but with keeping the juggling balls of cross-purposes in the air until the trick is complete. The corruption of *θυραῖος* to the literal-minded *οἰκεῖος* is likely; not so the reverse. *θυραῖος* 814 might also pick up *θυραῖος* here. It must, however, be admitted that one might have expected *ὀθνεῖος* in 811, picking up the same word from 810; and possibly Prinz was right after all in deleting 810–11, since 812 follows perfectly on 809 and the context is unfortunately riddled with suspicions of interpolation, cf. on 795 supra and 818 ff. infra.

815. The variant L P is probably the result of dropping **σ'** before **ὁρῶν.** The difference between *οὐ* and *οὐ . . . τι* is like that of our 'I should not have' and 'I should never have'. **οὐ γάρ . . . ἄν**: 'no, for if they *had* been *θυραῖα . . .*'. *κωμάζω*, like *κῶμος* 804, is used in a perfectly general sense for 'revelry', even without company.

816. ἀλλ' ἦ of surprised incredulity, cf. on 58. The same phrase recurs *IA* 847 in a similar context; *Σ ἀπατηθεὶς δηλονότι*.

817. δόμοις: probably with *ἐν δέοντι* as Ar. *Pax* 272 *κἀν δέοντι τῇ πόλει*, with **δέξασθαι** expexegetic inf.

818 ff. Disturbance of stichomythia, though rare, is occasionally found in Eur., e.g. *IA* 1438, 1461—a late play, however. A quickening-up by balanced division of the line, as 390, 1119, is common enough. But where, as here, an irregular disturbance includes an unbalanced mid-line *ἀντιλαβή*, a hardly tolerable position of *τε* (v. app. crit.), and words which seem to be put together from another part of the play (426–7) and anticipate a coming remark (826–7) the suspicion of interpolation begins to amount to certainty. Moreover, *Σ* V on 820 says that some texts omit 'these 3 lines'. As in V 819 is written as two lines, Wecklein took this to mean 818–19, the omission of which allows the stichomythia to proceed regularly and without badly jolting the sense, though 820 does not follow ideally on 817 and its text (v. app. crit.) is dubious. It is also very difficult to see how *Σ ταῦτα δὲ τὰ τρία κτλ.*, following *after* a comment on 820, can refer to 818–19; if 819 counted as two, then *ταῦτα τὰ τρία* should surely mean 819–20. Probably *τὰ τρία* is 818–20 as the older edd. took it, and either the interpolation has ousted a line of Heracles in place of 820, or possibly 4 lines are interpolated and 821 should follow on 816. The Servant might intend 821 as a reproachful correction (**μὲν οὖν**) of Heracles' question, which he has imperfectly understood.

822. ἔπειτα δῆτα of indignant surprise, very common in Aristophanes.

824. *Σ ὦ ἄθλιε Ἄδμητε.*

826. The object of **ᾐσθόμην** is left purposely vague. In noticing (**ἰδὼν**) Admetus' tears, his shorn hair, and distraught expression

Heracles had really *perceived* enough to interpret what he saw as a *πάνυ οἰκεῖον κακόν*, but he only now realizes its meaning.

827. ἔπειθε: 'he convinced me'; in spite of what I *saw* I believed what he *said*. The imperf. is probably the idiomatic use for a line of action which failed and in the event was reversed, cf. *ἔφραζες, ἐξένιζες* 1012–13, *ἔθαπτον* 1129.

828. κῆδος: from abstract to concrete (1) 'grief' (2) 'funeral rites' as an expression of grief (3) 'the dead' as the central object of the funeral rites.

829. βίᾳ δὲ θυμοῦ: 'doing violence to my feelings.' Monk compares A. *Sept*. 612 *βίᾳ φρενῶν*, and cf. also A. *Supp*. 798 *βίᾳ καρδίας*.

831. εἶτα as in 696 and *ἔπειτα* 822. There appear to be two variants in the tradition here: *κᾆτ' ἐκώμαζον* and *κᾆτα κωμάζω*. The latter by its shift of tense perhaps makes a better climax.

832. The inf. is exclamatory, and also epexegetic of the exclamatory gen. **σοῦ**. The gen. giving the cause or origin of an emotion (*θαυμάζω σε τῆς ἀνοίας*) can be retained when the verb is replaced by an interjection (*φεῦ τῆς ἀνοίας* S. *El*. 920), and, more colloquially, can be left even without an interjection if the quality causing the emotion is expressed or implied in it (*τῶν ἀλαζονευμάτων* Ar. *Ach*. 87); one can say *φεῦ τοῦ ἀνδρός* (Xen. *Cyr*. 3. 1. 39) or *χρηστῶ κοἰκτίρμονος ἀνδρός* (Theocr. 15. 75) but not simply *τοῦ ἀνδρός*. An apostrophe is not enough to carry such a gen. by itself; thus *IA* 327 *ὦ θεοί, τῆς ἀναισχύντου φρενός*, but *Or*. 1666 *ὦ Λοξία μαντεῖε, σῶν θεσπισμάτων* is probably to be linked with the next line. Again, the exclamatory gen. can be followed, epexegetically, by an inf.: *τῆς μωρίας, τὸ Δία νομίζειν* Ar. *Nub*. 818; this use is rarer in tragedy, but cf. *Med*. 1051 *ἀλλὰ τῆς ἐμῆς κάκης, τὸ καὶ προέσθαι*. It is obviously akin to the exclamatory inf. as in S. *Phil*. 234 *φεῦ τὸ καὶ λαβεῖν*. Here in **σοῦ τὸ μὴ φράσαι** the simple *σοῦ* is only possible as a gen. of exclamation because the epexegetic inf. follows. The **ἀλλὰ** both here and in *Med*. 1051 has itself the force of an interjection.

833. προκειμένου: v. on 551.

834. καί: Denniston, *GP* 312; supplementary information is required: since she is dead, where is she being buried? **ποῦ νιν**: Monk followed by some edd. *ποῖ νιν*, cf. *Hipp*. 1153 where M has *ποῦ*, and the corruption is of course an easy one, but the 'pregnant' use of adverbs as of prepositions is fairly common, cf. KG i. 545.

835–6. You will see the tomb by the side of the highway to Larisa just as you leave (**ἐκ**) the city's outskirts. Or perhaps this is one of the instances described by Jebb on *Ant*. 411 as the 'surveying' use of *ἐκ*, implying that the tomb is *in* the suburb. Van Lennep compares *ἐξορᾶσθαι Hcld*. 675. It was the usual practice to ribbon the roads leading away from the city with important tombs, starting just outside the precinct. That it is visible by the side of the straight road is not inconsistent with 1000, where the wayfarer is described as *δοχμίαν κέλευθον ἐκβαίνων*. A short path *ἐκ πλαγίου* (*Σ*) from the highway led to the tomb standing a little way back from the road-side. Tombs were visited mostly from the city, so that the path would be worn obliquely where the walkers took a short cut off the road. The tomb is imagined as *ξεστός*, of dressed stone like the tombs in the Cerameicus; the Servant speaks as if it were already completed and a familiar landmark.

836. προαστίου: the internal hiatus after *προ* is here perhaps defended by the original *ϝ* of *ϝάστυ*. Maas points out that there is no such excuse for *προ-άγγελος* (to say nothing of *προ-έδραμεν*) in the 'Gyges' fragment (Lobel, *PBA* 1950), which has no parallel in pre-hellenistic literature.

837. The absence of any hint in the text that the Servant here makes his exit is unusual in tragedy, but perhaps those of humble rank could more easily so depart.

The monologue of Heracles is admirably devised; so supreme a trial of courage and strength—**καρδία καὶ χεὶρ**—needs an explicit gathering of the self to meet it, especially after the recent carouse; and it also serves to inform the spectators beforehand of what is to happen instead of through a Messenger's speech after the event. They must be able to understand the significance of the veiled woman, but there could have been no human eyewitness of so fearful a struggle, and Heracles is spared the graceless task of describing and praising his own exploit. The alternative (850) of a descent to the underworld to demand from Hades and Persephone the surrender of Alcestis is probably 'vestigial' of the other version of her release (see Introd. xii).

839. The dubious omission of the augment in **γείνατ'** has led many edd. to assume a double form: *'Ηλεκτρύων, -ωνος* like *Ἀμφιτρύων* (as *HF* 17), and *'Ηλεκτρυών, -όνος* like *ἀλεκτρυών* 'cock'. Apollodorus has this short vowel. Thus *'Ηλεκτρυόνος ἐγείνατ'* following Blomfield is quite possibly right, though the *'Ηλεκτρυόνος* of Haun. cannot be taken as ancient confirmation of this. Wilamowitz (*Hermes* xiv (1879), 457 = Kl. Schr. v. 2, p. 4) would read *'Ηλεκτρυώνη 'γείνατ'*, adopting the form found in Hes. *Sc.* 86 but there pronounced in four syllables *'Ηλεκτρυ̯ώνη*, cf. the *Ἀλεκτρώνα* of *IG* 12. 1. 677. He believes this to be an independent name later identified with Alcmena, who was therefore called 'daughter of Electryon', a shadowy figure invented 'only to beget and die'. In any case, to Eur. reading his Hesiod it could only mean 'daughter of Electryon'. But in such a form (rather than a gen.) it would surely be more natural to use the name as an alternative to *Ἀλκμήνη*, not coupled with it.

843. μελάμπεπλον. It seems from *Σ* that there must have been an old variant *μελάμπτερος*, though the only attested form of 'black-winged' is *μελανόπτερος*, which (Ar. *Av.* 695) is applied to *Νύξ*, also as an alternative to *μελάμπεπλος* (*Ion* 1150).

844. **φυλάξω** is perhaps to be taken, as well as **εὑρήσειν**, with **πίνοντα.** The Nekyia may serve as a commentary on this passage, and may even have suggested it, though there the blood-drinking is a rite of quite different character; Eur. seems to have transferred it from the dead to Death, leaving the motive undefined.

846. Though all MSS. give *λοχήσας*, *Σ* notes a variant *λοχίας* (corr. *λοχαίας* Schwartz), and this is supported by the form in which the line is quoted in *Etym. Mag.* in cod. Flor. *λοχήσας* was perhaps a gloss on **λοχαίας ἐξ ἕδρας.**

848. Ar. *Pax* 316 is doubtless rejoicing over the addiction of Eur. to this phrase, cf. *Med.* 793, *Hcld.* 977.

851. Not the *πέλανος* in its technical sense of bloodless *χοή* offered to the dead, but the thick pools of blood, as *Rhes.* 430.

853. 'The stop after **τε** should be deleted, since **῎Αλκηστιν** is the object of **αἰτήσομαι** as well as of **ἄξειν**'—Maas.

860. Heracles leaves for the tomb, apparently without meeting the returning funeral procession, though his exit and Admetus' entrance must have been by the same side.

861–934. This *κομμός* consists of four anapaestic systems of varying length declaimed by Admetus, each followed by a stanza from the Chorus. The anapaests are of regular recitative type, with an occasional monometer and each closing in the paroemiac. The stanzas form two antistrophic pairs of quite different types: the first is in iambo-dochmiac with one iambelegus, and is interspersed with interjections *extra metrum* from Admetus. It is the earliest example of a typical form of Euripidean *κομμός* in which the metres are restricted to those which pass easily into recitative,[1] and it is possible that these lines were delivered in something less than the full singing tone, and even that they were given by the Coryphaeus alone. The second pair is pure lyric, sung by the whole Chorus (and ignored by Admetus).

861 ff. It is improbable that these opening lines had so unsymmetrical a form; the anaphora in **στυγναὶ** loses its effect unless each comes at the beginning of a metron (cf. **κείνων . . . κεῖν'** 866–7 and **οὔτε . . . οὔτ'** 868–9), and the diaeresis **ἰώ | μοί** is very weak. The transmission of interjections is notoriously unreliable. Hermann's guess is as good as any: *ἰὼ ⟨ἰὼ⟩ στυγναὶ πρόσοδοι | στυγναὶ δ' ὄψεις χήρων μελάθρων. | ἰώ μοί μοι· αἰαῖ ⟨αἰαῖ⟩.*

862. **ὄψεις**: by attraction from the surrounding plurals; possibly some slight support for the plur. *Supp.* 945.

863. **ποῖ στῶ** is a possible 'pregnant' use of the interrog., though **ποῦ**,

[1] See my *Lyric Metres*, p. 198.

ποῖ, and *πᾷ* (or *πᾶ*) are very confusedly transmitted in MSS. *Σ εἰς τίνα τόπον ἢ ἐν τίνι τόπῳ* could refer to **βῶ** and **στῶ**, without prejudice as to the interrog.

869. πόδα πεζεύων: a curious combination of extremely prosaic verb (see the instances in LS) and artificial construction with the internal acc. *πόδα*.

870. ὅμηρον: *Σ* paraphrases *ἐνέχυρον*, and gives two alternative explanations: (1) Alcestis stands surety for Admetus that he will come down to Hades too, since he will die of grief for her; (2) she is hostage for his life since she died instead of him. The first would be so allusively expressed as to be hardly intelligible; the second would be appropriate only if Death wished to ensure that Admetus should *live*. Possibly the metaphor is not be pressed; Death by taking Alcestis as a substitute for Admetus has kept some hold over the latter, e.g. ensuring that he shall know no more joy (868). It is noteworthy that in *Bacch.* 293 the only *apparent* sense of *ὅμηρον* is simply 'substitute', but that whole passage is so obscure that I should hesitate to press this.

871. Ἅιδῃ Θάνατος παρέδωκεν: the choice of verb here certainly seems to convey the notion of two separate personalities, the one conceived of primarily as King of the Underworld, the other concerned with fetching thither the individual victim. (See on 24–26.)

872–7 = 889–94.

⏑–⏑– –⏑– ⏑––	sync. iamb. trim. cat.
⏑–⏑– ⏑––⏑–	iamb. + doch.
⏑⏑⏑–⏑– ⏑–⏑	doch. + bacch.
––⏑– ⏑–⏑⏒	iamb. dim.
⏑–⏑–⏑–⏑⏑–⏑⏑–	iambelegus (⏑ **s** ⏑ **dd**).
⏑––⏑– ⏑––	doch. + bacch.

The short final syllable in *both* 874 and 891 might at first suggest that *φεῦ φεῦ* is to be reckoned in the line, which would then be sync. iamb. trim. cat., a headless version of the opening phrase. But the other three exclamations resist such treatment (note the final anceps in 875 = 892), so this phrase is probably to be related to the final clausula (894). In view of the unusual care to make word-end correspond throughout strophe and antistrophe, I suspect that the long initial anceps in 875 = 892—the only case in the stanza—is also deliberate, as a sort of compensation for the preceding short final anceps, but how this was conveyed, with the intervening *φεῦ φεῦ*, I would not care to guess. Of the two versions of the final clausula either is possible in sense and metre, but the strophe is more vulnerable to attack: **τὰν νέρθε δ' οὐδὲν ὠφελεῖς** seems to need some explicatory addition, as of a participial clause. Hermann proposed *στενάζων πρόσωπον ἄντα*, but *ἄντα* (with *εἰσιδεῖν*) is somewhat lame at the end of the clause, and the word itself may be the root of the corruption.

872. κεῦθος οἴκων: a lyric periphrasis for *οἶκον*, cf. fr. 1003N[2] *λῦε πηκτὰ δωμάτων*, parodied by Ar. *Ach.* 479 (and misunderstood by Pollux 10. 27).

874. The same words recur in a *κομμός El.* 1210 *σάφ' οἶδα, δι' ὀδύνας ἔβας*.

879. ἁμαρτεῖν: the inf. is as it were epexegetic of a *τούτου* which is omitted, cf. A. *Ag.* 602 (and Fraenkel ad loc.), where *τούτου* is expressed.

882. ἀτέκνους: the half-paradoxical theme is developed at length (also in anapaests) *Med.* 1090 ff., where its inappropriateness to the context betrays the rhetorical sentiment taken over ready-made. Here too the relevance is not very close, since **νόσους** 885 can hardly be taken in any other sense than 'illnesses'.

883. τῆς relative. The correct reading is preserved only in Stobaeus.

897. ῥῖψαι intrans. as in *Cyc.* 166. The reproachful question put to the Chorus informs us ingeniously of the dramatic scene at the open grave.

901. πιστοτάτας: 'most faithful to each other.' **σὺν**: perhaps adverbial, (cf. *Od.* 10. 42) rather than a case of tmesis.

903–10 = 926–33.

⏑–⏑– iamb. monom.
–⏑⏑–⏑⏑–⏑⏑– prosodiac + iamb. dim. cat.
⏑–⏑–⏑–– || (ddd ⏑ ss –)
⏑⏑–x̄–– ∧dd̄ –
⏑⏑⏑⏑⏑⏑ ⏑⏑⏑⏑– iamb. dim.
⏑⏑–⏑⏑–– ∧dd –
x̄–⏑⏑–– ∧d̄d –
⏑⏑–⏑–– ∧ds –

The exact point of division in 904/5 = 927/8 is a matter of indifference. After the first period labels are difficult. These colaria are usually called 'reiziana' on the assumption that there was a 'popular' form of metre which had a fixed number of longs but admitted between these either one or two shorts indifferently, as 'Senkungen'. There may have been such a metre, but if so it has no place in tragedy. 'Reizianum', since the name seems to have established itself, had better be kept for the aeolo-choriambic colon ⏓–́⏑⏑––, a catalectic form of the telesillean. It is a species, not a general category. Here the penultimate colon might be a reizianum, but from the context it seems probable that the initial long, like the other syllable marked above (in 906 = 929) is not anceps but a contraction of two shorts. The phrase ⏑⏑–⏑⏑–– (*Ἀθαμαντίδος Ἕλλας* A. *Pers.* 70) occurs in ionic contexts, and might possibly be so explained here, since – – ⏑ ⏑ – – is also an ionic colarion and the single-short of the clausula is a recognized way of bringing ionics to a close (cf. *Bacch.* 386 and the lyrics of Corinna). But in a context like *Pers.* l.c. where the regular ionic rhythm is strong it is at least arguable that ⏑ ⏑ – ⏑ ⏑ – – stands for ⏑ ⏑ ⊔ ⏑ ⏑ – – with protraction of the first long. It seems safest to leave these cola in the present passage as short varieties of the general 'enoplian' character so prevalent in this play; the single-short in the last line is analogous to that found in the clausulae of dactylic and ionic rhythms.

903 ff. The Chorus speaks with so collective a voice that it can give a personal anecdote of 'a relative' (**ἐν γένει τις**, cf. S. *OT* 1016). *Hipp.* 125 *ὅθι μοί τις ἦν φίλα* is a similar but less striking instance of this device. The notion that the Chorus is here the mouthpiece of the poet paying tribute to his friend Anaxagoras is not very well founded. It may have originated with the Stoic Chrysippus[1] who (ap. Galen 5. 413 Kühn) quotes *Alc.* 1079–80 and 1085, and in between them another passage of Eur. (fr. 964N²) in which Theseus claims to have learnt *παρὰ σοφοῦ τινος* the value of preparing oneself for the worst blows of fate by anticipating them in imagination. This, he says, is the lesson Eur. learned from Anaxagoras, who on hearing of his son's death said quietly *ᾔδειν θνητὸν γεννῆσαι.* (Cf. Cicero, *Tusc.* 3. 14. 29, and Terence, *Phormio* 241 ff.) The *point* of this is not relevant to the present passage, and, as Weber points out, in the version of the anecdote given by Diog. Laert. (2. 3. 13 *ᾔδειν αὐτοὺς θνητοὺς γεννήσας*) there is not even an 'only child'. It is true that the form of the Chorus's consolation here, a personal anecdote in place of the usual generalities (to which it returns in the antistrophe), is unusual and arresting, but that could be accounted for by the pressing need to provide some variety for this very hard-worked sentiment.

906. μονόπαις: 'an only child'; for this type of adjective cf. on 428. *παῖς* lends itself particularly to compounds of this kind; Wilamowitz on *HF* 689 quotes *εὔπαις IT* 1234, *καλλίπαις Or.* 964 and Pl. *Phaedr.* 261a. The appeal of the Chorus here is to an argument *a fortiori*; to lose an only child was far worse than to lose a wife; cf. the *μονογενὲς τέκνον πατρί* of A. *Ag.* 898.

907. ἅλις: *Σ μετρίως*, as in *Med.* 630.

909. προπετὴς: after his prime a man 'droops towards' the grey hairs of old age.

911. σχῆμα δόμων. This form of periphrasis is only found in apostrophe, cf. *Hec.* 619 *ὦ σχήματ' οἴκων*, *Andr.* 1 *Ἀσιάτιδος γῆς σχῆμα*, S. *Phil.* 952 *ὦ σχῆμα πέτρας δίπυλον*, and expresses the emotion of the speaker; it is something long familiar to him, of whose appearance he is made

[1] See Testimonia, Introd., p. xxxvii.

newly aware through the strong feeling that sharpens his perceptions.

914. *Σ τὸ διάφορον τῆς νῦν τύχης καὶ τῆς πάλαι.* The sentiment closely recalls that of A. *PV* 555–60; and in general the wedding-song and procession represent to one looking back in after years the summit of happiness and fortune (*HF* 10, *Supp.* 990, *Hel.* 722).

917. φιλίας: a more appropriate epithet for the new bride than the variant *πιστῆς*. **βαστάζων**: see on 19.

920. ἀπ' ἀμφοτέρων: 'on both sides', i.e. both of us, not 'each of us on both parents' sides'.

921. ἀρίστων: cf. *Med.* 5 with Page's note, S. *Aj.* 1304; *ἄριστος* and *ἀριστεύς* seem to be used like this interchangeably. **εἶμεν** opt. is certainly required here.

923. στολμοὶ: sc. *ἀντίπαλοι*, which carries the gen. **λευκῶν πέπλων.**

925. λέκτρων κοίτας: the inverse of the periphrasis *τᾶς ἀνάνδρου κοίτας ὀλέσασα λέκτρον* *Med.* 436.

926. An unusual sense of *παρά*, not quite parallel to *Hcld.* 611 quoted by Paley *παρὰ δ' ἄλλαν ἄλλα μοῖρα διώκει*, where the picture is of good and evil fortune chasing and passing each other, nor to Dem. 18. 13 quoted by Monk *ταῖς ἐκ τῶν νόμων τιμωρίαις παρ' αὐτὰ τἀδικήματα χρῆσθαι*, 'hard on the heels of', 'flagrante delicto'; here it is more vaguely 'in the midst of'.

928–9. The Chorus's consolation is seriously, not ironically, meant; the irony of the situation is left for Admetus himself to discover in his following speech.

930. φιλίαν: the affection between you; the tie which in dying she has broken, cf. 279.

932–4. *πολλοῖς . . . δάμαρτος* all MSS. except V, which with **δάμαρτας** gives a better construction, since *παραλύω* means 'detach from the side of', not simply 'part from'. It is thus more appropriate to have the wives in the acc. rather than emend to *πολλοὺς* with Canter in order to save *δάμαρτος*. The sing. *δάμαρτα*, however, would be more natural.

935 ff. This speech marks a crisis in the play, wherein Admetus at last realizes and makes explicit the bitter truth towards which the course of the action has been leading him. First there was the agony and despair of seeing Alcestis die, then the scene with Pheres to hit him in his self-respect and reputation. He sums up this double disaster lucidly, developing the thesis 'My wife is happier than I', paradoxical as it may seem. Her troubles are ended and she is *εὐκλεής*; he is entering on a life of grief and *δύσκλεια*, intolerable at home and in society. Conclusion: what profit is it to him to live? Now that he has reached this ultimate realization we can have what Aristotle would call the *περιπέτεια εἰς εὐτυχίαν.*

937. ἅψεται: like a weapon or a disease; so A. fr. 255 *ἄλγος δ' οὐδὲν ἅπτεται νεκροῦ*, S. *OC.* 955 *θανόντων δ' οὐδὲν ἄλγος ἅπτεται.*

939. χρῆν: for the tendency of MSS. to substitute *χρή* cf. 379, *Hcld.* 959 with Elmsley's note. **οὐ χρῆν ζῆν**, be it noted, in the sense that he had cheated Fate, **παρεὶς τὸ μόρσιμον**, not that he ought never to have accepted Alcestis' sacrifice.

941–3. The repetition *εἰσόδους . . . εἰσόδου*, though unsatisfactory, is hardly sufficient ground for Lenting's emendation *ἐξόδου*; the adjective *τερπνῆς* is only appropriate to a 'happy home-coming' here. The absence of its mistress means that the house is sad, listless, unfriendly, and there is no reason to suppose *Σ* wrong in associating words of greeting with *entry* (*ὡς ἔθους ὄντος προσαγορεύειν τὸν εἰσιόντα*). It is conceivable that 941 and 942–3 are a blending of two alternative variants, but if so they are too much involved to sort out now. After his repugnance at crossing the threshold with no friendly voice to make the act lucky Admetus dwells upon the next stage: two equally intolerable alternatives, staying in or going out.

The unforced homeliness and pathos of this 'domestic interior' is of the Eur. who is a forerunner of New Comedy. The cry in 944 could be echoed by the bereaved in all ages.

950. ἔξωθεν perhaps not simply = *ἔξω*, but with **ἑλῶσι** = *ἔξωθεν εἴσω*.

952. γυναικοπληθεῖς: a compound of Aeschylean form, cf. *Pers.* 122 *γυναικοπληθὴς ὅμιλος*, A. *Supp.* 29 *ἀρσενοπληθῆ ἑσμόν*.

955. αἰσχρῶς ζῶνθ': i.e. it is a disgrace that he should be alive at all.

960. Hesych. *κύδιον· κρεῖττον, αἱρετώτερον* (sc. *τοῦ μὴ ζῆν*), *Andr.* 639. There is no need to reject it here; Weil objects that its meaning would be reduced to that of *κέρδιον*, but the superlative is used by A. *Supp.* 13 *κύδιστ' ἀχέων* in just the same way.

962–1005. An ode on the inexorable power of Necessity: poetry, science, philosophy all agree in this lesson; even the skills revealed by Orpheus, and by Apollo to his descendants, can avail nothing against her, nor can prayer and sacrifice; even Zeus must harmonize his will with her, and the hardest matter is bent to her shaping. One of her laws is that the dead are dead and weeping will not restore them; Admetus must then cease repining for Alcestis and take comfort in her renown among men, who will pay her divine honours. Thus the Chorus emphasizes the irrevocability of it all, and rounds it off with a devout and chastened reflection on the only kind of survival which mortals can achieve. The *tragic* thread is now complete; enter Heracles with the veiled Alcestis, and in a triumphant final peripety the happy-fairy-tale thread comes uppermost. Not that *Ἀνάγκη* or our hard-learned wisdom is fallible; it is our understanding of the design of Necessity at any given time that may be faulty; the god has found a way where it seemed no way was: *τῶν δ' ἀδοκήτων πόρον εὗρε θεός*.

The shape of the ode is a common one in Eur. (cf., for instance, *Med.* 410 ff., 824 ff.): a general reflection, developed in the first strophic pair, is given its particular application—often in direct address—in the second pair.

962–81. *ἐγὼ καὶ διὰ μούσας* ⏑––⏑⏑––
μόνας δ' οὔτ' ἐπὶ βωμοὺς

καὶ μετάρσιος ᾖξα, καὶ –⏒–⏑⏑–⏑–
ἐλθεῖν οὔτε βρέτας θεᾶς

πλείστων ἁψάμενος λόγων –⏓–⏑⏑–⏑–
ἔστιν, οὐ σφαγίων κλύει.

κρεῖσσον οὐδὲν Ἀνάγκας –⏒–⏑⏑––
μή μοι, πότνια, μείζων

ηὗρον, οὐδέ τι φάρμακον –⏒–⏑⏑–⏑–
ἔλθοις ἢ τὸ πρὶν ἐν βίῳ.

Θρῄσσαις ἐν σανίσιν, τὰς –––⏑⏑––
καὶ γὰρ Ζεὺς ὅ τι νεύσῃ

Ὀρφεία κατέγραψεν –––⏑⏑––
σὺν σοὶ τοῦτο τελευτᾷ.

γῆρυς, οὐδ' ὅσα Φοῖβος Ἀσ- –⏑–⏑⏑–⏑–
καὶ τὸν ἐν Χαλύβοις δαμά-

κληπιάδαις ἔδωκε –⏑⏑–⏑–◡
ζεις σὺ βίᾳ σίδαρον,

φάρμακα πολυπόνοις –⏑⏑⏖⏑–
οὐδέ τις ἀποτόμου

ἀντιτεμὼν βροτοῖσιν. –⏑⏑–⏑––
λήματός ἐστιν αἰδώς.

The metre is straightforward aeolo-choriambic: pher., 2 glyc., pher., glyc., 2 pher., glyc. + aristophanean, dodrans (= –⏑⏑–⏑– ds), aristophanean. The aeolic base, after starting with the less usual ⏑–, is four times variable in responsion; there is no need to transpose *ἐλθεῖν* and *ἔστιν* in 974–5. Resolution, never admitted in the Aeolic poets, is occasionally found in this metre in tragedy; it could be avoided here by treating the dodrans as a dochmiac –⏖⏖⏑– (or by merely *calling* it a dochmiac). Periods are quite uncertain.

962 ff. *Σ* says censoriously *ὁ ποιητὴς διὰ τοῦ προσώπου τοῦ χοροῦ βούλεται δεῖξαι ὅσον μέτεσχε παιδεύσεως.* Indeed, Eur. often does not worry much, after the parodos, whether choral utterances are strictly in character, if the action requires a content not easily reconcilable with such realism; but to detect a note of personal boasting here is simply a naïve reaction to the prominent initial *ἐγώ*. Three sources of human wisdom all give the same answer, but they are not put in co-ordinated constructions. There is a zeugma in the first two; with

διὰ μούσας supply something like ἔμολον (cf. *Med.* 1082) out of **ἦξα**. *Σ* rightly paraphrases **μετάρσιος ἦξα** ('I have soared aloft in the heights') by περὶ μετεώρων ἐφρόντισα, but adds οἷον ἠστρολόγησα; the astronomy and physical speculations of the fifth century conveyed no other meaning to this later age. **λόγων**: the doctrines of philosophy.

965. 'Ανάγκας: the more philosophical formulation of *Μοῖρα*, in the next stanza half-personified as a goddess without a cult (like Death), yet, with a parenthetic touch of illogicality, addressed as **πότνια**, in a prayer like an apotropaic formula.

966–72. Neither mystical formulas nor medical lore can avail against the necessity of death. σανίδες were normally wooden tablets, covered with gypsum to make a writing-surface, used for posting up public records, cf. Ar. *Vesp.* 349, 848. *Σ* quotes Heraclides Ponticus (fourth century B.C.) as authority for the existence of a collection of Orphic σανίδες at a temple of Dionysus on the Thracian Haemus, and a temple would be a suitable repository for such a collection of texts. Plato, *Rep.* 364e, speaks of a 'babel of books', βίβλων ὅμαδον, attributed to Orpheus and Musaeus and offering λύσεις καὶ καθαρμοὶ ἀδικημάτων through certain sacrificial rites and liturgies (cf. also *Hipp.* 954). So here Orphic wisdom is preserved in magic prescriptions which nevertheless afford no 'remedy' for Necessity. **'Ορφεία γῆρυς** is usually taken as a periphrasis for the 'the poet Orpheus', an inversion of noun and epithet akin to that in βίη 'Ηρακληείη. Nilsson, however (*Harvard Theol. Rev.* xxviii (1935), 193), sees in 'Orphic voice' a more precise reference, to the utterances of the poet's severed head as it floated downstream (cf. Luc. *Adv. Ind.* 11); a red-figure vase of the late fifth century (Beazley, *ARV* 859/1) shows (on N.'s interpretation) Apollo bidding a young man take down on his tablets the words of the trunkless head between them. It is, however, uncertain whether this version of the legend was so well known that an allusion so slight as 'Ορφεία γῆρυς would be understood in this sense. Weber understands the words as the utterances of the Orphic Sibyl, recorded when the oracle was consulted. **ἀντιτεμὼν** 972 is explained by *Σ* as εὑρών, a *metaphor* from the herbalist's activities as in A. *Ag.* 17 ἐντέμνων ἄκος, *Andr.* 121 ἄκος δύσλυτον πόνων τεμεῖν, but here surely the **φάρμακα** are literal, the [recipes for the use of] herbs 'shredded as antidotes' which were the traditional lore of the Asclepiads.

973–5. The one god without a cult is usually Death, as in the famous fragment of Aesch. *Niobe* (161N²). The power of Ἀνάγκη is of course most dreadly manifest in death.

978. νεύσῃ: see on ἁγνίσῃ 76. The nature of the relation between Zeus and Necessity is always one of the nicest problems to be resolved, poetically or theologically. Here there is a kind of collaboration, an identity of purpose, expressed by the awful nod of Zeus.

980. *Χάλυβοι* as in fr. 472, A. *Sept.* 728, more commonly *Χάλυβες*. These remote and half-savage *σιδηροτέκτονες* (*PV* 714) on the south Pontic shores kept a literary monopoly of iron-working, even when the metal itself was found and worked all over the Greek world. They were a mining community on a great scale, and their products were credited with a peculiar hardness. Nature's most unyielding products can be 'tamed' and made malleable because all Nature is subject to the power of Necessity.

981. ἀποτόμου· *σκληροῦ Σ* (see on 118), cf. *OT.* 877 *ἀπότομον ἀνάγκαν* unpersonified. It appears there to be used of a steep *drop*; here, however, the picture is rather of a steep cliff-wall against which man dashes his head in vain, cf. H. Fränkel on *αἰπὺς ὄλεθρος*, *Dicht. u. Phil. des fr. Griech.* p. 61, n. 35.

984–1005.

καὶ σ' ἐν ἀφύκτοισι χερῶν	−⏑⏑− −⏑⏑−
μηδὲ νεκρῶν ὡς φθιμένων	
εἶλε θεὰ δεσμοῖς.	−⏑⏑−−−
χῶμα νομιζέσθω	
τόλμα δ'· οὐ γὰρ ἀνάξεις ποτ' ἔνερθεν	−−−⏑⏑⏒−⏑⏑−−
τύμβος σᾶς ἀλόχου, θεοῖσι δ' ὁμοίως	
κλαίων τοὺς φθιμένους ἄνω.	−−−⏑⏑−⏑−
τιμάσθω, σέβας ἐμπόρων.	
καὶ θεῶν σκότιοι φθίνουσι	−−⏑⏑−⏑−⏑
καί τις δοχμίαν κέλευθον	
παῖδες ἐν θανάτῳ.	−⏓−⏑⏑− ‖
ἐκβαίνων τόδ' ἐρεῖ·	
φίλα μὲν ὅτ' ἦν μεθ' ἡμῶν,	⏓−⏑⏑−⏑−− ‖
Αὔτα ποτὲ προύθαν' ἀνδρός,	
φίλα δὲ θανοῦσ' ἔτ' ἔσται,	⏓−⏑⏑−⏑−− ‖
νῦν δ' ἐστὶ μάκαιρα δαίμων·	
γενναιοτάταν δὲ πασᾶν	−−⏑⏑−⏑−−
χαῖρ', ὦ πότνι', εὖ δὲ δοίης.	
ἐζεύξω κλισίαις ἄκοιτιν.	−−−⏑⏑−⏑−−
τοῖαί νιν προσεροῦσι φῆμαι.	

Aeolo-choriambic continues, but in different cola: chor. dim. + dodrans (**d̄s̄**)—or these might be taken as a single colon, a kind of 'greater asclepiad' without introductory base, since the next appears to be a catalectic form of asclepiad; glyc., choriambic enoplian of the form −**ds**⏑ + dodrans **(⏑)sd**, 3 chor. enop., hipponactean clausula −− **ds** −. Period-ends are certain only at 990 = 1001 (hiatus) and the following two lines (conjunction of ancipitia). 992 *φίλα δὲ θανοῦσ' ἔτ'* ἔσται is only one of various possible emendations. The Aldine reading can only be a conjecture, and the absence of any verb for these two clauses would be harsh.

983. σ': Admetus has of course remained on the stage.

985. τόλμα: fortitude is man's only answer to the ruthlessness of Necessity.

989. σκότιοι is explained by *Σ* as *οἱ μὴ γνήσιοι ὄντες τῶν θεῶν παῖδες ἀποθνῄσκουσιν, οἱ μὴ ὄντες ἐξ ἀμφοτέρων θεῶν*, and *σκότιος* is of course commonly used of clandestine wedlock among mortals, though not as a direct adjective with 'child'. It is doubtful, however, whether gods' children would be referred to in such a way, and *σκότιοι* is better taken proleptically with **φθίνουσι** and **θανάτῳ** as 'fade in the darkness of death'. The play began with a reference to the death of Asclepius.

994. κλισίαις = *λέκτροις*, a use for which *IT* 857 *κλισίαν λέκτρων* is the nearest parallel.

995 ff. The tomb is not to be merely a mound of earth above the dead *and gone*; Alcestis is to be a **μάκαιρα δαίμων**, a beneficent *presence* to whom the wayfarer may do reverence and pray for a blessing. Earle aptly quotes Hes. *Op.* 121 ff. on the special status as *δαίμονες* of the departed heroes of the Golden Race.

1000. δοχμίαν: see on 575, 835.

1001. ἐκβαίνων or *ἐμβαίνων*? The latter is more straightforward: 'stepping on to', 'treading'; *ἐκβαίνων* with the acc. would be a pregnant use of the compound, implying 'stepping off the high-road on to the side-track'. Even if no close parallel can be found this seems a perfectly possible refinement of Greek usage, while unobvious enough to get converted into the lectio facilior *ἐμβαίνων*.

1004. εὖ δοίης: probably in such phrases *εὖ* is an old substantival use, *καλῶς διδόναι* (*Supp.* 463) being a late formation by analogy. *εὖ* may well be in origin a neut. of the adjective *ἐύς*: see Fraenkel on A. *Ag.* 121 *τὸ δ' εὖ νικάτω*.

1007. ὡς ἔοικεν: the guess of course is directed at his destination, not at his identity.

1010. δὲ introduces the particular instance of the general statement 'Friends should be candid with one another and not cherish secret grievances'.

1012. ἔφραζες: for the tense cf. on 827. *φράζω* is not used with the inf. in classical Greek except in the sense of 'order', and its use with a part. is rare, cf. *Od.* 19. 477, *IA* 802. It means 'reveal', 'make a declaration of an existing fact'.

1015. ἐλειψάμην: the unparalleled use of the mid. in this sense can be defended by the analogy of *χοὰς χέομαι* (as well as *χέω*) A. *Pers.* 220, S. *OC* 477, &c., and cf. *θύω, θύομαι*.

1017. See Introd., p. xxiii. The repeated **μέμφομαι** is not specially emphatic, but a common and probably conversational idiom, cf. *αἰνῶ μὲν αἰνῶ* 1093, *ἤλγουν μὲν ἤλγουν* *Andr.* 980.

1018. οὐ μήν: adversative, answering *μέν*, see Denniston, *GP* 335; this verse example can be added to the prose ones there adduced.

1023. The exquisite optatives are intended perhaps less to safeguard himself than to avoid obtruding mention of his own desperately real peril: 'But in an event which I trust will not happen, for I hope to return . . . .'

1025. L P's variant gives a perfectly possible gen.: 'as the price of many toils'. Paley quotes *Med.* 534 (where see Page's note), *Rhes.* 467.

1026 ff. Heracles leaves the time and place of these imaginary games undefined in his perfunctory narrative.

1027. πόνον: 'object of effort': the somewhat rare 'acc. in apposition to the sentence' has naturally acquired variants in the gen.

1028. νικητήρια: the 'appositional plur.', cf. *Hipp.* 11 *Ἱππόλυτος, ἁγνοῦ Πιτθέως παιδεύματα.*

1029. ἦν = *ἐξῆν*. **τὰ κοῦφα**: internal obj. of *νικῶσιν*; such as the foot-race and chariot-race, explains *Σ—τὰ περὶ ταχύτητος καὶ κουφότητος.*

1031. βουφόρβια: properly 'grazing cattle', then simply 'cattle'. Heracles does not say what he did with them; the woman was as it were 'thrown in' as an extra. The prizes are a reminiscence of *Il.* 23. 259 ff.

1032–3. ἐντυχόντι αἰσχρὸν ἦν: 'as I was there, it would have been poor-spirited . . . .'

1035. A hint to the audience that the struggle was a mighty one, as he had foretold.

1037. Admetus answers first the implication that he did not set store by Heracles' friendship. **ἀτίζων** (Scaliger's emendation, found also in one very late fragmentary MS.) is fairly common for *ἀτιμάζων* at this position in the trimeter. **αἰσχροῖσιν** or *ἐχθροῖσιν*? Nearly all edd. except Murray adopt the latter as a matter of course, referring to 1008 and 1011. But to assure Heracles that it was not because he considered him an *enemy* that he had kept silence is a singularly ungracious response to the gently reproachful 'I had hoped you would let me prove a friend'. 'It was from no wish to slight you' is Admetus' reply to that, 'nor that I thought it anything to be ashamed of'—*αἰσχροῖσιν* of course neut. To restrict **σ'** to *ἀτίζων* does not seem to me to make a 'harsh construction', as is usually claimed. The sentiment might refer to Pheres' accusations, but is more probably just a general defence such as any host might make about something he had kept concealed.

1041. ἅλις: *Σ ἤρκει τὸ ἐμὲ κλαίειν τὸ ἐμὸν κακόν*, cf. A. *Sept.* 679, and (in a personal construction) S. *OT* 1061 *ἅλις νοσοῦσ' ἐγώ.*

1045. There is little doubt that L P preserves the correct reading here;

Kirchhoff's over-ingenious adaptation of V, *ἄλλον τιν' . . . μὴ 'μέ·μιμνήσκεις κακῶν*, besides the strain on the punctuation, commits a solecism in the verb, since the pres. of *μιμνήσκω* is never used in tragedy.

1051. κατ' with **στέγην.** Hermann proposed *μετ'* in order to avoid this long-range connexion. Reiske's *δῆθεν οἰκήσει* is an improvement in both sense and rhythm.

1055. The sense is apparently 'am I to admit her to my wife's chamber and keep her there?' It is not certain whether the causal of *ἐσβαίνω* can be used without a preposition in this way, and on the assumption that *θάλαμον εἰσβήσας* was simply an attempt to correct *εἰς θάλαμον βήσας* (so V L P) Schmidt proposed *ἐμβήσας*, which is used with a double acc. *Cyc.* 467, *Hcld.* 845.

1056. *ἐπεσφρέω*, 'let in on to', or 'let in in addition' is found four times in Eur.; elsewhere we have only *εἰσφρέω*. The simple verb does not occur (see Wilam. on *HF* 1267).

1057–61. As often in a long *τε . . . καί* construction, there is a zeugma; instead of *καὶ ἐκ τῆς θανούσης* in 1060, the second limb acquires a new finite verb: *καὶ τῆς θανούσης πρόνοιαν δεῖ μ' ἔχειν*. The words **ἀξία δέ μοι σέβειν** are in parenthesis.

1063. προσῄξαι would appear, if correct, to have been formed by Eur. from *εἴκω* on an epic model (cf. *Od.* 4. 796 *δέμας δ' ἤικτο γυναικί*) in place of *προσέοικας*. Hesych. gives *προσήικται· προσέοικε.* But the word is suspicious at best, since one expects a part. continuing the construction *ἴσθι ἔχουσα.*

1065. μή μ' ἕλῃς ᾑρημένον: 'slay me not slain', cf. S. *Ant.* 1030 *τὸν θανόντ' ἐπικτανεῖν.* The perf. pass. of *αἱρέομαι* is hardly to be found elsewhere in this sense, but the expression is probably a proverbial jingle.

1067. θολοῖ: 'she makes turbid'; the word is used literally only of water.

1069. ὡς ἄρτι: 'only now do I *really* taste'.

1070–1. These lines are doubtless intentionally ambiguous, but in any case **ὅστις εἶ σύ** is meaningless. If this is a generalized warning ('whatever your station', 'even a king') the emphatic *σύ* (omitted by L) is quite out of place. Emendation is not easy; Hermann's *εἶσι* 'in whatever guise he (the god) visits' is most unnatural, nor do we really want the opt. *ὅστις εἴη* = 'everyone'. Earle suggests that *ἥτις ἐστί* (Wecklein) might have originated the trouble if the phrase had first been contaminated to *ἥτις εἶ σύ* from 1062 above and then 'emended' to *ὅστις*. *ἥτις ἐστί* would heighten the deliberate ambiguity of *θεοῦ δόσιν*, by which the Chorus intends *μοῖραν* while the audience can take it to mean the woman.

1075. ποῦ τόδε; sometimes explained as = *ποῦ τόδε ἔξεστι;* but perhaps the sense is rather 'But what sort of a wish is that?' Usually in this use of ποῦ a claim made by the other side is quoted with scorn or indignation, cf. S. *Aj.* 1100, *OT* 390, *Ion* 528 ποῦ δέ μοι πατὴρ σύ; Here the tone is milder.

1077. ὑπερβάλλω seems to be the verb required here (see app. crit.), rather than ὑπερβαίνω. The aor. given by B O D is found occasionally in prohibitions in Homer, but hardly ever in later Greek, and the fun made by Aristophanes (*Thesm.* 870 and Van Leeuwen's note) of Sophocles' μὴ ψεῦσον, ὦ Ζεῦ (fr. 453N²) shows that the construction was felt as outlandish. Monk is clearly right in substituting the enclitic **νυν** (the quantity of the vowel is common) for the νῦν with which it is often confused. Heracles is drawing the sensible inference from Admetus' last words.

1079. The better tradition θέλεις is quite possible here, θέλεις στένειν taking the place of στένοις: 'if you insist (as it seems you do) on mourning for ever', with the apod. more doubtfully expressed: 'how would that advance you?' Chrysippus, however, quotes the line with **θέλοις** (see Testimonia, Introd., p. xxxvii).

1080. The MSS. make this line another violation of Porson's canon, but Chrysippus (as above) quotes without the intrusive μ'. **ἔρως τις**: Σ rightly τοῦ θρηνεῖν ἔρως. Monk aptly quotes *Supp.* 79 ἄπληστος ἅδε μ' ἐξάγει χάρις γόων. It is quite unnecessary to suppose that Heracles in his next remark is wilfully or otherwise misunderstanding the reference of ἔρως; the Greeks never confused ἐρᾶν and φιλεῖν. In all this interchange Heracles is trying to reduce the situation to its most matter-of-fact terms, while Admetus insists that it is so bad as to make ordinary life impossible. 'This passion for tears is beyond my control'—'Naturally you find yourself weeping . . .'—'Destroyed is too weak a word . . .'—'Admittedly you have lost a good wife', &c.

1082. i.e. ἔτι μᾶλλον ἢ ἀπώλεσεν, cf. *Hec.* 667 ὦ παντάλαινα κἄτι μᾶλλον ἢ λέγω.

1085. **μαλάξει**: sc. κακόν from the next clause. **ἡβάσκει**: the correct reading is preserved only by Chrysippus (ap. Galen; see under Testimonia, p. xxxvii–xxxviii), the ἡβᾷ σοι of our MSS. being an obvious corruption of this. ἡβᾷ is used metaphorically (in the sense of violence, without any notion of youth) in *Or.* 696; the inceptive, a rare word, emphasizes the freshness of the grief which is just coming to its full vigour.

1087. Read νέοι γάμοι πόθου, F. W. Schmidt. Lesky, in his review of Weber's edition (*Gnomon* vii. 142), defends the reading of V B here, but the plur. **πόθοι** is surely very odd. The πόθος of L P—Maas calls my attention to the fact that P, contrary to all our app. crit., clearly has πόθος too—seems to be an attempt to make the phrase more normal. In any case **παύσει** is much better with a gen.; moreover, the idea in νέου γάμου πόθοι (or πόθος) seems to me too tastelessly coarse to be credible, or in keeping with the tone of this scene.

1088. οὐκ ἂν ᾠόμην: (Cf. Men. *Epit.* 193) 'I should never have thought it of you.' Heracles' words were deliberately intended to provoke this very reaction, and Admetus has every excuse for feeling shocked.

1090. Conceivably V is following a better tradition, and we might read *οὐκ ἔστιν ᾗ τῷδ' ἀνδρὶ.*

1092. ὅπουπερ ἔστι: a kind of euphemism for the dead, cf. *Hcld.* 946 *τὸν ὄνθ' ὅπου 'στὶ νῦν ἐμὸν παῖδα.* The audience of course is pleased with the unconscious irony of the phrase here.

1093–5. The sequence of thought and grammar in these lines is defective. *Σ* paraphrases 1094 *ἴσθι μηδέποτε καλέσων με νύμφιον*, and L seems to bear traces of the explanatory gloss. But the *ὡς* that conveys an emphatic assurance must have a finite verb (cf. S. *Aj.* 39, *Phil.* 117), whereas the part. **μὴ καλῶν** needs to pick up some construction from the previous line. The only possibility is *αἴνει*, or perhaps *αἰνεῖς;* understood out of **αἰνῶ**, with 1095 as Heracles' correction (though without any correcting particle) of this assumption. But, to say nothing of the grammatical *tour de force* of passing over **μωρίαν δ' ὀφλισκάνεις**, this is all rather feeble and pointless. To emend 1094—*ἴσθ' οὔποτ'* or the like—still leaves 1095 a weak echo of 1093. Wilamowitz excises 1093–4; I should prefer to cut 1094–5, since 1096 is more effective as a rejoinder to 1093 than to 1095, and 1095 alone is too tame an admission for Heracles to make. The interpolation appears to come from 331, 1095 being added to keep the stichomythia correct.

1097. νυν must appear to the hapless Admetus a non-sequitur. **γενναίων** is an appeal to his well-known sentiments (566–7 and the following chorus), sufficiently unobvious to have been corrupted in one tradition.

1102. Admetus' wish is carefully put into the form most appropriate to the real *ἀγών*, so as to evoke Heracles' pointed reply.

1107. 'I have my reasons too for asking this' (as you for refusing).

1110 addressed to the attendants.

1111. 'I would rather not. . . .'

1112. δόμους (Monk) is a necessary correction.

1118. The MSS. and *Σ* take this as a dat. *Γοργόνι καρατόμῳ.* The occasional elision of the -*ι* termination of the dat. sing. in Homer encouraged ancient authorities in the faulty transmission of a handful of supposed instances in our dramatic texts, but none of these will bear examination (see Jebb, Appendix on *OC* 1436). 'A beheaded Gorgon' in any case would have no terrors; cf. Beazley, *Pan Painter*, Pl. 5. 1, where Perseus turns his full gaze on the now headless Medusa. Nor do there seem to be instances of *καράτομος* as simply 'that from which the head has been cut off', the trunk, as *Σ* explicitly understands it; in *Tro.* 564, *Rhes.* 606, S. *El.* 52 it is used with abstract nouns (*ἐρημία, σφαγαί, χλιδαί*) as an indirect allusion to something concrete—slaughtered men, locks of hair. But the phrase *Γοργόνι καρατόμῳ* could hardly be a periphrasis for the trunkless *head* (so Paley), though it is true that this is the conventional use of the simile, cf. *Phoen.* 455, *Or.* 1520. *καρατόμος* (paroxytone) is used in the active sense in Eur. *Archelaus*, pap. Hamb. 640, l. 10 *ἐλθὼν Γοργόνος καρατόμος*. And it is the Gorgon-slayer in action that we want here, with Lobeck's **καρατομῶν**; for the verb cf. *Rhes.* 586 *καρατομεῖν ξίφει*. The gesture of the outstretched arm and averted head of the Gorgon-slayer would be familiar enough from many paintings, from the seventh-century relief in the Louvre (*Enc. Phot.* iii. 57) onwards. Méridier follows Weil in starting to break the stichomythia here instead of in the next line, by transposing *Γοργ. ὡς καρ.* to Heracles; 'Admetus must not make a joke against himself'—but it is not a joke. As spoken by Heracles it would be a satirical *réplique* more in tone with an adaptation by Giraudoux than with the Euripidean stage. And cf. Dodds on *Bacch.* 1268 for the decisive moment marked by breach of stichomythia.

1119. The MSS. all give *ναί* to Admetus: *ἔχω ναί* 'Indeed I have' (Murray's punctuation has a rather contrived air). Though *ναί* after *ἔχω* is strictly superfluous for a reply to the question *ἔχεις;* there is a similar redundancy in the answer of the oracle at Branchidae (Hdt. 1. 159. 4) to the question *Κυμαίους δὲ κελεύεις τόν ἱκέτην ἐκδιδόναι; τὸν δὲ αὖτις ἀμείψασθαι τοισίδε· Ναὶ κελεύω κτλ.* If *ναί* is transferred to Heracles, on the other hand, **νυν** would certainly be superfluous, and we should have to emend, with Monk, to the weaker phrase *ναί, σῷζέ νιν*. It is admittedly difficult to say precisely what the emphasis in *ἔχω ναί* is meant to convey, but we know very little about the everyday use of this word.

1121. Heracles unveils Alcestis, so that Admetus can see more clearly than in 1066.

1123–4. Murray's punctuation, with **λεύσσων**, is very involved; V B is more straightforward: *γυναῖκα λεύσσω τήνδ' ἐμὴν ἐτητύμως.* There is little to choose between this, with *τί λέξω;* in 1123, and *τί λεύσσω;* 1123, with *γυναῖκα λέξω κτλ.* 1124.

1125. κέρτομος: 'delusive', cf. *κερτομέω* 'delude' *Hel.* 619, *IA* 849. **ἐκπλήσσει**: 'drives me from my senses'. **θεοῦ χαρά** for 'joy sent by a god' is perhaps just possible, though parallels are hard to find. *θεῶν συντυχίαις* S. *Ant.* 157, and Eur. fr. 37 *δαιμόνων τύχας* are much less strange, since the notion of *τύχη* is often allied to that of *δαίμων*. Méridier accepts Buecheler's *μ' ἐκ θεοῦ*, perhaps rightly.

1126. The text is sound; cf. S. *Ant.* 289 for the same use of **οὐκ ἔστιν, ἀλλά**.

1127. Denniston, *CR* xliii (1929), 119, objects that the imperative **ὅρα** is not sufficiently prominent to take 'emphatic *γε*', and proposes to read *ὁρῶ γε—μή τι κτλ.* 'I *am* seeing—whether this is not some apparition' ('affirmative γε'). But the moment is surely too breathless for this somewhat comic stage repartee. *ὅρα μή* is in effect the equivalent of *δέδοικα μή*, and the *γε* merely 'assents' to the repetition of the same verb as in *ὁρᾷς* 1126.

1128. Evidently the conjuring of spirits was an art not well thought of; there is a touch of aristocratic contempt in Heracles' tone.

1129. **ἔθαπτον**: for the tense cf. on 827.

1130. **τύχην**: as often, 'this turn of events'. **ἀπιστεῖν** = disbelieve the reality of its existence; edd. are quite wrong who emend with Reiske to *τύχῃ*, which would mean 'distrust fortune'.

1131. **δάμαρτ' ἐμήν**: the repetition from 1129 underlines his incredulity.

1135. Admetus' good fortune is so overwhelming that Heracles throws in a conventional apotropaic formula.

1136–8 were deleted by Lachmann as interrupting the natural continuity of question and answer.

1137. **ὁ φιτύσας πατὴρ**: not as distinct from Amphitryon, his putative father, but simply to emphasize the appropriateness of Zeus' interest in him: as he begot you, so may he preserve you.

1140. **κυρίῳ** or *κοιράνῳ*? Schwartz's text of the scholia here is confusingly arranged, but there is little doubt that, as Murray's app. crit. states, the lemma gives *κυρίῳ* only: *μάχην συνάψας τῷ κυρίῳ* (*τῷ κ.* om. B)· *ἢ τῷ τῶν νεκρῶν κυρίῳ* (v.l. *κοιράνῳ*)· *φασὶ γὰρ καὶ τοὺς νεκροὺς δαίμονας· ἢ ἐκ τῶν δαιμόνων τῷ ταύτης κυρίῳ*. *Σ* in fact is giving two alternative explanations of the gen. **δαιμόνων**: either 'lord of the spirits', i.e. of the dead, a construction which would normally need the double article *τῶν δαιμόνων τῷ κυρίῳ*, or 'that one of the spirits who has her in his might'. The first of these two interpretations will not hold; the casual assumption of the equation *δαίμονες* = *νεκροί* is an anachronism for the fifth century. Only the exceptional dead became such spirits, as Alcestis (1003) and Darius (A. *Pers.* 620), and Heracles would not speak of Death as lord of those in particular. *κοιράνῳ* is a conjecture based on this mistaken meaning.

1142. This is enough to enlighten the audience; it was his first plan that was successful (846 ff.).

1143. **γάρ**: 'introducing the matter of the question as a reason for asking it'—Earle.

1146. **ἀφαγνίσηται**: 'be purified from consecration' to the nether gods, as effected by Death supra 76. As in *ἀφοσιόω*, the force of *ἀπό* in this verb can be of two kinds: either 'to render *duly* consecrate', or 'to *de*-sanctify' by propitiatory offerings to the surrendering powers. **τρίτον**: the most usual number of mystical significance. The mute Alcestis was of course performed by a walker-on, the original actor being now on stage as Heracles—but the perfect propriety of the reason here invented, and the advantage drawn from this limitation, in terms of drama, poetry, and good taste, need not be laboured.

1148–9. τὸ λοιπόν: not 'in future', which in English inevitably invites a *change* of behaviour, but 'continue to' practise piety. **δίκαιος ὢν** is probably to be assimilated to the imper. 'continue to show to your guests the piety of a righteous man'.

1150. Sthenelus: known from *Il.* 19. 123 as father of Eurystheus, cf. *Hcld.* 361; the rivalry between him and Amphitryon in an earlier generation appears to be alluded to in *Alcmena*, fr. 89N².

1152. 'Another time; just now I am in a hurry.'

1153. δόμον is clearly false; Wilamowitz corrects to *δρόμον*. V gives *ὁδόν*; B quotes both *δόμον* and *ὁδόν* as variant readings, but B itself and D have *πόδα*. But *ἐλθεῖν νόστιμον πόδα* is surely an impossible phrase. *βαίνειν πόδα*, cf., for instance, *El.* 1173, is another matter, since *βαίνω* = 'step', and *βαίνω πόδα* is merely an extension of *βαίνω βάσιν*. Dinarchus 1. 82 *οὐκ ἂν ἔφασκεν ἐκ τῆς πόλεως ἐξελθεῖν οὐδὲ τὸν ἕτερον πόδα* is sometimes quoted in support, but this is a quite different use of the acc., which defines the part affected where the verb does not apply to the whole; it is the idea of limitation involved which makes the acc. possible. Perhaps *νόστιμον πόδα* has got into the text here from a citation of *Hec.* 939, where it is used with *κινεῖν*. *ὁδόν* is quite possibly right.

1154. τετραρχίᾳ: *Σ* suggests that Eur. may be thinking of the four cities ruled over in Homer (*Il.* 2. 711) by Admetus' son: Pherae, Boibe, Glaphyrae, Iolcus, but a tetrarchy should be *one* of four kingdoms, not a group of four. This passage is in fact clear supporting evidence for the existence of a fourfold division of Thessaly in Eur.'s day, since it seems that by an anachronism he refers to the territory of Pelasgiotis. The meaning in any case is 'this city and all the surrounding province', and the word is used in the pomp of proclamation.

1157. βίον: the acc. as A. *PV* 309 *μεθαρμόσαι τρόπους νέους*.

1159–63. The exodos of *Andr.*, *Hel.*, *Bacch.*, and, with a different opening line, *Med.* (for which it is singularly inapt). It could well have been originally written for this play.